T0357560

THE NOTORIOUS VIRTUES

THE NOTORIOUS VIRTUES

Alwyn Hamilton

Viking

VIKING
An imprint of Penguin Random House LLC
1745 Broadway, New York, New York 10019

First published in the United States of America by Viking,
an imprint of Penguin Random House LLC, 2025

Copyright © 2025 by Blue Eyed Books, Ltd.

Visit us online at PenguinRandomHouse.com.

Library of Congress Cataloging-in-Publication Data is available.

ISBN 9780451479662 (hardcover)

1st Printing

Printed in the United States of America

LSCC

Edited by Kelsey Murphy

Design by Kate Renner and Anabeth Bostrup

Text set in Fournier MT Pro

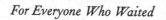

For Everyone Who Waited

The Descendants of
HONOR
HOLTZFALL

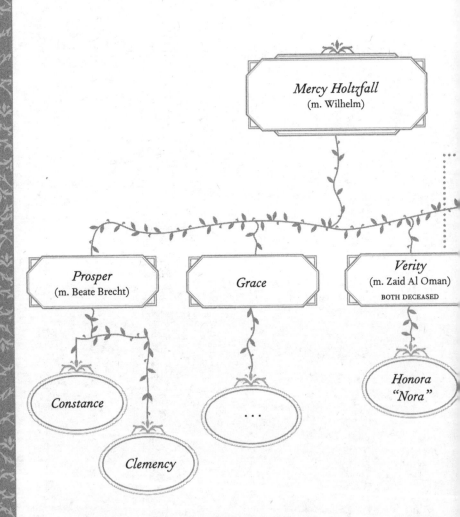

Mercy Holtzfall
(m. Wilhelm)

Prosper
(m. Beate Brecht)

Grace

Verity
(m. Zaid Al Oman)
BOTH DECEASED

Constance

Clemency

. . .

Honora
"Nora"

Sultan Oman
of Miraji
(Dethroned by the Rebel Prince)
DECEASED

Leyla Al-Oman
(+ Lord Bilal Emir of Iliaz, DECEASED)

Patience
(m. Georg Otto)

Valor
DECEASED IN TRIALS

Modesty

PART I

HONOR

THE CHARMED CITY

I t was known as the Enchanted Hour.

The sliver of day *just* before the clubs and bars and dance halls turned out their revelers. But after the factory workers and shopgirls had risen for another day.

The maids, cooks, footmen, and butlers had already hurried through predawn streets to get to their posts. They waited, as the sky lightened, for their sleepless employers to stumble home, discarding shoes and bow ties that their staff would tidy up behind them.

The lumbering delivery trucks had made their rounds, with their clinking glass bottles of milk, tightly bound stacks of newspapers, and cooling loaves of bread. But the sleek taxis and grand town cars still idled sleepily.

Yesterday was forgotten, but it wasn't quite today. Before the upper half of the city slept and after the lower half rose.

But the undying things in the woods never slept. They watched. They watched as a sleepy maid hurried to the back entrance of a white marble home, stumbling a little as she tucked her hair under her white cap. They wondered if she might lose her footing and cross out of the borders of daylight. They wondered if the footman shaking a cigarette into his palm might lean against a tree and come within reach.

And they wondered at the sight of the dark-haired girl, appearing and disappearing between the gaps in the grand houses. Walking alone through the streets in stockinged feet, her dress still dancing in the rising sunlight. Looking like the whole city belonged to her alone.

Because one day, it might.

Chapter 1

NORA

Honora Holtzfall was never late.

Everyone who arrived before the Holtzfall Heiress was unfashionably early. Everyone who arrived after her was embarrassingly tardy.

Except Nora was no longer the Holtzfall Heiress. Officially, she never had been, though every newspaper had called her that. She'd been the heiress to the Heiress. But now the Heiress was dead, and Nora was no longer guaranteed to succeed her as eventual head of the family. She was just another granddaughter of Mercy Holtzfall.

And there wasn't a person in Walstad wealthy enough that they could afford to keep Mercy Holtzfall waiting. Not even Nora.

Especially not Nora.

Especially not on the first day of the Veritaz Trials.

The clock above the bank on Bauer Street showed ten minutes to the hour.

Nora would just make it.

Obviously, in an ideal world, she would have arrived both on time *and* wearing shoes. But Nora couldn't have everything, no matter what the papers liked to say.

Today was the equinox. Allegedly the first day of spring, although Nora would have contended the chill in the air wasn't exactly vernal. But it meant that today, there would be exactly as much day as there was night. And even now, in a city lit with magimek bulbs, days like the equinox still held power.

Twice a year the immortal Huldrekall would willingly emerge from the woods. If they didn't ask the Huldrekall for a Veritaz tonight, they would have to wait for the first day of autumn before they could start the trials.

Stay out of the woods, little one. The old folktale refrain whispered in Nora's mind. *There you will find dangers you do not yet know how to face.*

Of course, every newspaper in the city had an opinion about the trials being held so swiftly.

At Least Wait Until the Last Heiress Is Cold
Before Picking a New One

Some couched it in feigned sympathy for Nora.

Let the Girl Grieve Before You Make
Her Compete!

But like most things, Nora agreed with her grandmother rather than the press. The sooner they held the trials, the sooner she could regain her rightful place in the family.

So tonight, Mercy Holtzfall, head of their family for the past three decades, would ask the Huldrekall which of her granddaughters was worthiest of being her heir.

It was a rite that stretched back centuries.

Held over generations.

Bound up in blood, custom, and ancient oaths.

And *still* Nora wouldn't put it past her grandmother to disqualify her if she was even a few minutes late for breakfast.

Nora turned onto Konig Street just as the metal grating of a kiosk clattered open noisily. Inside, the kiosk's owner began slicing open the thick bundles of morning papers, arranging them among packs of gum, cigarettes, and small charms, so that their headlines faced out.

The front page of *The Walstad Herald* caught Nora's eye. It was a picture of her sitting at one of the small tables at Rik's, taken just a few hours ago. Her head was thrown back in laughter, and a flute of champagne loosely dangled from one hand, while the other rested on Freddie Loetze's shoulder as if to say, "Oh, Freddie dear, you're too much." A diamond the size of a cherry glinted on her finger, and the thin strap of her effervescent dress slid off one shoulder, carelessly displaying her skin. Nora pulled up the same strap absently now. She looked carefree in the photograph only because she had taken a lot of care to appear that way. The headline was printed in fresh ink above it:

Cheers to Better Days Ahead for the Once (and Future?) Holtzfall Heiress

Nora waited for it: the intoxication that usually came with seeing herself on the front page. But she felt as sober as ever in the cool morning light.

Grief-Stricken Former Holtzfall Heiress Drowns Her Sorrows

Well—Nora plucked the *Gazette* out of the rack next to the *Herald—that* was definitely another take on things. There was a photo of her sipping from a frothy coupe with the blur of the brass band at Café Bliss behind her. She was still wearing her Lussier heels in that picture, kicked up brazenly amidst the chaos. She must have left them at the Ash Lounge, then. Or maybe the Ruby Rose Club.

Her fingers flicked through the rest of the broadsheets as the kiosk owner set them out. She was on the front page of most of them, obviously. News about the Holtzfalls always had papers flying off the stand before the ink was even done drying.

Especially since the murder.

Shock in the City as Verity Holtzfall Found Dead!

For a week, everything else had dropped off the front page as the same picture graced every newspaper in the city under a series of revolving headlines.

Nora's mother's lifeless body.

Lit by police headlights.

And the flash of journalists' greedy cameras.

Just hours before that picture, her mother had absently reached out to kiss her cheek before she left for the evening, as if Nora were a small child again. Nora had resisted the impulse to wipe at her cheek, which would have made her feel even more like a child. Instead Nora had said something flippant about not wanting to wear her mother's lipstick as rouge. Or maybe she hadn't said it. Maybe she had just thought it as she'd swept out the door without glancing back.

She wasn't sure, because in the moment, it hadn't mattered.

It only mattered a few hours later. When it became the last time she would ever see her mother alive. When she would next see her as a body on a newspaper cover.

That was how she'd found out. Leaving the Silverlight Café near dawn to a newspaper boy brandishing a broadsheet, calling out *Extra! Extra! Holtzfall Heiress Tragedy!*

Theo was waiting for her.

It was a burden to be as smart as Nora was sometimes.

Because in that moment, before Theo could even speak, before she'd fully caught sight of the picture of her mother's body, she'd put all the pieces into place. A Holtzfall knight sent for her, the cries of the newspaper boy, the carefully controlled grief in Theo's expression—her mother was dead.

And if she was dead, so was Alaric, Theo's brother—and her mother's sworn knight. There was no way to her mother except through Alaric.

Nora was an only child. But Theo and Alaric—they were like brothers to her. And in one night her mother and Alaric were both gone. The small circle of people she cared about had constricted around her so suddenly she could barely breathe.

That photograph of the crime scene was the last she saw of her mother's face.

And the papers showed it over and over and over under a carousel of headlines.

Verity Holtzfall Stabbed to Death
in Mugging Gone Wrong!

New Suspect in Holtzfall Heiress's Brutal Murder!

Mugger Confesses When Jewels Found
in His Possession!

Lukas Schuld Admits to
Stabbing of Verity Holtzfall!

Papers with her mother's body on them flew off stands. Even after Lukas Schuld confessed, speculation ran wild. What had Verity Holtzfall been doing in the 13th circle after dark? What kind of seedy business would draw the Holtzfall Heiress far from the safe upper circles of the city? How had her sworn knight failed to protect her? Had Alaric, whose body hadn't been found, been in cahoots with Lukas Schuld?

And when they ran out of things to print about the murder, they turned their lenses on Nora.

A New Heiress Must Be Chosen!
Who Is the Worthiest of Them All?

Grieving Former Heiress Not Seen
Since Mother's Funeral!

Driven Mad by Grief: Honora Holtzfall
Unfit to Compete in the Veritaz?

Those headlines had been like pebbles tossed against the walls of her solitude. Taunting her even as she sat a hundred floors up from where the photographers were camped on the street. They were waiting for the grieving daughter to make a scene.

Fine. If they wanted a scene, Nora would give them the whole show.

She had chosen a dress made of bright rippling streams of gold fabric sewn into waves that hugged her body outrageously. It was scandalously sheer with a tendency to slip dangerously around her shoulders, hinting at a mishap that would never happen, thanks to the charms sewn into the lining. The shoes were Charles Lussier, one of a kind, made from stained glass, charmed to be strong as steel. Her makeup exaggerated her Mirajin features, inherited from her desert-born father's side of the family. The brightest red lipstick in her arsenal made her look like she couldn't possibly be *in* trouble, she *was* trouble personified.

She had stepped out to show them that she was not beaten.

But the reality was, only one thing would truly show them she was still the heiress they all remembered.

Winning the Veritaz.

Spoiled Honora Holtzfall Gloats as Heirship Comes Within Reach

That headline was the *Bullhorn*'s. Obviously.

They'd run a picture of Nora wrapped in a white stole, which she had also abandoned in the course of the night, smirking knowingly into a camera. It was printed next to that familiar photograph: her mother sprawled in an alley stained with blood.

Pictures were worth a thousand column inches when paired like that: Nora seemingly celebrating only days after her mother's body went into the ground. To the *Bullhorn*'s disreputable credit, at least they stuck to their Holtzfall-bashing agenda even in the face of her tragedy.

"Does this look like a library to you?" The kiosk owner was eyeing the steadily increasing stack of newspapers Nora was holding with the sort of suspicion that suggested he didn't recognize her from the front of those same papers. "Choose one and move it along."

Ah. That was going to be a problem. Nora was one of the richest people in this city, but she didn't have any money *on* her. *Obviously.* Carrying cash was something that waiters and shop assistants did, not Holtzfalls. She sighed, working the small ruby ring off her finger. The papers were all one zaub apiece; the ring had cost her just over 10,000. "Here." She set the ring in the change plate. "This should cover it."

She tucked the newspapers under her arm and continued down the wide avenue to her grandmother's house. She heard him call after her, "If this thing turns out to be tin and glass, I'd better not see your face around here again!"

For the first time since her mother died, Nora felt a real laugh bubble up on her lips. She waved one of the papers over her shoulder, flashing her face on the front page at him. "That would be a lot of papers you'd have to stop selling."

She had the satisfaction of watching recognition dawn on him a moment before she spun back, dashing the rest of the way to the Holtzfall mansion.

Chapter 2
LOTTE

I swear on my oath. I will not—You wouldn't—Did my mother
She will not—I'd rather die.
I never—If you don't, I'll always—How could you—
I saw nothing.
You will never understand—

"Get up, you slothful girl."

In the restless moment before sleep dropped away, Lotte couldn't be sure if that voice was in her mind or not. But as she fought her way to consciousness through the cacophony in her head, she realized that none of the ghosts of the briar pit sounded as strident as Sister Brigitta.

The shovel-faced nun was glowering at her from the top of the briar pit, outlined by the beginnings of daylight. She looked indignant to find Lotte there. As if she wasn't the one who had thrown her down there in the first place.

Lotte didn't get up. She pressed the heels of her palms into her eyes. She wasn't sure how many hours she'd slept and how many she'd just lain with her eyes closed, hoping sleep might claim her. Between the icy stone floor and the voices of the dead, the briar pit wasn't exactly the place for a good night's rest. And from counting her meals, one a day, last night marked her sixth night down here.

Her punishment was seven nights.

Seven nights for talking back to Sister Brigitta.

Seven was a holy number among the Sisters of the Blessed Briar.

Where the convent now stood had once been the tower of an immortal Bergsra. Thousands of years ago, the Bergsra had given shelter to a young princess fleeing marriage to a cruel prince. The prince's men had besieged the tower for seven days in a vain attempt to retrieve the runaway princess. For seven days, the immortal Bergsra and the princess had watched as foolish mortal men tried to break open the tower with foolish mortal tools.

Seven days until his patience had failed.

The immortal grew a thick wall of brambles around his tower, ensnaring the attackers, piercing their bodies with thorns and binding them with branches. Their dying screams lasted seven more days. The princess drowned them out by playing the harp. And in the tower forever surrounded by brambles and bodies, the Bergsra and the princess lived many years in peace.

Until mortality claimed her too, and the Bergsra abandoned the tower, a crumbling monument to his love for a mortal girl.

Now all that was left of the tower was this pit filled with briars that couldn't be felled, and the voices of the men who'd died.

By my oath, I will obey.

She tried to push the voice away.

"Why *should* I get up?" Lotte still didn't move. Didn't let on how badly she wanted to be free of the briar pit and the voices. The Bergsra of the Blessed Briar hadn't been one for mercy. And neither, in Lotte's experience, was the high holy woman of his order. Which meant there had to be another reason her sentence was being cut short by a day.

"Because I am ordering you to," Sister Brigitta snapped. "And obedience to your betters is a virtue the lesser should learn." The *lesser*. The words shouldn't have stung the way they did after sixteen years. "Besides, you have been idling down here for *days* while my blessed sisters break their backs for the festival." Ah, there it was.

"So you're letting me out a day early because you want me to spare your holy hands and have *me* lug things down the hill for the festival."

The Blessed Sisters were the only people whose minds Lotte couldn't overhear. Sister Dorothea, who had been high holy woman before Sister Brigitta, had explained to Lotte that was because Lotte's curse was to overhear corrupt thoughts. The Sisters had sworn their lives in service to the immortals, and in doing so, their vices were absolved. But Lotte didn't need to hear Sister Brigitta's mind to know the truth. The flicker across the holy woman's face betrayed her, and Lotte felt an angry burn of satisfaction, even though she knew she would pay for the impertinence.

"It is amazing," Sister Brigitta said slowly, unknotting the briar belt she wore around her middle, "that one born with nothing but a curse from a mother who didn't want her could be so ungrateful for all she has been given. You would benefit from some humility today."

LOTTE'S BARE LEGS STILL STUNG FROM THE SMACK OF THE briar belt as she made her fifth trip from the convent down toward the half-timbered houses of Gelde.

The cold teeth of early spring nipped at the fresh welts, mud sucked at Lotte's feet, and the plates clinked in precarious balance, making every trip through the drab landscape painstakingly slow.

In summer, the village of Gelde shone.

The sun-drenched golden wheat that made up the village's livelihood haloed it, like all of Gelde had been touched by a holy light. But for months after the harvest, those same fields were nothing but a dun expanse of soil. It didn't matter how many oil lamps and colorful streamers were put up around the square, the village still felt dismal. And the smiles didn't cut through the murky thoughts that slid out of people's minds, Lotte's curse gathering them up eagerly.

She dropped the pile of plates on one of the trestle tables with a deliberate clatter. Sister Eva shot Lotte a chiding look. But she was new enough to the convent not to feel at ease scolding Lotte yet. Instead she turned away, green robes hemmed with brambled embroidery swishing imperiously.

With no other Sisters in sight, Lotte leaned against the trestle table, resting her cold aching body and squeezing her eyes shut. *Slothful girl*, the Sisters would say if they saw her. *What chance do you have of breaking your curse if you indulge your vices so?*

The chatter in the square this morning was still muted and clouded with the scraps of sleep. But inside Lotte's mind, it was a carnival of voices.

Lotte could usually handle the constant hum of other people's thoughts that ran at the back of her mind. But there were rarely this many people in Gelde.

Today the men of the village, alongside the workers who came into town for the season, would finish sowing the wheat fields for spring. The seasonal workers were men who couldn't find work in the cities, come to the countryside for a few weeks of pay and full stomachs. When the work was done, they would pile back onto the rattling buses to Walstad or Grenz or some other city. But tonight, before they were sent on their way, Gelde would celebrate. Every house would bring their best dish, Hehn's Bakery would make cardamom rolls, and there would be beer from the brewery. And the Sisters would gift the seasonal workers with a small piece of the briar to bless them.

And when they were gone, their thoughts wouldn't crowd Lotte's mind like this.

One seasonal worker in line at Hehn's Bakery was noticing the way Lotte's skirt rode up while she leaned against the table. From another man, she saw a flash of her bare knee reflected back at her. She saw in their minds how her ill-fitting smock strained across her body. Lotte could hear the hunger in those flashes. Even now, edges of other, more dangerous thoughts drifted close.

In all the noise, Lotte didn't sense Estelle until her hand closed around her wrist.

"Guess what I *just* saw in the bakery," Estelle hissed conspiratorially into Lotte's ear. The warmth of Estelle's palm felt scalding against Lotte's skin. The cold of the pit had sunk into her for the last six days. But if Estelle noticed that Lotte's skin was freezing to the touch, or that she hadn't been to the bakery for days, she didn't show it. The sudden contact of Estelle's hand on Lotte's arm flooded her mind with her friend's thoughts. And those thoughts were not consumed with where Lotte had been, only with what she wanted to tell her.

"What did you see?" Lotte stayed close to her best friend as they wove out through the crowd, the other voices beginning to fade from Lotte's mind as they went.

"No." Estelle pretended to pout prettily. "You have to guess."

Lotte knew what Estelle had seen. The second her friend had grabbed her hand, it had tumbled eagerly out of her mind and into Lotte's. But Estelle didn't want Lotte to guess correctly. She wanted to draw things out, basking in the attention of a secret, until she gloatingly dropped her morsel of information. And life was always easier when Estelle got what she wanted.

"Was it shocking?" Lotte played along.

"Scandalous!" Estelle clutched imaginary pearls.

"You covered the dough and for once in your life your mother didn't shift the cloth a quarter of an inch as if you'd draped it wrong?"

Estelle scoffed. "That will be the day."

"Your father actually had something unkind to say about someone?"

"I think my mother will stop correcting my every gesture *long* before *that*."

Lotte could feel the cold of the briar pit ebbing away in Estelle's presence. She'd been locked away six nights, with no company except ghosts. But right now, it felt like they were back at school, seeing each other every day, joined at the hip so tightly none of the other girls could fit into their little world.

Finally, Estelle's seams burst with the gossip. "Henriett came in to get rolls for breakfast, and guess what she was wearing?" This time she didn't wait for Lotte to guess. "It was one of the new dresses that Mr. Hinde ordered for his *daughter*." Henriett was a few years older than Lotte and Estelle, but they'd once all been piled together in the same small village classroom to learn what they could before they got jobs or married.

When Henriett had left school, it was to wed Lennart Hinde, the wealthy widower who owned the biggest house in the village. Everyone had toasted the health of the young bride and her not-so-young groom. Everyone had smiled and congratulated them and danced and consumed the food and beer that Mr. Hinde paid for. And all the while, Lotte could hear every single one of them thinking that it hadn't even been a full season since the first Mrs. Hinde had died. And besides that, Henriett wasn't *nearly* fit to raise a stepdaughter who was only seven years younger than she was. The girl couldn't cook or sew for goodness' sake, but all you had to do was look at the neckline of her wedding dress to guess that Lennart Hinde hadn't married her for her housekeeping.

The caravan of unkind thoughts behind the warm words had left Lotte feeling restless and irked.

The Sisters were always telling Lotte to repent. To discard any piece of her that was less than virtuous. But Lotte could hear in the minds of others how viceful they were.

Their thoughts were petty and rageful and jealous and greedy. And their words were so *dishonest* as they smiled in Henriett's and Lennart's faces.

And yet *Lotte* was the only one who was cursed?

She was the one who scrubbed convent floors until her hands bled, who slept half her nights in the briar pit, who had to spend her life in the convent until she was virtuous enough for her curse to lift. Why should she have to fight to be more virtuous than them? She heard it. How they enjoyed stoking the fires of their nasty thoughts in private, thinking no one knew.

But Lotte knew.

And as they watched Henriett whirl in her wedding dress and crown of flowers, curls splaying out around her joyously, Lotte indulged her own viceful tendencies. She had plucked a thought out of Estelle's mind and whispered, "I'll bet you she's already with child. That's why he *has* to marry her."

Lotte knew that Henriett wasn't, but a spike of vindictive joy had shot out of Estelle's mind in answer, crowding out the intense burning jealousy of seeing Henriett and her stupid flat freckled nose marry the wealthiest man in town. Knowing *she* was the one who deserved a lavish wedding, a husband who could keep her as a housewife with soft hands. Instead of a future spent rising before dawn to work in her parents' bakery, getting tough forearms from kneading dough and flour stains on her plain dresses.

"I was *just* thinking that!" Estelle hissed back, slapping Lotte's arm conspiratorially. That had been enough to draw a Sister's gaze as they melted into a puddle of giggles at the edge of the crowd. Lotte had spent the whole night scrubbing dishes after the wedding in punishment.

It had been worth it.

It was always worth it to have those moments of belonging.

The only good thing that had ever come out of Lotte's curse was the ability to make herself into the person Estelle wanted as a friend. Every day, over and over.

Now Lotte fell back into their pattern since childhood easily. "I'll bet you Henriett gave him the wrong measurements deliberately when he put in the order." That was a bet Lotte would have won. She'd overheard the scheme in Henriett's mind when she'd been walking the order form to the mail truck last month. She was angry that her husband was buying new dresses for his daughter and not his wife. So all she did was tweak measurements. Enough that they would be foolishly big on her husband's daughter but fit Henriett like a glove. The girl could have the dresses when Henriett was good and done with them.

She'd dropped the order in the mail truck and turned away. And it had occurred to Lotte that she could fix this. She could snatch the envelope back out and right this wrong. Spare Lennart's young daughter the humiliating moment of excitedly pulling on a dress only for the anticipation to turn to disappointment when the sleeves dangled past her wrists.

But that would be pointless.

The Sisters had made sure to remind Lotte every day that, in spite of her best efforts, she was far from *good*. Doing a kindness for Lennart Hinde's daughter wouldn't change what she was.

Besides, no one had ever rescued Lotte. Not a knight like in the stories of old. Not an immortal Bergsra shielding her in a tower from her enemies. Not even a well-meaning cursed girl from a selfish stepmother. No one had ever shielded Lotte from anything.

Estelle's face split into aghast delight at Lotte's "theory," and that was enough to overcome any guilt as they sank down onto the garden wall behind Mrs. Mueller's house. Absently, Estelle pulled a parcel from her pocket, wax paper wrapped around two cinnamon buns from the bakery. She handed one to Lotte, who tore into the still-warm pastry, sugary cinnamon steam rising from between the curls of dough, her empty stomach growling. They both swiftly dissected their pastries, Lotte handing the soft middle to Estelle and taking the flaky outside from her, even though she preferred the middle too, as they lapsed into the comfortable ritual they'd had since they were six years old.

But even as they ate their pastries, Lotte could hear the gnawing resentment at the back of Estelle's mind. *She* should be the one with dresses from the city. She suited city fashions better than Henriett did anyway. Lotte was searching for something in Estelle's mind to draw her out of her indignation when she caught the last edge of her spiteful thoughts.

It won't matter soon anyway.

When I'm in Walstad with Konrad, I can have all the dresses I want.

Thoughts didn't come like words did. Not slow and orderly, telling only the part of the story the teller wanted known. They tumbled out whole, messy and honest. In a blink, Lotte knew everything Estelle had been up to for the past six days. As if Lotte had been there and not locked in the briar pit.

Estelle had noticed the handsome blond-stubbled seasonal worker when he came into the bakery for his daily ration of bread. And when he flashed her a smile that made her insides turn over, she'd given him a spiced apple tart for free. They'd been stealing moments together ever since. In the shadows behind the barn after a day of labor in the fields. But still, she had held back . . . hesitating to give herself fully to a man who would be gone in a few days.

Until he'd said the words that won her over.

When *we* get back to Walstad.

And suddenly, Estelle didn't see a man anymore, she saw the city.

Tomorrow, while the town slept late after tonight's festivities, she'd slip out, take a seat on the bus that was carrying the workers back to the city. She'd cleaned out the money her parents kept hidden below the floorboards in the bakery and given it to Konrad for safekeeping. That would keep her going until she got a job. Something glamorous, like the cigarette girls she saw in the magazines. Or a waitress in one of the clubs, where she might see the Holtzfalls.

Estelle was leaving Gelde, and everyone in it, without a second thought.

Not even one for Lotte.

And she was smiling in Lotte's face. Like she had smiled in Henriett's face at her wedding.

She dusted sugar off her hands, saying something about needing to get back to the bakery before she got in trouble.

As Estelle stood to go, the warmth of her fled, and Lotte felt the cold of the convent crawl back over her. But now it stretched out ahead of her for years and years. Of being left behind again. Of being alone again.

And Lotte knew she couldn't allow Estelle to leave.

The Tale of the Woodcutter

The Woodcutter and His Wife

Stay out of the woods, little one. There you will find dangers you do not yet know how to face.

Now sit still, stay silent, and I will tell you the tale of the honorable woodcutter and his enchanted ax.

In the midst of the ancient woods, there was a tiny village called Walstad. It was small and poor, and the village folk, like all village folk, lived in fear of the creatures that dwelled in the dark between the trees. Creatures as ancient as the woods themselves.

There were the Nokk, who crouched in wells, waiting for children sent to fetch water so they could drag them down to the depths and drown them. Trolls, who could crack open the walls of the villagers' homes like eggs and devour them. The Weeping Orphans, who cried like lost children to lure soft-hearted mothers into the night. And the clever skin-shifting wolves, who stalked young girls gathering flowers and ate them whole.

On the outskirts of Walstad lived a young woodcutter and his beautiful wife. The couple was poor, but the woodcutter's work brought in enough that they neither went hungry nor cold. And they were happy.

Until one dark winter when the snow began to fall and didn't stop. Some said it was a war of the frost giant in the mountains that made the winter so fierce. But regardless of the cause, it snowed for days, then weeks, then months. The young woodcutter had worked hard for many months at his trade. But all the wood that he had cut, he had sold, keeping none for himself. Without a fire in the hearth, the woodcutter and his wife's house grew cold, their bellies went empty, and the creatures in the wood scratched at their doors.

And one morning, when the icy winds howled around their cottage and the woodcutter saw his wife poking around in the cinders for a scrap left to light, he knew he must take his ax and brave the dangerous woods.

But as the woodcutter pressed into the forest, he found tree after tree brittle with cold, shattering uselessly into shards of ice under his ax. He carried on, deeper and deeper into the woods, until he was hopelessly lost.

The woodcutter fought for hours against the bitter snow, looking for his path home, until he stumbled into a small clearing. Suddenly hail no longer lashed at his face, icy air no longer bit at his fingers, and banks of snow no longer reached up to his waist. Cold winds still battered the trees beyond the clearing, but here the air was as temperate as a spring day, the ground was clear and green, and the moonlight broke through dense winter clouds to shine almost as bright as the midday sun.

And in the middle of the clearing stood the most beautiful tree the woodcutter had ever seen. The bark gleamed like gold and silver, marbled through with rubies and sapphires that flickered in the moonlight.

The woodcutter raised his ax, but just before it fell, a voice called out from the tree.

"Please, good woodcutter. I beg of you, do no harm to my tree. For if you cut it down, I, too, shall perish."

The woodcutter was desperate. He and his wife would surely die if he returned empty-handed. But he could not ignore such a desperate plea either. And so he lowered his ax.

No sooner had he done so than a face appeared from the wood of the tree. Then an arm, then a leg, until finally, stepping out from the heart of the tree itself, in skin and clothes of golden bark, with hair of ruby leaves and veins of silver sap, appeared a Huldrekall.

"Thank you, honorable woodcutter." The Huldrekall was an immortal being, the powerful ruler of all living beings in the forest. And yet he bowed to the woodcutter. "For your good-heartedness, I will grant you any desire."

The woodcutter's wishes were simple. To return to his wife. To bring home enough wood to last them through this winter. And to keep her safe from the things in the woods that clawed at their door. The Huldrekall was surprised to hear such humble wishes. He pressed the woodcutter again. Told him that he could wish for all the jewels in the king's coffers and it would be granted. But the worthy woodcutter shook his head. And so the Huldrekall granted his simple wishes.

First, he gave the woodcutter a ring woven from the golden twigs of his tree. This ring, he told the woodcutter, would light and guide his path safely through the woods, leading him to wherever he wished to go.

Second, the Huldrekall reached up into the branches of his tree and plucked off a bough. In his hands, it twisted and shaped itself into a sharp ax, finer than any the woodcutter had ever seen. He gave it to the wood-cutter and promised him that this ax would cut down any tree in one blow. "If you cut down the trees around your cottage in a great circle," the Huldrekall said, "no danger from the woods will pass where the trees once stood."

This was his gift to the woodcutter, he said. And to his children. And their children's children. That for as long as his descendants wielded the ax, they would have the Huldrekall's protection.

Chapter 3

THEO

There was a time when knights did great deeds. When they rode into battle, rescued princesses, and hunted beasts.

But the battles had been won. Rulers no longer wore crowns. And the beasts were trapped in the woods.

So this morning, Theodric Rydder, sworn knight to the House of Holtzfall and oathbound descendant of Hartwin Rydder, was hunting a rogue heiress instead.

The revelers from the night were stumbling out of the Ash Lounge, blinking blearily into the dawn. Theo worked against the tide of tipsy patrons, keeping a lookout for her shock of dark hair amidst them. Last time Theo had retrieved Nora from here, he'd found her standing on top of a table, building a tower of champagne coupes, the crowd of 1st-circle bright young things cheering and gasping as the glasses teetered. When Theo had entered, Nora's head turned toward him. It was a tiny movement, but it was enough to send a shiver through the glasses, cascading them to the ground, shattering all around her and illuminating in the club's lights like stars.

In the morning light the broken glasses on the ground just looked like scraps of last night, mixed in with discarded gloves and lost baubles. Daylight sapped the glamour out of places like this. Only a few stragglers still lingered among the debris. Those either too drunk or too wealthy to be expelled.

In one sweep of the room Theo could see that Nora wasn't one of them.

Every Holtzfall was to have a knight with them at all times. Even Mercy Holtzfall's brothers had them. They were powerless in the wake of losing their own trials, but they were still appendages of the most powerful woman in the city. The last thing anyone needed was a repeat of Felicity Holtzfall's ransoming fifty years ago.

Or of Verity Holtzfall's murder.

Nora, as usual, thought she was the exception to the rule that governed everyone else.

Theo had been woken sometime in the middle of the night by Commander Lis Rydder, leader of the Holtzfall knights. And for just a second, before sleep cleared completely, he was back in the last time he was woken like this. The night Verity Holtzfall died.

The night Alaric had died with her.

And then Lis had spoken. "Honora is missing."

It was years of training that made it easy to let duty flood in and drown out the grief. *By my oath, I will protect them at all costs.* The refrain that guided the lives of the Rydder knights thrummed through him.

Nora had slipped her guard.

Of course she had. It was Nora.

The other knights had been taking bets for the past week on whether Nora would come willingly to the Veritaz Ceremony. Or if she would dig her heels in, demanding to inherit directly from her grandmother, the way she would have from her mother. Even though her mother had only had one daughter to inherit. And her grandmother had multiple grandchildren who were now eligible since Verity's death. In which case, the knights would no doubt be ordered to drag her in to compete.

And now, with hours to go until dawn and the beginning of the ceremony, she was missing. And Theo knew it was anyone's guess whether she was planning on coming back willingly. Because Theo knew Nora. Better than almost anyone did.

Which was why, amidst barracks of other knights, he was the one being roused in the dead of night.

"She hasn't shared her evening plans with me, Commander," he'd told Lis, reaching for the shirt and doublet that were carefully folded on the trunk at the end of his narrow bed.

Lis pressed her mouth together in frustration. It was as much a show of emotion as Theo ever saw from the Rydder commander. "She's a fool going out without a knight."

"A knight didn't do Verity much good." Theo knew even as he spoke that he was bordering on insubordination. "Commander," he added for good measure.

Alaric's name had barely been spoken since the night of Verity's death. And Theo didn't speak it now. But his absence hung in the silence between Theo and Commander Lis.

Theo's brother had been the best knight in a generation, chosen at only eighteen to become Verity Holtzfall's sworn knight. The one who was responsible for the life of the Heiress.

And he had failed.

Verity was dead.

Alaric was gone.

Not even knights were too valorous for rumors. And in the hours after the barracks had woken to the news that Verity Holtzfall was dead and Alaric nowhere to be found, the word that spread was that Alaric wasn't dead. That he'd failed to protect Verity and fled to avoid punishment. Like Sigismund Rydder had three hundred years ago, traveling across the sea to escape the retribution of the Holtzfalls when he had a dalliance with Meritt Holtzfall. It was years before he was found. But he was. Hunted down by other knights, his own kinsmen. When they'd brought him back, Fidelity Holtzfall ordered him to lash himself to death. And bound by the oath in their bloodline, Sigismund Rydder had done it.

But Theo knew his brother.

Alaric would never abandon his duty. He was the best of them. Not only because of his skills, but because of his principles. He despised injustice, cowardice, and disloyalty. He was the sort of knight they used to write tales of back in the days of the ancient woods. He would never abandon his duty.

As headlines filled with speculation about Verity, the barracks filled with speculation about Alaric. There was a trail of blood leading away from Verity's body. Like a wounded knight who might have gone for help. Or a body that had been dragged into the river. The knights who had trained with Alaric wondered who could have bested him in a fight. No one had landed a blow on Alaric in the training ground since he was twelve.

And then Lukas Schuld was arrested. Found with Verity's stolen jewelry. A scrawny man with an inclination for gambling and drinking. Not the type of man who could easily have defeated the best of them. And yet, there was no doubt in Theo's mind, Alaric would have kept his oath until the end.

Theo had always been glad for his oath. For his duty.

They were lucky to be born Rydder knights. Their father had taught them that. Most people went through life searching for their purpose. Many died without ever finding it. Rydder knights were born with their purpose. They protected the line of succession that protected the rest of the city.

They lived to die for the Holtzfalls.

"I'll find her." Theo pulled on his shirt. *By my oath, I will protect them at all costs.*

Commander Lis appraised him as he laced up his shoes. Theo felt sure she found him lacking next to his brother. But she nodded. "She needs to be at the house by dawn."

Nora wasn't wearing a locanz, of course, another rule she liked to exempt herself from.

All the Holtzfalls were meant to keep the small charm on them so they could be found at a moment's notice. Nora's locanz charm was a pair of diamond stud earrings that were magically paired with a wristwatch Theo wore so he could track her down. When caught without the locanz earrings Nora would dramatically declare that they didn't match anything in her closet. As if Theo didn't know her closet was the size of most people's homes.

But without magical means to find her, Theo followed a strange trail of journalists' whispers. A white stole left at the Ruby Rose Club, silver hairpins at the Paragon Hotel bar, a twenty-thousand-zaub bar tab at Rik's. Now Theo picked up a pair of charmed glass shoes from under a cocktail table at the Ash Lounge. He'd half expected to find Nora at the end of the trail of expensive breadcrumbs, sipping champagne and waiting for a ride to her grandmother's house.

But the sun was rising, and the city was beginning to rise with it. Which meant that either Nora had made it to breakfast in time on her own, or she was playing a dangerous game with her grandmother's patience.

Among the lingering revelers dotted around the lounge, Theo spied Freddie Loetze. Third in line to the Loetze shipping fortune and notorious rake about town. Nora, Theo knew, found him deeply boring. But there were only so many people in the 1st circle, which meant she also found herself in his company a lot.

Freddie Loetze was allergic to being alone. This time the salve to his solitude was a pretty girl with bright red hair that hung to her waist. Freddie was known for picking up girls with stars in their eyes, promising them the moon, and then dropping them like a bad habit. Nora, in turn, had made it her habit to pick them back up, hiring them into one of the many Holtzfall households. At this point, Theo guessed half the housemaids in employ of the Holtzfalls had been hired by Nora.

"Freddie." Theo moved through a maze of tipped-over chairs and discarded glasses toward where the other boy sat. He had to say his name twice more before the Loetze boy looked up, blinking blearily. Freddie's bow tie hung loose over a shirt that was no doubt only still crisp and unblemished due to the charms on his cuff links.

"A knight without an heiress, what a sight." Freddie's words were slurred and his eyes heavily lidded. "There are no Holtzfalls here, so you can be on your way." The scarlet-haired girl in the crook of his arm glanced up at the name Holtzfall. Now Theo saw her clearly, he realized she was wearing a dancer's costume, her makeup exaggerating her features for the stage. Bright gray eyes went to the symbol on his chest. The Holtzfall woodcutter stitched into the breast of his doublet. The symbol of the Rydder knights.

When Theo didn't move, Freddie waved one hand dismissively. "Shoo, boy, shoo."

Theo could have laid Freddie Loetze out like the foppish rag doll he was. He stood a full head taller than the other boy. The years Freddie had spent not lifting anything heavier than a canapé, Theo had spent relentlessly training. But Freddie wasn't worth Theo's sweat.

And so Theo waited, standing over the settee where Freddie was currently drooped with the redheaded dancer. Predictably, it didn't take long for Freddie to wilt. "*She* left." Freddie brought his glass to his lips before realizing it was empty; he waved and snapped his fingers at the barman, who ignored him.

"Nora," Theo clarified.

"*Nora.*" Freddie's lips curled up in a nasty snarl. "Awfully informal for a guard dog. That should be *Miss Holtzfall* when you're talking about your masters."

Theo was already turning away, but Freddie's words stopped him, his shoulders tensing in anger. Knights were meant to be above pettiness and ego. Theo knew his oath. He knew his place in the city and among the Holtzfalls.

There was a time when knights did great deeds, dueled enemies, and saved damsels . . .

"Do you have something to write with?" Theo asked the man at the bar, who was loosening the sleeve garters over his white shirt tiredly. The barman passed him a pen from his front pocket, and Theo scribbled down instructions on the back of a paper napkin.

"Knights," the barman snorted ruefully, rolling up his cuffs. Theo handed the pen back and returned to the booth where Freddie and the girl were.

"I thought you were leaving," Freddie groaned. "Listen, knightling—" His boldness ended with a flinch as Theo's hand skirted close to his face. But it wasn't a blow, he just handed the napkin to the redheaded girl. Instructions were scribbled on it of where to go if she wanted a maid's job in the Holtzfall mansion.

Some of the girls who found themselves in Freddie's company were foolish enough to really believe that he loved them. That he was going to make good on whatever promise he'd made. But most were smart enough to be in it for the money. And as Nora once said, being a Holtzfall maid paid well and required less faking it.

The girl took in the words on the napkin swiftly. Freddie made a clumsy grab for it, but the girl had the speed of a sober person and tucked it into the neckline of her dress. She met Theo's eyes, giving him a tiny nod of understanding.

Theo moved away, though not fast enough to miss Freddie's lewd joke about whether the napkin in her neckline was an invitation.

"You knights just can't resist a damsel in distress, can you?" the barman remarked as Theo passed by. He was almost at the door when the man added, "Your brother was right about you."

The mention of Alaric stopped Theo in his tracks.

But when he turned around, the bartender was gone.

Chapter 4

"**M**iss Honora." Margarete opened the door for Nora as she dashed up the Holtzfall mansion's steps, past the hungry flashes of cameras and shouting reporters, closing the door quickly on the chaos outside. The charms on the doorway instantly shut out the noise from outdoors, sealing Nora into the sanctuary of her ancestral home.

"May I take your . . ." The head maid hesitated, realizing Nora wasn't wearing a coat, in spite of the early spring chill. "Newspapers?" Margarete recovered elegantly.

"Thank you, Margarete." She didn't miss Margarete's quick glance at her stocking-clad feet as the long-suffering head maid took the papers. Unlike some of her ancestors, Nora wasn't a mind reader, but she knew Margarete was already worrying about all the city dirt Nora was bound to track through the house. The staff would be blamed if the carpets were any less than impeccable.

She needn't worry.

Nora might not be the type to make it home by midnight wearing both shoes. But she *was* the type to make a charm on the fly using nothing but a hairpin and two gold bracelets. It had taken Nora only a few minutes to scratch in the symbols that would shape the magical energy to its intended purpose, before attaching the bracelets to her ankles.

It was the sort of work most people would need to go to an expensive charmerie for. But Nora wasn't most people.

The soles of her feet were pristine.

"They're expecting you in the Blue Salon." Margarete curtsied.

They. Nora couldn't ask whether she was the last to arrive, at the risk of seeming like it mattered. Which of course, it did. They were in competition now. Everything mattered.

As Margarete turned away to store the newspapers in the closet, Nora quickly pressed her fingertips against the polished top of the nearest console table, channeling the innate magic of her Holtzfall gift. After generations, the Holtzfall bloodline was so oversaturated with magic that even without a charm, some of them could practice magic. There were empaths, clairvoyants, and on occasion, the odd mind reader, though not for a century now.

Nora could scry, which was to say she could read anything that had captured an image. Mirrors or photographs were best, but anything that caught a reflection would do in a pinch. She'd once read a reflection in a glass of champagne, albeit a slightly bubbly one.

A huge vase of roses occupied much of the surface of the table, but there was still enough clear space that Nora's gift ought to . . . *There!* As she flicked the image backward, she saw two bright blonde reflections captured in the polished wood.

Constance and Clemency being ushered in by their father.

Followed closely by Modesty and her mother.

Wonderful. All three of her cousins were already here. No doubt hoping to impress their grandmother. Punctuality might be a virtue, but there was such a thing as being *impolitely* early, some might say. Nora would probably say it behind her cousins' backs later, for instance.

At least Nora would get to make an entrance.

Her diamond bracelet was a vinder charm. The circuitry carved into the gold band was designed to move air around the wearer when activated. It had long since replaced the delicate charmed fans women once carried on hot days. Now Nora fed hers with a surcharge of magic as she approached the Blue Salon, turning the delicate breeze into a violent gust of air.

The double doors burst open dramatically, revealing her family on the other side. Five faces turned toward her, all wearing shock, annoyance, or a combination of both.

It was always nice to feel so welcomed by family.

"Nora!" Constance's hands were clenched in her lap. "We were beginning to think you wouldn't make it."

There were two empty seats left at the table. The hand that had been clamped around Nora's chest loosened its grip. She had made it to breakfast before her grandmother.

"You were hoping I wouldn't, you mean." Nora flicked a finger, sparking the vinder charm again to close the doors behind her. She didn't *need* to use magic. The point was that she could afford to. Constance's mouth opened then shut mechanically, stumbling for a polite retort, but her sister, Clemency, got there first.

"We were worried!" Clemency had the tact to look fretful. Constance and Clemency weren't actually twins, but they might as well have been. Constance was seventeen to Clemency's fifteen. They had identical Holtzfall blonde curls and milkmaid-pale skin. And today they were wearing matching dresses, one yellow, the other pink. They were porcelain dolls crafted from the same mold.

"We were just saying we ought to send a knight out to find you. Weren't we saying that?" Clemency waved vaguely to Sir Galdrick Rydder, one of the family knights, who was stationed like a silent statue by the door. Nora was only partly successful in stifling a scoff. Clemency didn't have the authority to send the knights for *milk*, let alone to fetch Nora. Besides, she was sure someone had been sent for her the moment they realized she'd slipped the guard at her apartment.

The breakfast table was dressed with a white linen tablecloth, seven elegantly patterned maiolica service chargers, fourteen pairs of silver forks and matching knives with ivory handles, and seven long-stemmed crystal glasses with needle-etched charm patterns designed to keep the drink inside cool.

And one ancient ax, buried blade first in the middle of the table.

Mercy Holtzfall usually favored calla lilies for a centerpiece, but today was a special occasion. The family had changed since their days as woodcutters in the forest, but their traditions hadn't.

Nora should be used to seeing Honor Holtzfall's ancient ax. But here, embedded in the table, it sent a twist of anticipation through her that it never had when it simply hung on the wall in her grandmother's office.

In spite of being the eldest cousin, Constance hadn't been given the traditional place at the right hand of the head of the family. That seat was empty, waiting for Nora. Which partly explained why Constance looked like she'd been sucking on lemons.

The end of the table, the place of least importance, was occupied by the previous generation. Or what was left of it.

Mercy Holtzfall once had five children.

Prosper, Grace, Verity, Patience, and Valor.

Three were still alive.

Only two were in the room.

Uncle Prosper, Clemency and Constance's father, slumped in his chair, toying sullenly with a silver cigarette case marked with charms to keep the cigarettes fresh. A waste of magic. Uncle Prosper had never given a cigarette a chance to go stale.

Aunt Patience was next to him, sitting ramrod straight and shooting her brother annoyed looks every time the cigarette case hit the table. On the other side of the table sat her daughter, Modesty.

Aunt Grace was conspicuously not invited.

That shouldn't have surprised Nora. Aunt Grace had no children to compete in the Veritaz. But Nora hadn't realized until this moment that she had been tacitly expecting her favorite aunt's support, since she was the only competitor there without a living parent.

But Aunt Grace was probably pouring herself into bed just about now, like Nora ought to be.

"Well, unfortunately for you all, here I am." Nora took her place at their grandmother's right hand, aware of Constance's face pickling even more as she did. Constance had clearly inherited her poker face from her father, if Prosper Holtzfall's gambling debts were anything to go by. Nora rubbed it in with an arch smile. "You can't get rid of me that easily."

"I guess we'll all have to work harder at it, then." Modesty laughed in a way that was clearly meant to cover up that she really meant it.

Aunt Grace and Verity Holtzfall had been sisters the way people said sisters were supposed to be. Friends and allies in all things. Nora had spent so much time with them both that it was easy to forget everyone else in this family loathed each other. Uncle Prosper and Aunt Patience resented Verity for winning their generation's trials. They resented Aunt Grace for not resenting Verity. And they resented each other for taking money from the family coffers, leaving less allowance for the other one.

For her part, Nora had always known her cousins didn't like her. They had been deferential to her while her mother was the Heiress. One day she would inherit all the family's money and magic, and unless they wanted to do something as distasteful as get a job, or they managed to marry well, they would spend the rest of their lives dependent on her.

She'd seen it happen with her mother's siblings. The deeper Uncle Prosper was in gambling debt, the more he'd drop by the apartment with a smile and a bottle of champagne for his "favorite sister." But when he was on a winning streak, he'd had no time for Nora's mother.

At the age when other children played dolls, Nora's cousins had begun playing the long game. They probably knew they weren't fooling anyone. But Nora had her part to play too, pretending she believed that their fawning was real affection.

Now the game had changed.

Since her mother's murder, the heirship was no longer *guaranteed* to Nora. And she could feel years of tamped-down resentment spilling over in her cousins. But the heirship wasn't wholly out of her grasp yet either. There was still a one-in-four chance she would be Heiress. Nora glanced around the table assessingly. Well, if she were the gambling sort, like Uncle Prosper, she would say her chances were better than one-in-four.

The disadvantage of keeping her cousins at arm's length was that Nora didn't know them well enough to be sure. Though underestimating Constance and Clemency seemed almost impossible. Somehow they always managed to limbo under the low bars she set them.

But the fact that Modesty had been seated at their grandmother's left didn't escape Nora's notice.

Neither did her perfect morning dress of ecru floral lace that accented her pale blonde hair and icy eyes, and complemented the décor of the house. Clever. She had dressed very deliberately to look like she belonged here, something that Nora with her Mirajin dark features could never quite pull off, no matter what she was wearing. No matter that she belonged here more than any of them.

"You were missed at Modesty's premiere last night." Aunt Patience finally broke the tense silence. "The papers are saying she gave a *radiant* performance."

Aunt Patience used to be an empath, able to read feelings on people. When she lost her own Veritaz, she had lost all her magic, including her Holtzfall gift. Apparently she'd lost her tact too. The attempt to focus the attention back on Modesty was embarrassing.

"Oh, yes, Modesty's *job*." The word dripped with disdain. Jobs were for needy people. As in people who *needed* money. Not Holtzfalls. Though if Aunt Patience hadn't started pushing Modesty into the cinema when she was only six, she likely *would* be broke by now. "Well, I must apologize for my absence. The truth is I really, really would just have rather gouged out my own eyes than spend two hours watching Modesty do almost anything."

Across the table, Uncle Prosper choked on a laugh he turned into a cough as Aunt Patience's normally hunched countenance drew up in sudden pique. Nora's mother and Aunt Grace used to laugh about Aunt Patience's legendary tantrums as a child. The neglected second-youngest Holtzfall. The daughter who sullenly accepted the scraps left of their parents' attention when Grace and Verity had used up their share. Until it suddenly overboiled into red-faced rage.

Nora had seen it only once, when she and Modesty were about seven, Aunt Patience shrieking and shaking Modesty over a lost silk glove. It had taken three knights to pull her off her daughter.

As Patience's face turned red, Nora wondered if sixteen years of resentment was about to spill out at her. Now, *that* was a performance Nora would watch. But Modesty glided in first, snipping her mother's sparking fuse.

"Oh, don't worry, dear cousin." Modesty's mouth drew into a self-satisfied smile. "You'll have the chance to see me at my next premiere! It's only that you missed the exciting news! Mr. Hildebrand is making a film about Temperance Holtzfall."

Temperance Holtzfall was their ancestor from six centuries ago, at the time of the last king of Gamanix. The young king had fallen desperately in love with Temperance and asked for her hand in marriage. But Temperance refused the crown, choosing instead to compete in her generation's Veritaz Trials. She gave up the certainty of becoming queen for a chance at her family's heirship. Everyone thought she was a fool. But her gamble paid off. Temperance

Holtzfall entered her Veritaz Trials alongside her six brothers. She was the only one to come out of them alive. Meanwhile, the king never married and died with no legitimate heir to his throne. Thus, the rule of kings ended, and the Holtzfalls took their place as the greatest force in the country.

There were always whispers about Temperance's children looking like the king, but Nora had a feeling those whispers were started by Holtzfalls wanting to elevate the grandeur of their bloodline.

"You don't say?" Nora pushed herself up from her chair, reaching for the silver teapot in the middle of the table. Her cousins were all politely sitting around with empty cups. But Nora knew she could get away with murder. Or at the very least, having a cup of tea impolitely early. "And he came up with that idea all on his own, did he?"

Modesty's Holtzfall gift was among the more insidious in the family bloodline. She could plant the seed of an idea in your mind and let it grow there until you thought it was your own. For instance, a director might think it was his own idea to cast Modesty, instead of someone with actual talent.

"And he wants *me* to play Temperance." Modesty brushed by the implied accusation. "After all, he says I do *look* the part of a Holtzfall Heiress."

That blow struck true.

All Nora had to do was look at the portraits that lined the walls of the Holtzfall mansion to know she was out of place in her own family. It was an uninterrupted sea of fair skin, pale eyes, and paler hair. Nora's dark hair looked like a blot of ink among her cousins' golden haloes.

The Holtzfalls might have tried to claim royalty through rumors about Temperance Holtzfall's children. But Nora didn't have to *claim* anything. She was royalty on her father's side. Her Mirajin features marked her out as descended from generations of desert-born rulers. She was the granddaughter of an exiled princess. Nora might not look like the Heiresses who came before her, but she looked like the Heiresses who would come after her.

"How thrilling for you." Nora aggressively stirred her tea with the silver spoon. "At least you'll get to playact being an Heiress if nothing else." The motion of the spoon sparked the charm engraved on the handle, designed to make the tea stronger when stirred clockwise and weaker counterclockwise. "You'll come to me if you need any tips from real experience, of course." Nora wouldn't need to stir so many times if Mercy Holtzfall would just serve coffee. But coffee, like Nora's other grandmother, came from Miraji, and Mercy Holtzfall begrudged its foreignness.

The drink darkened gradually as Nora's spoon clinked against the porcelain in the suddenly uncomfortable silence of the room. Nora had heard that there were families who gathered for meals because they actually liked each other, not because they were competing for a thousand years' worth of money and magic.

"Good to see everyone is here on time." The voice seemed to come from thin air, making everyone at the table scramble to stand. Everyone except Nora. "Punctuality is a virtue, you know."

"Not a virtue that has ever been tested in a Veritaz," Nora muttered into her porcelain cup as her grandmother stepped into the breakfast room, emerging from a panel in the wall that Nora had never noticed.

The Holtzfall home stood in the same place it had since it was nothing but Honor Holtzfall's cottage a thousand years ago. It was a hundredfold the size that cottage had been, sprawling wider with every generation, with new wings and secret passages and doors charmed to open to a half dozen other places scattered throughout.

Mercy Holtzfall was wearing a high-necked blue day dress, her blonde Holtzfall hair swept up. She wore a series of charms disguised as jewelry—rings, brooches, hair clips, and even buttons. At sixty,

Mercy was as beautiful as she had always been, her face unlined despite the four decades she'd spent ruling the family.

Her grandmother's personal knight, Commander Liselotte Rydder, followed behind. She had led the Holtzfall's guard for as long as Mercy had led the family, but she wore the same uniform as every other knight. A gray doublet with the family's crest sewn over her chest: a silhouette of Honor Holtzfall raising the ax high in the air. Nora had always thought it looked like the figure might drop his ax straight into the knights' hearts at any moment.

Commander Lis's gaze landed on Nora, her normally impassive face betraying a flash of annoyance. Wordlessly, she signaled to another knight positioned at the door, who silently exited the room. No doubt she was calling back whatever hunt she had sent out for Nora after she'd slipped out of the apartment last night.

"How did you all sleep?" her grandmother asked, gesturing at them to sit around her.

"Oh, I slept wonderfully, Grandmother," Constance piped up as she tucked her dress below her primly. "I felt like it was important to get to bed at a responsible hour to be prepared for today." She cast a not-so-subtle look at Nora.

"I wouldn't have been surprised if you hadn't." Mercy laced her fingers together over her plate. "I didn't sleep at all the night before my Veritaz Ceremony. A restless mind means you understand the importance of a day like today."

Down the table, Constance dropped her gaze, suddenly not so hungry for their grandmother's attention. Nora could have told her cousin that the question was a trap. Most conversations with her grandmother were.

"The Veritaz Ceremony is a family tradition in which every head of the family should expect to take part twice in their lifetime. Once when they are competing, and once when they are finding their successor. It is my great tragedy that this is my third time." Her grandmother's eyes drifted, not unintentionally, to Nora. Seventeen years ago, Mercy Holtzfall had sat here with her own children. Now two of those children, including the Heiress, were dead.

Valor Holtzfall, the youngest, had lost his life in the trials themselves. The five Holtzfall children had been skating on the frozen river when the ice collapsed. It was a test of their sangfroid. No pun intended. Though Nora was sure the irony of that concept wasn't what they were thinking of when the ice magically sealed over them. Aunt Grace had been the first to fight her way out of the frozen water, then she fought to pull her siblings out after her. But she hadn't reached her youngest brother in time.

Valor Holtzfall was just fourteen when he was buried.

And the Veritaz Trials continued.

Aunt Patience and Uncle Prosper had sat here seventeen years ago too. Neither of them won a single trial. In the end, the competition had come down to Verity and Grace. Nora's mother, Verity, had edged her sister out for the win. Barely.

Now, seventeen years later, here they all were. The next generation competing for the prize Verity Holtzfall hadn't lived to claim.

"None of you have been prepared to take part in the Veritaz," Mercy spoke to her four granddaughters, gesturing for a servant to pour the tea. "But that is for the best. The Veritaz is not meant to be prepared for, and it cannot be cheated. It will reveal the truth of who you really are. Which of you is cleverest, which of you is bravest, which of you is worthiest to carry on this family name."

Mercy looked around the table, taking in each of their faces. Nora's gaze followed her grandmother's. Clemency's and Constance's barely concealed excitement and terror, while Modesty feigned serenity. "I expect that several of you, like your parents, will want to tell me how the Veritaz isn't *fair*." This time her eyes went pointedly to Aunt Patience's sour face. "Predictably, like in life, the only ones who complain about fairness are the ones who *lose*. And I will tell you what I always tell those who come crying to me: Life is completely fair to those who *deserve* it."

It was a philosophy Nora had heard dozens of times, in every Heiress lesson with her grandmother. The poor were poor because they lacked the virtues of the rich. If they were as intelligent, as industrious, and as wise as the rich, they would be rich too. And within the Holtzfall family, virtue meant everything.

Around the table, all eyes were being pulled by the ax.

The Veritaz had evolved over generations. But the final aim of the trials remained unchanged: to be the first to retrieve Honor Holtzfall's legendary ax from the woods. Tonight, Mercy Holtzfall would give the ax to the immortal Huldrekall and ask him the same question Honor Holtzfall had asked a thousand years ago: Who is most worthy to inherit this powerful gift? And like every generation before theirs, the Huldrekall would agree to help determine which of the candidates was the worthiest.

Then the trials would begin.

They might come at any time and take any form. They might test bravery, or honesty, or temperance, or any of a dozen other virtues. The competitors might face the trials all together or separately. It might be clear as day that they were facing a trial or it might be disguised. But the outcome was the same: The victor of each individual trial would receive a ring that granted passage into the woods. And with that, a chance to be the one to retrieve the ax and become the heir.

There were as many ring trials as there were candidates. A fair chance for each of them to prove themselves. At the end, they might all have a single ring on their hand, and with it admittance to the final trial. Or a single one of them might have all four rings and the other three challengers would be disgraced. Or dead.

"Now," Mercy said, lifting a small finger and sending a spark of magic through the ax in the middle of table. "Who would like to go first?"

The table was silent. They all knew what they had to do. It was the reason they had been summoned here this morning. To tie their magic to the ax and agree to forfeit it to the winner.

A hefty wager for a gargantuan prize.

Modesty's starlet bravado was suddenly gone, Constance and Clemency's snideness faded.

Nora stood abruptly, her chair squealing across the floor of the breakfast salon.

The only reason to hesitate was if Nora didn't think she could win.

The ax was still sharp, even after a thousand years. Sharp enough for Nora to nick her thumb against the blade. She felt the magic inside her blood come to life, snagging onto the ax. Like an invisible thread twisting around the blade. The charm tugged on the magic inside her, threatening to unspool it all and drag it out of her. But it wouldn't yet. Not until the game was over.

Not to be outdone, Modesty stood next. Then Constance, and finally, Clemency.

Until all four of them were standing. Facing each other as the ax drank up their blood before even a drop could fall onto Mercy Holtzfall's spotless tablecloth.

Finally, their grandmother's gloved hand closed around the handle of the ax, tugging it out of the table and sealing the charm within. The magic of the ax would stay dormant until one of them reached it in the woods. The moment any mortal hand closed around the ax, the losers' magic would spool out of them until each one of them was nothing but an empty bobbin, while the Heiress would suddenly have four times the amount of magic she was born with.

And would inherit the generational treasury of magic to boot.

A weighty silence hung over the pristine breakfast table. They had arrived as cousins; they would leave here as competitors.

"Now." Mercy Holtzfall shook out her napkin, draping it over the ancient ax as servants swarmed in, bringing food to the table. "Honora, perhaps you'd like to start by telling us why you are so overdressed for breakfast?"

"Am I?" Nora sat back down, plucking a sweet roll from the tray in a carefully calculated act of nonchalance. "I like to think everyone else is just underdressed."

Chapter 5
LOTTE

It took about two weeks for the men to sow the fields in Gelde. And about two hours for Lotte to sow gossip among the women of the village.

To Sigrid Strauss she whispered that Estelle was seen kissing one of the seasonal workers behind the bakery. In Elsie Ghent's ear she dropped a few words about the money Estelle had stolen from her parents to run away with. Gossip, the Sisters would preach, was an unvirtuous habit. But Lotte was doing this for Estelle's own good.

Everyone knew the stories of what happened to girls from little towns who ran away to the cities. The lucky ones came back home with their tails between their legs. The unlucky ones . . .

Lotte knew the moment the gossip made it back to Estelle's father. The whole town did. In the blink of an eye, Mr. Hehn was flying across the square toward where a gaggle of seasonal workers were sharing a cigarette. Mr. Hehn wasn't an imposing man, but surprise and anger were a powerful combination. He had Konrad pinned against the glass of the bakery in one furious motion. Before the younger man could react, Mr. Hehn ripped the wallet out of Konrad's pocket.

"Thief!" Mr. Hehn spat, brandishing the wallet high in the air, even as heads started to turn at the commotion. "Damned city rabble! They're all swindlers and cheats!" It seemed Lotte and Estelle had been wrong about Mr. Hehn never having a bad word to say.

"I didn't take that," Konrad announced loudly, holding up his hands in a mockery of innocence, a smirk dancing around his mouth. "Your daughter *gave* it to me."

This time when Mr. Hehn lunged toward him, more men from Gelde moved swiftly in between them, holding him back while keeping the outsider in place. "You shut your lying mouth. We'll see what you have to say when we get some officers here!"

The nearest law enforcement was two hours away in the larger town of Lintzen. But mention of police was enough to get a real reaction out of Konrad. He jerked against the men holding him, and for a second Lotte caught the edge of a memory. Of strike lines being broken open by police and—

"What's happening?"

Estelle emerged from the bakery, dusting flour from her hands, just as the men of Gelde were marching Konrad off to be locked in the mill while officers were summoned.

Everyone's eyes were on Konrad, so it was only Lotte who saw Estelle's face drop into panic. Distantly, through the cacophony of angry voices in her head, Lotte wondered if she should feel guilty. Knowing she was ripping her friend's joy away from her. But the Sisters had been telling Lotte for sixteen years that she was a wicked, viceful girl. And maybe they were right, because there was no remorse in her.

Only satisfaction.

"What's happening!" Estelle moved to follow Konrad, but the women of Gelde who had gathered to watch the disturbance caught her first. The frisson of scandalous delight in their thoughts was at odds with the concern on their faces. *Stupid girl*, they thought as they fussed over Estelle. *Silly, slatternly girl.*

Estelle fought them, calling out Konrad's name, even as he struggled against his own captors. Estelle's panic crashed into

Lotte's mind, leaving her cold. Where had her panic been all the times the Sisters had dragged Lotte away to lock her in the briar pit?

The scuffling was threatening to turn into a full-blown brawl.

Lotte drew to the back of the onlookers. And suddenly she became aware of another sound. As it grew louder, and more onlookers' ears pricked up, Lotte realized it was an automobile.

One by one, people turned, torn between gawking at the fight and whatever new entertainment this was. Nothing interesting ever happened in Gelde, let alone two things at once.

Lotte had seen automobiles before. Obviously. There was the truck that brought the newspapers and the mail once a week, for starters. And the buses that brought the workers every season.

But the automobile slowing to a stop at the edge of the town square looked like a different monster altogether. It was bigger even than Lotte's sleeping cell in the convent. Light quivered across its inky surface like oil on water. And everything that wasn't black metal was silver: the door handles, the discs on the wheels, and a silver ornament on the hood—a man raising an ax, frozen seconds before he'd swing the blade down into the magimek engine.

When the automobile fell silent, the whole town seemed to fall silent with it. Though Lotte could still hear the murmur of fascination in their minds.

Two men emerged from the glistening black automobile. One was tall and broad, in his late thirties, wearing a gray doublet buttoned over a white shirt, and neatly pressed gray trousers. The sophisticated suit didn't fully hide the fact that underneath it all, he was twice as broad as any man in Gelde. The other stranger, who was considerably more compact, was clutching a briefcase in one hand and a bowler hat in the other. The buttons of a loud paisley vest strained a little under his suit as he stepped into the mud of the square, wrinkling his nose as it caked onto his well-polished shoes.

When he looked up, he seemed to realize the entirety of Gelde was watching him and tried to smooth out his features into something other than distaste. "Good morning," he said. "We are here looking for—"

Whatever he was about to say was lost as a cry came from behind Lotte. Konrad had taken advantage of the distraction, wrenching free from the men holding him, snatching the money out of Mr. Hehn's hand, and making a run for freedom.

He didn't make it far.

Lotte didn't even see the man in gray move. She just saw what happened next. As Konrad broke through the crowd, he went to shove past him. And a heartbeat later, Konrad was on the ground, unconscious. The large man was holding the wallet.

"Nicely done, Benedict." The man in the bowler hat cleared his throat. "As I was saying, we're looking for—"

"Give that here." Mr. Hehn barreled forward, interrupting the bowler hat man again. "That's mine." The man in the gray doublet, Benedict, extended the wallet toward Mr. Hehn wordlessly. Estelle was pushing forward behind him, but her father caught her, even as she cried out protests that Konrad was innocent. That she loved him.

"As I was saying." The bowler hat man raised his voice as Estelle struggled against her father. Lotte stepped forward swiftly, to draw Estelle back with her. If the bowler hat man was interrupted again, he looked like he might actually burst. "We're looking for—"

"Her." This time it was Benedict who cut the man off, his voice deep and sure, and his eyes were fixed on her. "We're here for her."

Lotte released Estelle swiftly. Sure that *her* meant Estelle.

But Benedict's eyes followed Lotte.

"I didn't do anything," Lotte burst out swiftly. More eyes were turning toward her now. Both men ignored her words.

"Are you sure, Benedict?" The man in the bowler hat was looking at her with the same vaguely averse expression he'd given the mud on his shoes. Lotte knew what he was seeing. She was in badly worn clothes that barely fit anymore, with muddy bare feet and welts on her legs, and she had no business being singled out by a man who drove a car like that.

"I'm sure." Benedict's eyes never left her. "She's the spitting image of her mother at that age."

Her mother.

Just the mention of her made everything else drop away. The pain of the lashes on her legs. The cold that had crawled into her bones. The mud that stuck to her bruises.

In the tales, mothers who were forced to leave their children always gave them a token. Something to let them know they were loved, and so that they could find them again later in the story. Lotte had nothing to prove her mother had even existed, but she had still prodded at the idea over and over again, like a tongue at a missing tooth, until it ached too much to bear.

Finally, when she was old enough for the last of her baby teeth to be gone, she had admitted the truth to herself. Her mother hadn't been forced to give her up by some wicked king or jealous immortal; she was just a woman who hadn't wanted a daughter.

And unlike the mothers in the stories, she was never coming back for Lotte.

"You knew my mother?" Lotte took a step toward Benedict, Estelle and Konrad forgotten.

"I know your mother." Benedict dropped to one knee in front of her, like a knight in front of a lady. Her mother was alive. The wound she had prodded at so many times as a child suddenly yawned open. "She sent me to get you."

Benedict's hand dropped to her shoulder. He must have said something else, because she could see his mouth moving. But Lotte didn't hear it. The only thing she could hear was his mind. And it was filled with a girl with blonde hair who looked identical to Lotte. Except instead of ill-fitting convent clothing, she was wrapped in furs and pearls. And with that image came a wave of protectiveness fiercer than anything she had ever known. A desperation to keep her safe. Agony that he hadn't been able to. But sureness that he would protect her daughter. It was so powerful that Lotte felt herself being dragged under by it.

And then Benedict's hand dropped away, and his thoughts vanished.

It was like a door had suddenly closed on a conversation, cutting it off. Leaving only the murmuring, confused thoughts of the crowd around her. She felt scraped out, empty, like she'd been shoved back out into the cold.

"Lotte." Sister Brigitta's shrill tone shocked Lotte out of her daze. It carried over the crowd as she pushed her way to the front. "Get away from those men! Now!"

The holy woman was moving toward Lotte, but before she could reach her, the man in the bowler hat stepped between them. "Good Sister," he said, "I regret that I have come armed with some paperwork this time. If you continue to keep Ottoline from us as you have done the past six days, this is a series of lawsuits we will happily bring against you and the Convent of the Blessed Briar." He started listing them, holding out various pieces of paper toward Sister Brigitta, even as she tried to move past him.

Ottoline. It took Lotte a second to realize that he meant her.

"It's not *Ottoline*." Estelle seemed to understand at the same moment. "It's just Lotte."

Just.

Lotte's anger and hurt at Estelle had been almost forgotten in the confusion, but it reared its head back up now. *Just*, she said. Like Lotte was nothing. *Just* an appendage of Estelle.

"Lotte." The man in gray smiled ruefully. "Your mother will hate that nickname."

Her mother. A woman who wore pearls and hated nicknames. In

a few moments she was taking a clearer shape in Lotte's mind than in sixteen years of imagining.

"Ottoline, Lotte," the man in gray addressed Lotte in a low voice that was only for her. "Your mother sent us for you, and if we're going to have any chance of— Well, we need to get you back to Walstad by dusk. But . . ." He hesitated. "If you don't want to come with us . . . if you are happy with the life you have here, then we will leave. And I will tell your mother you're better off left in peace. Away from your family."

Your family.

Even when she was younger, and more naïve, Lotte had never dreamed of a whole family. Only a mother.

When she had understood that her mother was never coming back for her, instead she'd dreamed of repenting enough to end her curse and being released from the convent. She'd imagined asking Mrs. Hehn for a job at the bakery. When she'd understood that she might never break her curse, her dreams had narrowed again. To simply being punished less, and allowed out more often. To having spare hours to come down and share sweet rolls with Estelle.

Now even those dreams had proved childish.

"Lotte." Sister Brigitta's voice rose to a screech as she finally shoved her way through the crowd. "You have shown yourself to be many wicked things while in our care, but you have never been stupid." Her voice was shaking, Lotte realized, surprised. Anger, now, *that* she had seen plenty of from Sister Brigitta over the years. But not this quivering panic that was making the woman's hand shake as her eyes darted between the two strangers. "Surely you aren't foolish enough to follow two strange men into the unknown!"

The unknown.

Everything in Gelde was known to Lotte. Every person's pettiest, nastiest thoughts. The shape of the briar pit where she was forced to sleep. The feel of a switch on her legs as punishment.

What her life had looked like so far. And what it would always look like here. Narrowing and narrowing until all she saw when she closed her eyes was darkness.

Whatever the unknown of the city was, it couldn't be worse than what she already knew.

Lotte drew away from Sister Brigitta. "Surely you can't think I'd stay?"

The color draining from Sister Brigitta's face was as satisfying as any pastry from Hehn's Bakery.

Benedict rose from where he'd been kneeling, nodding his understanding as he led Lotte toward the automobile.

"Lotte!" Estelle broke from the crowd, rushing toward her, her face suddenly alight. "After all our years dreaming of Walstad! We're finally going!" She clasped Lotte's arm in hers, moving with her as if they were both heading for the automobile, but Lotte pulled her arm free, shaking away the tendrils of opportunism in Estelle's mind.

A day ago, Lotte might have bent to her will. Might have believed that she and Estelle still belonged to each other. Might have cared to rescue Estelle from Gelde like Estelle had rescued her from the convent.

"No," she said, coolly drawing her arm away from Estelle's, relishing the shock in her face. In seeing Estelle, who had had everything Lotte hadn't her whole life, see this slip away. In *taking* something Estelle wanted for herself for once. "I'm going, not you."

Lotte watched understanding break across Estelle's face, her glee shattering into understanding.

Lotte didn't look back as she walked toward the automobile. But she was keenly aware of every mind in the square on her, of the mud clinging to her bare feet, the cold air nipping at her welts as she slid into the back seat of the glistening automobile.

She was barely in her seat when the magimek engine sparked to life. The man in the bowler hat had taken a seat across from her in the back of the automobile, and the man in gray was behind the steering wheel.

"I can barely wait to get back to the city." The man in the bowler hat sighed as Gelde drew away behind them. "That village is no place for a Holtzfall."

Chapter 6

NORA

Nora's cousins collected their coats on the way out of the Holtzfall mansion.

Nora collected her pile of newspapers.

Margarete had ironed and alphabetized them. *The Bullhorn* sat tauntingly at the top of the pile.

Spoiled Honora Holtzfall Gloats as Heirship Comes Within Reach

Nora rubbed at the nick on her thumb from the Holtzfall ax. The heirship was both closer and further away than ever now.

"Nora?" Constance's voice made Nora realize she had not been paying attention. Her cousin repeated the question. "What are *you* wearing tonight?"

Ah. She probably should have thought of that. Now that the private family matters were dispensed with, tonight would be the spectacle for the masses. Or at least the invited masses. In front of the wealthy and the journalistically inclined of Walstad, the ax would be handed back to the Huldrekall for the duration of the trials, and the contenders would officially declare themselves. It was an occasion to dress for.

"You'll just have to see." Nora flashed a smile she hoped came across as knowing. As in *knowing* what she was going to wear. Which she didn't.

Three large black automobiles were idling outside the mansion, drivers ready to whisk them all home to start preparing for this evening.

The crowd outside the mansion was twice the size it had been when Nora arrived, a mix of photographers and gawkers hoping to catch a glimpse of the would-be Holtzfall Heiresses. A few police officers kept the crowd in check.

The moment the mansion door opened, lenses started snapping like the mouths of hungry crocodiles. Modesty pasted on her movie-star smile, waving as she descended the steps. Constance and Clemency followed, doing a terrible job of pretending they were used to this kind of attention.

Nora let them have their moment, counting to five before she appeared at the top of the stairs.

Instantly, every camera turned toward her. Nora reached reflexively for the charm designed to shade her eyes from the onslaught of flashbulbs before remembering that it was pinned to the white stole she had discarded.

Journalists shouted questions as she descended the steps toward the idling cars. Nora caught the ones she could, lobbing back non-answers with ease.

"Nora, who do you think is your greatest competition for the heirship?"

"Are you suggesting I'm not the paragon of virtue in my family? How rude!"

"Nora, why weren't you at Modesty's movie premiere last night?"

"That little picture about the shipwreck? Boats make me nauseous. I didn't want to risk it, not even for the pleasure of seeing my cousin drown."

Nora enjoyed the quickly concealed annoyance across Modesty's face as the assembled journalists laughed. She couldn't take offense at Nora's little joke in public, or she would seem a bad sport in the papers.

She pressed through the crowd toward the waiting car, trying not to squint against the flashbulbs. Squinting would give her wrinkles, Aunt Grace had always said so.

And then to her right . . . something snagged at her attention. A flicker of something wrong as the throng ebbed and flowed, before the photographers crowded back around, obscuring her view. It took Nora's tired mind a moment too long to identify what had caught her eye.

Stillness, she realized. An island of stillness in the middle of the cacophony of movement. As men with cameras jostled, there was one body that was immovable. The only person out there not drawn in by Honora Holtzfall.

The crowd split again, and just for a moment she saw the mask, shaped like a golden wolf's face.

A shiver of warning ran down her spine.

And suddenly she was aware of them all around, the flashbulbs bouncing off half a dozen golden snarls in the crowd. Stalking her through the forest of people.

The Grims were here.

Wonderful, this was exactly what her day needed.

The Grims weren't a new phenomenon, though the name was hot off the presses.

The Egalitarian People's Party, they used to call themselves. It didn't exactly trip off the tongue. And Nora never understood how they could call themselves a "party" when they were neither holding political office nor celebrations of any kind of success.

Back when Nora was younger, they were idealist fools in drab clothing, ranting about the corruption of wealth. They would stand outside factories calling for strikes, which only ever ended with them losing their jobs. If they didn't want to work, there were plenty of others who did.

Each election, the Egalitarian People's Party campaigned with grand vague promises of "Reform" and "Change" and slogans like "More Magic and Money for All!" which obviously made no sense. Even as a child, Nora had reasoned that "more magic and money for all" also meant more for the rich. The rich would just be richer, and the poor would still be poor in comparison.

And then, about a year ago, there came the whispers of a new name.

A man had come from the countryside, though no one seemed to know exactly where. One backwoods village was much like another to city people. He had once been an honest farmer with a wife and children. Until one day, the Holtzfalls raised the tariff on his land with no warning. And since he couldn't pay, he and his family were turned out of their home in the dead of winter to be fed to the wolves. Literally. A hungry pack stalked them as they made their way to a neighboring village for shelter, finally killing the man's wife, his infant daughter, and young son. Only he survived. A man with nothing to lose, who came to the city looking for a fight.

His name appeared for the first time printed in great bold letters on the front page of the *Bullhorn*. *Isengrim's Letter to the People of Walstad*, it read self-righteously. In it, he told his tragic tale, how he'd come to the city and joined the Egalitarian People's Party, hoping to help build a better world for others like him. As if the fact that the world wasn't equal was somehow newsworthy.

The upper circles had scoffed. Isengrim's story sounded much like Honor Holtzfall's. Except where Isengrim had failed his family, Honor had proven his virtues and succeeded in saving them. If Isengrim were a good man, surely an all-powerful immortal being would have come to his rescue too. It just went to show, as Mercy Holtzfall said, life was fair to those who deserved it.

Isengrim offered an ultimatum at the end of his letter. The governor must pass a bill that allowed people other than the Holtzfalls to own land. The populace could not be eternally trapped, paying rent month after month, which could be raised on a whim, for the privilege of not being out on the streets. They should be given the chance to own their homes, just like the Holtzfalls owned theirs. And if the governor didn't pass this reform, Isengrim's letter warned, there would be consequences.

It was laughable. The Holtzfalls had carved the city out of the woods using Honor Holtzfall's ax. The city existed because of them. The Holtzfalls owned every piece of land where a tree didn't grow. No one was about to unmake the very laws that had *built* Walstad.

The newspapers had mocked the mysterious Isengrim ruthlessly. No one knew what he looked like, but that hadn't stopped *The Charmed City Times* from printing a caricature of a man dressed as a large baby, threatening a tantrum. *The Magic Mirror* showed the city as a beautiful woman, swatting at an annoying buzzing fly labeled: *Isengrim*. *The Walstad Herald* was the cruelest, printing a cartoon of a toothless wolf growling at the governor's door saying: *I'll huff and I'll puff* . . . With the governor safely behind his brick walls commenting in a little speech bubble: "He *is* a Grim fellow."

Of course, no reform was made. And Nora had forgotten the vague threat of *consequences* until, three days later, a bomb went off at Rikhaus Department Store. Nora hadn't been there herself. But Angelika Bamberg had held court at her birthday party on a yacht a few days later, telling all the details. A flash, a bang, screaming, and the glass cupola shattering and raining like diamonds around the shoppers.

No one was killed, but there were plenty of injuries. Angelika had a jagged scratch across her cheek, which, in Nora's opinion, she was making a bit of a meal of displaying, when there were charms that could have healed it overnight. And eighty-year-old Ursula Loetze was blinded in her left eye. Fortunately Ursula was the rare sort of person who could pull off an emerald-encrusted eyepatch.

After that, Isengrim hadn't seemed so toothless anymore.

Overnight, the Egalitarian People's Party was gone. In their place, proudly donning the name the *Herald* had given them, were the Grims, taking the wolf as their emblem and wearing masks to protect their identities. The Grims did more in months than the Egalitarian People's Party had in Nora's lifetime. They didn't call for factory strikes anymore; they shut them down completely, setting fires in the night or smashing machinery to pieces. Those who were arrested never gave up Isengrim to the police.

They'd set no more bombs since that first one, but the city had taken precautions, layering charms into the walls of any place meant for the wealthier members of Walstad society.

Nora had seen the Grims herself many a time since the Rikhaus bombing. Usually through car windows as they blocked off streets and chanted in their wolf masks, with cheap gold paint flaking off the tin surface. But they'd never dared come this close before. Not to her, nor to Walstad's 1st circle.

Then again, they'd never had a chance like this before.

All four Heiress candidates in one place. Photographers everywhere to witness them.

And as Nora watched, the Grim approached the police officer nearest her. And the police officer . . . stepped aside.

For the first time in the presence of the Grims, Nora felt something other than annoyance. She felt danger.

Nora reached for the shielding charm she wore as a ring before remembering she had traded it for the newspapers this morning.

Everything happened too quickly. She didn't even see where the attack came from. All she saw was a hand reeling back and something glinting before she was struck in the chest, the projectile exploding violently.

There was a cry from the photographers. Modesty paused, one foot inside the car, twisting back, hungry for Nora's downfall. Constance's and Clemency's faces were writ with shock. The Rydder knights jumped into action, two of them pushing into the crowd while more moved toward Nora.

Nora looked down at her dress. The front had turned blood red. Distantly, logic told her that she must have been shot.

Except there was no pain. There really ought to be pain with a bullet through the sternum.

Nora reached down, touching the red mark. Her fingers came away stained with . . . wine, she realized. She pressed her discolored fingers to her lips. *Cheap* wine. And it was dripping down her body as cameras flashed at twice the speed, eagerly lapping up the scene of the humiliated Holtzfall Heiress.

Modesty could barely hide her glee.

Well, that wouldn't do.

"I prefer champagne, for future reference," Nora called after the Grims, who had no sooner attacked than vanished. She reached up, slipping the sleeves of the ruined dress from her shoulders, revealing the white slip she had on underneath. "Well, I have been wearing this all night, it *was* beginning to go out of style," she announced to the photographers as she let the garment drop away from her body, pooling on the ground around her feet as the cameras went wild.

She could feel her skin tingling, alive with the thrill of controlling the situation to her advantage. With watching her cousins' faces curdle.

"Much better," Nora declared, shifting her pile of newspapers in her hand.

A heavy jacket dropped suddenly over her shoulders a second before Nora sensed the familiar presence coming to her rescue.

Theo was pushing down his shirtsleeves as his jacket engulfed her. He stood between her and the lenses of the cameras. Protecting her. The way he had since they were children. Since he had stood stubbornly between her and an immortal Brag horse that had wandered onto their country estate. She had been determined to ride it. Looking back, Theo was likely right, it would have been idiotic. But that rarely stopped Nora. What *had* stopped Nora was Alaric wrestling her to the ground and keeping her there until the horse disappeared back into the trees. While Alaric had held her down, both boys, only seven and eight at the time, had taken pains to explain that they were only doing their knightly duty. To protect her at all costs.

Now Alaric was gone. And Theo was left, still standing alone between Nora and her impulse to ride wild horses.

A silent conversation passed between them.

He wanted her to get in the car.

Nora didn't want to get in the car. Getting bundled away would make her look frightened. Which she wasn't.

But if she didn't get in the car, they both knew that Theo could pick her up and put her in the car.

Finally, with the smallest nod only Theo would see, Nora conceded.

They walked through the photographers, Theo shielding her as much as he could even as Nora smiled at the journalists. Nora gave the cameras one last wave as the car door closed behind her, the charmed windows shielding her from sight.

And in a few seconds, they were leaving the chaos of cameras behind, into the traffic of the city.

Inside, the car was silent.

Alaric and Theo had seen more sides of Nora than most people ever would.

They had been like older brothers always keeping her out of

trouble; she had stood between them and imperious demands from Modesty and Aunt Patience. They had played more games together as children than she ever had with her cousins.

They had even grieved together before.

Theo and Alaric's father had been the knight driving Nora's father when a milk van skidded off the road and struck them, killing both her father and theirs.

But for the first time Nora realized she had no idea what to say to Theo. It was impossible to see him without seeing Alaric.

Guilt twisted her stomach. Alaric had died defending her mother.

Then anger chased it away. Her mother had died because Theo's brother had failed to defend her.

"Are you all right?" Theo's tone was more formal than Nora had ever heard it.

"It was very cheap red wine," Nora said. "But I've had worse."

Theo didn't rise to the joke. He kept his eyes straight ahead on the road.

"I've spent half the night looking for you."

I didn't ask you to. But Nora knew how foolish that sounded. He hadn't been asked to. He had been ordered to. "Then it sounds like we both need some sleep."

They were heading west toward Silver Street and the empty penthouse that awaited her there. Nora leaned her head against the window. The stack of newspapers sat next to her. Her eyes fell again on the picture of her mother printed in the *Bullhorn*. Lying in that pool of blood in the alley.

Tears sprang unexpectedly to Nora's eyes. It was the champagne from last night, she told herself. Her mother always said that champagne made the women in their family emotional. And last night, Nora had drunk enough of it to drown every woman in her family in sorrow. She wiped angrily at her eyes with the neck of her slip. It came away black, and she wondered vaguely if mascara came out of silk. And then, in the blurred corner of her vision, something snagged Nora's attention.

There, in the picture . . . on her mother's throat. Light where the camera's flash hit something that wasn't dark blood. Nora snatched the paper up.

At her mother's throat was a necklace. Barely visible, the emerald chain twisted around at an awkward angle. But it was there. And on her hand, if Nora squinted, there was her ring too, and a bracelet.

Nora's heart beat faster. The police had barely needed any time to rule that her mother's murder was a mugging gone wrong. She was found in a darkened alley in a neighborhood known to be unsafe, her body stripped of valuables . . .

Except, Nora would certainly qualify those bits of jewelry as "valuable." And there they were, plain as day, still on her mother's body.

Mugger Confesses When Jewels Found in His Possession!

Lukas Schuld Admits to Stabbing of Verity Holtzfall!

That was what the headlines had read.

Nora had seen the photographs. The mugger in handcuffs while a cop held up her mother's necklace and bracelet for the reporters.

A necklace and bracelet. But no ring.

"Theo." Her voice rose when he didn't answer. "Theo, stop the car."

"We're in the middle of the road." Theo sounded exasperated, and for just a second, they slipped back into their old habits of bickering siblings. "I can't just stop the car, Nora."

"Fine, don't stop the car. Just don't take me home." Nora felt her heart racing.

"Where do you want me to take you?"

Good question.

Her eyes dashed down to the ink below the picture. *Photo by A. Wolffe.*

She was going on the hunt for A. Wolffe.

Chapter 7

AUGUST

August Wolffe was only still awake by the grace of four cups of coffee. He'd dozed off on top of his typewriter sometime around five this morning. Which now made three nights in a row he hadn't slept at home. He hadn't eaten a hot meal in two days. And all he had to show for it were a dozen photographs, twenty scribbled pages of notes, and exactly zero headlines.

He rubbed his eyes, strained from exhaustion and the gloom of the developing room, trying to focus on the pictures suspended in front of him.

For all their shouting about fair distribution of wealth, the *Bullhorn* was still a business. They paid by the headline. And August had nothing but a bunch of pictures of Modesty Holtzfall at the opening of her latest melodrama, waving under the marquee. A puff piece would be fine at any other paper, but not the *Bullhorn*. He could've written that her bracelet would buy half the city tickets to see her. But the Holtzfalls' obscene wealth wasn't exactly news.

August was already on thin ice.

Not just because every other journalist here had at least half a decade on him. Sometimes half a century. The *Bullhorn* was a place for idealists. For journalists who wanted to change the world by writing about how unfair it was.

A place for idealists . . . and seventeen-year-olds who'd been laughed out of every other paper for their age and inexperience. It wasn't that August Wolffe didn't care about the injustices of the world, he just cared more about righting his own station in life than telling everyone else how bad they had it.

He let out a frustrated breath as he leaned over the pictures spread across the table in the darkroom, his narrow shoulders straining against the suspenders that cut a line across his body.

"Is this newspaper so understaffed that you have to work the movie beat as well as the gruesome murder beat?" The voice startled August into looking up. Trudie, one of the newer secretaries, was leaning in the doorway, backlit by the bright magimek light strips of the bullpen against the red hue of the darkroom.

She was inspecting the pictures of Modesty still drying on the clothesline, with a single raised eyebrow that unsettled August, even though it was taking his tired brain a minute to work out why. "Do you write the housekeeping section too?" Trudie taunted. "*How to get tough ink stains out of shirts when you're too poor to afford a Fairweiss charm?*"

Trudie's accent was gone, he realized. That little rolling twang that marked her as a recent import from the countryside. And she wasn't talking in that breathy rushed way she usually did either. Like if she didn't get her words out quickly enough, someone might start talking over her.

She turned an uncommonly sharp gaze on him. "You're A *dot* Wolffe?"

Trudie definitely knew his name.

"I am." August's hand had already begun creeping toward the developing acid that was sitting on the table. "But I think the real question is, who are you?" August's hand closed around the bottle.

Fake Trudie's lips quirked up just a little. "Oh, how rude of me." And then, in a blink, where Trudie had been standing, another girl was lounging in the doorframe. "Honora Holtzfall, pleasure to meet you."

August almost dropped the bottle.

"I didn't really want to have to fight through a mob of journalists to get to you, so I ditched my honorable knight and borrowed a hair from one of your secretaries. I'm sure she won't miss it." She touched a small locket around her neck. A glamour charm, August guessed. All she'd have to do was feed a hair into it and she could look like whoever it came from.

Honora Holtzfall glanced down with sharp dark eyes. "Have you decided whether or not to throw developing acid at my face yet?" August realized he was still holding the bottle. He put it down quickly.

August had never understood the draw of Honora Holtzfall. She was just another wealthy girl in a city full of wealthy girls. But he'd never been alone in a darkroom with her before. He found himself scrambling to regain his footing. "I'd better not. Who knows how you'd get by without relying on those looks of yours."

Honora Holtzfall's lips drew into a genuine wide smile at the barb. Not exactly the reaction August had been expecting, but then again, it couldn't be anything she hadn't heard before. Every newspaper in town would tell you the Holtzfall girls were wealthy, beautiful fools and that was all there was to them.

Or maybe she wasn't smart enough to realize it was an insult.

"And then of course there's the small matter that developing acid is very different from the sort of acid that would peel my skin from my bones. *That* sort of acid is mostly used by mustache-twirling villains in chewing-gum comic strips and the terrible movies my cousin stars in." Honora swept him with a look he had never seen in any of the sultry pictures of her in the papers. "And frankly, I don't think you could pull off a mustache."

The challenge in her voice drew August to attention, quicker than any of the coffee. "You don't think it would make me look dashing?"

"Are you even old enough to *grow* a mustache?"

"So, you weren't expecting me to be so *young* and dashing."

"It worries me that as a journalist you don't know that *dashing* isn't a synonym for *annoying*."

"Big word, *synonym*. You should stick to two-syllable words. That's how many you need to order oysters, right?"

"Not if you want a proper dozen."

August almost laughed.

Honora Holtzfall seemed to remember herself all at once, drawing away from their duel as quickly as she'd raised her weapon. Her eyes dashed from his as she tossed the newspaper she was holding onto the table, sending his pictures scattering. "Since you clearly think I'm as stupid as I am beautiful, why don't you help me understand this?"

It was this morning's edition of the *Bullhorn*. August had been so wrapped up in finding his next headline he hadn't even seen today's yet. The photo he had taken of Verity Holtzfall's infamous crime scene graced the front page. The picture next to it wasn't his handiwork. It showed Honora Holtzfall, like he was used to seeing her, tipsy and carefree. The headline wasn't his either.

Spoiled Honora Holtzfall Gloats as Heirship Comes Within Reach

That had all the fingerprints of Walter Feuer, who despised the Holtzfalls.

"You didn't take the morning off from drinking martinis and come all the way down here to scold us for calling you a spoiled brat, did you? I mean, that can't have been news to you."

Honora's eyes dashed up from the paper so swiftly that they startled him straight into the snare of her gaze. Photographs didn't do her justice. That thought shot through August's mind too quickly for him to chase it away. "Firstly, you wouldn't catch me dead with a martini before midday. Secondly, your newspaper's tendency to spell *brat* with two *t*'s is really the only thing that surprises me." She flicked to the front cover. "My mother is wearing jewelry in this photograph. Do you see why that might be strange, or do I have to spell that out for you too?"

Now, that got August's attention.

He hadn't noticed any jewelry when he'd shot the picture. He'd been distracted by other things, like the fact that he was looking at the dead body of the Holtzfall Heiress, and getting out of there before the police confiscated his camera again. But as he peered at the image in the dim light of the darkroom, he saw that Honora was right. The flash of light at Verity Holtzfall's throat was from an immense jeweled necklace. And there was a ring on her hand. And a thin bracelet too, glittering in the flash of his camera.

He felt his heart pick up as realization dawned. "Muggers don't usually leave a million zaub's worth of jewelry behind."

Honora Holtzfall made a noise at the back of her throat. "Try thirty million. They're all from Rosenkwitz's Charmerie, you know." Rosenkwitz was the most renowned charmier in the city. Technically speaking, you could make a charm out of anything that would conduct magical energy. Tin or brass worked just fine for everyday charms. The heating charm in August's apartment was made from a half-rusted bicycle spoke. Though most winter months he and his mother struggled to scrape together enough to afford to power it. But charms worked better if the symbols were inscribed onto silver or gold. And then, of course, there were the rubies and sapphires imported at great cost from the Ionian Peninsula, ensuring anyone outside the upper circles was priced out. August could work his entire life and he'd never be able to afford a hatpin from Rosenkwitz's Charmerie. He could barely afford a *hat*.

No mugger in his right mind would've passed up the chance for charms like the ones Verity Holtzfall wore.

Which meant the mugging was a cover-up.

August had been hunting for a headline for days. Only for one to saunter into his darkroom in a pair of shoes that cost a year of his salary.

Honora's dark eyes were still fixed on him, her mind clearly far from just how many papers this could sell. "I am hoping, Mr. Wolffe, that you have a good explanation for why, out of hundreds of photos taken that night, yours is the only one where my mother is still wearing her jewels?"

And finally August understood why she was here. He forced his tone to stay light as he answered. Forced his eyes to stay on the paper so she wouldn't see the rising anger there. "Why, Miss Holtzfall, are you accusing me of being a criminal?"

"I don't know what I'm accusing you of yet." Even without looking up he felt her gaze sweep him. "But judging by how many times that shirt you're wearing has been darned, and the fact that you're working *here*, I don't think I *am* accusing you of jewelry theft, no." In spite of the insult, August felt his shoulders ease. He had spent five years fighting tooth and nail *not* to follow his father's lead. Getting jailed over false accusations from some rich girl would be a real kick in the teeth. "Besides," Honora added, "the *Herald* broke the story about Lukas Schuld, not the *Bullhorn*. And no one would be stupid enough to set up a man for murder only to be scooped by a better paper on their own frame job. Not even a dumb heiress like me."

Honora Holtzfall really wasn't what he'd been expecting, August had to admit. Not that he'd expected to ever come face-to-face with her at all. "I'll make you a deal." August fought to sound casual. "I'll tell you everything I know, if you get me into tonight's Veritaz Ceremony."

Honora drummed her fingers along the table. "Could I perhaps interest you in a large amount of money as a bribe instead?"

"Tempting," August lied. "But I'll still take that invite."

"Are you sure?" Honora said. "I am *very* rich, you know."

He did know. And he was all too aware of the empty cupboards in his apartment. Of the twice- and thrice-repaired clothes in his closet. He had no doubt that Honora Holtzfall could make his *Bullhorn* salary look like loose change. He also had no doubt that he would despise himself for putting a price on his integrity.

The murder of Verity Holtzfall being a cover-up was the sort of story that could make August's career. Stories like this came along once in a journalist's lifetime. A decade ago, a journalist at the *Herald* had broken the story that Albertine von Hoff had faked the kidnapping of her baby for ransom money from her famously tight-fisted father. Now that journalist ran the *Herald*. If August broke this story, he could leverage it into a real job at a good newspaper. One with a career path and a decent salary. But until then, he still had bills to pay. And the Veritaz party tonight, now, that was a headline.

"Wish I could help you." August shrugged.

It was no small ask, and they both knew it. The only journalists invited tonight to witness the ancient Holtzfall ax being handed over to the Huldrekall were the ones who could be counted on to fawn over the dresses, the décor, have a few drinks, and write a tidy little story about the glory of traditions being upheld. The *Bullhorn* didn't make the guest list.

"Do you own a tuxedo?" Honora Holtzfall sighed finally.

"Oh, sure, I wear it to drinks every weekend with the boys from the polo club."

"Get a tuxedo, and we have a deal."

A spark of exhilaration ran through August, the prospect of a story making him more alert than the coffee ever could. "It's a date."

"Believe me, it's very much not."

Chapter 8

LOTTE

*H*oltzfall.

The name pinned Lotte in her seat, even as the automobile raced into the unknown.

They got the papers once a week in Gelde. It was a whole other world pressed between flimsy pages. Estelle used to pore over them fanatically: ink and watercolor drawings of the latest fashions, announcements for events that had already passed, and gossip about people in an untouchably distant world.

With the same name appearing over and over again.

Holtzfall. Holtzfall. Holtzfall.

Holtzfalls clutching brilliantly white ermine stoles around their shoulders and stepping out of huge automobiles. Holtzfalls under lightbulb marquees, pearls and diamonds winking at the camera. Holtzfalls captured in flagrante in the clubs and bars of the cities, throwing money around like they *needed* to get rid of it as quickly as possible.

As far as Lotte was aware, there had never been a picture of a Holtzfall sitting in the back of an automobile with mud still drying on her legs. Some of it was sticking to the leather seats.

She had misheard. Or misunderstood. They didn't mean *she* was a Holtzfall. They meant . . . they meant—

It was only when they had fully drawn away from Gelde that

Lotte noticed how quiet it was. It took Lotte a few moments to understand what was missing.

And then she realized. She should be able to hear their minds.

She hadn't noticed in Gelde, in the cacophony of competing thoughts. But now . . . there was nothing. Not a stray scrap of memory or feeling invading her mind. It was as quiet as the convent.

Lotte had just got into an automobile with two complete strangers whose minds she was deaf to. They could be taking her anywhere.

"Who is my mother?" Lotte tried to keep her tone casual.

"Mmm?" The bowler hat man didn't glance up from the pile of papers he was arranging in his briefcase. But the driver's eyes flicked to her in the rearview mirror. "Well, I'm not sure she wants us to disclose that. And it is *my* job to keep confidences." He reached inside his jacket and handed a small card to Lotte. It was made of thick cream-colored paper with smartly printed black and gold ink lettering.

> *Mr. Clarence C. Brahm*
> *Chartered Executive*
> *Johannes & Grete — Family Office*
> *Lebkuchen House*
> *327 Brosell Street*
> *4th Circle, Walstad*

"Family lawyers operating at the highest level of confidentiality. You may keep that." Mr. Brahm patted the pocket of his jacket proudly. "I had my new secretary print a hundred, at a pretty cost too. My wife thinks it's a waste of money, but I know what image means to the Holtzfalls. And as I said, client confidentiality would dictate—"

"Grace Holtzfall," Benedict interrupted from the driver's seat. "She's your mother."

Lotte knew that name. She'd seen Grace Holtzfall in papers

alongside her sister Verity. They looked so similar that Lotte wasn't sure she knew which was which. And even now, as she tried to conjure an image, she wasn't sure which one she was picturing. But she kept returning to the image she had seen in Benedict's mind. Of a young girl with anger in her eyes and jewels on her neck.

"Why now?" Lotte said it aloud again, as if saying it out loud might make it feel true. "Why did she send you for me now?"

"Well, she actually sent us six days ago," Mr. Brahm was saying, visibly smothering his displeasure with Benedict for ruining his spiel. "But that holy woman kept insisting that you were on a pilgrimage. We didn't believe her, of course, but we searched the convent high and low day after day, and you were nowhere to be found—until today."

The briar pit. Suddenly Lotte understood. Sister Brigitta hadn't been punishing her at all. She had sent her down there to keep her hidden from these men. To keep her from her mother. Her mother who wasn't a poor unwed woman of sin who couldn't afford to keep her child. Her mother who was Grace Holtzfall, one of the wealthiest women alive.

"Did . . ." Lotte's teeth clamped down almost instinctively over the next words. She didn't want to say anything that would make them turn back to Gelde. But if she was going to be returned to the convent, she wanted them to do it now. She didn't want her mother to see her and be the one to turn her around. "My mother sent me away because I was cursed, didn't she?"

Mr. Brahm looked up from his papers, glasses falling from their perch on his forehead onto his nose. "Cursed?" She was suddenly aware of the lawyer's eyes roaming over her as if he might catch sight of a third arm she'd been hiding.

"Because if she did"—the words all came out in a rush—"you should know the Sisters of the Blessed Briar failed. They didn't manage to break my curse. So if she wants me back now because she thinks—"

"Lotte," Benedict cut her off, eyes on her in the mirror, "what are you cursed with?"

"I hear . . . thoughts." The words came out hesitantly. Lotte had never told anyone about her curse. The Sisters warned her to keep it quiet, or the villagers would shun her. "The viceful thoughts of those around me."

Mr. Brahm straightened in his seat. "You have the gift of mind reading?"

"It's a curse," Lotte said hurriedly. "A curse for being a child born to an unmarried mother."

In the front seat, Benedict made a derisive noise. "If every Holtzfall child born out of wedlock had one of the most sought-after gifts in the bloodline, I doubt we'd ever have a wedding again."

"He's right." Mr. Brahm was nodding enthusiastically "Why, there hasn't been a Holtzfall mind reader since—"

"Since Justice Holtzfall." Benedict's fingers drummed along the steering wheel. "I'd advise you to keep your gift quiet for now. And, Clarence," he said, addressing Mr. Brahm, "I'm sure we can count on your discretion. And on you loaning our young Holtzfall that hindern you're wearing."

"Of course! Naturally!" Clarence Brahm was already rushing to pull a small gold ring off his finger, holding it out to Lotte. As he passed it over, his fingertips touched her palm, just for a second. And Lotte was flooded with thoughts.

Mr. Brahm's mind read like an anxious clock. He understood that he was just a cog in the great machine that the Holtzfalls made tick. Just one of hundreds of attorneys who worked for the family. He had pulled himself up by his bootstraps to that position. Swelling with pride every time a promotion meant he could bring home a nicer cut of meat to his wife. But there had been no bootstrap to pull that got him any higher. Until Grace Holtzfall came looking for help discreetly. He knew it was risky to go against Mercy Holtzfall, but he would never rise further under her rule. If he could make himself indispensable to her daughter, though . . . treason wasn't treason if you were bringing the next Heiress to Walstad.

And then his hand drew away. And the thoughts were gone.

Along with the rest of the noise.

It was silent. Completely silent. The noise from a nearby village that she had been hearing like a distant buzzing was gone. And for a moment, it felt like she'd gone deaf.

Lotte turned the ring over, a pattern on the inside catching her eye.

It was the first familiar thing to her since they'd left Gelde. The same pattern was engraved on the pendants worn by the Sisters in the convent. "Why is it engraved with the symbol of the Blessed Briar?"

"Oh, that's not a holy symbol, Miss Holtzfall." Mr. Brahm's tone was patient and a little condescending. "It's just the charm circuitry."

"It's a charm designed to create a barrier to magical interference," Benedict said from the front again. "Most of us wear them to protect *from* magic, but in your case it will keep you from hearing the thoughts of every person who walks past."

The Sisters had been lying to her.

The Sisters, who had warned her time and time again that she would never break her curse if she was dishonest. They had been the ones lying, telling her they were too virtuous for her viceful curse. And deceiving her. They had been wearing charms because they had known who she was and what she could do.

All the while they had preached against magic to the whole village. They declared that magic didn't belong in mortal hands. They told tales of nameless neighboring towns where a charm used to mill the flour had turned all the bread to poison. They urged the people of Gelde to shun Christoph Richter when he used a charm to heal his broken leg.

And they were using charms to keep her prisoner.

As the lies fell away, for the first time, Lotte was keenly aware of herself. Every inch of her skin was sparking with apprehension and excitement, with joy, anger, and fear. And all of it was her own. For the first time, nothing was encroaching from other minds.

She was alight.

And she was going home.

THEY HAD BEEN DRIVING FOR HOURS, THE LANDSCAPE changing from fields to forest, when the automobile crested a hill and all at once, the gloom of the day shattered.

The city splayed out below them, alive with more lights than there were stars. Buildings speckled with glittering windows rose up so impossibly high, Lotte was sure they had been built by magic. Serrated gold and silver roofs threatened to scrape at the slate sky, piercing up through the clouds gathered overhead.

And then the road dipped and the city vanished from sight again. Like a creature that had crested briefly above the water for one awe-inspiring moment, only to crash down below the waves once more. They were almost there.

The storm that had been threatening since dawn broke in earnest now. Rain beat at the windows, slowly at first, then quickly, flooding the glass.

They hadn't gone far in the storm before the automobile slowed, then stopped.

"What now?" Mr. Brahm checked his pocket watch, looking exasperated. "We have to hurry, Benedict. We want to get into the city before rush hour."

But Lotte had already seen what Benedict had. There had been only a handful of people on the drive. Men dotting the fields in the distance. A pair of children sitting on a wall. But now sprawled across the narrow road was the body of a girl.

Lotte reached for the door, but Benedict quickly flicked a switch, and when Lotte pulled, she was locked in.

"Stay here," he ordered as he slid out of the driver's seat—as if Lotte had any choice. Still, she shifted to the opposite bank of seats to get a better look through the front window, her bare skin sticking against the leather as she craned.

The girl didn't move as Benedict approached her cautiously. Not even when he crouched inches away from her, reaching out a hand to check her pulse.

And then, in a blink, she vanished.

Lotte drew back sharply, her breath hissing through her teeth.

Mr. Brahm looked up. "What's that?" he asked, finally pulling himself out of the world of his papers.

Lotte hunted around in the gloom of the road for the vanished girl. She had to be somewhere. Girls didn't just disappear, not even with magic. She saw the flash of movement in the trees a second before the wolf launched itself out of the dark.

"Look out!" The warning ripped from Lotte's throat. Benedict was on his feet, drawing the sword at his waist as he spun.

His sword met the wolf's neck in one smooth motion, but instead of blood, there was a violent metallic clang as the creature went sprawling into the path of the car's headlights.

Lotte had seen wolves before. She knew they didn't glint.

Instead of fur and muscle, the wolf was all gleaming limbs and whirring joints. The rain pinged off its metallic hide noisily as it dragged itself back up onto its steel paws.

Stay out of the woods, little one, the stories went. *There you will find dangers you do not yet know how to face.*

The wolf launched itself at Benedict again, razor-toothed maw wide-open. But Benedict was fast, dodging out of the way with the same speed he'd used to lay Konrad out flat, the monster sailing over him.

Two more metallic figures appeared from the trees.

Wolves, Lotte remembered, hunted in packs.

There were hundreds of stories of the horrors that befell disobedient children who wandered into the woods. The shepherd boy who followed a lamb into the dark and never came home; the little girl who strayed too far from her grandmother's window, and all they found of her was a bright red coat in shreds.

A loud thump rattled above Lotte's head, jolting her as something hit the roof of the automobile. Another noise came from the right. Her head whipped around, and she was face-to-face with one of the wolves. It stared through the window with blank metal eyes. Up close, she could see every shiny slick detail of its face, down to the fake whiskers engraved on its snout. It looked more like a skull than a real beast.

Mr. Brahm cried out, scrambling back as far away as he could as the metal beast clamped its teeth around the silver door handle and started to pull at it like a dog worrying at a bone. Except a dog wouldn't have been strong enough to rip a door straight from its hinges. She crawled backward, casting around frantically for a weapon.

"Clarence!" Benedict's voice came from the road ahead as he fended off the wolves. There were three surrounding him now. The closest one's leg was damaged, hanging half off its mechanical joint, dragging along by a few wires. But the others were unscathed. "There's a luster in the glove box!" Benedict cried.

Mr. Brahm didn't move. He was drawn back into his seat, his

spectacles askew, his hat crushed below him, staring slack-jawed at the metallic monsters. Lotte wasn't even sure he'd heard Benedict.

But she had.

Lotte clambered up onto the seat, her panicked breaths coming short as she forced her mind to focus on those two things. *Luster. Glove box. Luster. Glove box. Luster.* She had no idea what a luster was. Or a glove box. The front seat was empty except for Benedict's carefully folded jacket.

The metallic wolf flung itself against the door again with a violent clang. Lotte tried not to flinch. The Sisters would have chastised her for being afraid of death. Death was the return to the matter they were made of, after all. They were supposed to welcome death and their return into the fabric of the earth itself.

And Lotte would welcome it one day. But not today. She would meet death *after* she had met her mother.

In the rain, Benedict's sword swung again, flashing the headlights into the front seat just long enough for Lotte to see the small compartment in the front panel of the automobile. The gap in the glass divider was just big enough for Lotte to fit her arm through. Her fingers scrabbled with the latch, shaking unsteadily. The wolf launched itself at the window again. The glass cracked under the impact, a spiderweb of fissures appearing. Another blow or two and the thing would be through.

She pressed her face against the divider, and finally she felt the latch give, revealing pens, a notebook, gum. And an engraved golden sphere.

Lotte didn't know what a luster was, but unless it looked exactly like an unsharpened pencil, she had to guess the sphere was it.

She reached for it even as the wolf rocked the automobile again. The window shattered as the luster careened forward. Lotte's fingers closed around it precariously as she heard a cry from behind her. Lotte wrenched her arm back through the divider, just in time to see the wolf's iron jaw closing around Mr. Brahm's collar, turning the paisley vest red with blood. His scream turned to a gurgle as the wolf dragged him out of the automobile. Lotte's vision blurred with panic as she turned the ball over in her hands, hunting for a button, a switch, something that might ignite whatever it was. Distantly, Lotte noticed she was bleeding. She had sliced her thumb open on the latch of the compartment without realizing.

The wolf that had dragged Mr. Brahm out rounded on her now, crouching back on its mechanized hind legs, as if it could smell the blood through its cold steel nostrils.

Lotte's hands shook, her blood smearing across the pattern on the surface of the ball.

Maybe now might be a good time to start praying.

And then the thing in Lotte's hand exploded into light.

It was like a firework bursting in the darkness, flooding the whole automobile, and then the road around them, turning the rain incandescent, drowning out the gray skies and momentarily blinding Lotte.

She screwed her eyes shut. She wasn't sure if it was against the light or against death. Like a child who thought the wolf's razor teeth wouldn't clamp around her flesh if she just hid under her blankets.

But she wasn't dragged out of the car, and no metal teeth sank into her throat.

She waited, eyes shut, listening to the sound of her ragged breathing, until the gloom of the storm crept back into the corner of her vision. Finally she dared to open her eyes, blinking away the last of the spots of dancing light.

Benedict appeared at the ripped-off door. There was a faint streak of blood on his forearm, and he was soaked through from the rain. "Are you all right?"

Behind him, a metal wolf stared up at her with unseeing metallic eyes.

Lotte jerked back on instinct. But the wolf didn't move. It was sprawled, dead, on the ground. Only it couldn't be dead when it had never been alive to start with.

"Talk to me, Grace." Benedict's voice became more urgent. "Are you all right?"

That broke through. Lotte might not be able to make sense of much right now, but she was sure of her name, at least. "I'm not Grace."

Benedict's face closed off as he realized what he had said, the fear instantly replaced with that same unreadable expression that he had worn since the convent. He reached out, taking the golden orb from her hands. "Well done."

"I didn't . . ." Lotte shook her head, still unsure of what she had done.

Benedict caught her shaking hand, turning it over gently. Quickly, he wiped the blood from her thumb with the sleeve of his shirt. She had already stopped bleeding.

"We need to go." Benedict stood up sharply.

Lotte was starting to come back to herself. "Mr. Brahm." She sat up straight, hunting for the lawyer. "He was hurt. He needs—"

She caught sight of him, lying prone at the edge of the road, a second before Benedict said the obvious.

"He's dead." She could see that. His once proud paisley-print suit was covered in blood and dirt. His glasses were askew, and his bowler hat was missing. His eyes were wide in shock and fear, staring up at the rainy sky. "He was just a casualty," Benedict said with the matter-of-fact voice of a man who had seen death before. "You were their real prey—this was an attempt to keep you from reaching Walstad."

Her eyes wouldn't leave Mr. Brahm. That was supposed to be her.

Her mouth felt numb as she asked, "Why would anyone care if I got to Walstad?"

"Your family cares." Benedict rubbed his face, looking worn through. "They care a great deal about you not making it to the city alive."

Even with her glamour back in place, walking through the *Bullhorn* offices with Honora Holtzfall felt like carrying a bomb. Any second, one of the other reporters would realize Trudie had never walked with this much careless assurance, and they'd draw and quarter the Holtzfall girl. And him with her.

But as they wove through the pit of crowded desks, not a single journalist looked up from the typewriter they were hammering away at. They were as oblivious to the most famous girl in the city as they were to the coffee going cold by their elbow.

August's own desk was littered with photographs, notebooks, camera equipment, and pieces of a broken magimek bird that he'd been trying to put back together. Just ten years ago, the way to get messages across the city was to fasten charms around the feet of real pigeons. Those disease-ridden birds had since been replaced with metallic birds, courtesy of LAO Industries. They cost three times as much as a living bird, but that was progress for you. August had bought this one secondhand, and it had died the first time he tried to send a message to the office. By the time he'd run all the way back with the headline in hand, the *Herald* had beaten the *Bullhorn* to the punch.

Honora perched delicately on the only uncluttered corner of his desk, crossing her legs with a flourish. She picked up the dented shell of the magimek bird, turning it over a few times. August ignored her. Undoubtedly the Holtzfalls had a whole aviary of the things.

"Move your legs," August instructed, nodding at the drawers that she was currently using as a footrest. Honora lifted her legs absently as she picked at one of the little gears in the bird's chest, forcing August to duck under her stockings. "The only reason I can think your mother might still have her jewelry in my pictures"—August started rifling through his drawers, looking for the right thing amidst the mess of paper and celluloid—"is that every other journalist got there *after* the police. I got there before them." He pulled out a sheaf of photographs.

"And how did you manage a thing like that?" Nora asked, peering down as he flicked open the manila file for her.

"Can you keep a secret, Honora Holtzfall?"

"I don't know." The heiress had turned the magimek bird upside down and was examining the charm inscribed on it. "Did you hear who Micha Bamberg was out with at the Netthaus last week while her fiancé was away on business?"

August didn't trade in gossip. He left that to Eudora Binks at the *Herald*, but Micha Bamberg was very much engaged to one of the Bittencourt boys. He couldn't remember which one; they all looked like identical rich jackasses to him. It was a business alliance, as most marriages among the wealthy families were. Honora Holtzfall herself was the product of one such merger, between the old magic of the Holtzfalls on her mother's side and new power of LAO Industries on her father's side. The Bittencourt–Bamberg wedding was designed to unify her father's industry with his father's shipping power. If she was stepping out on him, it would cost a lot of people a lot of money. August found himself leaning forward, interested in spite of himself. "Who?"

"Then I guess I *can* keep a secret." Honora, disguised as Trudie, winked disconcertingly. "So?"

August sighed. "There's this cop. In return for not sending a certain picture I took to his wife, he got me this." August pulled a small circular disc from under a pile of papers in his desk drawer.

"That's a police vox." Honora stopped her fiddling, her attention now wholly on the charm in August's hands. Police voxes were enchanted with a carefully guarded code, to keep the police's movements secrets from anyone who might want to eavesdrop.

"I heard about the body the same time as the police did, thanks to this. Except I was closer. I got there maybe a minute before they did. I took as many pictures as I could." He nodded to the photos on the desk. "And then I backed off before they could start asking me why I was at the scene of the crime before the rest of the press."

He leaned back in his chair, watching as Honora Holtzfall flicked through his photos with the intense detachment of an investigator taking in every detail. Not a girl looking at her mother's murder. First it was just a single picture of the body, the one that had run in this morning's paper. Then his photographs showed the cops arriving, obscuring Verity's lifeless form, until finally . . .

"There!" Honora held up the last picture. "The necklace is gone."

August leaned forward even as she returned to the picture before it. It was so plain as day he felt a fool for not seeing it before, in the mad dash to break the story first. The necklace draped around her neck in one picture, gone in the next.

He had taken three photos after the cops arrived. The last had been used by the *Bullhorn* the week of Verity's murder. It showed her without her jewelry, just like every other paper in town. It was pure chance someone had picked the earlier picture to run in this morning's story about Honora. It was the only picture in the whole city of Verity Holtzfall still wearing every piece of jewelry the mugger had supposedly taken.

Before August could speak, Honora took the middle picture out of the pile. It was of cops milling around the body. She pressed her fingers against it. There was a slight jolt in the air, like static electricity. She was using magic. Except she wasn't channeling it through a charm.

There had been rumors for *years* that the Holtzfalls brimmed with so much magic they didn't even need charms. But there were so many rumors about the Holtzfalls it was hard to know which to listen to. This was the first time August had ever seen anything like this. If this was true, someone ought to look into that *other* rumor about them owning a diamond as big as the Paragon Hotel.

Honora's magic acted on the pictures in front of her, making the still pictures come to life, as if it were a film reel instead of a static photograph. As August watched, the police officers paced around the crime scene, putting up barriers, sending out a vox call for help. All standard police procedure. And then . . . one cop quickly glanced around before crouching next to Verity's body. It happened so quickly that they wouldn't have noticed if they weren't looking for it.

The cop reached out, momentarily obscuring the camera's view, and when his hand came away, the necklace was gone.

"Well, I'll be damned . . ." August felt the hair on the back of his neck stand up all at once.

"*You* won't." Honora raised her hand, and the picture snapped back into place, becoming the same frozen image that August had taken. "But *he* will be when I find him."

She stood up abruptly, knocking one of the pictures off August's desk as she strode for the exit.

"Wait," August called after her. "What color dress are you wearing tonight? Should I get a boutonniere to match?"

But Honora was already gone, pulling the grated elevator doors closed behind her.

August slumped into his worn-out wooden chair. He could feel pins and needles in his fingers. The rush that came from being on the trail of a really good story. That need to chase it down. At times like this, he wondered if his father had got the same feeling when he saw a good mark with a fat wallet. And then he'd wonder if this ecstatic rush was what had driven his father to make so many mistakes. That got him in so much trouble.

Just then, the small magimek bird on his desk twitched, making August start. It flapped its little metallic wings a few times before resurrecting entirely, perching expectantly on his desk.

August had been working on that thing for a week, and Honora had fixed it in a few minutes. The infamous Holtzfall beauty, who was by all accounts flighty and foolish and self-interested . . .

August had a feeling he had already made his first mistake in underestimating Honora Holtzfall.

The Tale of the Woodcutter

The Enchanted Ax

Immortal beings always kept their promises.

The woodcutter found his way home by the light of the Huldrekall's ring.

The charmed ax the Huldrekall had given him felled the trees around his cottage as if they were nothing more than stalks of tall grass.

The woodcutter happily brought in the firewood to his wife, and soon their hearth was glowing. That night, as they sat by the fire warming their hands, the young couple did not hear any scratching of beasts at their door. Though outside they could see creatures' fearsome gleaming eyes just beyond the line of cut trees, as if they were held at bay by some invisible force.

The next day, the woodcutter, who now had more firewood than he would need all winter, went to his neighbors with parcels of logs over his shoulders to sell. As they marveled that one man had been able to cut so much wood in one night, he told each of them the story of the enchanted ax. Word quickly spread around the village of Walstad.

That evening, the woodcutter returned home, pockets heavy with coin. And the woodcutter and his wife slept with full bellies for the first time all winter.

The next morning, they were awakened by a knock on their door. It was a young widow from the village. She had lost her husband to the for-

est some months before, and her firstborn daughter had been carried away in the jaws of a wolf. She feared for her two remaining children. She had heard stories in town of how the things of the forest could not pass the trees felled by the woodcutter's ax. And so she begged that she might be allowed to build a home here, in the safe circle of trees that he had carved out. She promised the woodcutter that in return, she would give him a fresh egg from her chickens as payment every day.

The woodcutter, pleased with the idea of his wife having a fresh egg to eat each morning, agreed to her bargain.

Not long after, a family of shepherds from the village came knocking at the woodcutter's door. This family promised the woodcutter a bale of wool each month if they were allowed to stay. The woodcutter, who had seen his wife shivering in her thin smock, agreed to their bargain so that he might see his wife be warm. The next family were weavers, and they promised that they could pay by crafting the wool into clothes and blankets.

Before long, word of the woodcutter and his magic ax had spread beyond Walstad, and others began to arrive from neighboring villages. One family came from beyond the hills in the east, herding goats to trade their milk for safety. Another came from over the river in the western woods, asking if they might pay to live on the woodcutter's land with their rare craft of metalwork. From the south came a wealthy duke who had lost the favor and the protection of the king, and who paid in gold.

And then from the north, the enchantress came.

Or so they were called, back then, in more superstitious times, when the science of magic was new and mysterious.

The enchantress knew how to craft charms. She offered to pay the woodcutter in knowledge. To teach him and his descendants to use the magic that every one of us is born with.

With each new arrival, the woodcutter cut down more trees to make room for them. The village of Walstad grew larger, the woodcutter's wealth grew greater, and the danger of the woods grew farther away, always lingering just beyond the edge of the trees.

"We won't make it far in this car without being caught." Benedict's voice drew Lotte out of her thoughts, which were still on Mr. Brahm's body by the side of the road. It was only then that she realized they'd entered Walstad without her noticing.

The trees had been replaced by walls. The small road was now a wide paved avenue.

There were stories that started like this. Of ships that were swallowed whole by sea creatures so gargantuan that the sailors didn't notice they were in the belly of the beast until they looked up from the deck and saw that the stars had gone. And sure enough, all Lotte could see were towering buildings blotting out the sky, packed together so tightly she wasn't sure how the lashing rain that flooded the windshield could even get through.

Benedict was turning the automobile down a side street, away from the blur of traffic. "We'll have to go some way on foot, but we might be able to get a taxi a few circles up. That'll draw less notice."

The automobile looked like it had driven through a battle. Claw and teeth marks scarred its glossy black shell, the back window was shattered, and there were dents everywhere the mechanical wolves' heavy bodies had hit them. Even Lotte, who wasn't exactly an expert, knew they looked conspicuous.

"Because we're trying to keep my family from noticing us." Her lips felt numb. Everything on that road littered with wolves and blood had been a blur. Benedict gathering her out of the ravaged back seat to sit with him in the front and driving off at a speed that nearly made Lotte throw up. It wasn't until they were too far away that she realized she shouldn't have let Benedict leave Mr. Brahm's body behind in the woods. Mr. Brahm had a wife. A wife who'd be waiting for him to come home. A wife who'd want to bury him.

Lotte's family had killed Mr. Brahm, just because he was in their way. To get to her.

"All families are complicated." Benedict kept his face carefully neutral, his eyes ahead on the road as he pulled the automobile to a stop. "The Holtzfalls more than most."

Benedict killed the engine, and for a long moment, the only sound was rain hitting the metal carcass. Lotte waited silently.

The Sisters liked to say she had no virtues. But she had been patient her whole life. She had waited sixteen years for a family. She could wait Benedict's silence out.

"Seven days ago," Benedict finally spoke, "Verity Holtzfall was found dead." Lotte knew that name from the papers Estelle had pored over. Although when she tried to summon Verity Holtzfall's face, all of the Holtzfalls blended together into a shapeless mass of glittering blonde beauties. All except for Verity's daughter, Honora Holtzfall. The dark-haired desert princess who seemed to appear more than any of the rest of them. "I take it that particular piece of news hadn't made it out to the countryside yet."

"We only get the papers once a week." Lotte wasn't sure what she ought to feel, learning in one day that she had a family and that one of them was dead. But she could feel bitterness rising in her throat. "So that's why my mother sent for me? A Holtzfall is dead, so there's a vacancy in the family?" *Be compliant*, the Sisters' voices seemed to hiss in her head. *No one likes an impertinent girl. Your family will never want you like this.*

Benedict's mouth pulled up just a little at the edges. It was the first hint of a smile Lotte had seen on him. "You're not far off. Verity was the Heiress to the Holtzfall name. She's gone. A new Heiress must be chosen, by a contest of virtues. You're a Holtzfall. You have as much right to stand for the heirship as any of them. *That* is why your mother has sent for you. And that's why the rest of them want you dead."

Estelle used to hold up pictures of the Holtzfalls, pulling her own hair back into the fashionable short city cuts and asking Lotte, didn't she think Estelle looked *just* like them? Lotte had done what she did best and told Estelle what she wanted to hear. She'd never wondered whether she looked like them. Because she didn't. No matter what blood they might share, every Holtzfall she had seen in the papers looked like they could step into the part of Heiress without batting an eye. They looked like they belonged to their name.

Lotte meanwhile looked like she had never belonged anywhere. Or to anyone. Because she hadn't.

"What if I don't compete?" Lotte asked. She could feel that rising want turning to desperation. "I don't want to rule my family." *My family*—it felt so foreign on her tongue. She didn't want to be in charge of them, just to be one of them. "If I bow out of this contest, they have no reason to kill me."

"They'd have no reason to keep you either," Benedict said matter-of-factly.

So, this was her choice.

Most people just *had* a family. One that was granted them when they were born. But her family was being dangled like a prize just beyond some sort of game. She might almost have laughed. The Sisters had dangled her freedom beyond the same hurdles. *Prove that you are virtuous enough.*

But unlike at the convent, this was a *real* chance to prove she was worthy.

With a real prize at the end.

And it was so close. Almost within reach. She could feel it. She ached for it as she stretched out her fingers for it.

"Then I'll compete." It sounded simple said out loud, but Lotte felt that ache in her harden to determination as she said it. "If I have to win to have a family, then I will win."

Benedict nodded, as if he hadn't been expecting anything else. As if he already knew her more than she knew herself. He opened the door into the rain. "Then we'd better get you to the house before it's too late."

LOTTE TRIED TO MATCH BENEDICT'S PACE THROUGH THE chaos of the city.

They found a taxi, paying it double to accept them in soaking-wet clothes, after walking for almost an hour. Benedict told the driver to head north. Through the window, Lotte watched the city whip by. Men in black suits and women in colorful hats dashed up and down the streets. A girl extended a gloved arm lined with shopping bags, and an orange taxi pulled up alongside her, the light on top turning from green to red. They passed a restaurant. Through the gaps in the curling letters of its name, she glimpsed tightly packed bodies at small tables, knees and elbows knocking together, the window fogging with the heat of all their voices. Three stories up, a girl in a silk negligee leaned out a window, smoke from a cigarette clouding around her scarlet lips. A man in a slick suit pushed open a small metal door, spilling music out around him. It was far from Gelde. It was a whole new world here, and Lotte could feel herself coming alight with it, street after street.

Lotte could tell when the city started to shift around her. Shop fronts and high buildings became elegant white town houses with wrought iron fences and overflowing window boxes.

"Pull over. We'll get out here," Benedict instructed the taxi driver, handing over money. "We just need to get you to the house before sunset." Lotte could hear the urgency in his voice as he pulled open her taxi door. "Your mother will be there already."

Lotte hunched her shoulders instinctively against the rain as they kept moving, her whole body racing with anticipation.

They were almost there. Almost to her mother. Her family. Her chance to prove herself.

They rounded a wide street corner, and in an instant, the Holtzfall mansion appeared.

Everywhere else in the city, rain was relentlessly pouring down. But over the Holtzfall mansion, the skies were clear. It stood at the end of the street like a castle in an old storybook. The white stone glowed in the last of the daylight. Columns twisted up under wrought iron balconies draped in ivy, and turrets jutted up above a slate-gray roof. It was easily the size of Gelde. Next to the Holtzfall mansion, the automobiles that were pulling up and spilling out people looked like toys.

Lotte felt something catch in her chest. Something in her seemed to recognize her family's home as it came within reach.

They had barely taken another step when three figures stepped out of a nearby doorway.

They were dressed identically to Benedict. Gray doublets with a figure wielding an ax over their hearts. And just like Benedict, all three of them had swords at their sides.

Lotte felt Benedict's tension shift instantly as he stepped between her and the three knights, his hand dropping to the pommel of his sword.

Two of them were scarcely older than Lotte. A young man and woman, who drew to attention when they saw Benedict. The third figure, a man probably three decades older than Benedict, was the only one who didn't flinch at the sight of them. The only motion was his eyes flicking to Lotte, taking her in with the same easy efficiency that Benedict had in the square in Gelde.

"This is her." It wasn't a question. The knight seemed to know her the same way Benedict had.

They were here for her. Like Sister Brigitta locking her away. Like the wolves on the road. A last barrier to stop her from reaching the mansion. But there was only a weary resignation in his face as he took her in.

"Sir Emmerich." Benedict inclined his head, a bow of respect, but he never took his eyes off the three knights. "It would be too much to hope that you could step aside, I suppose."

Sir Emmerich's weathered face looked sorrowful. "We have orders." *Orders*. The word carried a weight that seemed to mean more than Lotte understood. "Benedict, my boy, this can't end well for anyone. Not even Grace's girl. If you just wait . . . it'll be dusk soon. No blades need to be drawn. No blood needs to be shed."

Benedict's answer to the older knight was wordless, his hand tightening around the sword at his side. Instantly, the two younger knights had blades drawn.

With the hindern on her hand blocking out the minds of others, Lotte had never been more aware of every feeling crackling through her. Fear flooded her whole body. Not only for herself, but for Benedict.

But neither of the young knights moved to attack. Both looked to the older knight for guidance. They were three against one, but they looked more scared than Benedict did.

"Then that is how it will be." Sir Emmerich had regret etched over every line of his face. "You know, you may cost a great many their lives tonight, my boy. But I will not begrudge you keeping your oath to her."

Lotte only understood a sliver of what was at play here, in the rain on the border of the hulking mansion they were guarding. But she knew that blood was going to be shed in her name. Again.

"On my signal," Benedict said low so that only Lotte could hear, "run."

And then he lunged.

Lotte stumbled back as Benedict's blade clashed with the suddenly drawn sword of the older knight. In one swift movement, Benedict had the younger man down on the ground, then his elbow slammed into the face of the female knight, bloodying her nose and sending her backward.

Lotte staggered in retreat before she remembered herself. *Run.* Not run away.

Her heart raced as the blades clashed, blood already pouring with the rain. Benedict was fighting for her. To give her an opening to get to her mother. Lotte wouldn't waste it. Not this blood. Not Mr. Brahm's blood.

She regained her footing just as the knight on the ground seemed to take notice of her. Lotte pulled the remaining strength she had to herself. After a night without sleep in the briar pit, after a betrayal, a near death by wolf, with one life crumbling around her, she could see the next life straight ahead, at the border of the mansion where the storm ended.

So she ran.

She ran for her life. For *this* life that she wanted so desperately. Benedict slammed his foot into the ribs of the younger knight as he tried to rise.

And in one violent movement, Lotte broke through the rain.

The sudden low sunlight struck her face, blinding her, forcing her to a stop even though her pounding pulse was telling her that she had to keep going. But without Benedict, she wasn't sure where. They had approached from a side street, and from here she could see the bustling front entrance, with streams of expensive-looking automobiles pulling up, pouring out people in grand clothing. Even as she hesitated, she saw a flurry of camera flashes go off, voices rising all at once as a dark-haired figure exited a car and was lost in the flashes.

Marching up to the doorway and declaring herself a lost Holtzfall while wearing a mud-caked dress was unlikely to get her very far.

A flash of movement at the edge of the lights and commotion caught Lotte's gaze. It was a plainly dressed girl with long red hair woven into a braid, moving around the commotion to another side of the house.

Keenly self-conscious of how casual she was trying to look, Lotte fell in behind the girl. She ran her hands through her hair, trying to shake off the worst of the storm. The other girl glanced at Lotte but didn't speak, ducking her head and pressing on. She had a slip of paper in her hand, the writing on it too small for Lotte to make out, although she could see a logo printed on the corner that read: THE ASH LOUNGE. Lotte stayed as close as she dared, worried the girl would be able to hear the pounding of her heart. The redheaded girl came to a small side door, far out of sight of the glamour of the main entranceway. She rapped swiftly.

For the first time since slipping on the hindern, Lotte didn't feel relieved to be free of the thoughts of others. She felt at a disadvantage, unsure what she was walking into.

Old habits came back easily.

Before she could think better of it, she slipped the hindern off her finger. Instantly, she became aware of the jumble of thoughts spilling off the girl. They were bundled in a nervous mess, but a few distinct images darted out.

A boy with a slimy smile that made her skin crawl even as she let him put his hands all over her, telling herself it would be worth it. It was a price to pay to enter his world. And then another figure, uncertain and blurred but larger, safer, solid and trustworthy, handing her a piece of paper. Instructions for a job in the Holtzfall mansion. Another way in. A way that meant she didn't have to do things that turned her stomach. That she could still serve the cause.

It was that simple. Come to this door and say that he'd sent her. And when she saw her chance—

Lotte slipped the hindern back on. It was enough. Enough to bluff her way in, even though she was sure the lie was written all over her face.

The door swung open. Held by another knight. Lotte fought her instinct to run. She kept her head bowed. But unlike with Sir Emmerich, no recognition passed over his face as he looked from one of them to the other.

"You've come for work?" He sounded faintly annoyed but not surprised. "On whose authority?"

"Sir Theodric," the girl with scarlet hair replied. Her voice was low and raspy and tinged with an accent Lotte knew didn't come from the city. His eyes went to Lotte, and she jerked a small nod, too afraid that a single word might give her away.

The knight made a vaguely exasperated noise, but he waved them inside. "Down the hall, get on some uniforms. In the kitchen, ask for Margarete." He kept talking, but it faded into distant noise under her pounding heartbeat as Lotte stepped over the threshold into her ancestral family home.

Chapter 11

AUGUST

I t turned out last-minute tuxedos were hard to come by.

August finally managed to borrow one from a tailor on Flint Street, on the proviso that the *Bullhorn* run an advertisement for the tailor, which was a promise he would deal with when he handed Mr. Vargene his article about the Veritaz Ceremony. He'd make sure to double up on pictures of the Holtzfalls' decadence to butter his editor up for that ask.

Guests had started to arrive at the Holtzfall mansion as dusk gloamed across the city. Even among the blasé rich, there was a buzz of excitement. It had been centuries since mortals and immortals walked together in the woods. But tonight, they had all gathered to wait for darkness to fall and the Huldrekall to emerge from the woods and begin the Veritaz.

And August would be there to capture it all on camera.

As well as the drinking and dancing and general wealthy debauchery that followed.

He tugged at the sleeves of his borrowed jacket as he waited outside the bustling pen of journalists and photographers. All too aware that the knights flanking the door were eyeing him with increasing suspicion the longer he lingered. Honora was bound to arrive soon. The sun was fading fast.

One overpriced car after the next pulled up to the front of the house, spilling out women in grand dresses and men in finely tailored tuxedos. The cars were streaked with rain, but the sky around the Holtzfall mansion was clear.

There really wasn't anything magic and money couldn't buy, even good weather. August might not be the one shouting for radical reform alongside others at the *Bullhorn*, but even he couldn't help wondering if maybe this charm might've been better used to stop the flooding of the tenement buildings near the docks instead of for a garden party.

"Good evening, sir." August recognized the carefully calculated tone from behind him. *Just* polite enough, in case August turned out to be somebody, but tinged with the fair certainty that he was most likely not.

August pretended not to hear, making a show of adjusting his cuffs. He didn't have any cuff links.

"Sir." The voice came again, as this time the man it belonged to stepped into view. August found himself eye to chest with the Holtzfall sigil of a figure wielding an ax, stitched onto an elegant gray doublet. Weren't giants supposed to have died out a hundred years ago? "May I help you?"

"Oh, not at all," August said. "Kind of you to offer though, my good man." He almost slapped the knight jovially on the arm, then thought better of pushing his luck.

The knight's brow furrowed, seeming momentarily baffled. "Sir," he said again, "most people usually go straight into the party when they arrive."

"Hmm." August nodded, as if the knight were sharing an interesting fact. "Is that right?"

The knight waited again for August to offer some sort of excuse for why he had been standing in front of the mansion for nearly half an hour now. But August didn't volunteer one. He was aware that he was rapidly running out of smart answers.

"Oh, well, I——" He stuck his hands in his pockets, as if hunting for his invitation. Too late, he realized the gesture had pulled back his jacket to reveal the small dented camera around his neck. The knight's demeanor changed instantly.

Damn. He was made.

"All right." The knight's firm hand dropped onto August's shoulder. "Time for you to go, journalist."

"No, no. See——" August forced a laugh as if this was all some big misunderstanding, though the knight was already marching August toward the boundaries of the weather magic, preparing to toss him out into the rain. "I've got a date."

"Oh, yeah." The knight looked skeptical, still moving toward the border of the charm where the rain was lashing. "With whom?"

"With me." Her words worked like a spell. Instantly, the knight released August, dropping into a deep bow.

"Well, at least you're in time to save my tux." August made a show of brushing off his lapels. "You know, I've got to return this by midnight or else——" Whatever he was going to say died on his tongue as he turned.

Honora Holtzfall was silhouetted in the last of the day's burnished sun. For the past half hour, August had seen women arrive in every dress imaginable. They came wearing thousands of peacock feathers, they came drenched in gold or wrapped in hurricanes of tulle. He'd imagined Honora Holtzfall would be wearing the finest finery of them all. Instead she was wearing a plain white slip that clung to her indecently. He barely had a beat to take her in before every other journalist waiting behind the barriers noticed her. All at once, the cameras started to go as they shouted questions at her. Flashbulbs went off like fireworks, engulfing Honora as she made her way toward him.

Honora Holtzfall ignored every single shouting photographer. She just kept walking, the flashes seeming to cling to her, and as August squinted against the onslaught of cameras, he thought he could see her transforming. She sailed through the army of press, until suddenly she was standing in front of him in a dress made of light.

She looked as if she had just broken through an incandescent veil and emerged with tendrils of it clinging to her. As she moved, the dress shuddered through every opalescent color light could be, from sunrise gold to sunset pink, a constant dancing prismatic color spectrum with every swish of her skirt. The dress trailed behind her like she was walking in her own spotlight.

August felt his hand twitch, aching to reach out for the ribbon of light along Honora's bare shoulders, except he was worried that she might break apart, too beautiful to be real.

"That tuxedo is *hardly* worth saving." Honora's eyes brushed him swiftly. He tried to find his footing again.

"Well, I was going to splash out at Rikhaus"—he buttoned the jacket up over the camera again—"but then I remembered that unlike you, I don't get by on appearances."

"I'll take that as a compliment."

"You shouldn't."

"Don't worry," she said, her sparring smile making her even more beautiful, "I own a mirror."

August was aware of cameras watching them curiously. Obviously wondering why Honora Holtzfall was talking to a stranger in an ill-fitting tux. Honora seemed oblivious to all of it.

"I would love to stand here accepting praise all evening, but I do need to get inside before sunset."

"Shall we?" August bowed sardonically, offering his arm. And suddenly Honora Holtzfall's bare skin was brushing the fabric of his suit, making the hairs rise on the back of his neck.

"We might as well."

And just like that, August Wolffe, the son of a thief and a laundress, journalist at a disreputable paper, walked into the world of the Holtzfalls.

"I have a question for you." Nora handed August the second glass of champagne she had plucked up on their journey across the garden.

"Usually questions are my job." August took the glass. He at least looked more presentable than he had in a rumpled shirt in the *Bullhorn* offices this morning. And once the sun set, people might not notice the tuxedo didn't quite fit.

"How many cops are in the pockets of the Grims?"

The question had been preying on her all afternoon as she had crafted the charm to make her incandescent dress. As she worked, she pictured it over and over again in her mind: the police officer outside her grandmother's house simply *stepping aside* for the man in the wolf mask.

And now another police officer was involved in faking her mother's mugging.

Nora was not naïve. She knew there were cops on the payroll of the city's criminals. But unlike the Grims, those criminals had money. Which could only mean that if there were cops aiding Isengrim, they were in it for the cause, not the cash.

"If I was taking a guess?" August took a swig of his drink as they skirted the edges of the party. "Not nearly as many as those in your family's pockets."

Nora scoffed. "Holtzfall tax money pays police salaries, if that's what you mean."

As they walked, the charms attached to Nora's shoes kept her high heels from puncturing the lawn. Lamps floated in thin air, dotted through the garden of the Holtzfall mansion. But here at the borders of the garden, the lights fought against the long shadows cast by the ancient woods.

August raised a shoulder in an infuriating shrug. "If you've already decided that the Grims are responsible for your mother's death, why are you talking to me instead of . . ." He waved his glass at the general crowd. The same gaggle of wealthy people who had been around her whole life. All she'd done for sixteen years was talk to them.

"Because I want to prove they did it. And then I want to take Isengrim down. And his entire Grim operation."

The Grims liked to blame the Holtzfalls for every tiny thing. If Isengrim got a splinter, there would probably be a soliloquy in the *Bullhorn* about how it was the Holtzfalls' fault. How they didn't pay the carpenter a decent wage to sand the wood down.

But more and more the Grims weren't just talking; they were taking action. And the only thing, generation after generation, that had ever truly threatened the Holtzfalls was the lack of a successor. A dead Heiress had Isengrim written all over it.

"You work for the *Bullhorn*."

"Well remembered."

"Your paper obviously knows how to contact Isengrim. You publish those *Letters to the People* he sends in every week." The letters were sloppily written, lie-riddled tirades that the *Bullhorn* had the gall to publish as news. Nora had never cared about them before, but a man who wrote letters was a man who could be found. Isengrim had eluded capture until now, but he hadn't had Nora hunting him.

"He doesn't exactly drop into the paper for coffee and cake,"

August said. "As far as I know, those letters turn up on my editor's desk, and he slaps them straight on the front of the paper."

"That would explain why they're riddled with spelling mistakes."

"Let's say Isengrim did order your mother's murder," August said, leaning back against a tree. "Why wouldn't the Grims have taken credit by now? Why wouldn't Isengrim have bragged in his letters that he'd struck a blow against the Holtzfalls?" They were close to the edge of the woods, and for a second, Nora thought she saw something behind him in the trees. Anticipation was building under Nora's skin. Soon the sun would set, and when it was gone entirely, the trials would begin. She should be mingling, reminding everyone of who the once and future Heiress was. But for some reason, she couldn't pull herself away from this conversation. And this irritating journalist with his irritating logic.

"The Grims playact at bravado. They know that if our attention turned fully toward them, we could end them." Nora's argument was rickety. The Grims had come for her in full daylight this morning. It had only been wine, but if they'd wanted to take a real shot at her, they could've. Which begged the question of why they hadn't. It could have been a knife in her sternum, not just a bad vintage.

"Fine," she said at last. "Who do *you* think it is if it's not the Grims?"

August didn't answer immediately, as if considering whether he could trust her with what he thought. Nora felt a spike of annoyance. "Then don't tell me. I don't actually care what you think." She made as if to turn away, to fold herself back into the crowd.

"Lukas Schuld didn't have your mother's ring." August's words made her stop. She glanced over one shoulder at him. "I looked back over the police report." August seemed serious for once. "When they arrested Lukas Schuld, they said he had your mother's necklace and bracelet. That was the evidence against him. Now we know he never had those until the cops planted them to frame him. But there's been no mention of the ring she was wearing in that picture."

"You think the cop who framed him pocketed the ring? Why would he risk that?"

August let out a short laugh, then seemed to realize Nora wasn't joking. "To sell it, obviously. Holtzfalls might pay cop salaries, but do you actually know how much a police officer makes in Walstad? Especially the ones in the lower circles." Nora ought to know that answer. Once a week since she was ten years old, she had been meeting her grandmother in her office for a lesson on the heirship. She had seen valuations for every property they owned in the city. Pages of records for rents and debts owed to them. She might even have seen salaries at some point. But Nora's mind was bright, not photographic. And it hadn't mattered at the time.

"So you think the cop who framed Lukas Schuld skimmed a little to make ends meet."

"I think that ring would *more* than make ends meet." August shrugged. "I might not know how to get to Isengrim, but I *do* know where cops take stolen jewelry to fence it."

Nora considered him. "So we find my mother's ring, track it back to the cop who took it, and ask a few questions about why he'd stage a murder to look like a mugging."

"What's this 'we'?" August asked. "I don't remember inviting you."

So. He was going to make her do this the hard way.

"Do I need a formal invitation to trawl pawnshops?" Nora pretended to adjust her diamond earring with a sigh. It was the easiest thing in the world for her to pull the stud out of her ear without August noticing.

"You're conspicuous in the first circle," August said. "What do you think you'll be below the tenth?"

Nora bent down under the pretense of adjusting her shoe, the diamond earring in her hand. "I think I'll be in disguise."

"This isn't a costume party."

"No." Nora's voice gained an edge in spite of herself as she straightened again, the diamond earring gone from her hand. "It's my mother's murder. And I'm going to find the person responsible." Nora's game with journalists was a careful balancing act she had learned as soon as she could speak. She showed them what she wanted them to see and only that. Never her true feelings. Never real anger or sorrow or joy. And never how clever she was. But August had already seen more than she'd intended him to. And for once, Nora wanted someone to see how *angry* she was. "And then I am going to destroy them."

The last time Nora had seen her mother, they had been crossing in their apartment on Silver Street like ships in the dusk. Verity coming back in from a meeting with Mercy. Nora headed out to . . . She couldn't remember what now. She also couldn't remember the last time her mother had stopped to tell her about her meetings with her grandmother. When Nora was younger, and her father was still alive, Nora would lie with her head on her mother's lap while she combed fingers through her hair, listening to her talk about the things that she would do when she was head of the family. Schools she would build. Artists she would sponsor . . . But that day, Nora's mother had kissed her and tried to push her hair out of her face, on the edge of saying something. And Nora had waved her off and vanished into the night.

"There are other people with something to gain from your mother's death, you know," August said, drawing her back to the present. To the party that was being thrown because her mother was dead. "People with the kind of money to bribe a police officer. People in your own family."

The music of the party seemed distant from where they stood in the shadows at the edge of the woods.

He meant Aunt Patience or Uncle Prosper.

The thought would never have crossed Nora's mind. But as soon as he said it, she understood. Aunt Patience and Uncle Prosper had lost their own trials to her mother. Lost their chance at ruling over all this. Verity's death gave them another shot at what they had lost, through their children.

"You're sure you want to accuse a Holtzfall of murder?" Nora felt the words, low and dangerous. There were certain people in her family she might not have the greatest affection for, but they were still her family.

"Are *you* sure Isengrim is guilty?" August shrugged calmly, taking another swig of champagne.

She had caught him on the back foot this morning, in the darkroom, looking disheveled and sleep-deprived. But he was standing his ground now. And though she hated to admit it, he did actually seem to know what he was talking about. He'd already started the work while she was off charming dresses made out of light.

This time, when she turned back to the crowd, it was to assess them.

Modesty. She roamed the party with her carefully trained smile and a waist-cinching green-and-gold dress, Aunt Patience hovering behind her like a shadow cast by her daughter's light. She had proven herself in the trials to lack many virtues. But true to her name, Aunt Patience had been able to play the long game elsewhere. With Modesty's career. With small investments of her Holtzfall allowance. Was it possible her aunt had been biding her time all these years, patiently waiting to snatch away her sister's prize?

Clemency and Constance. They were dressed like a matched set in pale cream gowns, their gloved hands flitted through the air anxiously as they spoke. Uncle Prosper stood with them, his avarice on full display in the gold of his buttons and silk of his necktie.

Aunt Grace was the only Holtzfall with no stake in this race. No daughter to give her a second chance at what she had lost. She alone, in the heavy atmosphere of anticipation, looked bored. Aunt Grace had come close to winning her own trials. It had come down to Grace and Verity in the end.

Both had won passage into the woods.

Verity had come out with the ax.

And yet even on that fateful day seventeen years ago, Grace had seemed as happy in the photographs as Verity was. And as her favorite aunt's gaze lazed over the crowd, it landed for just a moment on Nora. In that fraction of a second, Aunt Grace smiled and offered Nora a swift wink, like they were in on a secret together. And Nora felt the tightness in her chest ease. She had an ally in this still.

"Your theory would only hold water if any of my cousins had even the smallest chance at beating me in these trials. And that would be a very foolish gamble."

Chapter 13

LOTTE

The uniform was a little tight. But it was still twice as nice as the mud-stained dress that was now crumpled somewhere in the depths of the mansion.

Lotte had lost track of the girl with the red hair almost as soon as they'd been ushered into the bustling kitchens. The whole place was a flurry of identically dressed girls moving around stoves and ovens that ran hot with magic instead of fire. Trays as large as a person glided on rails above their heads. Sparks of unnatural energy ignited below an immense copper pot, and a cook flicked switches rapidly, setting an oven alight. Everything smelled mouth-wateringly rich, reminding Lotte that the only thing she'd eaten all day was the spiced bun with Estelle. A crackling piece of meat turned on a spit on its own, as a woman pristinely dressed in white arranged berries across perfectly iced cakes.

She had done it. She had gotten into the mansion. And she was trying hard not to gawk and get immediately spotted for the country girl she was.

She had to find her mother. She could still feel her heart racing as she thought of Benedict, drawing his sword in the rain. Lotte didn't know how long he could hold the three other knights at bay. How long before they would come after her. She had to find her mother before they found her.

"You." Lotte's head whipped around as an older woman snapped her fingers in her face. "You weren't hired to stand there. Go with Abigail and collect some used glassware."

The relief at being granted a way out of the kitchen must have bloomed all over Lotte's face, because the woman looked at her askance. "You're going to collect glasses only, you hear me?" she called out. "This isn't a chance to gawk at your betters up there."

A girl with chestnut curls peeking out from under her white cap appeared at Lotte's elbow. Abigail, she assumed. "Don't mind her." She rolled her eyes conspiratorially at Lotte. "The folks up there aren't better than us at anything. Except at being rich maybe."

"I didn't know that was a skill." Lotte's accent seemed to scrape harshly against Abigail's own city melodies.

Even her laugh was harmonious as she said, "I think you and I will be friends. This way." Abigail led her toward the wide hallway leading out of the kitchen.

They had just stepped over the threshold when everything around Lotte lurched suddenly. Instead of a tiled floor, Lotte's foot hit uneven grass. She stumbled, trying to find her footing, Abigail steadying her by her elbow. The contact of Abigail's hand broke through the barrier of the hindern, and Lotte caught a brief flash of amusement.

"First time taking a byway?" Abigail laughed again, but not unkindly.

They weren't in the hallway outside the kitchen. Instead they were standing in a sprawling garden, and as Lotte twisted to look behind, she didn't see the stoves and army of girls milling around anymore. The doorway behind them showed a grand ballroom. It was like they had passed through the whole house in just one step.

"A byway?"

"Charmed doorway." Abigail passed Lotte a silver tray. "The Holtzfall mistress doesn't like us traipsing through the whole house, wastes time on her money. So we take the byways to get around faster." She beckoned for Lotte to follow, gathering glasses as she went. Lotte followed the other girl's example, though her mind was only half on her work.

A full orchestra played somewhere in the garden. But when Lotte looked for musicians, all she could find were instruments floating in the air. Nearby, a fountain spilled out champagne as guests nonchalantly held coupes underneath to fill to the brim. She watched as a woman in a white-and-red gown downed her glass in one before dropping it to the grass. Abigail swiftly stooped to pick it up, her dove-gray uniform gliding in and out of the crowd like a ghost.

There had to be thousands of people in the gardens. And one of them was Lotte's mother. She didn't even know where to start looking for Grace Holtzfall. Her eyes dashed across every face as they moved, searching for the woman she had only ever seen in newspapers, her hands moving absently even as her heart pushed her forward.

Which was why she was looking the wrong way when she walked straight into a boy, causing him to spill champagne down his peacock-print suit.

Lotte staggered back. "Sorry." Then she remembered her disguise. "Sir," she added hastily. Her thoughts were already tumbling urgently. If she had survived wolves and knights only to be kicked out for spilling champagne . . .

The peacock-clad boy only grinned as he dabbed at his suit. "No need to worry. I was going to turn this into rags after tonight anyway. But I'll tell you what, you can make it up by having a drink with me. And please, it's not *sir*. Freddie Loetze at your service." A dart of recognition went through Lotte's mind. Except that wasn't possible. She didn't know anyone in this city.

Freddie Loetze held a coupe filled with champagne toward her expectantly.

"I can't." Lotte might be new to the city, but even she knew servants didn't drink with the upper class. And as she scrambled for an excuse, somehow it was the Sisters' sermonizing that slipped out. "Indulging in base vices blemishes one's work."

Lotte cast around for Abigail. She found her in time to see something unreadable pass over Abigail's face as she noticed Freddie. Abigail met Lotte's eyes just for a second. With a hindern on her hand she couldn't read her thoughts from here. But she thought she saw an apology in her eyes. And then she was gone, disappearing into the crowd. So much for being friends.

Lotte moved to follow her, but Freddie's hand darted out and closed around her wrist painfully, even as his smile stayed intact.

"You must be new." His bared white teeth reminded Lotte of the mechanical wolf on the road. "No one's taught you it's rude to refuse the guests." And in that moment, Lotte knew why he was familiar. She had seen him in the mind of the redheaded girl. The boy who made her skin crawl. And as his hand around her wrist broke through the barrier of the hindern, Lotte felt his thoughts climb all over her skin too. Her moralizing words hadn't deterred him. If anything, he was *more* interested. A holy little lost lamb here in the city. He looked forward to stripping all that righteousness away one piece at a time until she was ruined.

Lotte fought back the instinct to rip her arm from his. The last thing Lotte needed was to draw attention to herself. Even now, she could see a figure in uniform with his hands clasped behind his back, sword at his side, watching the crowd. Whatever danger this boy was, it was less than the knights.

She took the drink.

"Good." Freddie's grin widened. "How about we take a turn around the woods?" Lotte hadn't even noticed the woods until he waved his hand. The dark line of trees was well hidden behind the lights of the party. "They're teeming with magic, you know,"

Freddie said as he led her toward the trees. "That's where all of this"—he gestured at the lights around them—"comes from. LAO Industries draws the magic straight out of the woods and powers the whole city." He was pulling her farther from the lights of the party, toward the woods. "See, if you look closely through the trees, you can see some of the silver spikes they use to draw the magic out of the woods. You know Mercy Holtzfall carried those charmed spikes in there herself. The only woman in the city who has proven she is worthy of entering the woods to the creatures in there. Everyone else who has ventured in looking for magic has never come back out. If anyone else could figure out how LAO Industries does it we all could be as magic rich as the Holtzfalls."

"Your family is running out of magic of its own, isn't it?" The thought slid from his mind to Lotte's lips so quickly that she didn't have time to fully consider what she was doing. She just knew she had to say something to stall him. To keep this boy from drawing her into the darkness of the woods.

It worked.

The shock that rippled through him stalled his fake charm in its tracks. But he didn't drop her wrist. That was his mistake.

"Your father spent most of it on a deal with the Otto-Raubmessers, which seemed too good to be true. Probably because it *was* too good to be true. And now it's all gone. That's why you like to playact rich boy with girls like me who will be impressed by a couple of cheap baubles, instead of girls who might know the difference. And you promise them you'll marry them, because you know they're with you for the money they think you have. But the truth is, you're the one who is going to have to marry for money one day." The whole story was cascading freely from his mind right to Lotte's tongue, all the secrets he'd been keeping for months. "You won't be able to marry Nora, because she hates you. But if another one of the Holtzfall girls wins the Veritaz, you might have a chance—"

He ripped his hand free, but not before Lotte seized the thread of fear in his mind. "Who are you?" he hissed, his charming façade vanished now.

With his hand gone from her wrist, Lotte felt her own determination roll back over her. "I've been sent to find Grace Holtzfall." Let him think that she was someone who was supposed to be here. "Do you know where she is, or should I start telling everyone the truth about you while I hunt for her?"

She didn't need to read his mind to see the pure cold fury in him now. Wordlessly, he jerked his head.

And as Lotte turned, she saw her through the haze of gowns.

Everything else dropped away as Lotte moved toward her, unnoticed, through the crowd in her servant's garb. She'd had this dream before as a child, rushing toward a vague figure that she knew was her mother. She always woke before she reached her. But she didn't vanish now.

She was about to meet her mother.

Suddenly she was six years old again, and every single one of her childish hopes came rushing back as Grace Holtzfall turned toward her.

She was exquisite. That was the first thing Lotte couldn't help noticing. Blonde hair haloed out around a delicately featured face, a few short strands falling out of her fashionable bob and into her heavily lidded eyes. Remnants of bright lipstick adorned a full mouth, primed for pouting. The rest of it stained the rim of the nearly empty glass that hung loosely from her fingers. A sweeping feathered dress clung to her like it was made of cobwebs, slinking delicately away from porcelain skin and draping this way and that.

She looked exactly like every woman Lotte had ever seen drawn in a magazine. The kind Estelle would cut out and pin to her mirror and try to emulate.

And Lotte understood now why Benedict had known who she

was with such certainty. Why the knights on the street hadn't hesitated at the sight of her.

She saw her own face in her mother's.

Recognition broke across Grace Holtzfall's face too.

Lotte had imagined this meeting a thousand times, but all words seemed to die on her tongue. Everything she had ever thought she would say to her mother seemed unimportant now.

"Darling!" Her mother greeted her as if they were old friends who hadn't seen each other in a long time. "You're *appallingly* late, you know. We had to start the party without you." Her voice was bright and loud as she waved her drink at the celebrations, as if they were all for Lotte. And then her brow furrowed as she cast around behind her. "Where's Benedict got himself to?"

Lotte felt her stomach turn as she thought of her last glimpse of Benedict. Fighting to give her a chance to get here. But before she could reply, the last of the sun disappeared from the sky, and the sound of a bell rang, drawing the crowd around.

"It's time." Grace's smile was dazzling. "Are you ready to become the most famous girl in the city?"

The Tale of the Woodcutter

The Inheritance

Years passed in the safe haven of Walstad. As the town grew larger, the woodcutter grew richer and older. But no matter how many trees he felled, he never broke his promise to the Huldrekall, and he kept the ancient forest spirit's tree safe.

As the woodcutter aged, he visited the Huldrekall often. The woodcutter thanked his immortal friend for the great gift of his ax. But he also spoke of his uncertainty of the future. Unlike the Huldrekall, the woodcutter was only mortal. Soon his time would end. And without a new wielder of the ax, things would return to the way they had been.

He would have to pass his ax on.

The woodcutter and his wife had three children, and each was virtuous in their own way. His eldest son was the cleverest; his middle child, a daughter, was the kindest; and his youngest son was the most honest. But the woodcutter did not know which one was worthy of inheriting the ax and the responsibilities that came with it.

So once again, the Huldrekall offered his help to the woodcutter.

He instructed the woodcutter to give him back the ax that he had gifted him so many years ago. He told the woodcutter to go home and tell his children he had forgotten the ax in the woods and to send each of them to fetch it back for him.

Whichever of the woodcutter's three children returned with the ax would be most worthy of wielding it.

Chapter 14

NORA

It was time.

Mercy Holtzfall had taken her position at the edge of the woods as the last of the daylight ebbed from the sky around the mansion. Cameras took aim expectantly.

Everything else dropped away.

Nora's heart felt like a bird trying to escape its cage as the crowd moved around her, seeming to both part for her and surround her. Modesty glided through to Nora's left. And there, to her right, were Constance and Clemency. They clasped hands as they approached, born allies against Nora.

Being an only child was meant to protect Nora.

Her mother hadn't wanted this for her. And so long as she was the only heir of Verity Holtzfall, there wouldn't be a trial. She wouldn't have to experience the grief of losing a brother to the trials. Like Verity had lost her brother Valor. She would never have siblings turn against her. Like her Uncle Prosper and Aunt Patience had curdled against her mother.

An only child was, by default, the most virtuous.

As well as the least.

Until last week, Nora had never questioned if she was virtuous enough.

Well, she thought, as all four of them broke through to the front of the crowd, they would find out soon enough.

A hush fell over the garden as the girls lined up in front of their grandmother. Mercy Holtzfall cast a long, considered look over her grandchildren before turning toward the trees. She was holding the ax in her hand. It looked more at home out here, on the edge of the ancient woods, than it had buried in the breakfast table this morning.

The border between mortals and immortals had been drawn more firmly across centuries.

First by Honor Holtzfall wielding his ax. Then by his descendants. All to protect humans from the things that lurked in the woods. And then, as mortals grew more powerful, instead of fearing what lived in the woods, they had gone looking for it. Emboldened by charms and new weapons, people went seeking favors from immortals, like the one granted to Honor Holtzfall. Men returned with branches of immortal trees as trophies, women sought to seduce spirits into giving them half-immortal children like the ones who roamed the desert kingdoms.

Finally, just over a century ago, the spirits of the wood drew their own border in return. Overnight, no one could pass into the woods anymore. The boundary worked both ways now. Immortals couldn't come into the city to prey on humans. And humans couldn't pass into the woods to seek out magic. Every now and then, there was a rumor that a lost child had stumbled into the woods. Or someone might disappear and reappear decades later, looking as young as the day they'd vanished, babbling about the things they had seen. But those were only rumors.

As far as Nora knew, the woods were impenetrable.

When they were young, the Holtzfall grandchildren had tried running toward the trees as fast as they could, only to find themselves running in the opposite direction, back toward the mansion. Or sometimes they would just walk toward the trees for ages, only to find that the woods weren't getting any nearer.

The woods were closed to all but those deemed worthy to enter.

The Veritaz Trials were their chance to show they were worthy.

There would be four trials, one for each competitor. Each came with the chance to win a ring granted by the Huldrekall. At dawn, thirteen days from tonight, only those competitors who had won rings would be allowed to enter the woods and hunt for the ax.

There was a long moment of silence, punctuated by the occasional click of a camera shutter. And then, slowly, the darkness at the line of trees shifted. It happened so imperceptibly at first that it seemed as though the branches were just quivering in some imaginary wind, or maybe with the collective intake of breath from the crowd. And then a figure emerged from the dark. Except it seemed to Nora as if maybe he'd always been there at the edge of the woods.

Like he'd been watching them all this time.

He had the shape of a man but was tall and slender and impossibly beautiful in a way her mind struggled to grasp. Instead of skin, he seemed to be made of rough bark, which moved with him as effortlessly as water. Golden veins ran through the wood of his body so that he glowed from the inside.

Nora felt as if the air had been sucked out of her lungs. The Huldrekall had been around at the birth of the world, had known her ancestors as far back as they had existed. Nora was a big part of this city, but she suddenly felt like a very small part of the world.

"My old friend," Mercy Holtzfall spoke. It was tradition to ask for help the same way Honor Holtzfall had when he'd come to the immortal being in his old age. "I come to ask for your guidance, for I do not know which of my heirs is worthiest."

As cameras clicked, Nora wondered whether the ancient spirit even noticed them. All his attention belonged to Mercy. She extended the ancient ax to him, passing it over the border between the city and the woods, each remaining on their own side.

"I will guide your choice." The Huldrekall's voice sounded far away, as if it might be traveling from a deep hollow of a tree. "Who are your heirs?"

Constance stepped forward first, impatience practically bursting out of her. "I am her heir." Her voice rattled with nerves. A few lenses clicked, taking her in.

Modesty was next in order of age. "I am her heir."

Nora was next, younger than Modesty by only a handful of days. Her entire body lit up with pins and needles. Fear or purpose, maybe both. She felt the hundreds of eyes watching her, and the dozens of cameras, ready to take in her every gesture, her every mistake. She knew they saw her shaking.

But she wasn't trembling in fear. She was eager. Eager to join the trials to reclaim what was hers. To prove herself, though her mouth had gone too dry to speak.

She was still holding a flute of champagne in her hand. She drained it quickly as cameras snapped around her. Let them. She didn't care that she would undoubtedly see herself carelessly drinking in front of an all-powerful immortal being tomorrow.

"I am her heir," she declared.

Finally, the words came from Clemency. There was a small flurry of cameras snapping. She was the youngest, at only fifteen, and the papers would remind everyone tomorrow that Valor Holtzfall had been only fourteen when he had died in the previous Veritaz. The gambling halls would place bets on whether all the Holtzfalls would make it to the end.

Her grandmother opened her mouth to utter the official closing words of the ceremony. But another voice chimed in first.

"Oh, Mother, you've forgotten someone, surely." Heads turned, the crowd parting to admit Aunt Grace. Nora had only seen her from afar tonight, but up close she looked stunning in an emerald-green dress that was held at the back with lines of diamonds, and a long skirt designed to look as if she were wearing oversized feathers.

"Grace, dear." Mercy Holtzfall pretended to laugh. "You've had your time in the spotlight. Let the next generation have their turn." Her tone was light, but the words were sharp, especially those that were left unsaid. *You had your chance and you lost. You are unworthy.* But a sly smile spread over Aunt Grace's face. Her eyes locked with Mercy's in a silent battle of wills that Nora didn't understand.

"Mother, you're too funny." And when the crowd parted, there stood a girl in a maid's uniform. All eyes turned to the girl, though no one seemed to understand yet. But Nora saw it, so suddenly and clearly. The ethereal blonde hair, the delicate features and pale skin . . . The girl looked more like a Holtzfall than even Modesty.

"I'd like to present," Grace said, dragging out her words for the drama, enjoying the attention, "my daughter." The crowd exploded into noise, forcing Grace to raise her voice. "Ottoline Holtzfall."

All at once, the whole of the garden burst into madness. A blur of camera shutters snapping and flashes breaking through the dark. Modesty had gone still, but Constance and Clemency burst into instant outrage.

Uncle Prosper and Aunt Patience looked just as shocked, staring across the garden at their sister. A dozen voices shouted, asking questions, pushing to get close to Ottoline, even as every Holtzfall knight in the garden moved toward her. The cacophony drowned out whatever Grace Holtzfall said next. But Grace's hand squeezed her daughter's shoulder as she whispered into her ear, and like she was pulling the string on a talking doll, Nora saw the girl's lips move through the crowd.

I am her heir.

Chapter 15

LOTTE

I am her heir.

This morning, Lotte hadn't even been anyone's daughter. Now she was someone's heir.

The world exploded into light around her. Like it had on the road the moment the luster had gone off. She was blinded, a thousand voices crying out her new name, bodies jostling her frantically.

Lotte felt a hand close over hers. And with it came a powerful surge of protectiveness and purpose. She was being pulled through the crowd. And then a door slammed and Lotte was plunged away from the blinding flashbulbs and deafening shouts and into darkness and silence.

Like dropping through the surface of an icy lake.

She couldn't see anything, the echoes of the lights still too bright in her eyes. She leaned against the wall, struggling to catch her breath, tugging the too-tight maid's dress away from her chest. A pair of strong hands caught her clawing fingers, pulling them away before she could tear at the skin around her throat. His thumbs pressed into the palms of her hands, and his thoughts broke through the hindern. She was flooded with a profound sense of purpose.

"Breathe," his voice said.

The dancing lights from the cameras finally cleared enough that she could see.

The knight's sigil on his chest came into focus.

Her first thought was that death had finally caught up to her. She should run. Like Benedict had told her to outside in the rain. But there was nowhere left to run.

Her second thought was that death shouldn't be so handsome.

No, *handsome* wasn't the right word for the knight standing against her. He looked like something that had stepped out of the illustrations of the heroes in her prayer books. He was tall and broad, a crisp white shirt rolled up to his elbows under the gray doublet. His hair was the color of wheat, and just long enough that the locks at the front fell over his brow as he leaned forward. His nose was straight and strong, and his square jaw had just a bit of pale stubble, like he hadn't shaved this morning.

He wasn't handsome.

He was dashing.

He was heroic.

And suddenly he was bowing to her.

Releasing her hands, not reaching for a sword, but dropping to one knee, saying something Lotte didn't hear.

Lotte couldn't help it, she laughed.

It came from some deep hollow that had been carved out in her through the day. At the absurdity of this all. This time yesterday she had been sleeping in a pit, told that she was the most worthless creature to ever walk the earth. And now the most handsome boy she had ever seen was kneeling in front of her.

But the laughter didn't last long. She slumped against the wall, feeling everything catching up to her. "You're not here to kill me?"

"Given that I took an oath to protect the Holtzfalls with my life, killing you might be frowned upon." He looked up from where he was kneeling, his voice low and sure.

It was a hard habit to break, reading someone's mind, after sixteen years. Almost without meaning to, Lotte let her hand brush against his in the dark, feeling his calloused fingers under hers.

There it was again. That sense of purpose. Of sureness.

He had been born a knight. He had been born to protect the Holtzfalls. He would die protecting the Holtzfalls if needed. Like his brother had.

"Do you think the knights who tried to kill me on the way here took the same oath?"

He wanted to tell her that no Rydder knight would ever harm a Holtzfall.

She read that in his mind too.

But his eyes moved carefully over her face. Lotte wasn't sure what he saw there. But he knew that she wasn't lying. She was in danger. And that formidable sense of purpose reared its head in him as he got to his feet.

"I can't speak for my fellow knights." He extended his hand. "But I can take you somewhere safe." And she found that she wanted to follow him. His hand was wrapped around hers, sure and firm.

But as they turned, a silhouette pierced the light at the end of the corridor, blocking their escape. A woman wearing a knight's uniform, graying blonde hair pulled back from a grave face. Her hand rested on a sword at her waist.

The young knight moved on instinct to stand between the older knight and Lotte. To shield her, his spare hand dropping to his own sword.

The woman's eyes followed the gesture. "Theo." Her voice was formal. "You are dismissed."

Lotte felt like a rabbit who had finally been run to a dead end.

She waited now for the knight, Theo, to drop her hand.

She understood it through the hand clasped around hers. He was a knight. He was trained to obey orders.

But.

By my oath, by my oath, by my oath.

Lotte was suddenly aware of a war waging inside him. Between his orders and his oath. Fighting against every piece of training in him that told him to obey this woman.

"By your leave, Commander." Theo's voice was just as formal. "I should like to ensure her safety."

"Would you?" The commander's voice was cold.

Memories of thousands of hours training darted through Theo's mind and past the hindern on Lotte's hand. Drawn blades and sweat and days and nights of drills. She had taught him everything he knew. Alaric had died trying to save a Holtzfall. Theo would do the same if he had to.

Before either could draw a blade, the door Theo had pulled Lotte through swung open. The blinding lights and cacophony of noises streamed in behind Grace Holtzfall as she threaded her slender body through the gap, quickly pressing it closed behind her.

"Well, that was a success!" Grace gushed, pushing a stray lock of hair off her brow, seemingly oblivious to the tension. "I think they got a few good pictures before you were whisked away. We'll have to . . ." She trailed off, and for a second Lotte thought she had lost her train of thought. But her eyes had landed on the woman at the end of the corridor. "Commander Liselotte." Grace sighed, and finally the other woman's hand dropped away from her sword. "I suppose my mother would like a word?"

THE HOLTZFALL MANSION PASSED IN FLASHES.

Gilded hallways turned into an empty ballroom, turned into a wrought iron staircase that wound upward to a star-spangled dome, turned into a room filled with books and armchairs. There were too many doorways to possibly guess where they all led.

In the convent, Lotte could reach out from her bed and touch the opposite wall with her palm. Now, as they passed another room, she glimpsed a fireplace larger than her sleeping cell.

They turned into another long hallway, but this one was bare of doors or windows. Instead, portrait after portrait stretched the entire length of the walls. Lotte passed under the age-faded gaze of a man on two warped wooden panels. A woman in a white ruff, paint flaking from her face, making her pale skin look pockmarked. A man holding an ax on a velvet cushion. His eyes were the same color as Lotte's. The next showed a woman with Lotte's nose.

And then the hallway came to a sudden end.

Everything in the Holtzfall mansion was sleek polished marble, gilt surfaces, and varnished wood. But the wall ahead of them was entirely out of place. Like they had passed far beyond the house to the deepest, most gnarled part of the forest. As though hundreds of trees had grown over centuries and generations, their branches and roots twisting together into an impenetrable knotted wall. The gray-haired knight, Liselotte, rapped against the wood, and the branches spread apart, unknotting themselves and retreating into the walls. Behind was a large room dominated by an imposing desk.

Mercy Holtzfall sat, hands folded. Behind her, bloodied and battered but still standing, was Benedict. Lotte felt her stomach twist at the sight of him. His lip was split open, and there was a bruise blooming on his jaw. But he was alive. He was standing.

Even as relief flooded her, Lotte wondered what Benedict's survival meant for the other three knights. Wondered how many bodies had been made just to get her here.

Benedict's eyes went instantly to Grace. Their gazes locked with the ease of a long-formed habit. Of two pieces that fit together so naturally that neither of them made sense until they were together. And in the barest fraction of a moment, a thousand things seemed to pass between them. Lotte saw her mother's hand twitch, like she might reach for him.

Then Grace Holtzfall dropped her gaze and elegantly folded herself into a seat across from the desk. Liselotte took up position at Mercy Holtzfall's back, next to Benedict. Arms locked behind her, gaze straight ahead. Theo took an identical stance by the door.

Lotte didn't move. Everyone else seemed to know their place, but she had only just stumbled into this family.

"I don't intend to strain my neck." Mercy Holtzfall didn't look at her. "You will sit." The branches wove themselves tightly back together into a doorway behind them.

Lotte sat.

The desk was scattered with photo frames, pictures of children and grandchildren. One showed three blonde girls and a dark-haired girl wearing bathing costumes on the deck of a yacht. In another, five children, three girls and two boys, posed playing croquet, the youngest only as tall as the mallet he was holding. Another showed Grace and Verity Holtzfall as teenagers, both wearing ballgowns, leaning on each other with laughter. An army of Holtzfalls, past and present, surrounded Mercy in their silver frames, all staring out at Lotte from the life that had been taken from her.

"Well." Mercy Holtzfall finally spoke, but not to Lotte. "Isn't *this* familiar, Grace?"

"Oh, I don't know." Grace was hunting in her emerald clutch, and she pulled out a cigarette, slinging one long leg over the other, baring it scandalously. "You have crow's feet around your eyes now." The insolent ease with which Grace spoke to her mother jarred. This woman had tried to kill her twice today. "And I'm a little harder to intimidate than I was when I was nineteen. I don't suppose you have a light?" She held the cigarette toward Mercy, who frowned at her. "No?" Grace flicked her fingers, and a small flame sprang out of the diamond of one of her rings as she held it up to her cigarette.

The flame was licking the end of the cigarette when Mercy raised her little finger just a hair off the desk. Lotte felt it instantly. The snap in the air, a crackle of pure energy. The electrical bulbs that lined the walls flickered off for a moment before swelling up too brightly, until one of them splintered, shattering glass all over the floor.

And the flame of Grace's ring snuffed out.

Lotte held herself perfectly still. Sure that if she wanted to, Mercy Holtzfall could break her apart just as easily.

"Older, but not smarter." Mercy Holtzfall did not raise her voice as her little finger dropped back to the desk, her other fingers drumming out a quick sequence across the leather desktop. "Are you proud of what you've accomplished?" She raised one hand toward Benedict. "An injured knight, dozens more of them dead"—*dozens?* Lotte wanted to ask, but Mercy Holtzfall continued listing Grace's crimes—"our family humiliated, all so you could jeopardize our legacy with your mistake?"

Mistake. Lotte had thought time with the Sisters had hardened her. But it was different hearing that refrain from her grandmother. And Lotte felt her old treacherous anger rise in her. Anger she had felt so often at the Sisters. At their injustices.

"If I was a mistake, why not kill me years ago?" Mercy Holtzfall's eyes snapped to her, as if only just realizing that she could talk. "Why put me in a convent for sixteen years just to try to kill me now? You might as well have smothered me when I was born if I was such a *mistake.*"

Her grandmother sighed, leaning back. "You've clearly inherited your mother's sense of the dramatic"—Mercy Holtzfall considered Lotte—"if you believe I would kill my own granddaughter."

She was lying.

The wolves on the road.

The knights standing in her path.

She had held on to her life by the skin of her teeth to get here. And yet still, a flicker of doubt went through Lotte. She had only caught a brief glimpse of her cousins before everything turned to chaos. If anyone had a reason not to want her to compete . . .

"None of us would pretend to know how far you would go in the name of this family, Mother." Grace ground down the singed tip of her cigarette against the desk. "But the papers have all seen her now. It's too late to make her disappear again."

Mercy Holtzfall ignored her daughter, her gaze staying on Lotte. "You do not yet know your mother, Ottoline, so let me explain her to you." Her new name still jarred with unfamiliarity, but the condescension that dripped off it on her grandmother's tongue, that was familiar. "Firstly, she is unvirtuous, too unvirtuous to win the heirship seventeen years ago when she had a fair chance." Lotte couldn't help it, her eyes moved to Grace. But if she was bothered by her mother's harsh assessment of her she didn't show it. "Secondly, she is greedy, which is why she is using you to try to gain access to the family fortune now. Finally, she is foolish, because you and I both know that you will not win the heirship."

"You don't know anything about *me* either." Lotte tried to sound defiant, but her voice came out choked instead. "You don't know I'm worth less than them."

The words rang hollow. Lotte didn't belong here. She could see that just from walking among them in the garden. But she didn't belong anywhere else either. She glanced up at Benedict, the marks of the fight he had endured to get her here. She had told him she would fight to make them accept her and she would.

"Ottoline." Her grandmother's voice was needlingly gentle. "The good Sisters of the Briar have been reporting to me for years. I know all about you."

Those words struck Lotte hard enough to send her reeling back to the convent. Standing in front of the Sisters again. Being told for the thousandth time that she was selfish and lazy and covetous and ungrateful and dishonest. She imagined them writing the same to her grandmother.

But there were forces at play greater than Mercy Holtzfall. She had seen the Huldrekall step out of the woods tonight. She didn't need to convince her grandmother of anything.

The full truth of Benedict's words revealed themselves to her now. The only way to belong to this family was through a force greater than Mercy Holtzfall. It was to win.

"I don't care what you think of me." Lotte was aware of Benedict's gaze on her. He had risked his life to bring her this far. Mr. Brahm had died for it. She wouldn't do them the disservice of backing down now. "I will prove you wrong in the trials."

Mercy Holtzfall remained unreadable. And when she spoke again it wasn't to contradict Lotte. "We had better get you a dress. I won't have the papers saying my granddaughter works as a maid."

"You can't stop her from competing, if that's what you're planning." Grace Holtzfall's casualness sounded strained. "She's as much your flesh and blood as I am."

Finally, Mercy turned her attention to Grace. "Then I hope your flesh and blood doesn't let this family down as badly as mine did."

"**W**ho does she even think she is!"
It was the third time Clemency had asked the question in that indignant tone. The four cousins were clustered in a small circle in the aftermath of the chaos, under the floating stars that littered the garden's dark sky. Nora could sense the crowd casting them sidelong looks.

Nora kept her face carefully, pleasantly impassive. But her cousins were doing a terrible job of pretending.

"Did you see how outmoded her hair was?" Constance sneered.

"I mean, I knew Aunt Grace was a mess, but who knew she was *this* much of a mess?" Modesty scoffed into her drink.

"And *Ottoline*? What kind of name is that?"

Nora had been seven when she'd memorized the entire Holtzfall family tree, in preparation to take her place on it. Ottoline was the name of Honor Holtzfall's wife. Her name was as weighted by Holtzfall history as Nora's.

Nora knew what she was supposed to do. Join in against their new common enemy with something insipid and superficial. *And did you* see *how she was gaping at the cameras? You'd think her father was a fish.*

Who *was* her father anyway? Aunt Grace had had many dalliances since Nora had been old enough to know what a dalliance was.

But why not just marry her child's father? Ottoline would hardly have been the first Holtzfall born suspiciously early. Constance came seven months after her parents' wedding.

Nora disliked the furtive undertones and the glisten of gossip in the eyes around them. And now, running on close to thirty hours without sleep, she could feel her patience running thin. She'd lost track of August somewhere in the chaos and, to her annoyance, kept catching herself looking for him. Of course he'd be with the other journalists, waiting for the reemergence of the new scandalous creature from wherever Theo had whisked her off to.

"Sneaking in here like she has *any* right to be here," Clemency carried on loudly when she didn't get the reply she was after. "Who even *is* she?"

"She's a Holtzfall," Nora replied impatiently, finally cutting her cousin off. "Obviously." That milkmaid-pale skin that flushed pink delicately, and that pale hair that teetered over the edge of blonde, falling into nearly white. The kind that made all Holtzfalls except Nora look like every heroine tied to a railroad in the moving pictures. Waiting for someone to run in and save them.

And Theo had done exactly that.

"But she won't be allowed to compete, will she?" Constance was fretting. "She missed this morning's binding of the magic, it's the rules."

"There are no rules," Nora snapped again. She could sense her temper fraying. *Only tradition.*

"Besides, it's too late for her to bind her magic now," Modesty said witheringly. "The ax is already in the Huldrekall's hands deep in the woods. We can't just ask for it back."

"Then she shouldn't be eligible." Clemency all but stomped her foot. "We all had to wager our magic. She should too!"

"Modesty, dear!" Eudora Binks, the gossip reporter from the *Herald*, was approaching, wearing a frankly offensively canary-yellow dress. Modesty's expression of scorn shifted to one of placid silver-screen charm as she turned to face the journalist. "Darling, can I get a quote?" Eudora tapped a charmed pen against her notepad, releasing it so it began to write on its own, recording her every word. "How does it feel to have worked *so* hard, for so many years for your fame, and to have it *so very* overshadowed in just a few seconds by your cousin?"

Nora almost choked on her drink, turning away as she started to cough. Even for Eudora, that was a forward question. Usually journalists tried to stay on the Holtzfalls' good side when they were face-to-face, no matter what they wrote behind their backs.

For a moment, Nora thought Eudora was about to be on the receiving end of one of Modesty's famous eviscerations. More known for their volume than their verbosity but effective nonetheless. She made servants cry regularly.

But after a long tense moment, Modesty flashed the falsest smile Nora had ever seen. "Oh, don't be silly, there's room enough in the spotlight to share it with my new cousin!"

"Enough for her?" Clemency piped up angrily. "There's barely room in it for us all without her!" She gestured around the group of them. Nora was already moving away. She didn't want to be included in Clemency's point.

Nora became aware of a rustle running through the crowd of journalists. Eudora turned away from Modesty. Five figures were emerging from the house. The cuckoo in the nest herself, Ottoline.

She was no longer wearing the maid's uniform. They had changed her into a green evening gown. It was a little outdated, but not enough to be noticeable. In fact, the dress would have been unremarkable, except that Nora recognized it. That dress had belonged to Nora's mother. One of hundreds of slightly outmoded dresses she had left behind in her childhood bedroom in the mansion when she left the house to marry Nora's father.

She was wearing Nora's mother's dress. *Her* aunt and *her* grandmother flanking her.

And *her* knight standing guard.

Nora knew that spite wasn't fair. But neither was life. It snatched people away without warning. Either to death or to some intruder.

So many of Nora's people were gone. Her father. Her mother. Alaric. And now three more people who had unequivocally belonged to *her* were flocking around Ottoline Holtzfall. And the clawing vindictiveness was climbing rapidly through her. She briefly wondered if this was how her cousins had felt about her for sixteen years. Watching her *have* things while they craved them. She could hardly blame them for hating her. Nora certainly hated Ottoline.

"Well." Mercy Holtzfall smiled magnanimously at the crowd. "How blessed I am to discover I'm a grandmother all over again." That was a lie. There was nothing that happened in this family that Mercy didn't know about.

Lying to the city, Nora would understand. But she'd lied to Nora. Hidden another competitor from her. A cousin Nora knew nothing about, had no way to prepare for.

Nora knew, without question, that she was better than Modesty, Clemency, and Constance. But this wide-eyed creature, looking around the crowd like a newborn fawn seeing the world for the first time . . . she was a threat.

"And I *do* hope that you'll let my newest granddaughter enjoy her first party without badgering her too much."

The photographers in the crowd snapped pictures eagerly. Some had already rushed back to their offices. It would be a race now to be the first on the stands with this breaking news. *Extra! Extra! Another Candidate for the Holtzfall Heirship!*

Before she knew what she was doing, Nora was cutting through the crowd. Headed straight for Ottoline even as the remaining journalists flocked in around her, calling out questions. *Where have they been hiding you? Did you know you were a Holtzfall?* Aunt Grace gave a laughing response to a journalist, moving Ottoline's unfashionably long hair back off her face absently. The way Nora's own mother had done with her a thousand times.

Ottoline turned, answering a voice behind her. And in a second, her gaze locked with Nora's.

Nora didn't think it was possible for those eyes to go wider than they already were. But Ottoline's turned from saucers to dining plates as she caught sight of Nora. And just like that, she didn't look like Grace anymore. Nora had never seen Grace's face betray so much. And then the journalist who had called her name leaned forward, asking a question, breaking the moment between the two of them. Nora watched as Ottoline's face displayed every single thought that passed through her mind. Shock, then anger, then . . . tears sprang to her eyes.

The new Holtzfall was *crying*. She was trying to cover it up but doing a miserable job. And the journalists were fluttering and cooing over her. Nora could practically feel the resentment pressing against her ribs. If Nora had *ever* cried in public, the only thing she would have got from the papers was disdain.

"Do I know how to choose them or what?" Freddie Loetze draped himself over Nora's shoulder uninvited. He was drunk, obviously. But even sober, he was about the last person she wanted to see right now. "Here I was thinking she was just some country girl ripe for the picking." Freddie smirked. "Good thing I didn't get any further with her, since she's the secret Heiress-to-be."

"I'm still the Heiress-to-be." Nora had meant it to come across cool and flippant, but it slipped into defensive. Usually she was far better at tolerating Freddie Loetze. It had been a long day. And it had already started with her leaving Freddie Loetze at a club at dawn.

Freddie shrugged in that infuriating *okay, if you say so* way that people did when they were being patronizing and wanted you to know it. A sudden unintelligible screech of outrage came from a few paces away, drawing both their gazes. Constance spun away from her companions in a hurricane of skirt and huff. Nora caught a few in the crowd snickering behind their hands.

The hairs on the back of Nora's neck stood up as she glanced around. It was the same feeling that had come upon her the moment before the Grims attacked, a sensation of wrongness she couldn't put her finger on. If she could just concentrate . . .

"I mean, let's be honest. *She* probably is, though," Freddie muttered into his drink. "She doesn't just look more like a Holtzfall than you do. She looks like every worthy peasant girl who turns out to be a princess. And you're . . ." He waved at her.

Nora's fingers tightened around the glass she was holding. "I guess we'll find out what I am."

"Oh, come on, Nora." Freddie flashed her a grin. "You're one of us." Nora could feel her anger rising, even as she looked out across the garden toward Ottoline. The newest Holtzfall was surrounded by people fascinated by the perfect pretty doll. Theo stood protectively at her shoulder. Aunt Grace beamed on. Meanwhile, Nora stood alone with one of the most loathsome boys in the upper circles.

"Face it," Freddie was saying, "you can try all you want, you'll never be as good as—"

Nora's temper snapped. In one quick movement, she flung her champagne straight into Freddie's face, stopping him midsentence. She had absolutely no regrets. The champagne had gone warm anyway.

And suddenly Theo was across the garden in a few steps, coming between her and Freddie. "What happened?" He looked braced for a fight. Not that Freddie could do anything except retaliate with his own drink. And even that, Nora didn't think he had in him. "Nora, are you all right?"

But Theo was too late. Nora's embers of anger had risen into a flame, and she was stoking them.

"Oh, good, you're here. Give me your watch," she ordered Theo. She gestured at the locanz charm designed to look like a wristwatch. It was linked to her diamond earrings. She had worn them tonight as a gesture of goodwill to Theo. That she wouldn't vanish and lead him on a wild goose chase again. Her goodwill was long gone.

"Nora—"

"You can call me Honora or not speak to me at all, I don't care, but do pick one of the two." She ignored the sting that passed over him. "Now give me the watch. Neither of us wants me to have to ask a third time." Theo's lips pressed together, but he knew better than to argue with Nora when she was in a mood. He took off the wristwatch and handed it to her. She wrapped it around her palm before turning to address Freddie's inevitable ire.

He was sputtering as he blinked the drink out of his eyes. "Nora?" he asked, as if waking from a dream. He glanced down at himself. "What is this? Lustenberger Fine Reserve? Why is it all over my collar? I didn't think I was that drunk yet."

Realization dawned over Nora. But too late.

First, Eudora prodding at Modesty.

Clemency's little pique.

Constance's outburst a second ago.

Ottoline's sudden waterfall of humiliating tears.

And now Nora's own display . . .

Another cry split the garden, this time of delight. Nora felt her heart sink, already dreading what she was about to see as she turned toward the noise.

Modesty was holding her hand up to the lights of the party. On her ring finger was a plain wooden band. Nora's treacherously quick mind already understood, even as everything in her resisted the knowledge.

The ring was blackthorn wood. For temperance. Also known as the virtue of having enough self-control not to throw a drink in someone's face.

It had been a trial.

The first trial of the Veritaz.

And Nora had lost.

Chapter 17

Knights were meant to regard all the Holtzfalls equally, but as Modesty brandished her ring, Theo saw her as she'd been when they were children. The girl who used to speak to the knights like they were dogs. Who, once, when Alaric had refused her some petty thing, had gone crying to Mercy Holtzfall with scratches all over her arms, claiming that he had pushed her down. Alaric would have been beaten for it, but Nora had used her Holtzfall gift, finding the truth in a windowpane that had caught the reflection of Modesty scraping up her own arm. Modesty had hated them even more when her grandmother took Nora's side.

As they had grown older Modesty had learned to hide that side of herself. But still Theo felt engulfed with dread at the thought of Modesty having the power to command them like Mercy did now.

The crowd in the garden shifted toward Modesty, like winds changing a storm, pushing Theo away from Nora. From the certainty that she would be their next Heiress.

All the certainties of Theo's life were falling away. That he would fight side by side with his brother his whole life. That Nora would be the one to command them. That no knight would ever harm a Holtzfall.

You're not here to kill me?

He wasn't sure what had drawn him to protect Ottoline. The

cameras had been engulfing her, and through the storm of flash-bulbs he had been pulled toward her by something stronger than himself.

Theo had always followed his oath to the letter. But for the first time, he had felt the oath drawing him into action as if by some power greater than himself. Even now, through the press of the crowd, it was Ottoline he found himself looking for.

Movement caught Theo's eye instead.

Amidst the milling crowd, a single figure moved with purpose. A flash of scarlet hair, cutting her way toward Modesty. Theo recognized her. The redheaded dancer from this morning. Instead of silver sequins, she was wearing a gray Holtzfall maid uniform. And then Theo saw something slip from her sleeve into her empty palm. The light from the charmed stars danced down the blade of a long knife.

It all came together at once. Instinct, along with a decade of train-ing and, more powerful than both, a thousand years of an oath sewn into the fabric of his family's bloodline. The same oath that had made him protect Ottoline and stand against his commander.

Protect them at all costs.

Theo shoved through the crowd toward Modesty as the redheaded girl did the same. Theo reached her first, shouldering his way be-tween her and the crowd brusquely. An outraged cry emerged from Modesty's lips as she stumbled. "Watch it, you dumb brute of a—"

Theo slammed his arm up just as the blade drove down. The knife bit angrily through his shirtsleeve, drawing blood. He felt the pain shoot up his arm, but he pushed it to the back of his mind and forced the knife away. Modesty's outrage turned to a scream as she scrambled backward. More knights moved in, voices carrying over the crowd as they moved her to safety.

Theo pulled back, his focus on the girl. He was distantly aware of the commotion around him. Of screaming, jostling bodies, flashing cameras . . . Everything fell away as he stood between the assassin and Modesty Holtzfall.

The assassin, he realized with a distant sense of dread, who *he* had invited into the Holtzfall home under the guise of rescuing a damsel in distress.

Now whatever mask she'd worn this morning dropped away. He could see the wild fervor in her eyes, even as the bright flush rising in her pale skin screamed panic. She turned the knife over in her hand as she shifted from one foot to the other.

"You can't want *this*," she said in a voice too low for anyone else to hear. Her words trembled, but there was no backing down in her face. "You can't want to serve as a slave for the Holtzfalls for the rest of your life. We are trying to *save* you."

Theo could feel blood dripping down his arm. "I don't want to harm you," he said. "Drop the knife and this ends here."

The Holtzfalls had their stories of their ancestors. But so did the Rydders.

Hartwin Rydder had been born in a time when kings ruled Gamanix. When knights hunted monsters and saved damsels and fought battles. And his great acts of valor had won him the hand of Grete, the loveliest of the queen's maids. One day, Grete was picking flowers for her wedding bouquet when a Fossegrim, an immortal that lived in the nearby waterfall, heard her singing. The Fossegrim was so taken with Grete's voice that he desired her.

So he took her.

Immortals didn't understand mortal things. The Fossegrim made Grete sing day and night without food or rest, and he was astounded when her voice failed. Finally, the Fossegrim left his waterfall to gather mortal food to restore his songbird. Little did he know that Hartwin had been watching from the bank of the river. And when the Fossegrim left, the great knight saw his chance to rescue his love. Together, Hartwin and Grete fled.

They didn't return to the castle. They knew the king had no power against the will of an immortal. But no matter how far they fled, the Fossegrim followed. He was as tireless as the river. He flowed after them through the plains, mountains, and woods. Hartwin and Grete might have run as far as the waterless deserts of the far south if they hadn't stumbled into the village of Walstad first.

There, the Fossegrim was halted by the Huldrekall's promise. Just like the baying flesh-hungry monsters, he could not pass the trees. Hartwin and Grete threw themselves at the mercy of Honor Holtzfall. They had no worldly possessions to trade for the right to live on Honor's land, so Hartwin offered the one thing he did have: his loyalty as a knight.

If Honor Holtzfall allowed them to stay in the safety of Walstad, Hartwin would pledge his sword in eternal service to Honor and to his descendants. They sealed the oath in blood and in magic. So long as there lived descendants of both Honor and of Hartwin, they would be bound together by this oath. The Rydders would serve the Holtzfalls.

"Drop the knife," Theo urged.

The girl's lip curled into something between a sneer and a snarl. She plunged the knife forward sloppily. Theo moved, letting the blade skirt past him, grazing his ribs just enough to draw another streak of blood. It brought her near enough for Theo's hand to close over her arm and twist it hard. The knife fell onto the manicured lawn as Theo forced the girl to the ground, his knee pressing into her shoulder blade, hard.

The girl let out a small cry of pain, and then Theo heard her speak in a low hiss. "Your brother warned us you'd put up a fight."

The mention of Alaric hit Theo harder than any blow the assassin could have delivered. "My brother is dead," Theo said, voice low.

The girl didn't reply, but Theo felt something press into his palm firmly. And when he glanced down he saw a small crumpled napkin.

Their eyes met as Theo's hand closed over it, his heart racing.

And then the flash of a camera went off, breaking the moment. Dozens of photographers were eating up the scene, sending his hand flying up to shield his face. Releasing the girl just long enough.

"Magic and money for all!" She reared up briefly under Theo's knee with the Grims' war cry, her hand coming to her mouth. And then she slumped on the grass.

Poison, Theo realized. The girl had taken poison.

For a rare suspended moment, the immense garden was silent as everyone took in what had happened.

Theo stood, leaving the girl sprawled on the grass, red hair splayed out around her, dead.

Holtzfall children and Rydder children alike learned the story of Hartwin and Grete. How the knights came to serve the Holtzfalls loyally for a thousand years. For the Holtzfall children, the story ended when Hartwin took his oath. But the Rydder children knew what came after. When Hartwin and Grete settled onto Honor's land, the Fossegrim remained for years, watching them from the trees.

It didn't matter how far Honor Holtzfall and his ax pushed the border, the Fossegrim simply moved back with it. He lingered in the waters around Walstad, always watching from between the trees. The children of Walstad made up rhymes about the man in the trees. Sometimes the Fossegrim played his harp to accompany them.

Grete bore Hartwin children, those children bore their own children. None of them ever ventured past the border of Walstad. Her hair turned from gold to silver. And when old age took Grete, only then did the Fossegrim vanish from the borders of Walstad. But the Rydders stayed, and their grandchildren remained bound by an oath.

Protect them at all costs. Even if the cost was the life of a girl fighting for what she believed in.

Theo remembered the note crumpled in his hand.

It was the napkin from the Ash Lounge. On one side was his handwriting, giving her instructions into the house. On the other side was spiky, jagged handwriting with another address:

If you want answers about your brother, come to 113 Flint Street.

And then the silence was broken by a sharp burst of laughter from Grace, raising a drink to her lips, even as Theo quickly dropped the napkin into his pocket.

"Well, don't we know how to throw a party like nobody else."

The Tale of the Woodcutter

The Eldest Son

On the first day, the woodcutter sent out his eldest son. He gave him the ring for protection and his second-best ax. The eldest son, who was the cleverest, headed into the woods.

On the way, he encountered another woodsman, who was weeping in the road. The boy stopped and asked him why he wept. The woodsman explained that he had lost his ax in a river and without it, he would bring home no kindling and his family would freeze. The eldest son said he knew the river well, and only a few miles down there was a shallow part. He was sure his ax must have washed up there. Perhaps if he headed that way, he would find it.

The eldest son continued on his way, whistling as he went. He was nearly at the clearing where his father's ax had been left when he saw the Lindwurm, a great serpent curled around the trees, barring his path from the ax.

The clever eldest son knew that disturbing the beast would lead to his death, so he hatched a plan. Retracing his steps, he found the place in the river that he had told the weeping woodsman of. There, in the shallow waters, as he suspected, he found the other man's ax. He took it and went to find a witch in the woods who was known to him. Using his considerable wits, he created a charm to make the ax look identical to the one that his father had sent him to find.

He brought the ax home and presented it to his father. But as soon as the woodcutter held it, he knew that it was not his own ax.

His eldest son had failed. Though he was clever, he was not worthy to inherit.

PART II
VALOR

Chapter 18

THEO

The knights were restless. The barracks were sleepless.

A week ago a Holtzfall had been murdered. Tonight an assassin had come close to killing a second one. And on their own territory too. Where the Holtzfalls were meant to be safe. Where the knights let down their guard.

Finally, Theo gave up on sleep.

The training ground outside the barracks was empty. But out of habit, he took up position at the southern end and began moving through drills. Drills that had been trained into his very bones ever since he was a child. He moved through them now over and over again, until his muscles ached. Until his shirt stuck to him with sweat.

But he was fighting shadows, and those wouldn't be dispelled.

Liselotte Rydder had never contented herself to just command the knights. She had been the one to train them too, when her duties to Mercy Holtzfall allowed. On the days Lis trained them, every single young knight was made to stay until the worst one among them had perfected the drill.

Alaric had always been the first to master it. And always the first to be punished for complaining that he had to wait on the rest of them. For Theo, being a good knight had always meant trying to keep up with Alaric.

Your brother warned us you'd put up a fight.

It didn't mean Alaric was alive. Even if she was telling the truth, she could have spoken to Alaric months ago. Years. The same went for the barman this morning. *Your brother was right about you.*

But both had said it like they'd spoken this morning.

There were always knights, each generation, who stood out among the others. Who were earmarked to protect the next heir.

When Alaric and Theo's father died, and they came to live full-time in the barracks, there were whispers of favoritism as Alaric moved through the ranks swiftly. Their father had been the son of Liselotte Rydder's younger sister. The Rydder knights might all be descended from Hartwin and Grete, but some shared more blood than others. While Lis was only a commander to most, she was great-aunt to Theo and Alaric.

But it quickly became clear that any promotions Alaric received were for his talent, not his bloodline. He moved like the sword was an extension of his own arm. He seemed to know where an attack was coming from before his attacker did. It was inevitable that he would be sworn to guard Verity, the next in line to the family.

And it was impossible that he had been bested by Lukas Schuld.

Your brother warned us you'd put up a fight.

Theo turned sharply with an arc of the blade and caught sight of a figure watching him at the edge of the training ground. Even in silhouette, Lis's frame was one he would know anywhere.

Theo snapped to attention.

They faced each other silently across the training ground. Hands locked behind her back, Lis observed him with the same unreadable expression she had worn all through their training. But the inescapable sense that something had shifted hung between them.

"You're still dropping your shoulder on the parry," Lis said finally.

"Yes, Commander."

"You let the assassin's knife past you tonight as well." Rydder knights trained to guard the life behind them, not their own.

Dropping his shoulder would give the enemy a chance to get by. Keeping it raised meant taking a blade in the shoulder. It meant giving your life for the Holtzfall you were defending. "Your brother never had that problem."

Theo knew better than to expect any praise for saving Modesty's life tonight. But he had a feeling that was the only reason he was not being punished for protecting Ottoline. For disobeying a direct order.

Your brother never would have defied me.

Here, in the stillness of the night, Theo saw the grief that marked her countenance when she mentioned his brother. Alaric was more than just another fallen knight. He had been her favorite. Her nephew more than Theo ever was.

Theo was all too conscious of the note in his pocket.

In that moment, he could have told her everything. That Alaric might still be alive. That he might not have died defending Verity. It was his duty to tell her, as she was his commander. And as their commander, it would be her duty to find Alaric and bring him to Mercy Holtzfall.

Knights had been condemned for less than letting a Holtzfall die on their watch.

"Is it true?" Theo asked instead. "There were orders to kill Ottoline?"

Theo had thought he'd seen every aspect of the Holtzfalls in his years. But he'd never seen one of them face death like Ottoline Holtzfall had when facing him.

He'd never seen any of them talk back to Mercy Holtzfall.

He'd never seen any of them *want* for anything and not be afraid to say it.

He'd never seen one of them wear so much on their face at once.

"I ensured that you didn't receive those orders," Lis said simply. A bell went off in the barracks behind Theo, drawing him to attention.

"All knights are to report to the garden," Lis said, turning away from him. "Make yourself presentable."

This time, Theo did as he was ordered.

He donned a fresh shirt swiftly, with the sounds of the other knights stirring in the barracks around him. Hildegarde Rydder fell in beside him as they moved toward the gardens, fastening the end of her hair into a braid as they walked. "I saw you talking to the commander. Any idea what's happening?" she asked, tying her hair back as they moved toward the garden.

"Alaric was the one Lis would give a heads-up to, not me." Theo pushed the sleeves of his uniform up before catching himself and pushing them back into place. They cut through the servants' entrance, passing through the kitchen. It was mostly empty, except for a handful of maids polishing silverware, ready to be summoned if Mercy Holtzfall needed something.

Among them, Edmund Rydder, Hilde's brother, leaned against one of the counters, picking strawberries off a half-eaten cake. He was flirting with one of the kitchen maids.

Abigail, Theo thought the maid's name might be.

Edmund snapped to attention when he spotted Theo and Hilde, the maid quickly turning her attention back to the fork in her hand, polishing it fiercely, face going red.

"We've been summoned?" Edmund dusted crumbs from his hands.

"Can't get anything past you," Hilde shot over her shoulder as Edmund fell into step behind them. "Especially not pretty housemaids."

If Alaric had been the best of their generation, Edmund might be among the worst. He had the build of a knight, but he had always been lazy, since they were children, dozing through training and miming his way through drills. Mostly he'd been relegated to driving Prosper Holtzfall between his club, card games, his mistress's house, the racetrack . . . napping in the car while the aging Holtzfall son indulged his vices. There was no way out of knighthood if you were born a Rydder. Mothers of Rydder knights, on occasion, would deny the parentage of their children, hoping to give them a life outside the barracks. But the truth was always found out. There was no escaping blood and oaths.

Even for those as unsuited to the life as Edmund.

WHEN THE PARTY HAD ENDED HOURS AGO, THE WOULD-BE assassin's body had still been sprawled in the grass. Now eleven new bodies awaited them.

The sibling bickering between Hilde and Edmund died instantly as they stepped into the garden. Even as they watched, two footmen carried in a twelfth body, laying it in the grass next to the others. Theo felt a weight drop over his chest as he realized that he recognized that body. It was Sir Emmerich Rydder. One of the oldest and most venerated knights among them. He had served since Mercy Holtzfall's father.

Mercy Holtzfall stood over the bodies, Lis at her shoulder. When their commander caught sight of them, she gestured for them to come forward. As he moved Theo saw that all twelve were knights. Even without their uniforms on, he would have known them. They were faces he had seen all his life, faces of knights who had trained him and trained with him.

"Is that all of them?" Mercy Holtzfall spoke to the footmen from where she stood surveying the dead.

"Yes ma'am." One of the footmen bowed. His face looked pale and drawn. They had carried all twelve bodies here. To display them, Theo realized, for what reason he didn't know yet.

Death was part of being a knight.

Theo's father had died driving Nora's father. Sir Ulrich had been killed when a Holtzfall got into a brawl in a bar. Alaric—

Countless knights across countless generations, dead.

But this many knights dead at once . . . it hadn't been seen since the days that knights rode into battles. The last battle the Rydder knights had fought in was against King Domar II, who centuries ago had tried to send an army to take the Holtzfall ax and land when one of the many heirs named Valor was head of the family. Hundreds of knights had fallen in the name of their oath. To keep the ax in the hands of the Holtzfalls.

But they weren't at war now.

Theo's mind went back to the Grim assassin. Was this their doing? Three of the fallen knights bore the signs of a fight, Sir Emmerich among them. But there wasn't so much as a mark on the other nine.

More knights filed in swiftly. All of them came to solemn attention as they caught sight of the bodies lined up. Mercy Holtzfall surveyed them.

"These knights"—Mercy Holtzfall didn't raise her voice, but it carried across the assembled knights all the same—"failed to follow an order tonight."

An order.

The word was enough to make every one of them draw up straighter.

When Hartwin Rydder bound his descendants to obey the Holtzfalls, that oath was more than just words. Any Holtzfall might give the knights an instruction, but only the head of the family could give an order that bound them to obey through ancient magic.

Mercy Holtzfall scarcely gave them true orders.

She had given Theo three in all his life. And every single time was marked deep in his memory. First the order would claw at his mind, driving out any thoughts other than what he had been ordered to do. Then it gnawed at the body, slowly turning to a dull ache in the blood, until that ache turned to an agonizing pain that would wrack through the knight until there was no choice but to obey. Or to die for disobedience. Or failure.

"These twelve knights"—Mercy waved a hand over the dead matter-of-factly—"were ordered to keep Ottoline from the trials. At any cost."

Do you think the knights who tried to kill me on the way here took the same oath?

They had. These knights had all sworn to protect the Holtzfalls. And Mercy Holtzfall had ordered them to kill one. And they'd had no choice but to obey.

"Clearly, they failed."

The knights were too well trained to react, but Theo could feel the ripple of unease that passed through them. Temperance Holtzfall, Mercy Holtzfall's thrice-great-grandmother, had started to lose her wits as she entered her ninth decade of life. She was known to order knights on impossible quests, to find objects that only existed in myth. When they inevitably failed, the ancient oath that bound them would close its hand over their hearts and simply stop them.

The moment that Lotte had stepped forward, pronouncing, *I am her heir*, the hearts of these twelve knights would have stopped. Any one of them would have willingly given their lives for a Holtzfall. But instead their lives had been taken from them for failing to break their oath and kill one.

"And that failure lies at the hands of one of your own," Mercy was saying. "Sir Benedict."

This time the knights did move, gazes shifting to Benedict, who stood among them. He bore the same signs of a fight that Theo had seen on him in Mercy's office hours ago. He had wondered then who could have taken on the great Benedict Rydder and left a mark.

"I landed no killing blows." Benedict didn't cower under Mercy Holtzfall's gaze. The implication hung heavy in his words. *And I could have.* "I held them back, on orders from Grace Holtzfall."

"Grace Holtzfall is not head of this family, and never will be," Lis snapped. The commander of the Rydder knights wasn't one for great displays of emotion. But every knight who had ever trained with Liselotte Rydder knew that she was angry. The actions of the knights reflected on their commander. And Benedict had chosen loyalty to Grace over Mercy.

"Grace." Mercy Holtzfall considered him. "I have given you a lot of grace over the years, Sir Benedict. Because I love my firstborn daughter." Her voice sounded like a knife against the throat, even as she spoke of loving her children. "But you have cost twelve good knights their lives tonight, so it will not be up to me to decide your fate. It will be up to them."

Mercy Holtzfall turned to the assembled knights, all of them standing in perfectly disciplined rows in front of her. Hildegarde was the closest to her. She began, and Theo suddenly understood what was about to happen with a twist of apprehension. "As ax bearer of the line of Honor Holtzfall." Here were the words that preceded an order. Whatever Mercy Holtzfall said next, they would have no choice except to obey. "I order you, Hildegarde Rydder, to tell me the truth. Do you believe Benedict Rydder deserves to be executed for his betrayal?"

Theo had been given orders before. But not once to tell the truth. Whatever orders he was given might force his hand. But his mind had always been his. And now, he watched the order take hold of Hildegarde. "By my oath, I will obey," Hilde said.

Theo watched her struggle for a long moment. But if she was fighting the truth, then it would be no good. And finally after a painful moment the words seem to come from her as if ripped out. "I believe he should be executed."

As soon as the words left her mouth her shoulders bowed, as if in shame. Mercy moved to the next knight, repeating the same words.

The next knight voted for his execution too. So did the next. That was no surprise. It was Ingrid Rydder, whose father was among the dead on the grass. And then a no. And another. Benedict stood impassive, awaiting judgment as Mercy went down the line, one knight after the next echoing the ancient words. *By my oath. By my oath.*

Next to him, Edmund was quick to answer: no.

And then it came to Theo.

"As ax bearer of the line of Honor Holtzfall"—Mercy Holtzfall stood in front of him—"I order you, Theodric Rydder, to tell me the truth. Do you believe that Benedict Rydder deserves to be executed for his betrayal?"

"By my oath, I will obey." The words fell out of Theo's mouth as he felt the oath take hold. Like a hand wrapping itself around his chest, forcing the words out of him, finding the disloyal thought that was buried deep within his mind. *Benedict is not the one responsible for this. You ordered knights to break their oath. To kill a Holtzfall.* Theo pushed that thought away. "I do not believe he should be executed."

And as soon as he had obeyed, the hand released his heart. The oath was fulfilled. And Mercy moved on. Until every vote had been cast.

Only three more knights voted to spare Benedict than those who voted to condemn him.

It was enough.

And all the while, Benedict had stood impassive.

A knight to his core.

Chapter 19
LOTTE

Grace Holtzfall was leaning against a floor-to-ceiling window that overlooked the city, tilting a newspaper to catch the morning light. An emerald-green scarf patterned with colorful birds was tied at her brow, so her blonde hair foamed up elegantly at the back of her head. She had a long strand of pearls wrapped twice around her neck, which swayed over a peacock robe. When she lifted her arms, light from the windows streamed through the sheer fabric, making the sleeves look like wings. Lotte hesitated in the doorway to the sitting room, watching Grace, her mother, a near stranger.

She was stillness in a flurry of movement.

Six hotel maids in matching black uniforms and white mobcaps were milling around the sitting room, setting out breakfast, plumping pillows, and gathering discarded pieces of clothing.

A sudden pang twinged in her chest. It could have been this way, always. Waking to find a mother waiting for her. Sleeping in a bed instead of on a cold floor. Having a family she belonged to. Being a Holtzfall was beyond anything she could have fathomed. But now she saw it. Now she ached for it.

It wasn't too late.

She could still have this life.

As long as she won these trials. As long as she didn't fail like she had last night.

Grace Holtzfall seemed to suddenly become aware of her as she shifted in the doorway. "Good news, darling," she said in greeting, "you're famous!"

Grace held up the newspaper. It took a moment for Lotte to realize it was a picture of her under a headline that read:

Secret Holtzfall Daughter Shock!

It was easy to see why the newspaper used the word *shock*. She looked like a startled animal, the flash illuminating her face. There were a dozen other papers scattered around the living space. Her face stared up from all of them.

Lotte, still half-drunk from sleep, was suddenly more aware of herself than she'd ever been. Like she could feel every eye in the city on her. Even as she caught one of the maids staring at her, the girl looking away quickly.

"You're even bigger news than Modesty winning the first trial!" Grace Holtzfall was saying. "Front page on almost every paper! Patience will be fuming. But maybe my sister will learn everyone is sick of looking at her daughter's face. Although, of course, it would be a lot better if the news were of *you* winning the first trial."

That landed painfully. Lotte had stood defiant in front of her grandmother. So sure she could prove her worth. Her right to belong to this family. To stay in it. Only to fall at the first hurdle.

Questions had been spinning around her, too many for her to answer as people with cameras penned her in. And then she'd caught sight of Honora Holtzfall. So at ease while Lotte felt so out of place, watching her struggle, contempt in her eyes. And Lotte had ached to even pretend she was as at ease as Honora looked. And in that moment, one journalist had stepped close and asked, "Do you think you'll ever be one of them? Even if you do win? Do you think you deserve to win the trials after *lying* to everyone for ten years? After turning your back on a friend this morning?"

In the blur or exhaustion, she hadn't even wondered until later how the journalist knew about Estelle. Everything had just caught up to her at once. The day. The lack of sleep. Before she knew what was happening, her vision was blurring. There were tears in her eyes. Lotte had turned away, trying to hide it. But it was too late.

Crying wasn't a sign of temperance.

"I won *all* the trials in my generation, you know," Grace was saying. "I mean, all but one. Verity won the ring for selflessness with that nonsense with the birds." Lotte had no idea what the nonsense with the birds was. "And I suppose one is all it takes. My point is, if I can triumph, you should certainly be able to. All that time in the countryside *ought* to have served some good."

Some good. The words were so similar to something the Sisters of the Blessed Briar might have said. *A night in the briar pit will do you some good. Scrubbing the kitchen floor instead of sleeping will do you some good.* Lotte felt like a child who had been running toward her mother's arms, only for her mother to move out of the way at the last second, and anger and hurt rose up. "Is that why you *abandoned* me there? Because you thought it would make me good?"

Grace's face was a changing carousel of emotions, none of which Lotte could read with the hindern on. But it settled quickly into blithe smiling again. "Oh, you know what I mean. Everyone is always going on about how much simpler life is for the peasants." Grace Holtzfall waved her hand vaguely. "Not corrupted like us city dwellers."

Lotte wanted her mother to say that she hadn't abandoned her. That she had always wanted her. That she'd given her up against her will. She wanted her to say that Mercy Holtzfall was wrong last night. That she hadn't just brought her back for the competition, for the money. That she loved her whether or not she was good enough to win the trials.

Lotte moved uneasily toward the impeccably dressed table. It was piled high with pastries, and a polished silver teapot steamed. She hadn't eaten since yesterday, and her stomach turned over as she picked a flaky swirl topped with berries. She felt immediately uncouth and out of place as pastry crumbs scattered across the white tablecloth.

Last night, Lotte had barely taken anything in, stumbling exhausted to a bed. But in the daylight, she could see that her mother's hotel room was immense. From the ceiling, a golden chandelier shaped like drooping palm trees illuminated polished wood with gilded edges and stark cream furniture that looked untouched. The walls were papered with a bright blue sky, penned in behind golden arches. Flocks of painted exotic birds were dotted around the room, and as she watched, a bright green bird took off from its perch and landed on another one, painted feathers stilling.

All her childhood, Lotte had imagined her mother living in some hovel, the kind the Sisters warned awaited young girls who got too big for their country boots and tried to make it in the big city.

"I always thought you couldn't afford to keep me."

"You were right." Grace didn't meet Lotte's eye, but there was a bitterness to her words that Lotte couldn't mistake. "There are costs in this world that are greater than money, Ottoline." Grace slid down across from her, flashing her bare leg under the silk robe. "And now I can't afford *not* to have you back. The winner of the Veritaz decides whether *everyone else* in the family gets anything or nothing at all. And I can't pay for this room with my beauty."

As Lotte reached for a second pastry, she was aware of her mother's eyes following the movement. She pulled her hand back, not wanting to look greedy.

"Everything was fine when Verity was the one holding the

purse strings. But Prosper and Patience hate me for not turning on Verity with them. Their children are not going to give me a single scrap. I might have been able to count on Honora once, but my mother has gotten to her over the years. If I'm to afford to keep you, we have to win." *We.* Grace moved, brushing hair off Lotte's face with a smile. The tiny gesture made Lotte ache. She had watched Mrs. Hehn move hair from Estelle's face a thousand times, even as Estelle would shake her mother away like an inconvenience. Every time, Lotte would watch enviously, and feel her own skin ache for someone to care about her like that. In that moment, Lotte would have done *anything* to keep her mother. To keep being someone's daughter. Whatever her mother wanted her for, it was enough to be wanted.

There was a sharp rap at the door, shattering the moment between them.

"Come in!" Grace dropped her hands, and Lotte felt the cold rush in. The door swung open, admitting an older woman in a sharp gray uniform. She had one hand wrapped around the arm of a young maid like a vise.

"Miss Holtzfall, my apologies for disturbing you," the older woman fawned, "but I caught this little sneak trying to send a message to the *Herald*."

The woman in gray held out a note. It was scribbled hastily on a piece of paper, *The Paragon Hotel* marked in gold writing at the top. Grace's gaze scanned the paper quickly before flicking it away.

Lotte read it as it landed on the table between the pastries and fresh fruit.

G.H. and daughter at ~~odds~~ over the trials

Lotte hadn't realized they were being watched. She felt the hairs on her neck stand up in fear. But Grace only sighed, as if this were a common inconvenience.

"You think my *discussions* with my daughter are the business of the *Herald*?"

The maid finally looked up. "The papers will pay good money for any word on the new Holtzfall. If I didn't do it, someone else would."

Lotte slipped the hindern off her finger. The desperation under the defiance poured off the young maid. She couldn't lose her job. She was supporting her mother and two little sisters. If she lost this job, they might be turned out onto the street. But she had pride. She wasn't going to beg.

"If they *had*, someone else would be the one being dismissed right now." Grace yawned.

"Do you know how much we get paid to work here?" The maid's fear uncoiled into anger now. "Do you know how much we make for cleaning up after you day and night, breaking our backs, carrying up tray after tray of food that you barely touch!" Lotte could feel the cramp of hunger in this girl's stomach. "And you're talking about needing money while you wear diamonds. You have *everything*, and you leave *nothing* for the rest of us."

Lotte knew what it was to be hungry. To be desperate. But Grace looked impassive. "Well, luckily, you no longer have to worry about making your pitiful salary anymore."

"Don't—" Lotte started, but Grace was already rising from her seat, moving toward a side table.

"And of course, before you go, we will have to make sure you cannot try to tattle on us again." She pulled out from a drawer what looked like a small pocket watch with a mirrored surface, turning a dial before snapping it open. She held it in front of the girl's face, as if she were showing her the reflection. A small spark of light coursed from the ring on her mother's finger into the pocket mirror, sparking whatever charm this was.

And with her hindern resting on the table, Lotte heard the girl's memories slip away. They glided out of her mind and into the mirror. The memory of frantically scribbling the note in the linen closet before Matron Winterhalter walked in, catching her in the act. The memory of hearing the argument. The memory of coming into work this morning, eager to set eyes on the new Holtzfall girl. Gossiping about her while they changed into their uniforms at the crack of dawn.

Grace snapped the mirror shut again. The girl's mind stumbled into the present moment, clouded with confusion. Lotte could hear her struggle to make sense of things. To bridge the missing hours. The rising panic as she realized she had lost her job and had no idea what she had done wrong.

"That will be all." Grace Holtzfall waved a hand coolly.

In a moment, the girl was gone, pulled out of the door by the matron. Grace was already turning away, the other maids going back to their work as if nothing had happened. But Lotte's whole being had gone cold.

"You *stole* her memories."

"It's a simple memorandum charm." Grace dropped the small mirror onto the settee lazily.

Lotte could still hear the young maid's memories inside. Like a distant conversation muffled from another room. Then Grace rested her hand on her cheek again. "It's to protect us." Her mother wore a faintly amused look on her face, and Lotte felt a flash of it through her palm, of Grace enjoying her naïveté at how things worked. Her mother expected a demure wide-eyed country girl. She wanted that. Lotte couldn't show her the angry convent-raised ingrate she had grown into instead. "There is a great deal you're going to have to learn if you want to be part of this family, Ottoline."

Chapter 20

AUGUST

August woke to the sound of a newspaper hitting his desk. The last thing he remembered was deciding to close his eyes, just for a moment, after rushing his article to print.

Now Honora Holtzfall was staring up at him from the front page. And his editor was staring down at him.

"Mr. Vargene." August swiped his hand over his face in a quick bid to clear the last of the sleep. "I must've—"

"Fallen asleep at your desk." The newspaper editor clapped him on the shoulder. "Every decent newspaperman does it at some point." In the months since he'd started working at the *Bullhorn*, Mr. Vargene had referred to him as the boy photographer. This was the first time he had called him a *newspaperman*. August pulled himself up straight. "This is good work." Mr. Vargene held out a check. August could already see two zeros on it. The list of bills he could pay was forming in his mind. As he reached for it, Vargene pulled it back slightly. "How did you get in anyway?"

Randolf Vargene was a genial-looking man with surprisingly well-groomed salt-and-pepper hair. August had only been at the job since last autumn, and he hadn't found the time to go to the barber's more than once. It was almost like Vargene made a point to wear his hair cropped and combed back, so that the scars on the side of his face would never be hidden.

If he didn't know better, August might think he'd been clawed from temple to jaw by a wild animal. But the truth was a machine at the LAO factory had overheated from running through the night and exploded.

He'd come out of it with scars, a cash payoff from Leyla Al-Oman, the owner of LAO, and a deep hatred for the whole of the upper circles. August wasn't about to fess up to striking a deal with Nora Holtzfall, granddaughter of both the women his chief editor hated most.

"One of the new maids working at the Holtzfall mansion is from the neighborhood. She snuck me in."

Vargene considered him. The chief editor had used his payoff money from the LAO accident to found the *Bullhorn*. Most of the men here shared his hatred of the upper echelons of the city. The rest, including August, shared the hatred of not having a paycheck. But he worked hard not to let on to that fact.

August tamped down the impulse to embellish his lie. *Keep your lies simple*, that was what his father had always taught him. "Sounds like a good person to know," Mr. Vargene said finally, and August felt his shoulders ease as the man handed over the check. "Just don't get her fired, and keep up the good work. You'll go far here."

"Yes, sir." August had plans to go far, but not at the *Bullhorn*. His ambitions extended beyond a one-floor office with lights that flickered occasionally. It extended to the *Times*, to the *Herald*, even. And the way he was going to get there was by breaking the story of a lifetime: the murder of the Holtzfall Heiress.

He scrubbed the sleep from his face with one hand, checking his watch. He'd better get going. The pawnshops would be opening soon.

"ANY LUCK?"

The voice startled August as he left the third pawnshop of the morning. She was leaning against the window, between the stenciled-on *Best* and *Prices in Walstad!* She was glamoured as Trudie again, but she was still unmistakable. Even if he wasn't starting to recognize Honora Holtzfall's demeanor, she was the only person in the 12th circle wearing clothes that cost a month's salary.

"Don't you have trials to be at or something?" August asked, exasperated. But some treacherous part of him was glad to see her.

Nora sniffed. "I don't go to trials. Trials come to me."

"A cotillion, then? Or some luncheon?"

"No one has gone to a cotillion in the past century. And the luncheon isn't until two."

August sighed, leaning back in the doorframe of the pawnshop. "Do I even want to know how you found me?"

"I put a locanz charm in the heel of your shoe last night. It's paired to this." Nora tapped the wristwatch she was wearing. It was far too bulky for her, and the hands of it were pointing straight at him. August braced himself in the doorway, pulling up his shoe to examine. "Other one," Nora said.

Sure enough, there was a small diamond stud earring embedded in the heel of it. He was suddenly remembering Nora in the garden, fiddling with her earring, crouching down to adjust the strap of her shoe next to him.

"A Holtzfall following a journalist instead of the other way around, that's new." August went to offer the stud back to Nora.

She made a face. "I don't want that—it's been in your shoe. Besides, I'm here about rings, not earrings."

He'd told her last night that she wasn't going to come trawling pawnshops with him. But clearly Honora Holtzfall was used to getting what she wanted, one way or another. He thought about arguing with her or trying to ditch her. But he had the feeling that wouldn't do him much good. Besides, right now they wanted the same thing: to find the truth about Verity Holtzfall's murder.

He gave in. "No luck here. There's about a dozen more pawn-shops in the city that are known for trading in stolen goods." She was wearing black leather knee-high riding boots. "I'm so glad you're wearing sensible shoes."

"They go with the coat." It was less a coat and more a cape, paired with close-fitting leggings. She looked like the woodsman who had hunted down the big bad wolf.

They moved down the street, toward the messily whitewashed shop front of the next pawnshop. Laundry hung off the balconies from the apartments above them, partially obscuring the painted letters above.

Buy and Sell Diamonds! Fine Silver! Old Charms! Watches! And More!

Inside, it looked like someone had tried to move the contents of an entire house into a single room. Mirrors were propped precariously on top of desks, which were balanced on top of rolled-up carpets, which were piled on top of low coffee tables. Possessions that immigrants from the countryside had brought to the city with them, only to find out they couldn't fit them in their tiny apartments here.

They moved carefully among stacks that looked liable to topple over at any second.

This part of the city wasn't exactly the safest, but dying by a breakfront credenza would be a real indignity.

Nora nudged August, gesturing toward a locked glass cabinet in the corner. It displayed the promised *Diamonds!* that the front window had advertised. There were even a few real ones by the looks of things. But no emeralds.

"You'd suit that bracelet very well, miss." A man was emerging from the back room, dusting crumbs from his garishly colored tie. "You have a wrist made for diamonds."

"I actually prefer rubies. But diamonds will do in a pinch."

August leaned over her shoulder, pretending to inspect the contents of the cabinet with her. "Try not to sound *so* first circle," he whispered to her, quietly enough that the shop owner didn't hear. Nora's head turned, her face suddenly inches from his.

"Oh, I see," the shopkeeper said, even as August pulled away quickly. "It's a ring you're after, is it? Runaway wedding? What is it? Parents don't approve? Or is the young lady in a blessed state?"

Nora opened her mouth, but before she could say something that would blow their cover, August piped up, "Well, I *would* propose, but she's got expensive tastes." He turned to face the shopkeeper, giving him a conspiratorial eye roll. "Do you have anything a bit more valuable? Something with an *estimable* provenance, maybe?"

The shop owner's brows descended in confusion, clearly not picking up on the hints August was dropping.

"Which word was it that lost you?" Nora asked, running a finger over a nearby desk and picking up grime as she went. "*Estimable* or *provenance*?"

"Means a fancy origin," August provided. "For instance, something that used to belong to a veritable heiress."

"Ah." The man's genial grin wavered. "You're talking about the Holtzfall mugging."

August felt the pull of the story rise eagerly in his chest. "What have you heard? There's a rumor going round that it might've been the Grims." He didn't mention that was less a rumor and more Nora's working theory.

"Depends who's asking." The shopkeeper raised one hand, conspicuously rubbing his fingers together in the universal sign for *bribe me*.

August glanced at Nora. Nora took her empty hands out of her pocket. "Don't look at me."

"*You* don't have any money?"

"I never carry money. What would I need it for, buying milk on the way home?"

"How much do you think milk costs . . . ? Never mind." August sighed, turning back to the man. "Oskar Wallen is asking, how about that?"

Even Nora reacted to that name.

Everyone in the city knew Oskar "The Ears" Wallen.

The shopkeeper's hand dropped to his side warily. "You're not one of Oskar's." But he didn't sound all that sure of himself.

August shrugged. "I'm new."

"Then maybe no one's told you that Oskar normally sends something to grease my cash register. Nothing comes for free, not even to the Draugr of the Docks." That was an old name for Oskar. From back when he'd been a bloody enforcer controlling the bribes at the seaport. That meant this man had been in the game longer than August had been alive.

"We don't have time for this." Nora pushed by August. She rested her fingers on the glass counter. It was polished and clean, unlike most of the shop. There were some silverware sets, displayed in pride of place under the counter. But Nora wasn't looking at what was under the glass. August had seen Nora use her Holtzfall gift once, on the photographs of the murder scene. Now Nora carefully spun back the reflections in the top of the display case, like a picture show played backward at high speed. They watched money changing hands, items sliding over the counter to pawn, and then . . .

She stopped the image. August followed her gaze to the frozen image in the glass.

It wasn't a flattering angle on anyone, reflected from below like that. But even without a face, the police badge was obvious on the man's chest. As was the reflection of the ledger as the officer flipped through it, taking notes as he went. "Do you think Oskar might be interested in knowing the cops are looking at your books?"

The shopkeeper's eyes shot from the reflection up to Nora and August. And then down again, and back up. For a moment, August thought he had recognized Nora, even through her glamour.

"I've heard that maybe *all* of Verity Holtzfall's jewelry didn't make it into evidence. But if it was pawned, then it wasn't pawned here."

"Do you know where it might've been?" August tried to sound casual, even as his pulse thrummed with the rush of following a story.

"There are rumors that Winsch's has been closing in the middle of the day. And that he took a taxi to a jeweler. A good one in the third circle. He'd have to have *something* to make closing his shop down worth his while."

Of course. No one would risk selling the Holtzfall ring as it was. They would need a jeweler to break it apart. Reset the stones, sell it piecemeal.

Nora pulled her hand away, releasing the image, their double act falling easily into place as August took her cue. "Oskar Wallen thanks you for your information."

"And you'll keep *your* information?" the shopkeeper called after them, even as the bell above the door dinged on their way out.

"We should probably stop for bribe money on the way to Winsch's," August said as he turned up his collar against the spring cold. "Blackmail only gets you so far."

WITH A BIT OF BRIBERY, MR. WINSCH ADMITTED HE'D SPOKEN to a man about an emerald ring. He couldn't say whether the man was a cop or not, but he'd seen the ring. Mr. Winsch had made him his best offer, but he'd been shot down. They asked about the identitat charm above the door, but Mr. Winsch told them that hadn't been powered for years. It was just for show to deter burglars.

Three more pawnshops later and they were no closer to an answer. "We can either head north toward—" August was saying when he realized that Nora wasn't walking beside him anymore. When he turned around, she was handing over the last of the bribe money to a woman squatting in the doorway of a large tenement building. She dusted her hands off before catching up to him.

"Any Holtzfall would have to be *idiotic* to ignore a beggar during the trials," Nora responded to the raised eyebrow August gave her. "It's practically the oldest trick in the book. Any one of them could be a test in disguise." Nora checked her bulky watch. "It's nearly two, I should be getting to Hugo Arndt's little campaign luncheon."

August had thought she was joking about the luncheon.

The fact that it was Hugo Arndt . . .

After Verity Holtzfall's murder, Hugo Arndt had abruptly announced that he was running against Governor Gerwald. He was one of the 1st-circle crowd, who promised that he'd put an end to Isengrim once and for all. August had figured he was joking. Or that he'd get bored and find something else to spend his money on.

"First circle is that way." August nodded north. "Bring me back some truffles."

"Don't be ridiculous, truffles won't be in season until—" Nora cut herself off as they rounded a corner and came face-to-face with a man toying with a knife.

Nora instantly reached for a charm, but August grabbed her hand. "Nice morning, isn't it, Joachim?"

August ignored the look Nora gave him as Joachim checked his watch.

"Afternoon now," he said bluntly, spinning the knife in his grip. "Oskar Wallen sent me to find out how come you're throwing his name around town."

Damn.

"Well, I can be a little late for lunch," Nora said. "Since there won't even be any truffles anyway."

Chapter 21

LOTTE

Lotte had never had the luxury of boredom before.

At the convent, if Lotte was ever caught idle, she'd either be punished or given another chore. But Grace had poured herself into bed with the casual nonchalance of someone who hadn't just taken hours of someone's memories. And Lotte was left . . . idle.

After help from the maids, she had figured out how to make the water run in the bathroom. It had been gloriously, magically hot. Hot enough that after years of washing in an icy pump at the convent, she thought it might make her skin melt off. She'd stood under it for what felt like hours. Watching blood and grime wash off her. Watching the convent, Estelle, Gelde, years of solitude and lies leave her. When she emerged, scrubbed raw and dripping wet, there was a fresh plate of pastries and fruit, and tea waiting for her on a small table by the window.

The maids moved around her efficiently, clearing away her breakfast when she was done. And then Lotte was left alone in the sprawling suite of the Paragon.

Waiting for the next trial.

Within a few hours, Lotte was restless. She'd opened every cabinet and drawer and cupboard in the suite. She'd tried to go into the hallway, but a maid had stopped her, pointing out kindly that she wasn't dressed. When Lotte had gone *looking* for the green dress from last night, it had vanished. Whisked away to be cleaned.

Out the window, the city sprawled in every direction. To the north, she could see the woods, bordered by a crescent of large houses, the Holtzfall mansion the largest of them. The woods stretched beyond sight, but somewhere, far away, they met the ice sea to the north. In the days of Honor Holtzfall, everything in every direction would have been covered by trees. But Lotte felt just as bewildered by the city as people must have once been by the woods.

She thought back to when Estelle would flip through magazines picking out the marvels of the city. Shops that served frozen desserts, kept cold by magic. Places where you could watch moving pictures or hear live music. Lotte would have no idea where to start if she wanted any of those things. But she also had a feeling that whatever trial was coming next, it wouldn't come for her locked away here. If she was going to win, she had to get out there.

Although the maid was probably right—wandering the streets of Walstad wearing nothing but a hotel bathrobe wouldn't end well.

The door opening startled Lotte out of her thoughts. She turned, expecting to find yet another maid entering. Instead, letting herself into the suite like she owned the place was Modesty Holtzfall.

And behind her . . . Theo. Lotte felt an aching flash of gratitude for a familiar face. She took an involuntary step toward him, but she stopped as he kept his eyes straight ahead, not meeting her gaze.

He walked like a soldier, rigidity in every inch of his body. Maybe she had misread him last night. Maybe she had overstepped the boundary that was supposed to exist between knights and Holtzfalls. Suddenly in the daylight their conversation in the dark hallway, his offer to take her to safety, felt illicit. And Lotte was suddenly painfully aware that she was wearing nothing but a bathrobe.

"Cousin!" Modesty air-kissed each side of Lotte's face, as if they had been the best of friends their whole lives. "I thought you might be an early riser like me." It was nearly noon. "After all, word is you were raised in a convent."

Lotte drew back sharply. "Where did you hear that?"

"Oh, you know." Modesty sank onto the settee, Theo taking up a guard position behind her. Lotte's eyes strayed to him again, but his were still fixed ahead. "Around."

Around. Lotte needed to know who was talking about her. If someone knew she was from Gelde, how long until they knew what the people of Gelde thought of her? The viceful, convent-bound girl. Unworthy of winning a game of virtues.

Lotte perched awkwardly on the sofa next to her cousin, and let her arm brush Modesty's, breaking the barrier of the hindern, enough to skim the thought that was at the top of Modesty's mind.

Modesty hadn't *heard* she was from Gelde. She had gotten up early this morning to press their grandmother for information. To know where this new cousin had come from until finally, a challenging glint in her eyes, Mercy Holtzfall had told her she was raised in a convent. Which dashed Modesty's half-formed plan of leaking to the papers that she'd been raised in a brothel overseas . . .

Modesty was threatened by her.

She might have *already* won a trial, the first trial of the Veritaz. The heirship was within her reach.

And yet it was Ottoline on the front of every paper.

And this morning, the reporters were waiting outside the Paragon Hotel, not Modesty's apartment.

"So it's true. My, what a stacked deck Aunt Grace has with you in a game of virtues." The playful smile never left Modesty's lips, but a small thrill of danger went down Lotte's spine.

Her family had already tried to kill her before she got to the trials.

And now Lotte was alone in a room with someone eyeing her as competition. For the trials and for attention.

There is a great deal you're going to have to learn if you want to be part of this family, Ottoline. Her mother was right about that, no doubt. But, no matter what the Sisters had told her grandmother, her family didn't know anything about Lotte either. They didn't know she had spent a decade playing at friendship with someone who always needed to be the shiniest thing in the room.

Lotte had been six when she was finally released from the cold solitude of the convent to go to school with the other children. The Sisters had told her again and again that she would be punished if she indulged her curse to steal thoughts from their minds.

Lotte would have promised anything if it meant being allowed out of the convent. She saw the children from the village at weekly prayers with their parents, full of laughter and warmth that she craved. But the other children had been wary of her. Their mothers knew each other, their fathers worked or drank together, or both. She was the strange parentless child from the convent. The desperation to get them to welcome her had clawed at Lotte's chest.

It hadn't taken long for Lotte to realize that the same way they pulled away from her, they pulled toward the bright-eyed baker's daughter. And it was impossible not to hear Estelle's mind. Her thoughts spilled out of her like a beacon, too bright and loud for Lotte to ignore. And Lotte saw that she was her path in.

Her chance came during a game Lotte didn't know. A razor-sharp thought flashed from Estelle's mind. She was so much better at this game than everyone else. It was *embarrassing* for them. And so boring for her. If only she could find someone who would be a decent match. Latching onto that thought, Lotte had stepped away from the fence, toward the game.

Lotte could keep up with Estelle because she knew every move before someone made it. She anticipated where one girl would dodge; she knew where another boy was hiding. Winning would have been easy for her. But she let Estelle win, narrowly. Because no matter that she thought she wanted to meet her match, Estelle still wanted to win. To be the most important, interesting, popular person in the room. And Lotte could make sure it happened.

And as an out-of-breath and muddy Estelle flung up her hands in victory, she had already decided that she liked this new strange girl from the convent on the hill, who was almost a match for her, but not quite.

Lotte had used her curse over and over again to stay Estelle's friend. To whisper a thought passing through Estelle's mind just in time for Estelle to gasp and slap her on the arm and say, *I was just thinking that*. To agree with every opinion she had before she voiced it. And tell her what she wanted to hear.

She had found her way into Gelde through Estelle.

And she could do it again with Modesty.

She needed a way *out* of this hotel room to start with. A foot into this family. Into the trials. She just needed to make Modesty believe she wasn't a threat to her in this game. That she was the naïve little country girl lost in the great big city.

"I guess news travels a lot faster in the city than I'm used to." Lotte widened her eyes a little more than was natural, pitching her voice higher. Instantly, Modesty's expression eased. And finally, Theo's eyes flicked over to her. Lotte forced her gaze away from him. She was suddenly sure he could see through her. That he could see her trying to hide the angry ambition he had witnessed in her grandmother's office.

She told herself it didn't matter. So long as Modesty didn't see through her.

"Anyway." Modesty toyed with a tassel on the couch with forced indifference. "Do you know what you might wear to Hugo Arndt's luncheon today?"

"Hugo Arndt?" This time the naïveté wasn't an affectation.

"I'm not convinced he has the strength of character to stand against the Grims if he's elected governor. But we do have to hear him out. So—what do you think you'll wear?"

Modesty wanted to outdress her, Lotte realized. That's why she was here. And with that, she saw her path. She could give Modesty what she wanted. And get some clothes and out of this hotel with it.

Lotte arranged her face to what she hoped was endearing helplessness. She could feel Theo's gaze on her, threatening to burn it away. But she kept it fixed.

"Well, maybe I could borrow something from my mother." She didn't want to lay it on too thick, but as she thought of the cameras she'd seen in Modesty's mind, waiting outside the Paragon, she added, "I don't think I can be seen out in this, after all."

Modesty took the bait. "Oh, dear cousin, that won't do at all! You *must* let me take you out to buy something suitable!"

Chapter 22

THEO

Theo might have thought he'd imagined the Ottoline Holtzfall of last night. That girl burning with anger and want. Except—

Modesty had demanded Theo as her knight this morning. Commander Lis said it was because he had been the one to save her from the assassin. Theo was sure it had more to do with Modesty wanting to take him away from Nora.

But even though he was assigned to Modesty, he couldn't let Ottoline step out in front of the cameras wearing nothing but a bathrobe. On the elevator down he was all too aware of the flashes of bare skin every time she moved.

When they reached the lobby, Theo turned for the back entrance. "No." Modesty snapped her fingers at him. "The car is at the front."

He could already see the flashes of cameras through the grand glass doors of the Paragon Hotel. Modesty forged ahead, Ottoline following.

Seconds before they stepped out, Theo turned sharply, stepping in front of Ottoline so fast she almost walked into him.

"Here." He pulled off his coat, draping it over the bathrobe. Shielding her as best he could.

And then he saw it, in the second before he stepped away. Like he had in the dark hallway last night, though the shape of her was clearer to him now. That porcelain skin flushed from the heat of the shower. Her damp pale hair glowing that unnatural shade of blonde that only Holtzfalls seemed to have. The sharp wanting in her eyes.

And in that second, he wasn't so sure that she didn't know exactly what she was doing by walking into a sea of cameras half-dressed.

He pulled away swiftly. And she was gone again. Back to wide-eyed innocence and country accent.

He watched for the sharpness, but he didn't see it again.

There was certainly no sign of it in the girl who was now letting Modesty drape her in dresses like she was some life-sized plaything. Theo stood to attention in the doorway of the private room at the back of Rikhaus Department Store. Shop assistants ran to and fro, bringing dresses and shoes and jewelry for Modesty to appraise as she lorded over them like an empress.

He wasn't surprised that only hours after winning the first Veritaz ring, she was already abusing her power. He'd been able to envision a future with Nora as Heiress easily. But one with Modesty as head of the family . . . He saw the line of dead knights from last night all too clearly.

"Are you *ready*?" Modesty demanded to the curtain of the dressing room, just as Ottoline pulled it back. She wore a silk emerald gown that clung to every part of her body, dipping dangerously low at the back in a way that made it impossible not to trace the curve of her spine. Theo dropped his eyes swiftly, suddenly feeling like even more of an intruder than he had seeing her in the robe.

"I don't think so." Modesty waved her back into the dressing room. "It's not *you*."

The door opened behind them. Theo's hand was on his sword in a second, attention snapping back to his duty. But it was Hilde who entered, followed close behind by Edmund. Neither one of them looked like they'd slept since the vote in the garden in the small hours of the morning. Edmund caught Theo's gaze, giving him a quick eye roll behind Hilde's back as she sketched a bow to Modesty.

"We've come to relieve Sir Theodric," Hilde said.

Modesty's mouth pressed together in displeasure even as she turned her attention to a platter of jeweled rings a shop assistant was bringing in now. "On whose authority? Nora doesn't have *dibs* on him, you know. And you." She flicked a finger at Edmund. "Didn't I already send you away this morning? Or was it another one of you knights? You all look the same after a while."

Hilde ignored the second part. "On Commander Liselotte's authority." Which meant Mercy Holtzfall's authority. Even Modesty couldn't fight that.

"Very well." Modesty waved a hand now adorned with rings. "You can go."

Edmund followed Theo out. "How did you draw the short straw?"

"What does the commander need?" Theo knew better than to speak poorly of any Holtzfalls, even out of earshot.

"Guess who's nowhere to be found? I'll give you three guesses. The first two don't count."

"I don't know where Nora is." Theo and Alaric's father had warned them when they were young that being a Rydder now was not like it was in the old days. It was mostly standing guard at doors and driving the Holtzfalls places. He'd forgotten *and looking for reckless runaway Holtzfalls* from his list of duties that became rote. "She took my locanz charm last night, which I'd say means I'm the last person she wants to find her right now."

Theo had seen Nora's storms before. One would last a few days of silence and then it would be gone. She hadn't spoken to them for two weeks soon after her father had died, even though it was Theo and Alaric she had sought out at his funeral. And though she'd come to their father's funeral too.

She's grieving, Verity Holtzfall had said in apology for her daughter then. Everyone had seemed to forget that Theo and Alaric were grieving too. But Holtzfalls always came first.

Edmund rubbed the back of his head tiredly, making his hair stick up awkwardly. "I don't know what to tell you, Commander Lis's orders." He clapped Theo on the arm. "See, this is why the rest of us don't make friends with them."

It was well past midday, and the sky had begun to storm as Theo stepped out of the department store, turning his collar up against the weather. He could do what he had done before, move through the places that the 1st circle haunted until Nora finally decided to make herself known.

If you want answers about your brother, come to 113 Flint Street.

The napkin was still in his pocket.

He knew he should've destroyed it by now. It had his handwriting on one side, inviting a Grim into the house. And on the other side, the Grims inviting him in return. It was tantamount to treason. Especially since he'd had his chance to hand it over to Commander Lis. But if he did, he would never get answers about Alaric.

The rain began to slip its fingers under his shirt as Theo hesitated on the corner. Rikhaus Department Store was in the 7th circle. Only five circles away from the address. He knew better than anyone that he wasn't going to find Nora if she didn't want to be found. He could waste the rest of his day looking for her.

But that was what he had been commanded to do.

He had never disobeyed a command before. Not until last night, refusing to stand down from Ottoline. His whole life, Theo had believed that his duty and his oath were one and the same. That he was serving a proud purpose.

But again he saw the twelve knights lying dead on the ground. Ordered to do something against their oath. They had sworn, like every knight, to protect the Holtzfalls with their lives. And they had died for failing to kill one of them.

Theo, too, had refused to let her be killed. But he was still alive.

And, he thought, turning away from the upper circles and moving south, Alaric might be too.

113 FLINT STREET TURNED OUT TO BE A BOARDED-UP BETTING shop in the 12th circle of the city.

The windows had been plastered with posters advertising everything from a play that had closed months ago to medicine that promised to heal you for a fraction of the price of charms.

Theo knew that in all likelihood, this was a trap. He would be a fool to take instructions from an assassin. To walk through a door with no idea what was on the other side and the slim hope that it might be his brother.

But fool or not, he didn't walk away.

Suddenly, through a torn poster, there was a flash of movement, a face looking out onto the street quickly before vanishing. Theo's hand was already on his sword, heart hammering in anticipation of a fight. Slowly, the door opened a sliver, revealing a girl, her face hidden behind a sharp-snouted metallic fox's mask.

"Look at that," she said, her voice tinny through her disguise. "The lapdog slipped his collar long enough to come play with the wolves."

Theo felt every muscle in his body tighten, ready for a fight. But Theo had been trained to be a good knight.

A good knight waited for his opponent to make the first move. Behind the mask, the girl's eyes swept over him once before she finally stepped aside. "Come in before someone sees you."

A good knight knew better than to walk into enemy territory alone.

And yet, Theo followed the fox inside.

The room was dimly lit, the only light from a flickering bulb in the middle of the room. Offshoot energy, siphoned illegally from LAO's supply that ran like a nervous system of magical energy through the city.

"It looks like I owe you twenty zaub." A man's voice came from the darkened corner. Theo fought his impulse to draw his sword toward the voice. "I didn't think he'd come."

A truck rumbled by outside, the glare from the headlights splintering in between the posters, casting a spiderweb of light across a floor littered with betting slips. The rest of the room was filled with people in tin animal masks. A dozen of them or so.

An older woman in a doe mask leaned in the corner, a broad-shouldered man in a boar mask, a blonde girl with a scratched-up mouse's mask, a hawk, a bear, a squirrel, an owl . . . The only thing he didn't see was a wolf. No sign of Isengrim.

And then the truck was past, and the room was thick with gloom again, though Theo could still see the glints off the masks as they shifted. His nerves felt more awake than he could ever remember. Like the blood from his ancestors who had been stalked in the woods by creatures like these was waking up.

After years of training, when they were finally put into duty, Alaric had been known to complain that he could feel himself rusting like a toy soldier. Standing around, guarding them when there wasn't much to guard against. But serving the Holtzfalls had always given Theo purpose. And he felt that purpose alive in him now. If it came to a fight, he was badly outnumbered, but he would go down a knight all the same.

"I didn't even think your little pet project would get close enough to deliver the message," the fox girl said.

"Your *messenger* tried to kill a Holtzfall," Theo said into the darkness. He saw the redheaded girl's wide-eyed gaze, sprawled on the grass. "She's dead."

The brashness of their chatter dropped instantly into silence.

"You're lying," a woman's voice cracked, thick with the kind of grief that meant she knew he wasn't. "It would have been in the papers."

"No," another man in a mask said, "*they* don't want the city knowing we got that close to them." Theo had no doubt that *they* meant the Holtzfalls. "Foolish girl. What was she thinking?"

"Saskia knew what she was getting into," the girl in the fox mask snapped. "It was her idea to use that Loetze boy to try to get into the ceremony in the first place." She turned her fox grin at Theo. "But you made it so she didn't even need him. Who says chivalry is dead?"

Theo felt the twist of the knife in his stomach. "Even if she'd managed to kill Modesty you had to have known she wouldn't have made it out alive. Is that what you do, send people to die for your cause?"

"At least Saskia chose what she was dying for," the fox girl said, her voice crawling through the darkness. "Unlike you and your dozen brothers-in-arms."

The Grims couldn't know about the twelve dead. It had been only knights lined up in the garden last night. And the footmen who had carried them in.

"I'm not here for a debate." Theo's hand had never left his sword. "I'm here because you claimed to have news about my brother."

As his eyes adjusted to the gloom, Theo could see the masked figures casting looks between each other, a wordless conversation. Finally, the fox girl moved toward a door at the back. It looked like it might have led to a stockroom once. She pulled it open sharply, revealing a kneeling bound figure. "I guess you could say that."

Theo knew his brother even before the fox girl ripped the bag from his head.

Alaric looked worse than Theo had ever seen him. He was battered and bloody. He squinted against the light suddenly shining in his eyes, drawn with sleeplessness. One of his eyes was blackened, a gag shoved into his mouth.

But he was alive.

Alaric was alive.

It somehow seemed to Theo simultaneously impossible and inevitable. Impossible that Alaric wouldn't die executing his oath. Impossible that he *could* have fallen from something as average as a *mugger*. Impossible that he could be alive and not have found his way back to his duty.

Theo instinctively took a step toward his brother, but the fox girl crouched down in a flash, pressing a blade to Alaric's throat, pulling his head back. Only then did Alaric's gaze seem to focus on Theo.

"We're not fools, knightling, we know we're no match for you in a fight, but I think they can hold you off long enough for me to slit his throat if you try anything."

Theo forced himself to stay rooted, his hands clenching at his sides as questions went through him. "Alaric." He tried to steady his voice. "Are you all right?"

Somehow, even around the gag in his mouth, Alaric managed to give Theo a rueful half smile that Theo knew was meant to reassure him, and a bare nod, before the knife pressed into his throat harder.

"How?" Theo demanded, his mind reeling. How could Alaric still be alive when Verity was dead? Was Lukas Schuld working for the Grims? "Was Verity Holtzfall's death your work?"

"Are you asking us to confess to murder?" The fox girl tsked behind her mask. "That would be foolish of us, wouldn't it?"

The knife shifted as she moved, drawing a bead of blood from Alaric's throat. Making Theo tense.

"You didn't bring me here to watch my brother die." Theo tried to keep his voice steady. How many of them had it taken to wrestle his brother to the ground? To bind and gag him.

"No," the fox girl said finally. "We brought you here to strike a deal. It's simple, really. You can have your brother back. He's more trouble than he's worth to us. All we want in exchange is for you to bring us one of those little magic rings."

They wanted a Veritaz ring.

That's why the Grims had come for Modesty last night with a knife. When just hours before, they'd only come for Nora with cheap wine. It was why the redheaded girl had suddenly turned from messenger to would-be assassin. The difference was the wooden band on Modesty's hand.

"You want a way into the woods," Theo realized aloud.

Desperate men had been known to try to get into the woods. To seek their fortune like people used to in the old days. Knights had found them on the Holtzfall property before, trying to press their way into the trees. Held at bay by the ancient magic that shielded the woods. But somehow Theo didn't think wandering the woods and hoping to be granted an immortal gift was what the Grims had in mind.

The only sure passage into the woods was a Veritaz ring.

"If there's enough magic in those woods to power this city"—the boar surged forward angrily—"there's enough for all of us."

The solitary lightbulb flickered. "That's how Isengrim intends to keep his promise of *magic and money for all*?" Theo asked. He was aware of his brother watching him. Aware that he had neither agreed nor refused them right away. "By taking it from the woods?

"And how do you think you're going to succeed where so many others have failed?" Even in the decades since LAO had begun to draw the magic from the woods, there were still those foolish enough to try to steal magic from the power lines that ran through the city. It always ended in their death, surges of untethered magic stopping their hearts. Taking it straight from the soil of the woods like LAO did was the only way. And whatever charms Leyla used to do that were a closely held secret.

"Much like how we're not going to confess to murder, we're not about to tell you how we're going to get into LAO. Isengrim is done asking the Holtzfalls to do the right thing. We have to *take* our equality by force. And if needed"—she jerked Alaric's head up by his hair—"by blood."

The Grims were asking him to betray his oath. Veritaz rings weren't simply wooden bands. They were immortal magic, bound to the victors. The only way they could be removed was if an heiress took it off willingly. And no heiress was going to give up her ring by choice.

But she might with a knife against her throat. Or if they sawed off her finger.

"This really is very simple, but you knights seem simpleminded, so I'll lay it out for you plainly." The fox girl's knife pressed harder against Alaric's throat, a fervor in her face. Theo had seen the same one in the eyes of the redheaded girl a moment before she took poison. The Grims had no hesitation in choosing death for their cause. "It is twelve days until the Veritaz Trials end. Bring us a ring by then with a Holtzfall attached to it or not, or else we will slit your brother's throat. Equally, if we see a chance to take a Holtzfall ring, and you stand in our way, we will slit your brother's throat. Tell anyone about us and we'll—"

"Slit my brother's throat. I know."

"Wonderful, you get it."

Alaric made a noise against his gag. Theo felt like her knife was pressed to his own throat. His brother was gagged, but he could see it in his eyes, urging him not to betray his oath. But the fox girl jerked him back, and the knife drew blood again. "You decide, knightling. Your oath or your blood. Which do you value more?"

"So are you going to tell me how it is that you know Oskar Wallen?" Nora asked the back of August's head. The stalls of Silverlight Fish Market were pressed so close together they had to move single file behind the man with the knife, Joachim. Ahead of her, Nora could see the tension written in August's shoulders.

She'd been hoping that at some point in the journey down to the docks, he would have taken it upon himself to enlighten her. She was, after all, mostly here because she was curious. And because if August was murdered by the city's most notorious gangster, she would have to find a new journalist.

"Why do they call him *Ears* anyway?" Nora asked loudly as they wove their way through the crowd.

"Because." August finally stopped, turning to face her in between a stall selling mackerel and another one loaded with still-twitching shrimp. Both of the stalls were layered with charms to keep the fish from spoiling. "He hears everything that happens in this city. Do you think you could be talking any louder?"

"Probably." Nora shrugged. August's nerves didn't touch her. It didn't matter who this man was. She was a Holtzfall. He might be untouchable to the police, but she was untouchable to everyone. And she was wearing so many charms that she challenged anyone to get within six feet of her if she didn't want them to. "Who are you afraid will hear anyway? It can't be a secret that he does his work around here."

"Oskar's never in the same place twice," August said. "How do you think the cops haven't caught him?"

"I assumed rampant bribery."

August made to turn away, but Nora caught the pocket of his jacket, turning him back to face her. "How do you know Oskar Wallen?" she repeated, lowering her voice, conscious that the man August had called Joachim was waiting expectantly for them a few feet ahead.

August hesitated, and Nora watched as he surrendered. "He came up on the streets with my father." Nora knew the broad strokes of Oskar Wallen. Born fatherless to a laundress who was dead before he saw six years. Oskar Wallen started life picking pockets, then falling in as a runner for the gangster of the moment, Leon Junge. When Leon Junge was killed, Oskar Wallen started his ascension.

"So your father works for Oskar Wallen?"

"They worked for Leon Junge. When Junge died and Oskar climbed up, my father went straight. But Oskar paid for my father's burial." He skipped over his father's death so swiftly that Nora knew he didn't want questions or sympathy. "He isn't a man who forgets an old friend. He's also not a man you keep waiting."

They reached a small metal door that led into a brick building overlooking the market. Joachim banged his fist against the metal, letting it reverberate. The door swung open almost instantly, held by a man whose hands looked like they could've cracked a normal person in half.

As they stepped over the threshold, Nora felt the familiar snap of magic in the air a second before her glamour slipped off her. Her hand flew to the locket, but it was no good. The second she sparked it back to life, it extinguished again.

August glanced at her over his shoulder. "No charms around

Oskar Wallen." He was seeing her real face for the first time all day. And Nora watched him take her in swiftly, the way he had last night at the ceremony.

"I wish I'd known." The slight thrill of danger, of being without her charms, traveled up her spine. "I have so much uncharmed jewelry I never get the chance to wear."

They traveled up a short flight of stairs and emerged into a large empty room. It had all the trappings of a disused customs house. A large window overlooked the river. The remnants of old shipping crates littered one corner. The only other thing in the room was a hulking oak desk flanked by two equally hulking men, and a very much non-hulking man sitting behind it.

He was backlit by the warehouse's single immense window, so for a moment all Nora could see of the figure sitting at a desk was a silhouette with two translucent protruding ears.

"Oh," she said, not bothering to lower her voice. "*That's* why they call him Ears."

Next to her, August went tense, but from the desk there came an amused voice. "All the better to hear you with, my dear."

Oskar Wallen took on a firmer shape as they moved toward him. A man in his early forties, wearing a well-tailored three-piece suit. The vest was a bright paisley print, with an impeccably paired pocket square and cravat. The knot was pierced by a pearl-encrusted tie pin in the shape of a bee. But even though his garish clothes and his ears stood out, nothing else about him did. He had the same haircut as every man in the city, and a bland sort of expression that would fit right in with a crowd of bankers and lawyers.

"Miss Holtzfall." He inclined his head in greeting. If Oskar Wallen was surprised to see a Holtzfall in the company of a journalist, he didn't show it. "Auggie, what's this I hear about you saying all around town you're working for me?" His tone was mild, but Nora couldn't help feeling there was a definite right and wrong answer to this. "Don't tell me you've finally come around after all these years?"

"Just following up a story." The casual shrug August gave belied the nervous energy she could feel pouring off him.

"And what story might that be?"

"We're looking for the cop who stole my mother's ring to fence it." Nora ignored the look August shot her. "But since you already knew we'd dropped your name, you also already knew what we were asking about. You just wanted to see whether we would lie to you."

Oskar Wallen's hands folded together, obscuring the smile on his face. "I would *hope* a Holtzfall in the midst of the Veritaz Trials would be too smart to lie." He wasn't wrong there. Although Nora didn't think even the Huldrekall would turn Oskar Wallen into a trial.

He leaned back in his chair. "This ring you're after, what was it? Ruby?"

"Emerald."

"Of course. Green always flatters blondes." Oskar's own bejeweled fingers drummed across the table thoughtfully.

"You've heard something," August said. It wasn't a question.

"I hear a lot of things." Oskar tapped his ear.

"You tweaked a shielding charm to turn inward instead of outward. That's why charms don't work in here." All the while they had been talking, there had been another part of Nora's mind working away at this minor mystery. And the final piece had just clicked together. "A disruptor charm would do the same, of course, but it wouldn't account for such controlled range. And if the disruptor spilled out beyond the walls of this building, merchants might start to wonder why their fish is rotting and their ice is melting when they have charms on their stalls. The only other option would be to charm the whole building, but that amount of work would be impossible to duplicate daily if you really are moving offices that often. And there's no real reason that a charm that is meant to shield from outside magic couldn't be turned inside out. Very clever."

Oskar's grin spread far enough now that she could see it behind his clasped hands. "As are you."

"I'm aware."

Oskar considered the two of them before turning his attention to a newspaper on his desk, leafing through it languidly. "Your grandmother, the one who *isn't* a Holtzfall, they say has an excellent mind for business. I've heard you take after her more than Mercy Holtzfall."

"If you know who has my mother's ring," Nora said, skipping over whatever bait he was throwing her way, "why not just take it for yourself? It's worth millions of zaub."

"It could be worth billions, and it still wouldn't be enough money to risk being caught with evidence from the murder of the century."

Nora had a feeling she knew where this was going. "So what's your price to tell us?"

"Information." Oskar turned to the front page of the newspaper now. Ottoline's face stared up at them. "Her father." He tapped the picture. "Who is he?"

Nora could have been given a hundred guesses, and she still never would have thought the city's greatest mobster would ask about Aunt Grace's dirty laundry. "You'd rather have gossip than money?"

"Gossip. Leverage." Oskar leaned back in his chair. "Your grandmother, I mean the Holtzfall one, went to a lot of trouble to hide her existence. I'm curious as to why."

Blackmail, then.

"Aunt Grace and my grandmother have lied to me for sixteen years," Nora hedged. It should have been easy to just agree to this price. Her grandmother and Aunt Grace hadn't shown any loyalty to her yesterday. She didn't owe them loyalty either. "Why would they tell me the truth now?"

"If the truth was something your aunt was willing to just *tell* you, it would probably be useless to me. You're a clever girl. There are other ways to find out." Oskar leaned back in his chair, his attention returning to the papers, Nora could feel August's gaze boring into her, but she kept her eyes fixed on Oskar Wallen. She didn't want to see whether he was urging her to agree or to walk away, either was likely to make her want to do the opposite.

"Here it is, Miss Holtzfall: If you bring me a little leverage, I'm sure we could track down who has your mother's ring. If you don't, then you and Auggie will have a grand time interrogating every pawnshop owner in town. I'll even be gracious and let you continue to drop my name. It's really no skin off my nose. But you'll likely wear holes in your shoes before you get any answers."

Chapter 24

LOTTE

When Lotte had told Modesty that news traveled faster in the city, she still hadn't expected there to be pictures of her from only hours ago in this afternoon's papers.

Every newspaper stand they passed on their drive from the department store to the luncheon showed Lotte leaving the Paragon Hotel wearing a dressing gown, Theo's coat draped over it. Modesty beaming at the cameras beside her.

At this rate, this evening's papers would likely show her entering the Arndt mansion in a silk emerald-green gown with diamonds on her wrists and neck, Modesty still beaming beside her.

Lotte didn't pretend to understand why the currency of newspaper coverage had value. Why it would matter to Modesty Holtzfall that this made girls like Estelle envious, who lived far away from the life they were flaunting. But as the cameras devoured them on the steps to the Arndt mansion, Lotte understood that for whatever it was worth, it was a currency she had right now, one that Modesty wanted.

"Vultures," Modesty said unconvincingly, picking up two glasses of champagne from a tray as they entered, handing one to Lotte. Lotte might be affecting the role of a wide-eyed country girl, but it didn't take much pretending at that moment. The ceiling of the Arndt mansion was elaborately decorated with scenes from stories of the ancient woods. Trolls rampaging through villages, knights receiving swords from immortal beings, girls spinning gold. And climbing the columns of the ballroom were wreaths of flowers so elaborate that some garden somewhere must've been stripped bare.

When she pulled her gaze back down, she realized people were staring at her. She might as well *have* turned up wearing a dressing gown.

Finally, a girl in a blue gown fringed with pearls broke off toward them, her dress clinking excitedly as she moved across the room.

"Oh, I've been *dying* to meet the newest Holtzfall arrival!"

"Angelika!" Another girl, with chestnut hair fashioned into an elaborate braid, joined them. "Don't put it like that. You make it sound like she's a new baby they've just announced."

The first girl, Angelika, wrinkled her nose in amusement. "Oh, please, I doubt anyone will make the mistake of sending rattles as welcome gifts."

"No one has sent *any* welcome gifts so far," Lotte said.

Angelika, Modesty, and the brunette laughed. Lotte belatedly managed to school her face into vaguely beatific amusement as if she'd meant it innocently and not sarcastically.

It didn't take long before Lotte was being passed around like a doll all the guests wanted to marvel at. They didn't seem to need answers to the questions they tossed at her.

"Where have they been hiding you away?"

A briar pit in a convent while you sipped champagne.

"So you grew up in the countryside? And this is your first time in Walstad? How quaint! Why didn't you come visit the city before? There's so much more to *do* here. At least that's what I find, it's pure boredom on my country estate."

Because not all of us have the freedom of wealth.

She sipped her drink to drown out the answers she wanted to give. And every time she finished a glass, someone seemed to hand her a fresh one.

On festival days, Lotte and Estelle would sometimes manage to sneak a mug of beer each. And half the time, the dregs of it got dumped in Carlotta Feuer's flower bed when they'd hear someone coming.

But champagne was a different beast altogether, and somewhere around when the speeches began, Lotte realized that the bubbles had gone to her head.

Hugo Arndt, Lotte noticed through a slightly light head, was a well-dressed man with a blinding grin. As he rose to a podium, Lotte found herself being shuffled to stand with a gaggle of others in green. It took her a second to realize that it was her family. A sea of Holtzfall green at the center of the room. Her mother had come from . . . somewhere. Grace smiled at her approvingly, and Lotte felt her heart soar. She wanted her mother to smile like that at her for the rest of her life.

"My friends!" Hugo Arndt began, leaning on one side of the podium, a glass dangling carelessly from his hands. "You're all here—well, let's be honest, you're all here because I have a well-stocked cellar, for one." He raised his glass as a laugh ran through the crowd. "But you're also here because I think we can all agree that it's time for one of our own to be in charge. We need a leader who understands what a grave threat the Grims pose to *us*. And I saw it myself last night." He gestured into the crowd toward Modesty, who pressed her Veritaz-ringed hand to her chest as if surprised she was the topic of conversation. "Governor Gerwald *says* he is going to put measures in place. I have it on good authority that in his little speech on the vox tonight, he is going to decree a curfew for anyone below the fifth circle." A ripple went through the crowd. "But I say!" Hugo Arndt raised his voice again. "That a curfew is not enough! We need to use our resources to root out the problem: that bloody pest Isengrim! And can you really trust our current governor to have our best interests at heart when, just last month, he was talking about equal vote reform?" Another laugh went through the crowd.

"An equal vote?" This time she didn't have to play up her country girl ignorance. There had been a vote for the governor in Gelde too. Every three years, a small ballot box wheeled through town and the people of Gelde lined up and made their choice.

"Oh, you know." Modesty waved a hand. "The Grims seem to think it should be one vote per person instead of votes being weighted by income. But then *imagine*. The governor would have to pander to the whole city instead of working for the people like *us* who pay for everything, including his salary." Modesty laughed. "Ridiculous notion that people like *them* should get the same vote as us."

Lotte had thought she'd understood what wealth was. Lennart Hinde had been the wealthiest person she'd known before Walstad. In Gelde, that meant ordering dresses from the city and eating meat every night of the week. But this wealth, this was something different. This was power.

Her face was already hot from the champagne, but she felt it rising now with anger. Lotte knew from years of experience that she had trouble keeping her anger at bay, even knowing it only made things worse. She had spent more than one night in the briar pit because she had snapped at one of the Sisters.

And under the influence of the champagne, she felt herself dangerously close to saying something. Something that would undo all the doe-eyed ignorance she had labored over today. She had to leave. Before she revealed in front of her whole family what a lifetime in the countryside had really made her. Not an innocent little good girl. An angry wild creature.

As laughter rippled through the crowd again, Lotte turned, swiftly pushing her way out of the ballroom.

And straight into Honora Holtzfall as she came through the front door.

Lotte had probably seen Honora Holtzfall's face more than she'd seen her own. She seemed to grace every magazine and newspaper that they got in Gelde. She dominated gossip columns, fashion spreads, and event announcements, over and over again.

Estelle had hated her with the sort of spite that only came from jealousy. *She's too foreign to actually be pretty*, Estelle was fond of saying. *She just fools us into thinking she's attractive because of all the money.* But in person, Lotte realized, Honora Holtzfall *was* fooling everyone. Because no photograph had ever done her justice.

Lotte didn't know where her eyes should come to a rest on the sharp, sweeping planes of her face. Her sleek cheekbones conspired with an elegant nose to make Lotte feel suddenly self-conscious, like every feature on her own face was snub and provincial.

Meanwhile, Honora Holtzfall had the look of someone who had never cared less what anyone thought of her.

"Making up for lost time with the champagne consumption?" she remarked, and Lotte realized she was still holding an empty glass. "You have sixteen years of catching up to do."

She considered trying the innocent country girl act that she'd been using on Modesty all day. *Gosh, I've never had such nice sparkling wine before. I didn't think these bubbles would go to my head like this.* But Lotte was just sober enough to know she was too drunk to pull it off. And more than that, she was too angry. Angry at this room full of people laughing at people like her, born with nothing. Angry that she felt so outside of it all. That she felt nothing like a Holtzfall.

"I don't know, how much champagne do you think it takes to make up for all those times they locked me in a pit without anything to eat or drink?"

Honora let out an impatient sigh. "You're as dramatic as Aunt Grace."

"And you're as ignorant as the rest of them in there." The Sisters had often chastised drinkers in their sermons, preaching that alcohol led to foolish drunken brawls. Lotte wasn't sure exactly if this was a brawl, but she was in the mood to fight someone.

Honora sighed again, but she looked faintly irked. "Since you're new to this family, I find it's my sad duty to inform you that I'm a great deal smarter than anyone currently here. Yourself included, obviously."

Lotte somehow didn't doubt that. She could see the canny look in Honora Holtzfall's eye. And it made her angrier. "And with all those smarts, you still think all of this is *fair*? That you get more of a vote than everyone else?" She waved a hand vaguely. "That if that man in there charms the four hundred people here, then it doesn't matter what any of the thousands of other people he governs think?"

Honora Holtzfall considered her soberly. "That politics aren't fair isn't news to me," she replied finally.

"So why don't you *do* anything about it?" Lotte could feel it clawing at her chest. The unfairness of everything.

"Because nothing in the world is fair. Some of us get champagne and murdered mothers. Some of us get convents and living mothers dropped into our laps at opportune moments. It's better to learn to live with your lot in life than complain like it will make a difference."

Lotte's mind felt soft and indistinct with the champagne, so she wasn't sure what she was angry about anymore. She was angry about the vote. About Mr. Brahm dying. About the maid's memories being stripped from her this morning. She was angry that she had to pretend to be silly and foolish to survive. About being passed around like a fairground novelty. She was angry that this could have been her whole life and she wouldn't feel so out of place. She wouldn't see how unfair it all was. She was angry that people like Freddie Loetze and Hugo Arndt and, hell, Modesty Holtzfall thought their wealth made them deserve power over others. "Do you just not care because the world is unfair in your favor?"

Outlined in the darkened doorway, in the glow spilling out from the ballroom, Nora looked like an immortal spirit in the stories. The ones made of light that led the worthy to safety and the unworthy over the edge of a cliff. And for a moment, Lotte thought she was going to say something else. Something truthful. And then another figure appeared behind her, and all of a sudden the light moved and she was just a girl again.

Theo. He had vanished from the department store, replaced by another knight whose name she didn't know. Only to reappear now, shaking rain from his hair, eyes moving between the two of them.

As undressed as she had felt this morning wearing a bathrobe in front of him, she felt even more bare now draped in silk and diamonds.

"As much as I'd like to send you into the streets of Walstad tipsy and alone, if you were abducted, I'm sure they'd blame it on me somehow." Nora raised a shoulder, elegant even in her disdain. "Get Ottoline back safely," Nora instructed Theo without looking at him, and then she was gone. Vanished into the bright glittering fold of the party that Lotte had left behind.

After that, Lotte didn't entirely remember how she got back to the Paragon. She remembered Theo guiding her to an automobile. She remembered the city spinning by as dusk turned to night. She thought she might have fallen asleep at some point.

She was half aware of being lifted.

And of a mind that was not her own breaking past her hindern as her head lay against his chest.

Your oath or your blood, a voice she didn't know whispered in her mind nastily. *Which do you value more?*

The Tale of the Woodcutter

The Youngest Son

The second day, the woodcutter sent his youngest son, the most honest, into the woods.

He gave him the Huldrekall's ring, his second-best ax, and the same instruction he had given the eldest son.

On the road, the youngest son, too, encountered the weeping woodsman. The woodsman told him the same story his brother had heard: He had lost his ax to the river and his family would starve. The youngest son looked at the ax in his own hand. Well, of course he could not give him this ax. This ax was his. The youngest son had never liked to share. So he simply explained to the man that he himself needed his own ax, so he hoped that he found his ax in the river. And then, thinking no more of it, the youngest went on his way.

Soon he reached the circle of trees and the sleeping Lindwurm. And he, too, retreated. When he returned home empty-handed, he explained that he didn't see the point in risking his life for one ax. They had money, he said to his father, they could afford to buy a new ax. He was honest.

But he was not worthy.

Chapter 25

NORA

Nora had done a bad thing.

But as she took her breakfast at sunset on the balcony overlooking west Walstad, she wasn't sure yet whether she felt guilty or just hungover.

She was wrapped in a bright silk robe against the spring chill, her feet propped on the opposite chair with charms around her ankles. Their healing magic worked at the blisters that were either from a day spent traipsing all over the city with the journalist or from a night moving through the upper circles with her own kind. Both she had done in improper shoes for the occasion.

Two days ago, Nora had refused Oskar Wallen's deal.

No matter who Ottoline's father was, those secrets belonged to her family. Nora had been raised as the Heiress; she knew the importance of putting the family first.

But there was nothing quite like *time* to erode good decisions.

Time and watching the whole city fall for Ottoline and her fakery.

That day at Hugo Arndt's luncheon, Nora had come dangerously close to respecting her new cousin. Even if she was misguided, at least she was honest. And the anger . . . Nora knew that anger.

But as fast as she'd sparked to life in front of her—that Ottoline was gone. The next day, Gisela Gruessing had held a birthday party. Ottoline had been all doe-eyed innocent while she let Modesty trot her around like a show pony.

She seemed to be fooling the newspapers too.

Ottoline leaving the Paragon, wearing nothing but a robe. The headline gushing that she *must* be a Holtzfall. Being seen in public dressed so scandalously was *just* like something Nora might do.

And all of that might not have been slowly eating away at Nora if it weren't for the waiting and the wanting.

It had been four days since the night of the ceremony and the first trial.

Four days since Modesty had won her ring.

Four days of Modesty gloating and no new trials to equal the playing field.

Four days of waiting for another chance to prove she was the worthiest of the heirship while the newspapers whispered that she wasn't.

The trials had stalled. The hunt for her mother's murderer had stalled. Nora's whole life was at a standstill. And she didn't like where it stood. The stabbing grief that had pierced her so violently in the days after her mother's murder had turned to a dull ache that only seemed to ebb when she was with August, looking for answers.

Looking for Isengrim.

But in the quiet moments, Nora's whole being was made up of rage and grief and the desperate, gnawing need to win. The urgency to be tested again and succeed.

And she couldn't push that away. Because if she did, all that was left behind was a small nasty voice telling her that none of it mattered. Becoming Heiress again wouldn't restore things to how they used to be. Neither would finding Verity Holtzfall's killer.

Her mother was gone. Aunt Grace had a new daughter taking

all her attention. Her grandmother's focus was slowly shifting to Modesty. The newspapers would never admit she'd ever done anything right.

Who was she even trying to prove herself to?

"Are you going to finish that?" August had asked late in the afternoon the day before. "Or does it need more caviar on it?" He meant the half of a sandwich that had been sitting on greaseproof paper in front of her going soggy. They were taking a break in a grimy-windowed café in the 11th circle. It was just them and some factory workers who were on strike, the rain drumming its fingers on the window. "We'd better go if we're going to make it three blocks and back before curfew."

"Curfew?" Nora had scoffed disdainfully. "You can't expect me to be inside by sunset. I only woke up at noon."

"Sure, no one expects *you* to obey curfew." August reached across the table, helping himself to the sandwich. "But we're below the fifth circle here."

Governor Gerwald had announced the curfew the same day as Hugo Arndt's campaign party. To keep the Grims in check, all lower-circle residents were to be off the streets by dusk. Anyone caught out or caught *gathering* would be arrested on sight.

Hugo Arndt had brought voxes into the ballroom as the governor's speech was broadcast. He gave a mocking commentary of his political opponent as the ballroom laughed along.

The jails were already filling up by all accounts.

"They're not going to arrest us." Nora waved August's words away impatiently.

"No, they're not going to arrest *you*," August corrected her. "And until we crack this case open, I'm low on bail money, so unless you want to pull some strings and get the whole curfew repealed—"

"Why does everyone seem to think I can fix everything wrong in the world?" Nora was on edge, Ottoline's tipsy accusations coming back to her. *Or do you just not care because the world is unfair in your favor?*

"Because you could," August said absently, taking a bite of the sandwich. "If a Holtzfall said jump, the governor would say, 'How high?' If a Holtzfall said ride through the city naked on the back of a horse, the governor would say, 'Silver dapple or chestnut?' If a Holtzfall—"

"Do they pay you by the word at the *Bullhorn*?" Nora cut him off. Since turning down Oskar Wallen, she had spent almost every waking hour with August. Hunting for some sign of her mother's ring. She liked to think she was beginning to know him. "Are you going to pretend to be an idealist now?" Nora asked. "Is that how you're going to get that pay raise if you can't make your career off of my mother's murder?"

You'll likely wear holes in your shoes before you get any answers.

Oskar Wallen's parting words were proving true. In a way. Nora's shoes were too expensive and too well charmed to wear holes in, but her patience was thinning.

"Oh, come on." August didn't rise to her annoyance, which irked her even more. "I know you'll be just devastated to be without me after dark. But there must be something else you'd rather be doing tonight than following me like a shadow."

His words landed harder than he knew. When she'd been the next Heiress, she was the sun that the rest of the world moved around. So bright that everyone else became her shadow. But now she *felt* like a shadow of her former self. The main purpose of her life had become waiting for some immortal being to test her in some abstract way to prove her value to her family and the city.

"Since you mention it, there is somewhere I need to be." Nora was too rich to storm off. Instead, she hailed a taxi, paid it triple, and found her way to Aleksandra Flipp's birthday party.

Aleksandra had flooded the ballroom of the Flipp mansion and set several small ships afloat on it. One that served champagne out of the portholes. Another that fired sweet bonbons out of its cannons to the crowd.

And once *again*, amidst it all, was Ottoline. Never mind that Ottoline had never even met Aleksandra before and Nora had known her since they were both infants. The fact that Nora had nothing but disdain for Aleksandra and her tendency to open every conversation with ebullient flattery was beside the point.

And as the night wore on, the artificiality of it all, of Ottoline and the fact that her little act was *working*, began to eat away at Nora until she couldn't think of anything else.

It was a few hours into the party when Nora found that she had drifted toward Modesty through the shallow waters at the edge of the ballroom. Nora's dress had been charmed to billow around her in the water and dry the moment it was out. The beginning of an idea was dancing across her mind. Suppose she did want to know who Ottoline's father was. Aunt Grace wouldn't tell Nora the truth. But if her own daughter asked about her father . . . "So what's your end-game when the newspapers lose interest in her?"

Modesty glanced up from the tart she was picking berries off and throwing in the water, where small fish were eating them. "By the time the papers lose interest, I will be the next Heiress." It was meant to needle at Nora. Obviously. But she decided to let that go for now, since she was working an angle here.

"*Whoever* the next Heiress is will be stuck with her one way or an-other. Another family member begging for handouts, just like your mother always did." To Nora's surprise, Modesty didn't bristle at *that*. Perhaps all she and Modesty had needed all along was a com-mon enemy.

"So what are you suggesting?" If Modesty was suspicious of Nora's sudden interest in their new cousin, she didn't show it. "Arsenic?"

"Or," Nora replied drily, "she becomes the problem of her *other* family." Modesty wasn't as bright as Nora, so she gave her cousin a second to catch up.

"Eudora Binks started a rumor that her father is an immortal." Modesty eyed Ottoline across the artificial sea. She was nursing a glass of champagne. Clearly she'd learned her lesson about over-indulging at the campaign luncheon. "Allegedly, she was born nine months after their Veritaz Trials."

"Please." Nora's scoff was genuine this time. There were still parts of the world where half-immortal children were common, but Gamanix wasn't one of them. "No one is ever going to accuse Aunt Grace of being so worthy and virtuous that a forest spirit fell in love with her."

"Then why hasn't *someone* tried to claim her? For the money or the fame or any other number of reasons." Modesty had clearly thought about it. Nora hated when the worst person she knew made a good point.

"Well, since you two are so *close*"—her tone was mocking— "perhaps she'll tell you who he is." Nora raised a shoulder carelessly. "Perhaps it just hasn't *occurred* to her she has a father yet."

Modesty had only managed to use her gift on Nora once, in a moment of carelessness when they'd been children. They'd been playing a game of rounders in the garden of the mansion. Nora had been winning. Modesty had bumped against Nora, bypassing her hindern. And suddenly it had occurred to Nora that she shouldn't win. She ought to lose. Modesty deserved to win instead.

It was only when the game was over and Modesty was victorious that Nora realized her cousin had used her Holtzfall gift to plant an idea. It had felt like a violation of the thing Nora held most precious in the world: her mind.

And now she was going to inflict the same on Ottoline.

Nora was powerless to move the trials forward, but if she could find out who Ottoline's father was . . . She had told Oskar she wouldn't trade her family's secrets for his information. But that was days ago. Things had changed.

Modesty understood her. Wordlessly, she sailed across the ballroom toward Ottoline. And Nora watched as Modesty pulled off a glove, casually dropping her hand against Ottoline's arm.

No matter what her bloodline was, Ottoline wasn't family. She didn't deserve Nora's loyalty.

Still. If Oskar Wallen was in fact a test sent by the Huldrekall, she knew she had failed.

THE COFFEE WAS GOING COLD IN NORA'S HANDS NOW. SHE sparked a ring on her hand, warming it even as she let the chilly spring air pull her hair off her face as she looked out over the balcony.

The skyline blazed in the setting sun over the city that sprawled around her, seeming to set the city on fire. Except . . . Nora drew to attention as something in the distance caught her eye—the *illusion* of the city being on fire didn't usually come with smoke.

Nora rose, her healing feet hitting the tiled floor of the balcony as she pressed against the wrought iron barrier. The smoke was rising in a column from somewhere west. Near the 6th circle.

Nora was moving before the police sirens wailing on the street below even reached her. Her whole being sparking to life with anticipation.

What was that old expression? Where there was smoke, there might be a trial that would finally allow her to prove her worth to an immortal being.

She was sure it went *something* like that.

"A ribbon around the waist might tie it together?"

"Not in green, though."

"Gold, maybe?"

"Yellow makes you look sallow."

"I didn't say yellow, I said *gold*."

The blandness of the conversation between Modesty, Constance, and Clemency was at odds with the restlessness in the room. It was obvious in the strained casualness of the conversation between her cousins, and Lotte could feel it rising in her too. Like a wave threatening to draw down her every thought into a maelstrom of anticipation.

She had been in the city for four days now.

Four days of dresses and parties and more dresses and parties.

A ball where the entire room was filled with pink clouds on which drinks and food drifted by. A gathering to show off a painting collection in which each frame was held by a beautiful young girl, standing perfectly still all night. A birthday with a flooded ballroom and ships full of champagne.

And no more trials.

She was starting to feel her eyes strain from playing the wide-eyed country girl in the city. She could feel her patience waning every time someone pointed at the magimek lights with a grin, saying, *I bet they don't have this out in the countryside.* Last night it had been a gaggle gathered around, pointing at the flooded ballroom and prodding at her to say *water* in her non-city accent and laughing.

And every time their hands brushed against her arm in condescending kindness, the truth of them revealed itself. The ones who didn't want to be here but needed to be *seen* here. The ones who bought things they didn't even care for but needed to be seen having. The way they drifted toward the people they thought had power or popularity that would reflect well on them. The ones who weren't having any fun but needed everyone to think that they were having more fun than the person next to them. The way all they were ever thinking about was what everyone else thought of them in their world, and outside it through the papers.

All except for Honora Holtzfall, who seemed like an unmovable island amidst the shifting tides around her. Lotte thought she caught Honora watching her a few times. But any time she turned to face her, Honora's attention was elsewhere and Lotte felt foolish for thinking her cousin might care a jot about her.

All of them were on tenterhooks, waiting for the next trial.

But Lotte was the only one waiting for the chance to prove she was worthy of being a Holtzfall. And not just a temporary sideshow in their world. That, too, she read in their minds.

The papers were also spinning their wheels since the last trial. While they waited, they recounted tales of Veritaz Trials past. Waking up at dawn was a hard habit to break, which meant Lotte had hours before anyone was awake to read every paper cover to cover.

That was how she came to learn about the past trials of the Holtzfalls. About Valor Holtzfall, her mother's youngest brother, dying on the ice. About Earnest Holtzfall III trying to flee his generation's trials by going abroad and seeking refuge with the royal family of a foreign nation. But the trials didn't care about man-made borders. The ruins of the royal castle, ripped apart by a trial of bravery, were a tourist site now. Lotte read about Charity Holtzfall ironically not winning the ring for generosity because she didn't give her shawl to a shivering woman. That explained the strain in her cousins' smiles as they stopped the automobile every time they saw a beggar on the street to give them a jewel or a coin.

Only Modesty seemed at ease, flaunting the wooden band on her finger. Sure of her place.

Last night, sleepless after yet another party thrown by yet another person Lotte didn't know, her doubts had become harder to ignore. In spite of lying in the ocean of expensive sheets stitched with the Paragon's insignia, she had a feeling of being at the bottom of the briar pit again, the voices whispering nastily in her head. What if the Sisters were right all along? What if she wasn't good enough? Unworthy of all of this? What if she failed the next trial too? Where would she go if she couldn't prove that she was good enough to be a Holtzfall? And just as she began to finally drift off, crawling out of some dark corner of her mind she had never looked at before, there came a new thought.

If her mother's family didn't want her, maybe her father's would.

She'd awoken that morning with the idea firmly rooted in her mind. Growing and taking shape into a desperate need to know. Lotte had only ever fantasized about her mother coming back in her life. If she'd thought about her father at all, she'd imagined him as the type of man who would cast aside a poor pregnant woman and force her to abandon her child.

But now she knew her mother was far from poor, which meant her father was something else entirely.

She paced the suite at the Paragon Hotel, waiting for Grace to wake up.

"Who's my father?" Lotte asked as her mother finally stepped into the sitting room around midday. For a second, Lotte thought she might have seen something flash over her mother's face as she hesitated.

"Goodness, Ottoline," Grace said. "Can I sit and have breakfast before I start trying to remember all the men I slept with seventeen years ago."

Lotte wondered if that answer was meant to scandalize her into silence, little innocent country girl that she was. But Lotte stood her ground. "I'm not asking you to remember *all* the men. Just one."

Grace took her time, pouring herself a cup of coffee from a silver pot. She took a sip, avoiding Lotte's gaze. And when she looked up and found Lotte still watching her, she made a frustrated noise. "I honestly couldn't tell you, Ottoline."

"You're lying."

"And *you* are giving me a headache." Grace rose abruptly, taking her coffee with her. "I'm going back to bed. Oh, good, Benedict," Grace greeted the knight as he stepped through the door. His eyes darted between Grace and Lotte, taking in the tension. Benedict's injuries from the night of the ceremony were beginning to fade, but they still made Lotte wince. "Can you drive Ottoline to . . ." She waved a hand vaguely in the air. "Her thing?"

"Dress fitting." Lotte didn't care about the dress fitting. But it irked her that her mother didn't care enough to know. Didn't seem to care where she went or what she did. Didn't seem to want to spend any time with her after they'd been separated for sixteen years. "For the governor's victory celebration." The election for the governorship was two days away. Whoever won, the Holtzfalls were expected to show up in style.

"Yes," Grace said, her hand dancing vaguely in the air as she faded back toward her bedroom. "That."

They drove mostly in silence through the streets of Walstad, Lotte sitting next to Benedict in the front seat. Finally, they pulled up outside of the tailor. All of Lotte's clothes so far had come from sprawling department stores. But this was a small white-fronted boutique, with a bell for entry. Lotte hadn't seen her grandmother since the night of the ceremony, but she had apparently taken enough note of them to decree that they were all to procure their dresses for the governor's victory celebration here. Instead of getting something flashy and modern at one of the department stores.

Through the window, she could see her cousins already there, looking through bolts of green fabric with the easy air of people born to this life. And Lotte made her decision.

"Benedict." Lotte caught the knight's arm, crossing the hindern into Benedict's mind deliberately. "Do you know who my father is?"

She didn't expect him to tell her. But she did expect the question to bring the answer to the surface of his mind. She'd be able to snatch it from there. But there was nothing.

When Grace Holtzfall had confiscated a few hours of memory from the servant girl, Lotte had been able to read the absence that was left behind. Like a gap in her mind that she was struggling to bridge. But in Benedict's mind, there wasn't a gap, there was a chasm.

His mind was riddled with so many missing memories that he had stopped trying to fight his way across them. He accepted them as scars born from serving the Holtzfalls. If he knew nothing, he could never betray them, even against his will. He could only do his duty.

By my oath. They were the same words she had heard in Theo's mind the night he had pulled her out of the swarm of journalists. And again when he had draped his coat over her the morning after. The words she had learned guided the knights in their duty.

By my oath. It echoed around the fissures in his memory. His oath to protect Grace at all costs. Even if that meant forgetting.

Once, he'd known the answer to the question Lotte had asked him. But that memory was locked away now. One moment he was stepping into Mercy Holtzfall's office, the next he was driving Grace down unsteady roads to a convent.

He sat with her in a stone chamber for months on end as she alternated staring out a window and screaming her rage into the empty fields that stretched on and on around it.

Benedict pulled his arm away, breaking the contact and pulling Lotte out of the memory of her mother.

In a swift movement he was getting out of the automobile, opening the door on her side formally.

"Benedict—" She felt a stab of guilt. He knew what she had just tried to do. She wanted to explain. She wanted to tell him about the gnawing feeling that she *needed* to find her father. But he had been the one to bring her here. To risk his life to get her here. She couldn't tell him she wanted a different family.

"You are late to meet your cousins, Miss Holtzfall." His voice was formal, and he didn't meet her gaze.

Lotte felt shame pricking at the nape of her neck as she walked away from him. She had never felt shame for reading a mind before. Not even when she had thought it was a curse. But then, she had never been caught either.

The three younger knights who had been assigned to protect them were stationed just inside the door of the tailor's. Lotte was aware of Theo watching her as she hurried into the small shop, but she kept her own eyes straight ahead. Sure that if she looked at him, he would see what she'd just done.

Now Lotte sat restlessly as dresses were draped and pinned. For three hours. She was waiting her turn, sitting on a plush sofa, when a small metallic bird flitted into the shop, landing between Theo and Hildegarde.

Hilde pulled the note it was carrying from between its talons, reading it swiftly before passing it to Theo, then Edmund. Lotte watched their faces shift one after the other. "We have to leave."

"Now?" Constance asked into a glass of champagne she had just refilled.

"Now." Theo's tone didn't invite argument. "Every Holtzfall is to go to the house immediately, for your own safety."

"Fine." Constance made an exasperated noise as Clemency sighed dramatically. Modesty seemed to be the only other person picking up on the sudden change in both Hilde and Theo. Something was happening. Lotte was already standing, even as the pair of cousins moved languidly. "I'll just have to find my clothes."

"No time," Hilde said at the same time as Edmund said, "You're wearing clothes."

Even Edmund looked serious.

Lotte was not used to being in the dark like this. Her whole life, she had thought hearing people's minds was a curse. But it had been part of her too. And now she found herself almost unconsciously pulling at the hindern on her finger.

"My dress isn't even hemmed," Clemency complained.

"Now."

This time, even Constance and Clemency seemed to realize something was wrong.

The answer crashed into Lotte the second she took off her hindern.

Inside the boutique, it was still and quiet. The walls here, like most expensive places in the city, were charmed to mute disturbances from the street.

But Lotte's mind was flooded with noise. A mass of seething hatred, desperation, and anger poured off the city, moving through the streets outside. The wave of voices crashing into Lotte threatened to carry her away into chaos. But, like flotsam among it, she managed to pick out some distinct shapes.

It had begun as civil protests against the governor and his curfew. Curfew that had cost people jobs, freedoms, what little distractions they had at night.

Civil protests that were meant to stay civil.

But anger stoked fast.

Protests turned to riot.

And Lotte could feel it now, echoing deep in her chest, the desire to rip the wealth of Walstad down to size. It was a moving storm that no Holtzfall would want to be caught in.

As she picked up the maelstrom of voices getting closer, the knights were already shepherding them to the back entrance of the tailor's. One of the shop girl's eyes followed them as they pushed through the stockroom, hands knotted around a silk sash.

Two black-and-silver automobiles were stationed at the back door. Hildegarde Rydder loaded Constance and Clemency into one. Modesty headed toward the second one.

Lotte was moving to follow her when the sharp edge of a thought cut across her mind. A second later, a small gaggle of rioters rounded the corner.

Two wore wolf masks. The third was a girl in a fox mask.

Next to Lotte, Theo jerked, his arm coming across her body, shielding her instinctively.

Your oath or your blood. Which do you value more?

She had heard those words, distantly, in Theo's mind the day after the Veritaz Ceremony. Only now did she understand them. The memory was clear and focused.

His brother, Alaric, was alive.

And his life was in Theo's hands.

A choice between Alaric and his oath.

Two impossible choices wrestling each other like wild animals as he hunted for another way. A third answer.

But here, in this moment, the choice had come.

He could hand Modesty over to them now and break his oath to save his brother. Or he could help the Holtzfalls all escape and let them kill Alaric.

His oath or his brother.

No.

Lotte spun to face Theo, so her back was to the masked figures. "I'm going to faint," she said in a low voice. Theo's eyes snapped to her face. "If you catch me, Edmund will get Modesty out of here."

A flicker of understanding passed over Theo's face. She could leave Theo's hands clean. She could buy him some time to find a way out. A path between his oath and his brother.

And with that, Lotte let her knees go slack.

Chapter 27

THEO

otte fell without questioning that he would catch her. And he did, arms going around her, lowering her to the ground. Edmund faltered for just for a second as Theo stopped, his eyes going to Theo, then Hilde, for guidance. But Hilde didn't hesitate.

"Go!" she ordered Edmund, wrenching open the door of the automobile. She was right, there was no time to waste. In a second, Edmund was in the driver's seat, peeling off behind Hilde, leaving Lotte and Theo behind.

Theo felt the war raging in his chest still as Modesty, wearing the ring, vanished out of his reach.

The fox girl called something out, the three Grims taking off behind the automobile, even as her gaze stayed on Theo for a long moment before she turned and followed. They wouldn't catch up. Edmund was a reckless driver at the best of times. Modesty was safe.

Theo turned his attention to Lotte now.

She was limp in his arms, but this close, he could see that she was faking. Her eyelids dashed open quickly.

"They're gone," Theo confirmed, righting Lotte, feeling the warmth of her leave him as he pulled away. He tried to right his mind too.

Just because she didn't have a ring didn't mean she wasn't in danger. He could hear the sounds of the approaching mob. Of windows smashing, raised voices. Some voices carried a chant about abolishing the new curfew. Others were just raised in inarticulate anger.

Lotte had just saved him. It was his turn now.

Theo passed his jacket to Lotte. "Here. Put this on," he said even as he stripped off his doublet, proudly emblazoned with the Holtzfall woodcutter. He draped it over a nearby railing, divesting himself of signs he was sworn to the enemy of the rioters.

Lotte wrapped his jacket around herself, covering the expensive cut and fabric of her half-made dress. "What now?"

"We need to get back to the first circle before anyone realizes who you are. Keep your head low." Theo said, turning the collar of the jacket up, his thumb grazing her face involuntarily. Lotte tucked her hair in the back, though there was almost nothing that could be done to hide the Holtzfall blonde. Together, they moved out from the back alley behind the shop, merging into the protest swarming through the streets. The Old Kingsway was crammed with people. Some held placards, but for others, marching was an excuse to turn to rioting and looting. They passed smashed automobiles. A shop window was shattered, rioters dragging the expensive clothing off the mannequins. The city had descended into chaos while the heiresses had been trying on dresses.

To the north, toward the 1st circle, Theo could already see the flicker of shielding charms going up around homes.

Everything he had ever been taught as a knight was alive in Theo as he moved both of them through the crowd. Every time they were jostled, he crushed the instinct to fight back. They had to go unnoticed in the midst of an ever-growing crowd.

The anger was thick in the air in the low light of the setting sun, threatening to turn more dangerous with every moment they moved toward night. And he was walking through it all with a Holtzfall. It wouldn't matter she'd only been one for a few days; there were those who would gladly rip any one of them limb from limb for having more than they did.

Finally, Theo saw an opening in the crowd. They broke free into a side street, cutting away from the chaos. Breathless, they pressed themselves into the side passage, watching the people stream past.

Theo's oath thrummed as he tried to think of a path to the 1st circle.

Lotte had kept her head low as instructed, but she raised it to him now as she felt his gaze on her. She looked the same as she had when he'd pulled her out of the crowd of photographers that first night. The affectation of blithe innocence was gone. Her eyes were lit with real feeling. Real fear.

"You're a mind reader." If he'd had any doubt before, her expression was enough to confirm it. "That's how you've been playing Modesty's game. That's how you know—" *Know that I'm a traitor.* No. He wasn't, not yet. Thanks to her.

Theo's heartbeat was slowing, and there was some part of him that wanted to reach out for Lotte. To press his fingers into her pulse and see if it skipped with a lie. But she just leaned back against the wall of the alley across from him. "I won't tell anyone your secret if you don't tell anyone mine."

She made it sound like an even deal.

But if her Holtzfall gift were found out, she would become one of the most exceptional Holtzfalls in centuries. Meanwhile, if it was discovered that Theo had even considered breaking his oath, he would be executed.

She didn't seem to realize the power she had over him.

Lotte pulled his jacket close around herself. "What are you going to do?"

Theo glanced out at the crowd. "There's a chance we might be able to break through the riots at—"

"About your brother I mean."

"I don't know." Saying it eased a weight off his chest. He had lain awake nights trying to find a third option. One that meant neither delivering a Holtzfall to the Grims nor turning his back on his brother. Theo had been loyal to the Holtzfalls his whole life. But still he found his gaze straying to the ring on Modesty's hand far too often.

And today, Lotte had saved him from making that choice.

"We're supposed to rescue Holtzfalls," Theo said finally, "not the other way around."

"I owed you one." Lotte rubbed her hand over her face ruefully, as if erasing the last of the liar. "For not telling Modesty that I'm a liar and a fake."

Theo let out a laugh in spite of himself, and a small smile pulled at Lotte's mouth.

That was when the screaming started.

Theo drew up straight, reaching to shield Lotte without thinking as the shouting from the riots was suddenly interspersed with cries of pain and panic.

"That'll be the police cracking down on the rioters," Theo said. "We need to get out of here." Theo reached for Lotte's hand again, but she curled her fingers back. Stopping him from bypassing her hindern. From inadvertently letting her into his mind. He thought of all the other times the hindern barrier must have been broken. The first night in the hallway, the moment he had shielded her from the cameras—he wondered how much she knew of him.

"You already know my worst secret," he said. "I have nothing else to hide."

Lotte's gaze searched him for a long moment, and he found himself wondering what she was thinking. Wishing he could read her mind as easily as she would his.

She took his hand.

They moved together to the other end of the alley, Theo silently focusing on what they needed to do. Hoping that Lotte could draw that from his mind. That she would know that if it came to it she should run and he would fight.

The rioters were more spread out here. Theo and Lotte passed through unnoticed in the eddies of people moving toward the larger swell of the protest.

They stuck to smaller side streets, making their way north. It was painstakingly slow work, and Theo could feel the tension running through him anytime someone came close enough that they might recognize Lotte.

Until they reached the 6th circle, and the side streets disappeared.

Here, in the wealthiest parts of the city, there was nothing but wide tree-lined avenues with nowhere to hide. And here was where the police had run the protestors aground.

A fire was blazing where Muirhaus Department Store stood, smoke billowing through the streets and sparks dancing over the rooftops. No doubt that had drawn the police like a beacon because here they were, locked in a line against the rioters in their wolf masks.

As Theo and Lotte rounded the corner a called-out order came, and the line of police sparked their weapons to life even as they pulled their own masks over their faces. Thick charmed gas masks. In one violent burst fumet charms exploded into streams of smoke that engulfed the protestors. They were LAO inventions meant for this exact purpose, to end revolts before they could start, the inhaled smoke bringing the protestors to their knees in agony.

And it did.

Screams of pain ripped through the crowd, bouncing off the high white marble walls of the expensive town houses even as the police drew immobilidat charms from their belts. He felt Lotte tense next to him, no doubt reading what was next even before the officers began firing into the crowd, striking the writhing figures through the smoke randomly.

With each protestor who was hit by the immobilidat charm, one more scream died away. The charm gripped their muscles, paralyzing them in place, turning them into living statues of agony.

"The smoke, it's coming this way," Lotte said. And she was right—as the gas-mask-wearing officers waded into the subdued protestors, the smoke from the fumet charms was billowing down the street toward Theo and Lotte.

Theo's mind raced. This wasn't an enemy he could throw himself in front of for Lotte. They couldn't outrun this. Fleeing in any direction would only lead them back into the riots.

But there was no other choice.

They both turned, aiming away from the smoke. But before they could even take a step, a sudden burst of air buffeted them back. Theo shielded his face, rooting his feet against the blast automatically even as Lotte staggered. But as he glanced back over his shoulder, he saw the smoke change direction with the sudden gust of wind, moving away from them now, back toward the police.

Another burst of air came, pushing it back farther, and as Theo drew his gaze ahead again, he saw a familiar dark-haired figure moving down the street. Hands raised, twisting a gold bracelet on her wrist, sparking violently with magic.

Nora was wearing what looked like a silk dressing gown.

In the middle of citywide riots.

Of course she was. She strode forward with the confidence of someone who had an army at her back, flashing them a smile as if to say *fancy meeting you here*. Like they'd just run into each other on a casual afternoon stroll.

"I saw a fire," Nora offered as an explanation as she came within earshot.

"And you ran toward it?" Lotte asked.

"I thought it might be a trial." Nora's eyes were drifting past them, to the police in their gas masks, manipulating the frozen figures as if they were dolls, pushing them to the ground. Clearly she still thought it might be a trial. Theo knew Nora well enough that he could tell she was taking in the scene, looking for some way she could prove herself to the Huldrekall. Lotte's gaze followed Nora's, as if drawn in by the same hope, and Theo felt apprehension rising in him.

"It's not a trial," he pressed, his oath thrumming in his blood, urging him to get them both to safety. "It's a riot."

"It could be both." Nora didn't move. The smoke was billowing back toward them again. And Theo was more aware with every passing second that the rioters were closing in. Lotte, he might be able to keep concealed. But Nora . . .

"No." It was Lotte who spoke now. "It can't be a test. They're too—" Her voice caught for a second. "The anger is so real."

"And you know *all* about the Huldrekall and the history of the trials, do you?" Nora raised her eyebrows at Lotte.

"I know enough that I'm not staying here to prove something to no one."

Lotte turned, but Theo drew her back. "We can't double back. They'll come up North Street."

"Or the Kingsway," Nora added, finally unstitching her attention from the chaos, seeming to accept that there was no trial here.

"The first circle will be sealed off by now."

"The factory won't be."

Theo followed Nora's gaze. Over the top of the delicately gilded white mansions around them loomed the four immense brick towers of LAO factories.

"We won't make it three blocks out in the open like this," Theo argued.

"We only need to make it one," Nora said.

Theo had learned it was easier not to question Nora, even when her mind had skipped ahead too swiftly for anyone else to follow it.

They ran then.

All three of them. Running from the encroaching riots. Running from the fumet charms that were bursting all over the city now, filling the streets with cries of pain.

Suddenly Nora took a sharp left, leading them up the steps of a town house.

It was an innocuous-looking façade, identical to the ones on either side. But Theo watched as Nora deftly twisted up the door number, revealing a combination lock hidden below.

She flicked in a quick code: 14-15-18-01. The door came open under her hand, and all three of them pressed inside, slamming the door on the swelling sounds of the approaching riot behind them.

Theo's hand was still wrapped around Lotte's.

Chapter 28

NORA

Honora Holtzfall was born into two inheritances.

On her mother's side, she came from worthy woodcutters with good hearts and virtues stretching back generations. People who had carved this whole city out of the woods, one tree at a time.

On her father's side, she came from royalty and industry.

Mercy Holtzfall owned the city, but her other grandmother, Leyla, powered it.

In the marble entranceway of the house, Nora could feel the hum of magical energy through her slippers. She ran her fingers across the tiles until she found the small concealed handle embedded in the floor. She pried it open, revealing the staircase into the underground passage.

"A ladder wouldn't be simpler?" Theo asked.

"You've known me since I was six. Have you ever seen me *climb*?" It was easy to fall back into bickering like siblings with Theo. And then her eyes dropped to where his hand had been gripping Lotte's a second before.

She reminded herself she couldn't trust anyone's loyalties. "Last person down, close the hatch."

Nora's grandmother, her *other* grandmother, had shown Nora the tunnels as soon as she was old enough to keep a secret. Leyla Al-Oman had been forced to run before. It made her into the sort of woman who always had an escape route. She had built these tunnels in secret while digging to make room for the power lines that fueled the city. Sure enough, the huge silver and bronze coiled wires met them at the bottom. Wires like these stretched all the way from the woods into the enormous magimek generator at the center of the LAO factory, and then back out across Walstad. They hummed with the pure magic that was being drawn out from the woods.

Leyla Al-Oman, the exiled desert princess, had been a fascination when she had first arrived in the city. A young noblewoman fleeing the revolution with a newborn in her arms. Everyone had wanted to hear her stories of princes and djinn in far-off lands. They invited her to salons to tell the sweeping romantic saga of her mother, a Gamanix-born woman, stolen away into the harem of the handsome young sultan, Leyla's father. Seductive stories of her youth in the colorful gardens in the midst of the desert, safe behind walls. And then the tragic tale of how the sultan, her father, had been usurped by a band of rebels led by his own son, a treacherous radical prince.

Leyla had indulged them because it meant gaining their ear. And once she had that, it was easy to turn the conversation to other subjects, like their money. She called it an investment so that she could do what she did best: invent, create, build.

She started with an invention she had brought from the desert. A light that could run without oil or fire—on magic alone. In a matter of months, every wealthy home in the city had magimek glass lights. It had earned her investor, Roland Bittencourt, millions.

And it had got Leyla the attention of Mercy Holtzfall.

Which was what she had been after all along.

They were both young women then. Neither of them had seen thirty yet. But they each had lifetimes behind them already. Mercy had won her trials and stepped in as head of the family when her own father died young. Leyla had been cast out by her country and rebuilt her life in a new one. Nora knew that it was rare for either of her grandmothers to meet an equal. And they had hated each other as much as they needed each other.

The Holtzfalls represented the history of Walstad. But Leyla represented the future. With or without Holtzfall backing, Leyla would soon become one of the most powerful people in the world. Mercy could either become an ally in Leyla's rise—or her rival.

And the Holtzfalls only survived so long as the city needed *them* more than they needed anyone else.

So Mercy Holtzfall came in while Leyla still needed something—a way into the woods. Leyla wanted access to the bottomless well of magic that coursed through that most ancient part of the world. And Mercy Holtzfall, who had a way in thanks to the Huldrekall's original ring, could give her that access.

More than three decades later, both sides of Nora's family were stitched into the fabric of what made Walstad tick.

The tunnel sloped up gently at the end, leading straight into the main industrial floor of LAO Headquarters. In the factory, brick and metal rose three stories high, housing monstrously sized machines. Half-finished automobiles and other magimek creations littered the factory floor.

And, in the midst of it all, there was Leyla Al-Oman. The most brilliant woman in the city, sitting on the floor, machine parts scattered around her, a huge glass magnifying her work. They called her the inventor princess. The silk-stockinged magnate. The blue-blooded industrialist. Nora mostly called her Grandmother.

"You should have a coat on, little princess." Her grandmother spoke in her native Mirajin without looking up. "You will catch sick."

As usual, Leyla's office was kept at a temperature that Nora could only describe as lobster-boilingly hot. The exiled desert princess didn't tolerate the cold well. Finally she looked up, her eyes dashing across the scene in front of her, Nora, in nightwear, trailed by a knight and a rogue cousin. She had likely read about Ottoline in the papers, but Leyla had never been able to tell Nora's blonde cousins apart at the best of times. So Nora was a little surprised when, again, in Mirajin, she nodded at Lotte and asked, "She is the new competition? I could kill her if you want."

"No," Nora answered in Gamanix. She understood her grandmother's native language well enough, but she knew she spoke it like a child learning their letters. "I don't want you to kill anyone."

Leyla Al-Oman made a noise at the back of her throat as she jutted her chin toward a wall strewn with cushions in the corner. A signal to Theo and Ottoline to get out of her way. They took the hint.

"What are you fixing?" Nora asked as her grandmother turned her attention back to her work.

"A problem." Her grandmother gestured angrily with a wrench in the general direction of the front of the building. "Those people with the signs." There was no word in her grandmother's native language for *strike*. "I caught two of them trying to steal from me. Trying to steal plans for the charms in the woods. To sell to my competition, no doubt. So I fired them. And now the ones I didn't fire are angry. And now they have signs. People with signs lead to terrible things, you know. Things like democracies." Nora didn't remind her grandmother that Gamanix was a democracy. Just not a foolish democracy like in Miraji or Ionia, where every person got just one vote. "If they don't want to work, I will replace them. I will make machines that can work for me."

Now that she looked, she could see it. Pieces that might fit together to make a jointed mechanical hand.

Nora's eyes flicked quickly over the design. "You'd have better results if you used a different charm sequence for the thumb than for the four fingers."

Her grandmother paused, her eyes only needing to dance over her work for a moment to see the truth of what Nora was saying. She started to recurve the circuitry on the thumb joint.

"Your mind is wasted on their endless revelries, little princess," her grandmother said in her gravelly accent. "Perhaps it would be better if you lose these foolish trials. You could be here more."

There were few people that Nora would allow to lie to her out of kindness, but her grandmother was one. The truth was, they both knew what happened if Nora lost the heirship for good.

Nora found out about her parents' marriage when she was a child. From Modesty, of course, who had heard it from her mother in a moment of pique and wine.

Thank goodness my mother didn't win her trials. Modesty had stuck her nose up in the air on one of those many occasions where Nora was being given something the rest of them weren't. *Or she would have had to marry your foreign father.*

From there, Nora had learned the truth. Mercy Holtzfall might have given Leyla Al-Oman a way into the woods, but she was not one for sharing power. They had struck a deal the night before Grace and Verity were due to enter the woods for the final trial: Leyla's only son would marry Mercy's Heiress, whichever daughter that might be.

Verity Holtzfall emerged from the woods with the ax. And a year later, Nora's birth was the final seal on the contract between the two women.

Nora watched her parents closely after that. Even as a child, she'd been able to see that they didn't love each other like the people did in the stories and movies. But they were kind to each other, and they laughed together, and until the day her father died, they would sit together every night and talk about what they had done that day. And her father would smile when her mother spoke about hers. They were friends, if nothing else.

And they both loved her.

And when she inherited, she would be the one to bring LAO into the Holtzfall empire.

Or she could also be the reason it all fell apart.

The chaos on the streets of Walstad broke around the factory like an angry sea against an unyielding shore. Lotte could just make out the edges of the shielding charm from the towering window of the factory. Like an invisible wall of magical energy that closed around the building, impossible to pass.

Nora claimed that her grandmother had once shielded a whole city this way.

Although ultimately, it had fallen to rebellion.

She had gotten used to feeling ill at ease since arriving in Walstad. Moving through glittering parties and gleaming shops and conversations she had nothing to say in. But for a moment, fighting through the riots, she had felt like herself again. She knew what it was like to be that angry. She understood the rage pouring through the streets more than she did the vague indifference of the Holtzfalls. She had been angry for so long at being punished for the circumstances of her birth. Being told that she was worth less than the people who had more. Because she was unvirtuous and cursed and they were good.

Leyla Al-Oman kept her office sweltering hot, but Lotte was still wearing Theo's jacket over her dress. She was aware of the collar of his shirt sticking to his skin as he stood next to her, both watching the chaos from the window.

She thought that she might have got used to him by now. But she was still conscious of how stupidly, heroically handsome he looked.

Heroes didn't betray their oaths. But they didn't turn their backs on their brothers either.

That contradiction, that battle raged within him. She could feel it like a thrumming heat every time he closed his hand over hers. She ached to do something. To find the third choice for him, the way out where he betrayed neither her family nor his. But there was nothing. Nothing Lotte could do except keep his secret.

As night fell, the police moved through the streets with militaristic thoroughness, voices blaring through the voxes, ordering the rioters to return to their homes. Deploying more fumet charms. More weapons.

"What are those?" Lotte asked as the police rolled small metallic charms through the streets. She had her answer as rioters' legs gave out below them.

"Stoffel charms," Nora said from where she was working with her grandmother, her silk bathrobe over pajamas pooled out around her elegantly amidst the tools and metallic parts. "Produced here at LAO. Standard police solution."

"Another solution would be lifting the curfew." She didn't even bother trying the silly innocent act with Nora; she'd seen through her already.

"She speaks her real mind for once!" Nora feigned shock. "And stone-cold sober this time." She passed the small screwdriver she had been using to her grandmother. "I like you better like this. You're the descendant of a woodcutter, not a fawn."

Lotte liked herself better too, but she wasn't going to admit that to Nora. "I have no idea who I'm the descendant of." The words slipped out. Nora paused, halfway through engraving a charm on a piece of metal.

"Your father." Nora didn't raise her eyes, but there was an unusual interest in her voice. "Aunt Grace hasn't told you who he is?"

"Your guess is as good as mine. Probably better, even." Nora had been a Holtzfall all her life. If there had been a man coming and going in her mother's life, maybe she would know.

Or she might know where Benedict's memories were kept.

Nora seemed to consider Lotte for a long, silent moment, but when she spoke again, it was to her grandmother in a foreign language. And the moment between them was gone.

They didn't say another word until Nora abruptly set down the charm she was building and declared, "Well, we can't possibly stay here tonight, sleeping on anything other than a silk pillowcase will cause mayhem to my hair."

For a second, Lotte thought Nora was crazy enough to believe she was just immune to the fray outside. The police were dispersing it, but still—

And then she clicked her fingers, and from the corner, a metallic dog rose to its mechanical haunches. It looked eerily like the wolves Lotte had seen on the road. Lotte's eyes drifted to Leyla Al-Oman, who was intently looking at her work.

Nora's earlier words danced through her mind. *I don't want you to kill anyone.*

And for the first time Lotte wondered if Mercy Holtzfall hadn't been lying to her that first night when she said she'd never kill one of her own family. Lotte wasn't Leyla Al-Oman's family. But Nora was. And she was Nora's competition.

Nora clicked again, and another dog came alive, then another and another.

Until there was a pack.

MODESTY WAS THE FIRST TO SPOT THEM WHEN THEY EN-
tered the mansion, her eyes darting up, the words on her lips dying

as she saw them. Two Holtzfalls and a knight, surrounded by a pack of metal dogs. They had marched them through the streets like a magimek honor guard, through the dying fray of the riots, all the way to the mansion unscathed.

The look on Modesty's face was something even Holtzfall wealth couldn't buy as, next to Lotte, Nora scratched one of the metallic dog's ears. "Sorry we're a little late."

Mercy Holtzfall, as usual, was unreadable as she surveyed them.

"Knights and dogs to the barracks" was all she said finally. "We were about to sit down for dinner."

They were to sleep at the safety of the mansion too. Mercy Holtzfall's orders. After a painfully awkward family dinner, a servant walked Lotte to a room with eggshell-blue wallpaper and a view of the woods. But she had barely closed the door when there came a knock.

Nora stood there, somehow wearing a change of clothes that fit her perfectly while Lotte was still wearing Theo's jacket. There was something unreadable on her face in the dark of the hallway as she leaned in Lotte's doorframe.

"I don't know who your father is." She picked up the conversation from hours ago as if there'd only been a small lull. "But I do know how we might be able to find out."

The windows of Johannes & Grete stared knowingly down at Nora as they approached through empty streets littered with debris from the riots. *Knowing* she wasn't here with good intentions.

Most candidates were on their most virtuous behavior during the trials. But breaking and entering to steal birth records wasn't an ideal demonstration of virtue. And then there was the whole manipulating and lying to her cousin part.

That wasn't ideal either.

It was closer to dawn than dusk now. The jail cells would be heaving, but the streets were silent. Over the vox, a citywide lockdown had been announced. Anyone seen on the streets before dawn would be summarily arrested.

Obviously, that didn't apply to Nora and Lotte.

They were challenged once, by two officers marching down the street.

"Stay where you are!" one of the men bellowed as he caught sight of them, raising a charmed weapon. Lotte stopped instantly, but Nora didn't even break her stride.

"No." Someone was going to have to show her new cousin what it meant to be a Holtzfall. "Shan't. We have places to be."

"Miss Holtzfall." One of the officers recognized her, his hand going to his companion's weapon, forcing it down. "You shouldn't be out. The city is in lockdown."

"We're well aware." Nora didn't stop walking, leaving the officers no choice but to part for her. "That's why we're trying to make our way home, if that's all right with you."

"Allow us to accompany you—"

"And take you away from your duty?" Nora said, brushing by the officers. "What would my grandmother make of *that*?" They had no choice except to let them pass.

When they were out of earshot, finally she felt Lotte's shoulders ease. "What if he hadn't recognized you?"

"Everyone recognizes me," Nora replied absently. Her gaze flicked back to the officers. She wondered if she would know the cop from the photograph if she saw him. The one who'd stolen her mother's jewelry. But all of them looked the same to her now, in their gray uniforms.

She would never identify the man who'd taken her mother's jewelry without Oskar Wallen. She had known that the day he had made her the offer. Ottoline's father's name in exchange for the man who had set up Lukas Schuld. She'd just been too stubborn to admit it then.

She had manipulated Modesty into pushing the desire to find her father into Lotte's head in a low moment. But the ripple of hope that flickered painfully across Lotte's face when she asked about her father was enough to make Nora feel small.

She told herself it didn't matter. Lotte wanted to know, so she was helping her. Whatever happened to that information after . . . But the truth was that if someone offered Nora either of her parents back and it was a manipulation—she would burn that person's whole life to the ground.

The only small comfort against the guilt slowly climbing through her chest was that she was almost sure this wasn't a trial in disguise.

Which meant she was just being a bad person on her own time.

The large white office building up ahead was dark. And so were the rest of the windows on the street, as well as the streetlights. The power was out for three blocks.

Several blocks of the city *had* lost power in the riots, but mostly in lower circles. This one . . . Nora had asked Leyla to cut all magic to this block. It would be blamed on the protests damaging the power lines. It was actually one of the perks of being the granddaughter of the two most powerful women in the city.

"Johannes & Grete is where every piece of legal information that has ever existed about this family resides," Nora began telling Lotte as they approached the immense office. "They're—"

"*Family lawyers operating at the highest level of confidentiality.* I know." Lotte's arms were wrapped around her elbows uneasily. "My mother sent one of them to get me from the convent."

Nora scoffed. "Has our grandmother had him fired yet?"

"No," Lotte said. "She had him ripped limb from limb instead."

Nora didn't have time to unpack whether her cousin was joking. They had reached the front door. "Well, we're not going to get an invitation." Nora pressed her hand to the door, feeding a small snick of magic to the lasa charm she wore on her hand. The door swung open.

"Don't worry," Nora said as she strode inside. "Unless they were smart enough to feed their security charms off a separate power grid, all of their alarms are deactivated."

"Yes." Lotte's voice was dry, but she followed Nora nonetheless. "That was my exact concern. You read my mind."

Nora scoffed. "Believe me, if I had a gift like mind reading, we wouldn't be doing *this*." If she had a gift like mind reading, she could simply *know* the secrets Oskar Wallen was keeping from her. *Know* why Lukas Schuld was lying. But Justice Holtzfall had been the last mind reader in the family, and that was over a hundred years ago.

Nora had been to Johannes & Grete before, for an introduction as the next Heiress. She had walked down this same long marble hallway, listening to Mr. Grete talk about how his firm had served the Holtzfalls exclusively since the days of Ernest Holtzfall.

Nora realized that Lotte wasn't following her anymore. She had paused in front of one of the offices. There were three names on the door. Lotte pressed her finger against one. *Clarence Brahm.* "He's the man who came to get me," Lotte said. "He was killed by mechanical wolves on the road."

"So you *weren't* joking." Nora's voice carried through the empty building.

"Why would I joke about that?"

"I don't know you very well. It's possible you have a dark sense of humor." But Nora's gaze was on the name on the door. She had been angry that their grandmother hadn't told her about Lotte. She'd thought Mercy had done nothing to protect her from this threat to the heirship. But maybe she had tried.

"Our grandmother wouldn't hurt you, you're a Holtzfall." Nora believed that. She wasn't so sure about her other grandmother though. Leyla Al-Oman had done many things to survive in her time.

"That's what she said too." Lotte sounded skeptical. "Whether or not she meant to kill me, she *did* kill him. He had a wife."

Nora wondered whether he had children. Instead she said, "And what *we* have is three hours until the sun rises. Do you want to spend them worrying about a dead man's wife, or do you want to find your father?"

Nora knew it was contempt for her callousness that she saw in Lotte's gaze. Good. She didn't want her cousin to think this charitable act was going to become a habit.

"The records room is at the end of this hallway." Nora turned away.

The door opened as easily as the first one. For a moment, all they could see was pitch blackness.

Nora flicked her hand, activating the lumen charm she wore as a ring, casting a pool of light. She had thought maybe she only remembered this room as cavernous because she had been smaller last time she was here. She was wrong. It must've made up more than half the building, ringed on all sides by cramped and triple-occupied offices. People packed in so there was space for the Holtzfalls' records.

The marble checkerboard floor made the enormity of the place look like an optical illusion from a magazine. And filling the whole room, row after row of filing cabinets, stretching back before vanishing into the darkness far beyond the small circle of light on Nora's hand.

"This," Nora said, her voice seeming to echo around the labyrinth of cabinets, "is every single piece of paperwork ever belonging to our family. Every contract, every deed to every piece of land in Walstad, every debt owed to us. And every record of a Holtzfall birth, marriage, or death."

"And you think that includes mine?"

"You're a Holtzfall, aren't you?"

"Even if my birth record is here," Lotte said, scanning the room, "there's no guarantee that it lists my father's name."

"There isn't," Nora admitted. "But our grandmother tends to be thorough. Here." Nora extended a lumen charm in the form of a small gold band to Lotte. "This aisle covers the time since our grandmother took power. You take the north end, I'll take the south, and we'll work toward the middle."

Lotte looked at the ring blankly. "Are you bribing me to take the farther end?"

A smart retort was on Nora's lips, and then she realized Lotte once again wasn't joking. "Do you not know how to use charms?"

"Why would I know how to use charms?"

"I don't know." This, she hadn't anticipated. "Who doesn't know how to use *charms*?"

Lotte pushed up her sleeve. In the glow of the lumen was a faded scar. "Once, a traveling circus came to town. My friend and I tried to imitate the magician's card tricks after they left. The Sisters gave me a lash for every card in the deck in punishment. And that was *pretend* magic."

Nora's eyes flicked from the scar up to Lotte's face. There had been opportunists around the Holtzfall family over the years. Disgruntled siblings of the heir apparent, greedy distant relatives who brought shame to the Holtzfall name. Lotte was far from the first pretender to the heirship to appear over the generations. But for the first time, Nora found herself wondering if Lotte wasn't trying to take something from them, but get away from something.

With a dramatic sigh, Nora sparked the ring in her hand with magic. "There." She dropped it into Lotte's palm. "That should last a few hours at least." And then she added, "You can get rid of that scar with a charm too, by the way."

Nora started with the cabinet closest to her. She worked her way through methodically. One after the other. Her mother's birth records flashed under her hands as she searched. Then Aunt Grace's.

Valor Holtzfall's birth and death records.

Holtzfall after Holtzfall. But there was no sign of Ottoline.

Until suddenly, Nora became aware that she wasn't reading by the light of the ring anymore. Sunlight was filtering through the skylight above. It was dawn, which meant the lockdown would be lifted soon.

"We need to go," Nora said, moving toward Lotte. "Even I can't pass *this* off as an innocent nighttime excursion."

"We haven't found anything," Lotte said, rubbing the heels of her palms tiredly across her eyes.

"We'll find it tomorrow night." Nora waved a hand dismissively.

She was half disappointed, half relieved. The further she got down this path, the more the idea of selling Lotte's father's name to Oskar twisted her stomach. Her mind was tumbling over itself, trying to find another way. Another path to the answer she craved about her mother. "Now, where shall we get breakfast?"

Chapter 31

LOTTE

A jet of flame erupted from the small pin in Lotte's hand, blasting up from the balcony, well above the roof of the Paragon Hotel, nearly taking Lotte's eyebrows with it.

If anyone were watching from the street, they might think that the Holtzfalls had somehow acquired a defiant infant dragon. But no, just Lotte.

"Better," Nora commented from inside Lotte's room, where she was going through the closet and pulling out clothing at an impossible rate. "By which I mean: better than when you were accomplishing nothing. But that charm exists to light candles, and I think you not only reduced the hypothetical candle to a pile of wax there, but also incinerated the dining table."

"I don't need magic to light a candle." Lotte came in from the balcony, poking the small diamond-headed pin through the lapel of Theo's jacket, frustrated. The tips of her fingers were turning red where she had been holding it, and she could feel her skin was close to blistering. She wasn't sure if it was from the excess of magic or the fire. The idea of having magic at all was sitting on Lotte like an ill-fitting coat. After years of the Sisters preaching against it, shaking the discomfort was hard. She could almost feel Sister Brigitta at her back waiting with a rod. "I could just use matches."

"You could." Nora pulled a face at a dress she'd just extracted from the closet, a lacy thing that Modesty had insisted looked perfect on Lotte, before tossing it on the growing heap on the floor. "You could also strike flint and steel. Or maybe hit two rocks together until they spark. Or just wait for a lightning strike and—"

"I get it," Lotte interrupted. She dropped into a chair, surveying the array of charms Nora had produced from . . . somewhere. Charms to disguise her appearance, charms to unlock doors, charms to shield herself in case a Grim should throw wine at her. Or something more lethal. Nora's words.

Nora had tried to talk Lotte through how to use the charms, several times, with the impatience of someone for whom it came far too naturally to be able to effectively explain it.

"Magic is energy." Nora had a tendency to press two fingers to the spot between her eyebrows when she got frustrated that someone wasn't as quick as her. It was amazing there wasn't a permanent dent in her forehead. "Everyone," Nora went on as patiently as she could, "is born with varying amounts. Those in the first circle, closer to the woods, tend to be born with more. Those in the lower circles—well, it is part of the reason they are poor. But magic is formless, shapeless energy. Until it receives a conduit. A charm. The patterns on charms are all designed to shape a thread of magic to a certain purpose. Like a loom."

"I don't think that's how looms work," Lotte said.

"Oh, I forgot"—Nora rolled her eyes—"because growing up in the countryside makes you an expert in all bucolic crafts?"

"Looms aren't a *craft*," Lotte said, "they're a tool to make clothing. How do you *think* clothing is made? Do you think dresses are made by magic?"

"They are in the city. I think we're getting off track."

So far, the only way Lotte had been able to activate the charms was through her blood. Blood, life force, and magic were all tied together. Nora's fingers pressed deeper into her forehead. Smearing blood across a charm was a crude, if effective way to power one, according to Nora. It was Lotte's blood that had ignited the luster in the woods that had stopped the wolves. And yet still she felt unsettled at the idea of this intangible power laced through her veins.

Lotte wrapped her finger in a cloth napkin that had come with their breakfast, the pinprick on her index finger blooming bright across the white fabric. Just blood. If she really had so much power, shouldn't she be able to see it?

Walstad hadn't just . . . bounced back from a full-blown riot by dawn, seemingly much to Nora's surprise. When she reluctantly accepted that nowhere would be open for breakfast, they had wound up back at the Paragon, ordering room service.

Room service was news to Lotte.

Up to now, she'd just *waited*. Hoping the maids might turn up with food. Nora didn't seem like the waiting kind.

Nora tossed another dress aside. This one landed on the coffee table, knocking a newspaper off it to the ground.

Lukas Schuld to Be Executed Without Trial for Murder of Verity Holtzfall

The headline was from the *Bullhorn*. Underneath it was a letter marked: *Isengrim's Fourth Letter to the People of Walstad*.

It was easy to forget that Nora was grieving. That she had lost her mother less than a fortnight ago. Lotte wasn't sure of the right thing to say. But her cousin swiftly turned her attention to the mountain of clothing she had made. "I really did think Modesty had better dress sense than this." She was gesturing at the pile of clothing. "I mean, if I'm being honest, she probably does, and she was making sure you wouldn't outshine her in all those photographs she's been using you for." Nora's gaze was sharp. "But of course, you knew that."

Lotte held Nora's gaze. There was no accusation in her cousin's eyes, but Lotte still felt the need to defend herself. "I have to play a different game to fit here than you do."

"No," Nora said, "we're playing the same game. I just started with a lot more pieces on the board." It suddenly occurred to Lotte that somehow Nora understood her. More than Estelle ever had in a decade. And then Nora stood abruptly. "We should get moving. It's nearly noon. Surely the department stores have recovered from bricks through windows by now."

GOING THROUGH THE WORLD WITH NORA WAS DIFFERENT than with Modesty.

Modesty had seemed to move through the world with a constant sense of need. Need for photographers. For attention. For clothes.

Nora had never needed for anything.

The dresses Modesty had picked were safe, they were unassuming. As they walked through a department store, stepping over the glass from a shattered window, Nora pulled out dresses made of cascades of silk and tulle, pearls and sequins that Lotte couldn't help but run her hands over.

Lotte had pretended for years to fawn over the flashy clothing and jewels in the magazines with Estelle. But maybe she'd never cared because she just thought she'd never have them.

It was amazing what *having* brought out in the wanting.

And Lotte found that she wanted to be part of this world the same way that Nora was, on her own terms. Not pretending to be the little overwhelmed country bumpkin they expected her to be. But the only way to do that would be to win the trials. To prove she was as good as them. Better even.

When they finally left the department store, the newspaper kiosk on the corner was changing over the papers. The front page of every single one was dominated by the riots.

Each under wildly different headlines.

City Revolts Against Curfew!

Stricter Measures Needed as Lower Circles Push Back Against Safety Precautions

Trade Cut Short Due to Inconvenience on the Streets

"Well, it looks like you were right." Nora picked a copy of the *Bullhorn* from the stand. "It wasn't a trial after all. Or if it was, none of us came out of it with a ring."

Whatever warmth she was feeling toward Nora cooled at the mention of the trials. They were competitors, she reminded herself. And there would be another trial soon.

"You really thought the Huldrekall would stage a trial that wrecked the whole city?" Lotte asked. The front page of the *Herald* showed wreckage. "People died."

"People die in trials, it—" But whatever Nora was going to say cut off. Something flashed over Nora's face as her eyes suddenly darted across the edition of the *Bullhorn* in her hand.

"What?" Lotte's heart jumped as she craned over Nora's shoulder, trying to see what her cousin had seen. Some sign that they had both been wrong. That this had been a trial. One they had failed.

But Nora folded the paper up quickly. "I need to go. I just figured out why there are so many spelling mistakes in Isengrim's letters."

Chapter 32

AUGUST

The first thing August noticed was that his desk was occupied by a pair of expensive shoes, crossed one over the other at the ankle. As he got closer, he could see those shoes were attached to legs, and those legs were attached to—

"What time do you call this?" She looked at him over the top of the newspaper. Her real face was on the front page. Nora was wearing glamour, of course, but there was still something unmistakably Nora-ish about her.

"Well, I'd call it lunchtime. Why? What do *you* call it? The banqueting hour? Feast o'clock?"

"No one respectable holds a banquet before sunset." She folded the paper over, smoothing the edges. Her fingers were stained with newsprint. "Doesn't work start at nine a.m.?"

August had made it back to the *Bullhorn* by the skin of his teeth after covering the riots yesterday. Just before the police started using force and charms. Half the *Bullhorn* had been locked down in the building overnight. Some of them worked, some of them tossed balled-up paper wads into baskets, some dozed at their desks. Until finally dawn came, and journalists could venture home without risking their skulls being cracked open. August had headed home to let his mother know he was alive. And take a shower and a nap.

But he didn't tell Nora that.

"What would you know about work?" He sat on the edge of his desk, swatting her feet out of the way.

"I know what time the people who work *for* us are supposed to start." Out of anyone else's mouth, it would have been the sort of comment that deserved nothing but his disdain. From Nora somehow it was funny. Foolishly, August found himself wishing he could see her real face instead of her glamour.

"I don't have any more leads." August rubbed his hand tiredly over his face, craving a coffee. Last time he'd seen Nora, she'd walked out in a snit. "If that's why you're here."

"Well, then lucky for me, I cracked your newspaper's stupid little code." She slapped the paper down, slightly harder than was necessary.

Code? That woke August up. "What code?"

"Oh, come on." Nora tossed the newspaper down on the desk. It was dated two days ago. The front cover was emblazoned with *Isengrim's Fourth Letter to the People of Walstad*.

Nora looked at August expectantly. August looked blankly back at her.

"Yes, it's an old newspaper," he said finally, in the same slow patient voice that one might use with a child holding up a rock they thought was interesting.

"Where do you get these letters from?"

August shrugged. "I told you, it's not my department." The letters from Isengrim moved a lot of papers, but the journalists weren't all that fond of them. Half the time it meant someone was getting bumped off the front page.

"But if you had to guess," Nora pressed.

"Mr. Vargene," August acknowledged. "He's our editor in chief. He's the only one I've ever seen with the originals. So I guess Isengrim addresses the letters to him, and he puts them in the layout."

Nora tapped her foot against the desk in a quick, almost nervous rhythm. "These letters are riddled with mistakes." She tapped a place where there were two *g*'s crowded tightly together at the front of *aggain*.

August shrugged. "Typesetting error. It happens when we're in a rush to put something out."

"That's a lot of typesetting errors," Nora said. She was watching him intently. There was something about Nora that made August want to be able to rise to answer her. But he really had no idea what she was looking for here.

Nora sighed and started reading aloud from the page. "*Meannwhile*, spelled with two *n*'s, *amidst the Holtzfalls' games our city suffers! The peoople of this city have oonce again*"—she tapped both double *o*'s, an easy mistake on a trigger-happy typewriter—"*beenn distracted from the true issues of this city's working class by the antics of its most privilegged few.*" She tapped the double letters and spelling errors as she went. "*While yoou slept, preparing for another backbreaking day of wvork to pay for their lifestyle.*"—the *v* almost blended into the *w* next to it, but it was there—"*they gather to decide which ammong them is the lesser evil. The one who will govern over you until your graandchildren are the onnes doing the backbreaking work in their namess.* With two *s*'s in *namess.* But then the mistakes stop. Everything after that is spelled exactly right. But if you put all the mistakes together . . ."

All at once, August saw it. "Noon," he read out. "Gov Mans." It was the paper from the day before the protests. With instructions of where they were to gather to scream their rage against the wealthy.

"Yes." She sounded exasperated. Clearly she'd been waiting for him to catch up. "You really didn't know about this?" And he realized suddenly what she must've been thinking: That he'd been leading her on some wild goose chase all around Walstad in hunt of answers, when all this time the way to the Grims was hidden right in his newspaper. That he'd been lying to her. But his look of confusion seemed to convince her. And finally, the carefully controlled tension she had been wearing since she arrived melted off her.

He'd never bothered to look all that closely at the Isengrim letters. They were just inflammatory hyperbole. Not exactly journalism.

How many of the other journalists knew? Was he not in the loop on this since he'd failed to scream his political allegiance to Isengrim from the rooftops?

"And then there's today's." Nora tossed down this morning's edition, *Isengrim's Sixth Letter to the People of Walstad*. She'd already circled the letters. They spelled out a time only:

Eight tonight

So. That's how the Grims were arranging meetings that the police couldn't bust up.

Back before Isengrim, the Egalitarian People's Party would boldly flyer the whole city, letting them know where their rallies would be held. It might as well have been an invitation to come bust the place up. But the cops couldn't bust up a rally they couldn't find . . .

"So eight o'clock, where?" August asked.

"Here I'd been hoping you might know that," Nora said, leaning back in the chair. "And you have the gall to write about me being brainless."

"I mean, if you really think it's a good idea for *you* to go to a Grim rally, then I might stand by that." Nora had never wavered, not since the night of the Veritaz, in her belief that the Grims were behind her mother's death. That whatever the police officer in the photos had done had been on the orders of Isengrim. That Lukas Schuld had confessed to protect Isengrim. That finding answers would lead her to the man who most wanted to bring her family to their knees.

And now she'd found a way to get to him directly.

"Well, you know, I've been hoping to speak with the famous Isengrim. Discuss the weather, the rising price of wheat, which wealthy people he might have killed lately . . ."

August understood Nora well enough now to know that trying to dissuade her when she had an idea set in her mind was impossible. But he also had to try to be the voice of reason.

"You know who you are, don't you?"

"The entire city knows who I am."

"Exactly. And you want to go into the wolf's den."

"Only if I can find it. Whatever the code for the location is, it's better hidden than the time."

Nora's eyes locked with his, and August felt the thrill of danger go through him. But also the thrill of getting a step closer to answers. To the story he needed. The lure of the con, his father would call it.

"Do you really expect me to believe you're not smart enough to figure this out before tonight?"

Nora had five different copies of the newspaper spread out in front of her, highlighted and scribbled all over and cut out. So far she had managed to anagram *Isengrim Followers* into *Remising Wolf Loser*, but that didn't seem to help much.

"Find anything?" August asked, setting down a paper cup carefully next to her increasingly insane decoupage project. She had dropped the glamour now they were safely locked in August's darkroom, all lit up on this occasion for Nora to work. No one would disturb them here.

"Nothing yet." She took a sip of the coffee and pulled a face. "This is terrible."

"You're welcome," August said.

"Thank you for the terrible coffee," Nora amended.

"It's from the terrible machine out in the hallway. You owe me two zaub."

"Add it to my tab. I promise I'm good for it." Nora pressed her fingers between her eyebrows. "This cannot be that complicated if it is meant for hundreds of people to understand. And hundreds of people are *not* smarter than I am. They must have a cipher key or something that we don't."

She was getting irritated. August had never seen Nora irritated. Honora Holtzfall glided through life without a single trouble. He had to admit he was enjoying watching her get frustrated, energy sparking off her wildly—it made her fascinating to watch. This maddeningly entitled, fascinatingly frustrating heiress.

"This isn't even true, you know." She rapped her knuckles against the subtitle of the letter: *Holtzfall Factory Wage Cut 12% as Heiress Steps Out in Diamonds*.

"They're sapphires?" August asked.

"Rubies. And my grandmother raised wages just last month. Isn't there some sort of rule against printing lies?"

August shrugged, sipping on his coffee. "It's a letter from Isengrim, it's meant to be inflammatory, not accurate. I mean, look at this." He leaned over, tapping the note next to it. "*Isengrim's Sixth Letter to the People of Walstad*. I know education in the countryside isn't what it is in the city, but I swear we've had at least two letters a month for the past year."

In an instant, Nora went still, her eyes darting over the headline. "I need a pen," she said urgently.

"What did you do with the last pen I gave you?"

"Pen," she repeated, not looking up, as though if she dared take her eyes off the paper, the letters might escape her.

"I'm not made of pens, you know." August pulled out the pencil that was behind his ear, intrigued as her mind raced ahead of his, and Nora snatched it from his hand. She leaned over and started scrawling under the libelous headline.

Holtzfall Factory Wage Cut 12%

"Bifntzuff," August read aloud the jumble of letters she'd written under *Holtzfall*. "Brilliant, you've cracked it."

She ignored him and kept writing, scrawling more unintelligible letters under *Factory* and then moving on to *Wage*. August opened his mouth to say something, but before he could, he realized that this word wasn't gibberish. Underneath *Wage* she'd written the word *quay*.

"Nora . . ."

"Sixth letter," she said out loud, barely concealed excitement in her voice. "*Isengrim's Sixth Letter to the People of Walstad*. Count six letters back from *w*, it makes a *q*; six from *a* makes a *u*; *g* becomes *a* and *e* becomes *y*. And *quay* looks an awful lot like a place to me."

August felt his own heartbeat rise, matching Nora's voice in excitement as he watched her continue. As another word appeared below her pen.

"Won," he read as she wrote the three-letter word below *Cut*. "Who won what?"

"Obviously it's not *won*. Or it is, but it's not the verb."

"One," August translated, suddenly realizing. "Quay 1 12."

He felt it again, that sudden charge of energy flaring in the air that separated him from Nora as the realization of what this meant sparked in both of them.

They had a chance at getting close to Isengrim.

"What do you say, Miss Holtzfall." August glanced up, a grin on his face, a smile slowly creeping onto hers. "Fancy an evening walk down by the water?"

PART III
PRUDENCE

Chapter 34

LOTTE

The wealthy of Walstad handled a blackout like they did just about everything else.

With a party.

Leyla Al-Oman, Nora's *other* grandmother, had cut the power to about three blocks last night in order for them to break into Johannes & Grete. Just one block would seem suspicious, according to Nora. The Bamberg mansion was within the radius of the blackout. And Angelika Bamberg was taking this opportunity to throw a blackout party.

There were no official invitations on such short notice, but Lotte had begun to understand that, as big as Walstad was, the upper circles didn't work so differently from a small town. Somehow, when something was happening, everyone just *knew*.

Guests were to bring a candle for the price of admission.

Lotte took a long taper from the dining room of the Paragon Hotel. It would burn down quickly, but that didn't matter. Lotte wasn't planning on staying long. She and Nora had made a plan to find each other at Angelika's, and then they would slip out for the short walk to Johannes & Grete to make another attempt at finding information about Lotte's father.

When Angelika opened the door to the mansion, she was holding a thick pillar candle, like the ones the Sisters had used in the convent.

"You'll need a light." Angelika beamed, holding out the candle. Lotte thought of the small charmed pin she was wearing and the cascade of fire this morning.

She tipped her candle forward to catch the flame.

It seemed to Lotte like every mirror in Walstad had been moved to the Bamberg mansion. They were set up in such a way as to catch the light from the candles in people's hands and those scattered around the room.

Lotte suddenly understood the dress that Nora had insisted she wear tonight.

It looked like old-fashioned chainmail, gathered tightly at her waist and loose around her shoulders so that it draped around her collarbone, before collapsing into a skirt of chain links so tiny that they looked like cloth. The silver chain links had been polished until they shone, and every step Lotte took, the light of the candles seemed to find her. And so did the gazes of the partygoers.

"Ottoline." Modesty beelined toward her as she entered, her smile tightening. "I don't remember that dress!"

"Oh, you don't?" Lotte dropped into her act, although it felt more jarring this time. "It was just in my closet."

Lotte's eyes skated briefly past Modesty, looking for Theo before she was aware of what she was doing. He was stationed by the door, along with other knights. She could feel their shared secrets stretching out between them like an invisible thread. His eyes pulled toward her before she could look away.

Lotte quickly returned her gaze to Modesty even as her smile tightened further. "It's a little flashy, don't you think?"

If Lotte had any doubt that the dress was impressive, Modesty's attempt to make her feel ashamed of it would have been all the confirmation she needed.

And then the party swept her away from Modesty.

Lotte drifted, keeping one eye on the door for Nora as she felt the wax of her candle growing warm under her fingers. She half listened to conversations she couldn't take part in. The upper circles talked about the riots, by way of talking about restaurants they liked that had been looted for food. They talked about maids who hadn't turned up to work this morning because they were locked up. Some for disrupting the peace. Some for breaking the lockdown and venturing out before dawn, trying to make it to work on time.

They talked about how terribly inconvenient it all was.

Minutes turned into an hour, and there was still no sign of Nora. Lotte felt the restless nervousness rising by the second. Nora seemed to keep to her own schedule at the best of times. But tonight wasn't exactly the best of times. Lotte's candle was beginning to burn close to her fingers, wax dripping on the marble floor of the ballroom.

Leyla Al-Oman could keep the power cut for another night, *maybe*. Tomorrow, people would start complaining if their power wasn't back. If Lotte was going to find out who her father was, tonight was her last chance.

Her fingers danced nervously across the charms Nora had given her. She had spent hours this afternoon trying to spark them smoothly, like Nora did. But then there hadn't been a good reason she needed to learn to use them.

Now there was.

Lotte couldn't wait for Nora anymore. She made the decision abruptly, moving through the ballroom in a ripple of chainmail.

She headed straight for Theo.

His hand twitched toward her for just a second, and then he seemed to remember that he was Modesty's guard tonight, not hers. Lotte had been brought here by Edmund Rydder, who was watching her now. He might not be the knight Theo was, but she had a feeling he would still notice if she tried to just walk out into the street on her own.

"I need you to pretend to drive me home." Lotte kept her voice low, aware that Hildegarde Rydder wasn't far out of earshot, though her attention was trained on her charges, Constance and Clemency.

Theo's eyes traveled carefully over her, taking her in.

He knew she wasn't just trying to escape another never-ending party. He knew she was up to something. But he just inclined his head ever so slightly.

"Then we should go quickly, before you have to faint again."

SHE CAUGHT HIM UP ON THE BRIEF WALK TO THE OFFICES OF Johannes & Grete. The light from the last of her candle illuminated the space between them on the dark street as she told him about wanting to find her father.

The building loomed large without Nora striding confidently next to her. But Nora's grandmother was true to her word—it was still dark and seemingly empty, just like yesterday. Lotte fumbled a little with the charms she was wearing, conscious of Theo watching her, before finding the one Nora had said was made to open locks. She pressed her hand to the door with the ring on it, but no matter what instructions Nora had given, she couldn't seem to feed magic into it gently.

The lock shattered.

Theo moved, instantly reacting to the explosion, pressing her back into one of the columns on the portico of the building. She felt that surge of protectiveness again as his body pressed against hers. She wasn't sure whether she could feel his heart hammering through his mind or his chest pressed against her.

"It's fine, sorry, it's fine," Lotte said hurriedly, feeling her face flush, although she wasn't sure if it was with embarrassment or his sudden closeness. "That was my fault."

Lotte pretended to focus all her attention on the lumen charm on her hand as he pulled away, keeping her eyes on it as she moved toward the doorway. But she had a feeling she might blind them if she tried another charm at this rate. So instead she held the still-burning candle ahead of her as they moved through the same hallway she and Nora had gone down last night.

Heading toward the Holtzfall vault.

In the cavernous marble-tiled records room, it took Lotte a second to orient herself. To find where they had left off this morning when sunrise had halted their progress. She pulled open a drawer, carefully keeping the flickering candle away from the sheets of paper.

She had seen the records for her cousins yesterday. Thick cream certificates of birth with proud official stamps and signatures. Declaring both parents' names on them.

Patience Holtzfall and Georg Otto.

Prosper Holtzfall and Beate Brecht.

Verity Holtzfall and Zaid Al-Oman

She tried to summon it in her mind's eye. A name printed in black and white next to *Grace Holtzfall*. The answers that she could feel her heart stretching toward even now as she flicked through the papers.

A movement caught the corner of Lotte's eye. She whipped around, heart in her throat, a lie stumbling its way to her tongue as she expected to find a guard there. But there was no one.

"What is it?" Theo's hand was already on his sword.

"I thought—" Lotte scanned the records room, hunting for the movement she'd seen.

There. Something in the shadows was shifting, barely visible in the moonlight streaming through the glass dome above. Lotte hesitated, her breath coming sharp and shallow. This time Theo saw it too. He drew his sword warily, moving in front of Lotte.

The movement rippled out toward them.

It was the floor. The floor was moving.

The white-and-black marble was cracking, crooked, bent shapes rising from the once mirror-smooth surface. Like a figure was trying to pull itself free from the glossy stone.

A hundred childhood stories told by Mrs. Hehn rose to Lotte's mind. About the sorts of creatures that lived in the ancient woods, the Huldrekall that were born from trees, the Backahasten from water, or Mossmen from soft earth. And the ones that tore themselves brutally out of boulders and cliffs and craggy stone faces. And came to eat disobedient children when they refused to go to bed.

Lotte knew it with ancient certainty as it tore itself out of the marble flooring, a hulking thing born of glossy black-and-white checkerboard.

It was a troll.

Chapter 35

NORA

"You still look rich."

"I've had a lot of practice."

Nora and August were making their way toward the docks through the early evening crowd. The curfew was firmly in place across the whole city, and all around them, gaits seemed hurried as people rushed to get home before nightfall. Every few blocks, they passed a small scattering of police officers keeping their eyes on the crowd and their hands on their weapons. Nora was wearing her glamour, but there was nothing she could do about her clothes. She hadn't had time to go home and change.

"Here." August shucked off his heavy brown coat and handed it to her.

The coat was too large, but it was pleasantly warm from August's body. It smelled of shaving cream and what she had started to recognize as newspaper ink.

Without the coat, he stood out starkly against the water and warehouses that surrounded them in his white shirt, suspenders carving dark lines across his tall narrow body. Nora stuck her chilled hands in the pockets as August rolled down his sleeves from where they were bunched up around his elbows. Shop fronts turned to warehouses and sidewalks turned to wooden docks, and the crowds began to thin.

"This is really how you want to spend your evening?" August said, fastening his cuff. "Isn't there some party you could be at?"

She was meant to be at Angelika Bamberg's party. She and Lotte had made a plan to break in and continue the hunt for Lotte's father this evening. But this might be her *only* chance to get to Isengrim. And if she did, then she could shrug off this guilt too. She didn't need to help Lotte find her father and sell the information to a gangster.

"There are *many* parties I could be at," Nora said evasively. "But I read in *Modern Mode* that to snag a man you should occasionally take a night off from your usual routine and try new hobbies. And I'm going to assume that also applies to snagging men that you'd like to see spend the rest of their lives in jail for murder." Let the papers miss her. Let them speculate over where she was and who she was with. They'd never guess she was crashing a Grim rally. Getting Isengrim to admit to what he had done.

Nora was glad August was here with her. The only times she found that her mind wasn't worrying at the trials, like a dog at a meatless bone, was when she was with him. When he was challenging her, not succumbing to her too easily.

Truthfully, she probably *should* be thinking only of the trials. Waiting for them, preparing for them. But August's world seemed so far away from hers, she had a hard time imagining any trials coming to find her this far downtown.

Each dock was painted with bright white letters along the wooden slats. As they got closer, Nora noticed others emerging from the streets and between the piled crates that marked where the water began. Couples trying to feign casualness, as if they were just taking a stroll arm in arm at the docks at sunset . . . while there was a curfew. Or young men moving quickly, their hands deep in their jackets, walking with purpose in the hopes no one would stop and ask what that purpose was.

All of them slowly but surely veering toward the warehouse

doors marked with *112*. Nora let a young woman go in front of them, watching as she pressed toward the entrance and passed through the darkened door into the shadows beyond.

Nora didn't like walking into a party without knowing what was on the other side.

"It's not too late to turn back," August said, echoing her own uncertainty. "We might still get answers from tracking down your mother's ring."

"We both know that's a dead end without Oskar Wallen's help." Nora fought the impulse to slow her steps as the warehouse doors loomed closer. She checked the charms on her jewelry. "Besides, I'm used to rooms full of people who hate me—I have a family."

The warehouse was packed wall to wall, with even a handful of children sitting on shoulders to see over the heads of the crowd. There was a makeshift stage at the front with a large zungvox set up on it to project Isengrim's voice to his assembled admirers. Nora and August maneuvered their way toward the front, until the crowd was too packed to pass any farther, and they stood wedged off to one side.

A woman bumped into them, jostled by the restless crowd around them. "Sorry," she said, gripping the worn felt hat that covered her pale blonde hair. "I'm so sorry. I'm so nervous. I've never been to something like this before. Have you?" She was babbling, and she didn't wait for an answer. "My husband got arrested for striking. They've been holding him for weeks, and we can't pay for a lawyer to get him out. And then my neighbor told me about the Isengrim code and I just thought . . . some days it seems like the only way he will ever come home is if we bust open the doors of the prison ourselves."

The woman was as slight and delicate as a feather, and her voice was sweet and singsong and breathy. Nora couldn't exactly imagine her wrenching open a prison door. "Why are you here?"

"We heard rumors the LAO factory is getting rid of all its employees," August piped up before Nora could invent a lie. "My wife and I need those jobs. We've got little ones to feed. Can't have poor baby Chastity starving."

The woman smiled and nodded along at August's ridiculous story, the crowd around them shifting her away after a moment.

Nora shot August a look. "Moving a little fast, aren't we? Seems like just yesterday we were eloping in a pawnshop, and now we're married and raising a child."

He shrugged ruefully. "That was five whole days ago; our relationship has evolved."

"Well, we're *not* calling our daughter Chastity."

August glanced sideways at her. "Don't you have a cousin named Modesty?"

"Exactly, and look at *her*." She shifted from one foot to another, keeping her eye firmly on the stage, waiting for the appearance of Isengrim. The man who might be able to answer all her nagging questions about her mother's murder.

"How about Prudence?" August asked.

"No, she'll get called *Pru*. That's an old woman's name."

"Benevolence?"

"Don't be ridiculous." It was a pointless game to play with August. Even if she felt anything other than constant annoyance for him, what world existed where an heiress married a journalist? Not the world of Mercy Holtzfall, certainly, and not the world of Isengrim either. "Benevolence is a boy's name."

Suddenly the chatter around them died down. Something was happening onstage, the first sign of movement. And then through the darkened door behind the zungvox appeared a slender figure in a gold-painted deer mask. Behind her was a man in a boar's mask, then a fox. A bear. A falcon. A hare. A doe. A hound. They crowded onto the stage like animals coming out of their den, flanking either side of the stage protectively. Dozens of them in their snarling gold masks. And finally, behind all of the lesser beasts of the wilderness, came the wolf.

It was as if a bomb had gone off in the room. Everyone broke into rapturous applause at the sight of Isengrim. Except for Nora.

Her body ran cold at the sight of him.

He was just a man, she reminded herself. A man in plain work clothes and a ridiculous wolf mask that was more fit for games at a garden party than a stage. But the crowd reacted as if he were a hero of old returned to life. A savior from . . . what? Their poverty? Her family? The way the world was doomed to work?

August nudged her in the side, bringing Nora back to herself. *Clap*, he mouthed. Nora realized she had been staring fixedly while everyone around her cheered and stomped.

Begrudgingly, she put her hands together for the man who might have ordered the murder of her mother.

"I heard he wears the mask to hide his scars," a man said loudly behind them. "The ones he got from the wolves that killed his family."

Oh, I'm sure that can't possibly be apocryphal. Nora bit her tongue against the words. *That's why the police haven't identified him yet, too many men with disfiguring claw marks across their face in this city.*

Isengrim raised his hands, gesturing for silence as he leaned toward the zungvox. "People of Walstad!" His voice was distorted through the machine. Nora couldn't tell if his accent was Northern or Southern, if he was old or young. He could be anyone. "You glorious people, who have been mistreated too long. Stepped on, looked down upon, not seen or heard by those who think they are so high above us! Know that I have heard you." The crowd roared, and Nora could feel it. The desperation in their voices. The urgency, the yearning for someone to help them. For someone to save them. And Nora felt a swell of anger mingled with purpose that she couldn't wholly put her finger on.

"Tomorrow they will trot out the pantomime of an election for all of us once again. Pretend that we have a choice as the victor celebrates before the polls even close because our votes are not counted."

Was the election tomorrow? Nora had forgotten completely. She hadn't even decided what she was going to wear to the victory celebrations.

"The voices of the rich matter to our governors! Ours do not, so we will make them heard another way!"

The crowd around them cheered. Nora listened, hackles rising. Grim protests always ended the way they had yesterday, broken up by the police, with violence, injuries, death. Isengrim was leading them into a battle he knew they couldn't win. Into another losing fight like the riots. Sure, they'd smashed up some windows. But it meant hundreds in jail cells, several dead. If Isengrim thought any governor would flinch at the idea of citizens of Walstad beaten down in his name, he was wrong. And the people here were cheering in his name. They were willing to march into a losing fight for him.

She imagined the blonde girl being dragged away to join her husband in prison. The governor would watch it through the window of his mansion, bragging to Mercy Holtzfall how effective he was at keeping the peace. And meanwhile, nothing was being solved. They thought Isengrim was offering them freedom, but he was only offering violence.

Even as Isengrim spoke, Nora's eyes moved to the door behind the stage. Isengrim would have to leave that way. There had been a brief time in their history where the Holtzfalls had ruled like kings. Where they were the judge, the jury, and the executioner. Nora would be a fair judge. She would follow Isengrim, and she would make him admit what he had done to her mother. And then he would take Lukas Schuld's place on the executioner's block.

And when the wolf's head was cut off, the body would die. She could end the Grims. She could end this war in the streets of her city. She could find another way for them.

But right now, Nora and August were hemmed in on all sides by the crowd.

Nora nudged August, gesturing with a tilt of her head. Together, they moved to their right, pushing past people, around to the side of the stage, Nora's heart hammering as they went.

They were halfway there when there came a noise like a sledge-hammer cracking against wood, loud enough that it carried over the zungvox. Isengrim's words faltered, the crowd turning toward the wall where the noise had come from.

A noise like a battering ram slamming into the warehouse wall.

And then it came again. And again.

An uneasy mutter ran through the crowd. "The police?" someone near August and Nora wondered aloud. No, Nora knew the weapons the police used. They came from her grandmother's factories. Those would elegantly disintegrate a wall. This bashing was crude and primitive.

With a shattering noise, a section of the wall exploded, and the crowd erupted into screams, pushing backward, trying to move away, though the crowd was too dense for them to gain much room.

Nora pushed forward heedlessly, and as the dust cleared, she saw what had broken through.

It was an arm. Too large to belong to anything human. It was immense and rough and gray, like a stone brought to life. It withdrew through the hole it had created, and in the gap there appeared an eye, the corner of a face. And then came a roar so deep and guttural it shook the walls.

The crowd erupted into chaos. But Nora stayed rooted.

It was a troll. Made of *sidewalk*, from what Nora could tell.

Of course it was. Because a Veritaz Trial by troll was *exactly* what Nora needed right now.

Be good or I'll turn you out for the trolls to eat.

It was an old refrain. One every child had heard from their mothers at some time or another. Even children without mothers, like Lotte, had heard it. Maybe, once upon a time, it was a real threat. Back in the days of towering dark woods, when trolls still roamed in the night. But children hadn't feared trolls in hundreds of years.

But now that there was one standing between them and the door, a strange, ancient fear spread through Lotte. As if her bloodline remembered being afraid of trolls, even if she didn't. And it felt like a hundred generations were screaming at her to run.

Marble knuckles dragged slickly across the ground as it pulled itself fully free from the checkerboard flooring, tombstone teeth clashing together with a noise that echoed around the filing cabinets.

Theo moved with a sureness that could only come from years of training, placing himself between Lotte and the troll. "I'll hold it off," Theo said, voice low and sure, without looking at her, turning his sword over in his hand. "You run. Now."

She couldn't run. Lotte might not know all a Holtzfall should, but unless this was some elaborate security measure Nora had neglected to mention, she was sure of one thing: Finally, after days of waiting, after letting uncertainty worm its way into her chest so deeply that she had tried to look for a way out from the Holtzfalls, *this* was the next trial.

Her chance to prove that she belonged.

And she wouldn't win by running.

But she wouldn't prove anything by dying either.

Every story Lotte had ever heard about trolls flicked through her mind at once. There must be something that would help her. Trolls were stupid. They were vulnerable to iron, like all things born of magic. They followed their prey by smell. They hid in mountains in the day because sunlight turned them back to stone.

The lumen charm.

Lotte lifted her shaking hands, fumbling for the ring on her finger. If there was ever a time . . .

She tried to focus her mind. To feed magic into it slowly and surely—

The troll roared, advancing on them, its heavy marble feet crashing into the floor with every step. Actually, now *wasn't* the time. Lotte moved to Theo, quickly, slicing her hand open across his sword, blood welling painfully in her palm. The blood streamed down her fingers, sparking the lumen charm on her finger to life.

In Nora's hand last night, the ring emitted a warm glow that cast enough light for them to see by. Now, brought to life by her magic-drenched blood, it bloomed into life like a falling star.

The light bounced off her chainmail dress with a thousandfold the power of the candles, turning her from a girl into a blazing silhouette and flooding the entire hall. The troll roared in anger, its arms swinging violently as it raged against the sudden light. It staggered sideways into the filing cabinets, sending them crashing down, paperwork raining around it.

"Lotte," Theo urged, "we have to go."

But still, Lotte hesitated. This was a trial, she was sure of that. But how was she supposed to win it? Was the test just to *survive*, if she fled and escaped with her life would that be enough? Or was she meant to trick the troll into surrender like clever Hans in the stories?

The troll swung blindly, trying to find the source of this false sun. Its arms sent two more filing cabinets crashing to the ground. But no paper scattered from these ones. They crashed hollow and empty. And behind them was . . . a safe.

A safe without a combination or a keyhole, without a handle even. All Lotte could see was a tightly fitted metal door made of thick iron. But all at once Lotte felt certainty wash through her. If she were hiding a secret child, a safe with no lock was exactly where she would hide it.

"Lotte!" Theo called after her as she moved toward the safe, her hand raised, the light blazing against the troll. With her other hand, she tried to dig her fingers around the door to prize it open. But it wouldn't move. She circled the safe, trying to find something on it, a charm or a lock. Some way to open it.

The troll roared again, and Lotte staggered, catching herself on the safe with her sliced-open hand. She pulled away, blood smeared across the safe. But instead of the blood marking the metal door, the safe seemed to drink it up, the smear of red disappearing into the iron.

And with a whispering click of the lock, the door swung open, spilling the contents across the floor.

Holtzfall blood to get into Holtzfall secrets. And now those secrets were scattering out.

Lotte wasn't sure what she'd expected inside. Paperwork, maybe. A certificate of her birth like the ones she'd seen for her cousins.

Instead, glass tablets slid across the floor around her. Still holding the light high as she advanced, Lotte snatched up one. It wasn't just glass, she realized. It was two pieces of glass with blood pressed between them. The etched pattern across the glass surface gave it away as a charm. On the back of the one she was holding was a small label written in faded black pen.

Child J.

Lotte could feel her heart in her throat even as she fell to her knees, frantically rifling through the glass tablets. *Child T. Child R. Child H. Child F.* Some of them had numbers too. *Child S2. Child S3.* But she didn't see an L. She riffled through frantically until in her hand she saw a small tablet marked *Child O.*

Not Lotte. Ottoline.

She still forgot that was her real name sometimes. Lotte's hand closed around the glass a second before Theo's hand closed around hers.

She could feel it racing through his mind, the desperation to get out of here. The troll was still raging, thrashing against the light pouring from the lumen. Last night with Nora they'd been in and out without leaving a trace. Tonight . . . well, any chance of concealing the fact that she'd been here was gone with the troll. Would her mother know that she'd been here hunting for her father? Would she care?

She tightened her hand around the glass. *Child O.*

And they ran.

Chapter 37

NORA

The troll's fist hammered at the warehouse wall, splinters flying, making the gap larger and larger as it roared and fought to break through.

Well, this was incredibly inconvenient.

The crowd was screaming and pushing, trying to scramble backward, even though there was nowhere to go. From the stage, someone was shouting into the zungvox, but it was lost in the din.

Nora fought the flow of people, shoving forward heedless of whether August was following her. This was her challenge to face. She had to get to the troll before it broke through the wall and started wreaking havoc. But the press of the crowd was too strong. The troll slammed its shoulder against the warehouse wall, finally shattering it and stumbling through into the fray of people.

All right. Nora was done with shoving. She needed magic—now.

The troll staggered forward, stone nostrils flaring hungrily as it scanned the crowd through its scraggly hair. Nora found the charm on her wrist. She poured more power into it than was reasonable. Air emerged from her in a violent spiraling blast, forcing the crowd out of her way on either side, giving her a clear path to the troll and sending it staggering back toward the wall. Its head cracked against the wood, dazing it for a moment.

Nora started to move, her focus single-minded, wind rushing

in her ears, reaching for more charms as she went.

"Honora Holtzfall!" The cry came through the chaos. "It's Honora Holtzfall!" A middle-aged woman was pointing at her, finger shaking. She looked more afraid of her than of the troll.

Nora had inadvertently let down her glamour when she had poured her magic into the new charm. Keeping up appearances hadn't exactly been high on her list of priorities when a troll was smashing its way into the room.

"She's come to spy!" someone shouted from the stage. The Grim girl in the fox mask. Perfect. Because of course this trial had just been *too* easy.

Eyes turned on her. Even with a troll in their midst, Nora somehow was the most fascinating thing in the room. Were they really going to try to stop her? The only person in this room with enough magic to prevent the troll from killing them all?

Nora knew better than to argue with a mob.

And this one was already beginning to circle. She was the enemy that Isengrim preached against. And here was a chance to tear her limb from limb. Nora was all too aware they outnumbered her, no matter how much magic she had.

The fox girl leaped off the stage. The Grim in the boar's mask called after her, but she didn't stop. For a moment, Nora's attention flicked to the stage. There was something faintly familiar about the tinny voice inside the boar's mask, but she didn't have time to worry about that now. The fox girl pulled a knife from her waist as she plowed through the crowd. Nora shifted her magic into the ring on her right hand as the girl reached her and slashed the blade mercilessly toward Nora's face.

Nora dodged out of the way, grazing the ring against the girl's arm as she moved. A bolt of cracking energy surged out from the ring and through the fox girl's body, sending her twitching to the ground.

The Grims were very much wrong about Nora if they thought she was prey. They were the ones dressed as the wild animals that howled at the edge of the woods, beyond civilization.

But she—she was the woodcutter's heiress. She was the one who hunted wolves.

"Stay down," Nora warned the fox girl. "And I won't have to hurt you."

With a roar, the troll dragged itself to its feet with its scabby knuckles scraping the ground. She had bigger problems to turn her attention to.

Running from the troll would make her seem a coward. It could cost her a trial.

But if she stood her ground, it was only a matter of time before someone got hurt. Nora could defend herself. But she couldn't defend five hundred people at once.

Her mind raced for another solution. For some way that she could win this trial and keep everyone alive.

The only thing she could do to protect them was run.

At least she was wearing charmed shoes.

Nora jumped over the fox girl's body and ran straight for the troll.

It had looked inhumanly large from across the room, but as she got closer, she realized it was actually only grotesquely huge. The thing lumbered toward her, clearly oblivious to the fact that it needn't waste its energy. She was coming to it.

Nora would have to time this right. She kept her eyes on the troll's wide loping gait. Its arms were swinging wildly, and people in the crowd scrambled to get clear. She checked her index finger, unspooling magic from her charm in anticipation.

The troll lunged at the same instant that Nora flung herself onto the ground. Its fist cracked the wooden slats of the dock just in time for Nora to drop through, plunging toward the water below.

Her hand with the charmed ring hit first, magic sparking as the diamond touched the surface and the water below her turned to ice.

Nora's knees and wrists bashed into the ice, scraping away skin. The small sheet of ice teetered dangerously on the rest of the river.

Still, it wasn't bad for a charm meant to cool a drink.

Nora didn't stop there. Pushing more of her magic into the ring and turning more of the river to ice, she crawled her way under the dock, heading toward dry land.

The troll's fist slammed suddenly in front of her, right through the dock, ugly gray fingers scraping the top of the ice, barely missing Nora as she staggered back. The sheet of ice behind her was already unsteady as it melted into the river.

Nora's mind worked fast. He could smell her, she realized. That was what the old tales said about trolls. They sniffed out misbehaving children in their beds and gobbled them whole. He could find her even through the slats of the dock. She had to keep moving.

She pushed more magic into the ring on her hand, driving the ice farther forward as she forged an unsteady path across the water, half her attention on the glassy walkway, half on the sound of the troll's lumbering footsteps above. She heard the occasional scream as he barreled by a person, the crash of crates clattering around him, hitting the dock. She really hoped that August had enough sense to get out of the way. To get himself home before this all inevitably summoned the cops. But no matter what happened, the troll was still following her, with whatever ancient magic fueled the Veritaz setting its tiny, simple dirt-and-rock mind on her intently.

Finally, Nora broke free from the underbelly of the quays and docks onto open river.

Here, the water was choppier, and she found herself pushing out the magic from her ring farther to steady the ice float she was on. She could feel it heating uncomfortably on her hand. The charmier had designed it to be tapped against glasses of champagne at garden parties, not used on whole bodies of water.

The troll was on the embankment walkway now. The road behind it was already becoming chaos, automobiles veering to avoid the troll. If she didn't do something soon, someone was going to get hurt.

She rested the diamond ring on the ice below her, and she pushed the charm to its limit. She forced the ice outward, farther and farther, the gold band scalding her finger, but she pushed, until finally the ice reached land.

Forming a clear path between herself and the troll.

It took the bait.

With one slow, lumbering step, the troll moved onto the ice. Instantly, fissures appeared under its foot. Another heavy step, more cracks. Nora stood her ground, watching as the troll got closer and as the fissures got bigger and bigger. Her heart beat faster and faster as it got closer.

And with a greedy roar, it reached for her, its fingers almost brushing her.

It happened in a moment. Like a highball hitting the ground, wasting a perfectly good drink.

The troll hit the river with a roar.

The ice shattered, plunging both of them into the water.

It sank like the stone it was born out of.

Chapter 38

NORA

She surged to the surface, gasping for breath, frantically swimming toward the embankment. Until suddenly a hand closed over Nora's, dragging her out of the water, pulling her sopping wet onto the embankment.

"I'd give you my coat to warm you up," she heard August say. "But you're already wearing it."

So he was too much of an idiot to run. She would have told him that too, except she was shaking violently from the cold. Nora pulled her shivering hand out of August's, holding it up to the faint light of the distant streetlamps.

There was no Veritaz ring there.

She had failed. She had outsmarted and out-magicked a troll. But she didn't have a ring on her hand.

Because she had run.

The trial didn't care that she hadn't run out of cowardice, or even to save herself. She had run to give grace to the Grims.

She had run to save the same people who wanted her family dead.

And she had lost the trial because of it.

She wanted to scream, but again, she was shaking too violently. Instead she ripped herself away from August, peeling off his coat and dropping it to the ground as her freezing fingers scrabbled for a charm that would warm her up.

"Nora," August called after her. "Nora, where are you going?"

Home, but that word wouldn't come out. The apartment on Silver Street hadn't been home since her mother died. "Away. Away from this *pointless* pursuit. What does it even matter if I find out who killed my mother? She'll still be dead. And I still won't be Heiress. Because I've been doing this instead of competing."

August was a still silhouette at the edge of the water, his coat a sopping heap at his side, as he said, "You mean this pointless pursuit you strong-armed your way into."

He was right. And she had been an idiot. An idiot to think the trials would wait for her to cross out of August's world and back into her own. The trials had followed Earnest Holtzfall all the way to Albis. They could follow her a few miles south.

Here, standing on the edge of the water, Nora didn't have the words for the rage and the sorrow, the fear and the disappointment currently running through her. None of this—the Grims, the police, the missing jewelry, her mother leaving her here alone in the world—none of it was important next to the heirship.

Nora was born to be the Heiress. And it was about to be taken away from her. That was two trials down now. Two trials failed out of four. One for each of the heiresses who had sat around the breakfast table, tying their magic to the ax. Which meant there were only two left. Nora only had two more chances to earn back her entire future.

And all of this, it was a distraction. She had failed because she was distracted.

Because she had put the lives of the Grims, of all people, ahead of the heirship.

But if Nora tried to say any of that, she feared it would come out in a guttural scream that would ripple across the city. That would shatter her to pieces after she had spent day after day carefully holding herself together.

So she settled back into her imperious heiress persona. She put away the daughter who wanted the truth. Who wanted revenge.

"I really do wish I could fit tracking down murderers into my schedule, but my diary is very full these days." She flicked sopping wet hair out of her face. "I'm meant to be an heiress, not a journalist. So why don't you do your job and I'll do mine?"

She was turning away when August spoke again. "Why do you even want it?"

"What?" The question pried open her defenses.

"The heirship." August still hadn't moved from the bank of the river. "Why do you *want* it?"

Of all the questions journalists had ever asked Nora, this had never been one. It had never even crossed her mind. It was like asking why someone would want money. The answer was so obvious it didn't need to be spoken out loud. Except August seemed to be waiting for her to say it, and when Nora opened her mouth, she found the answer wasn't there.

"Because," she said, "it's mine."

"It's not, actually," August countered, taking a step toward her now. "It *was* yours. Now it's not. And half the time it doesn't seem like you'll even know what to do with it if you get it back."

"You don't *do* anything with the heirship, you *are* the heir or you're not." Nora spoke slowly, like he might be simple.

"Exactly." August closed the distance between them in a few steps, and suddenly Nora could see his expression up close in the flicker of lights from the street. "None of you *do* anything. Holtzfalls haven't done anything for this city in hundreds of years. You just *have*, and you take from the rest of us, and you get richer and we get poorer."

"You're starting to sound like the Grims." Nora felt disgust shudder through her. "If you want me to give away all my money so badly, I'll start by writing you a check for the last few days."

"I don't want your fucking money, Nora." August's voice rose. "I just think you could do something with it other than buy dresses and throw parties. Unless what you really want for the rest of your life is to do nothing but sit on a heap of gold."

"It's not *money*, it's power," Nora snapped.

"Power is only power if you use it!"

"What, then?" She hated that he sounded like Lotte. That he sounded like the Grims. That he sounded right. "If you know everything, what should I do with the heirship? Feed the poor and heal the sick, like I'm some worshipped hero of old? Solve all the injustices of class and raise up humanity? You think it's that easy to upend the entire hierarchy of the world?"

"No." His gray eyes were fixed on her intently. "I don't think it's easy. But I think you could do it." His gaze carried a challenge, like when they'd stood in his office and he'd told her she could break the code. "Tell me now with all your money and all your magic you couldn't change this entire city. This entire country. That you truly don't think you could make things better. Tell me that now, and I'll never ask you about the heirship ever again."

Nora knew better than to lie during a Veritaz Trial. Honesty was something the trials had challenged the Holtzfalls on year after year. But this wasn't a test sent by the Huldrekall. This was another sort of challenge August was throwing at her.

And she wasn't going to lie to him.

"You will never ask me about it again," Nora said finally. She had let him joke, about their future, their children. But even then, she'd known there was a time when they would have to part ways. That there was no future here. She turned away and walked up the bank to the streetlights. "Because you and I, we will never see each other again."

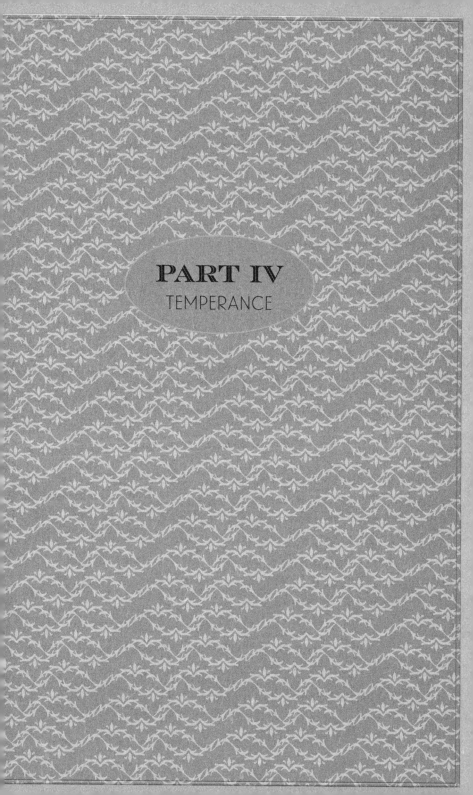

PART IV

TEMPERANCE

Chapter 39

THEO

"**E**xtra! Extra! Holtzfall Heiress Defeats Troll! Wins Second Ring!"

The newspaper boy's voice met them as they got close to the Paragon. It was late, but the kid brandishing newspapers was surrounded by people handing over their half a zaub for the news. Bellboys from the hotel and upper-circle residents alike.

Finally, Theo relaxed his grip on his sword. If a ring was won, that meant the trial was over. He had been on guard for the marble troll storming past the charm and coming after them. But even as his tension eased, he felt Lotte draw tense next to him. She swiftly checked her own hand, but even in the dim streetlights they could both see there was no ring there. And in spite of himself Theo felt a dart of relief. A ring would only draw the attention of the Grims to Lotte.

The newspaper ink wasn't even dry yet; it stained Theo's fingers as he handed over the half a zaub. But her face was clear on the front page.

Modesty.

Behind her was Angelika Bamberg's house. Or what was left of it.

The rest of it was consumed in flames.

Back in Grace's suite in the Paragon, they read the article. It was short and hastily written, the reporter from the *Herald* clearly rushing to be the first to break the news and get it on stands.

Details of the thrilling events at the Bamberg mansion are still coming in, but the way this reporter heard it, all the Holtzfall heiresses were in attendance when a troll suddenly wrenched itself free of the Ionian stone floor in the Bamberg ballroom. Details of what happened next are scattered since many guests were both tipsy and panicked, but everyone agrees the troll's rampage was ended with a fire started by Modesty Holtzfall. Which seems to have earned her a second win and a second ring in the Veritaz Trials.

"What are you going to do?" Lotte asked. He was aware of her on the settee next to him, searching his face. The secrets they shared hung heavy between them. Modesty had two rings now, and the whole city knew that, the Grims included. Theo's options were narrowing with every day.

"I don't know." It was the truth. Another truth was that it would be easy to break his oath. He had been with Modesty all week. He had driven her place after place under the guise of protecting her from another attack from the Grims. And all the while, at any time, he could have taken a left instead of a right and delivered her to their door. Exchanged her for his brother.

But Theo couldn't do that. He couldn't turn his back on what the Grims might do to a Holtzfall with a ring to get it from her. It wouldn't just mean betraying his oath. He could not be the sort of person who traded one life for another.

If it were Nora with two rings, he could have just . . . asked her for one. No matter what kind of mood she was in, if it were for Alaric, Nora wouldn't hesitate.

The idea of Modesty giving up anything was laughable.

"What if we *did* ask Nora?" Lotte said. And Theo realized that she had read his mind without meaning to. Her hand was resting next to his on top of the newspaper, of the picture of Modesty wreathed in fiery victory. He was sure that half the time she didn't even realize why she was doing that.

"Nora doesn't have a ring." Theo didn't draw his hand away.

"Not for a ring," Lotte said, "for *help*. Nora is—well, she was right about this." She held up the glass charm she'd taken from the vault. "She has answers the rest of us don't."

She wasn't wrong. Over the years, Theo couldn't think of a time Nora hadn't had an answer. But still, Theo hesitated. Their whole lives, Nora had trusted him with her life, but Theo had never had to trust her with his.

Mercy Holtzfall had let a dozen knights die without a thought. And there were days when Nora was more her granddaughter than she was Verity's daughter.

"Nora despises Modesty," Theo hedged. Even admitting aloud that he wasn't sure of Nora's loyalties felt treasonous. "Her answer would probably be to throw Modesty to the wolves."

Lotte leaned back into the settee, her chainmail dress starkly at odds with the plush velvet. She was turning the small glass charm over in her hands absently, fingers closing around it intermittently.

"There will be other trials," Theo said. Other rings. Other chances for her to stay a Holtzfall. For him to buy time from the Grims. He wasn't sure who he was reassuring. Her or himself.

And for the first time the thought crossed his mind . . . if Lotte won a ring, would she give that up?

"More trials," Lotte echoed remotely. "And for all we know, Modesty might win them all."

HE WASN'T SURE WHEN, BUT SOMETIME IN THE EARLY HOURS of the morning, they'd both drifted off. Distantly, Theo remembered that he'd been telling Lotte about his brother. That she'd been telling him about the convent. About the scars they'd given her. About the things that he was too late to protect her from.

He woke in the sitting room at the Paragon with a jolt.

His half-lucid mind hunted for whatever it was that had roused him. The sun was barely rising through the curtains, casting a ribbon of light over her face, the mirrored dress dancing in the sunlight.

And then Theo realized someone was standing over her.

A maid in the Paragon Hotel's pale blue uniform, a small white apron tied around her waist and a white cap covering her hair. She had every right to be in the room. If the maids didn't clean when the Holtzfalls were sleeping, nothing would ever get done. But something wasn't right. Her stillness. The hardness in her eyes watching Lotte. And even as she noticed him stirring, her eyes dashed up, and a sly smile danced over her face. She brought one finger to her lips.

"Quiet now," she whispered. "If you wake her, I'll have to kill her."

He knew that voice, he realized. It seemed so out of place from this primly coiffed girl in her pinafore. The last time he'd heard that voice, it came from inside a fox's mask. "Unlucky she didn't win the ring last night." The fox maid gestured to Lotte's bare hands. "If she had, I could just saw her finger off and be done with all of this."

As he glanced at her, Theo realized Lotte was awake. She was faking sleep. Staying perfectly still, but her chest wasn't rising and falling as it had been. Theo held himself still with effort. "What are you doing here?" He kept his voice low, but every nerve in his body was vibrating with the need for action.

"Well, being a Grim doesn't exactly pay the many bills I owe to the Holtzfalls." The girl gestured at her uniform. "But if you mean right this very moment, I want to know how Honora Holtzfall found out about our meeting place last night." The fox maid leaned on the back of the couch, watching him over Lotte.

"Nora?" What would Nora want with the Grims? Unless she

somehow knew about Alaric. Knew that them having him likely meant they were involved in her mother's murder . . .

"Nora." She said it with a mocking singsong voice. "What a familiar way to refer to your master. How did she know where to find us?"

The fear that went through him wasn't for Nora, he realized—Nora could take care of herself—but at what the Grims might do in reaction to Nora. "No one knows how Honora Holtzfall knows half the things she does."

She is smarter than you.

Than all of us.

You don't want to cross Nora's path if you know what's good for you.

"She was on a wolf hunt." Her eyes narrowed, as if she didn't fully believe he was as ignorant as he seemed. "Traitors don't fare well in our world."

Theo might have laughed if the words hadn't made him so angry. "You are the ones who asked me to be a traitor." He clenched his jaw.

The girl sighed dramatically. "You just don't understand that we're on the same side yet. Knights are supposed to be the champions of noble causes, you know. Our cause is noble even if our blood isn't."

The fox maid ran her tongue along her teeth thoughtfully, something new passing over her face as she looked down at Lotte. She drew out something that looked like a small pocket knife.

Theo felt every muscle tense in his body as he prepared to move across the room before she could slice Lotte's throat. "She's not your enemy."

The fox girl's eyes flashed. "They are all *our* enemies. They have enslaved your family for a thousand years with an oath made by your ancestor. Just like I am a debtor in *my* city because they cut down some trees a thousand years ago." The fervor that danced across her face was raw. But in that moment, Theo saw something of himself in it. The purpose that drove him, that had pushed him every day to train, to fight, to stand by the Holtzfalls because they shielded this city. He saw it in her now. This was *her* purpose. "But once you get us that ring, we will be able to draw enough magic out of the woods to fight back."

Fight back. He had seen the kind of violence they were capable of the day of the riots. Theo could see it in her now. More than equality, the Grims wanted retribution. They didn't just want to rise to meet the Holtzfalls. They wanted to bring them to their knees.

"But until we have that magic"—the knife flicked open, sparking with magic as it did—"maybe we can borrow some."

Theo surged to his feet as he recognized the Raubmesser charm. But the girl was fast, moving until the knife hovered a hair's breadth above Lotte's face. She didn't stir. She stayed completely still, trusting Theo not to let it get any closer.

Raubmesser charms were illegal. Unlike the Holtzfalls and the other families of the 1st circle, who were born overflowing with magic, most were born with only scraps of it in the blood. Enough to feed a heating charm for a few days of winter, maybe. Or to get an automobile from one end of the city to the other before it sputtered out.

Many people chose to sell their little allotment of magic when they got old enough. Pawn it off to a charmier for a few hundred zaub. If not, they'd usually use it up before they hit adulthood. But a Raubmesser charm, that had the power to drain someone's magic straight out of their blood. It had been outlawed as soon as it was invented, the charmier who created it sent to prison for the rest of his life.

Still, every so often, in the more dangerous parts of the city, someone would find themselves cornered in a dark alley with a knife to their throat, mugged for their magic. And now a knife was hovering dangerously close to Lotte's neck.

"If you hurt her"—Theo fought to keep his voice even—"you will not make it out of here alive."

"I wouldn't be the first of us not to."

The face of the redheaded girl at the Veritaz Ceremony flashed through Theo's mind. The cold certainty on her face as she chose to die. The Grims truly believed they were fighting to change the world.

"I can give you something better." It was desperation that pushed the words from Theo's mouth. Desperation to keep his oath. To protect Lotte. To buy time to find a way to save Alaric—without giving them a ring.

"Better than an heiress's worth of magic?"

"How about a factory's worth of magimek?"

The fox maid paused. "We told you we have ways of getting into LAO to get the charms we need."

"Leyla Al-Oman caught employees trying to steal from her. I assume that's your plan out the window. You need another way in." The words tasted like treason on his tongue, but it was too late to swallow them back. "I know another way in."

The maid flipped the pocket knife closed then open again, then closed again as she considered. "LAO is charmed and guarded to the gills. Even your brother couldn't give us another way in." Theo felt his fingers clench, trying not to picture them trying to force the information out of Alaric.

"I can." The guilt twisted in his stomach at the idea of betraying Nora. Nora, who had led them to safety through the secret passage into her grandmother's factory. Who hadn't even hesitated to tap the code into place in front of him. Who had never imagined he would use this information against her.

"Today," the fox maid said. "The factory will be empty for the election. We go today."

No, I need more time. But he bit back those words. More time for what? There was no one he could warn. No one he could turn to for help. Not without risking Alaric's life. Not without revealing his own treason. "Fine. Today."

The fox began to answer when the door to the suite opened suddenly. The energy of the entire room shifted in an instant. With one swift movement, the knife was gone and the maid was gathering the remnants of the mess around the room. Eyes respectfully on her feet as Grace floated in, trailing a dress made of white silk emblazoned with pearls.

The noise brought Lotte's eyes open. Theo caught her gaze, saw in it everything she had just heard.

"Oh, good, one of you is already here," Grace addressed the maid, oblivious. "Get me a hangover tincture, won't you? I don't have time to sleep this off before we leave for the governor's victory celebrations."

"Of course, Ms. Holtzfall."

"And hurry, or don't expect a tip," Grace ordered as the maid moved toward the door.

"Of course, Ms. Holtzfall," the maid said again, turning for one last curtsy. As she came up, she caught Theo's eye. She pressed one finger to her lips before closing the door.

"We'll leave for the governor's victory celebration at midday," Grace was informing Lotte, tossing her handbag and gloves on the ground.

"I thought the polls didn't close until sunset." The lightness in Lotte's voice rang false, but Grace didn't seem to notice.

"The polls are a formality, darling." Grace didn't break her stride. "Besides, it's never too early to celebrate *someone's* victory." Theo watched the pointed words land on Lotte like a jab. The door to Grace's bedroom slammed behind her, leaving Lotte and Theo alone.

The weight of their secrets thickened the air between them.

"You traded my magic for a whole factory." Lotte spoke first. "Was it because you saw just how unbelievably bad I was at using it?"

Theo ran his hand over his face tiredly, but he couldn't help but smile. "You're right. It was a bad trade. But I'm oathbound not to let her slit your throat."

A long silence passed before Theo spoke again. He thought back to Lotte's words from last night. "You were right," he said. "We need Nora."

Chapter 40

AUGUST

The lights started flickering first thing in the morning.

They gave out entirely just before lunch.

A collective groan went around the bullpen as it went dark. The only light now was the reedy sunlight that had managed to fight through the storm clouds that were gathering. The police report of Verity Holtzfall's death that August was holding blurred suddenly in the gloom. He rubbed a hand across his face, trying to focus.

He'd barely slept last night after their little misadventure with the Grims and the troll. August had never thought he'd see a troll outside of the woods, and now there were photographs of one splashed all over the front of papers. Meanwhile, the one he'd taken last night at the rally idled at the bottom of his desk drawer.

It showed the troll standing off against Nora. It was impossible to mistake her. And impossible to publish without revealing the fact that she had been in the midst of a Grim rally last night. Mr. Vargene wouldn't have it. A Holtzfall in their midst was a dangerous thing to admit.

August slammed the police report shut. Reading it over and over wasn't doing him any good, but he'd needed something to focus on instead of gnawing on his anger with Nora. And at himself, for thinking that she might have been better than her upbringing.

Which then became anger at himself again for giving a damn.

The *Bullhorn* was probably the only paper with this many people sitting around desks today. Every other journalist would be out chasing election stories. But the *Bullhorn* knew it was already a done deal. The upper circles had voted for their own. Hugo Arndt would be the next governor, and the lines of expectant voters in the lower circles wouldn't do anything to change that. Mr. Vargene wanted stories that were *actual* news from them.

And August *almost* had one.

With or without Nora, he *needed* to get to the bottom of this story.

The Grims' promise was that they would raise everyone up. But August had always known better than to trust anyone else to better his place in the world. Not his father, not the government, and not the Grims. He ought to have known better than to trust an heiress.

He needed to make the front page. He needed to make something of himself in this life.

"All right, all right, settle down and listen up." Mr. Vargene emerged from behind his glass door where the words EDITOR IN CHIEF were stenciled. "It's not a power outage. Looks like LAO has doubled the costs for the lights in this building." He held up a letter on thick cream paper. August recognized the stamp of LAO Industries at the top. "Now, I'm sure the fact that LAO is in bed with the Holtzfalls has nothing to do with the fact that we're the only building on the block to get our rates hiked."

August shifted in his chair uneasily. Was it a coincidence that the day after falling out with the granddaughter of the owner of LAO, they'd raised the rates on this building? He'd seen the kind of spiteful anger Nora was capable of. And more than that, he'd seen what the Holtzfalls were capable of.

"So here's the thing, I can't make this paper without printers, but I can make it without five of you. Which means you've got until the end of the week to give me something that'll convince me you're going to help me sell papers, or you're fired."

"End of the week?" August called over the sudden outcry. "That's in two days!"

"Well done, you can count. Now show me you can come up with a decent story." The cacophony of dissent reached a crescendo. But Mr. Vargene was louder, grabbing their newspaper's namesake from his desk. It was mostly a prop; August had only seen him use the bullhorn once before. "You've got a problem? Take it up with LAO or our good friends the Holtzfalls," he boomed into the metal mouthpiece before barging back through the door of his office.

Half of the people were already on their feet, but August was closest. He dodged around desks and over chairs, pushing through his boss's door and slamming it behind him. "Did you hear what I *just* said, Wolffe?" Mr. Vargene said. "I don't want to hear it."

"I've got a story. I've been looking into Verity Holtzfall's murder."

"The mugging?" Mr. Vargene asked. He'd started pulling open desk drawers.

"That's the thing, sir, I don't think it was a mugging." August knew he didn't have the whole story yet, but if he got fired . . . there were bills and empty cupboards at home. "I think the Grims killed her. I've been looking into it—"

"We're not printing that." He pulled out a bottle of brown liquor from his desk, and a single glass. "Now get out."

"Sir—" August protested.

"Listen, Wolffe." Randolf Vargene poured himself a drink. "If you don't understand why people read our paper, then you're not as bright as I gave you credit for. Lots of people who aren't Verity Holtzfall get mugged and killed in this city every year. Do you want our readers to think that we're giving the Holtzfall Heiress's mugging more of our attention than anyone else's because she's worth more than them?"

"No, but—"

"When's the last time you were at the pictures?" He didn't wait for August to tell him that he didn't have enough time off or money for the pictures. "Ever notice how there are good guys and bad guys? People don't go to the pictures to watch the good guys do bad things. And people aren't going to read our papers if we remind them that sometimes the good guys have to do bad things. Isengrim is the good guy, he's the people's champion, the Holtzfalls are the bad guys." He gestured at the dark bulb above his head. "You want to try to tell the people their champion is a criminal and the people who tax them to death get another win?"

The editor finally paused for a sip of his drink. It took August a moment to realize he was waiting for an answer this time. "I've got a feeling I'm supposed to say no."

What he actually wanted to say was *it shouldn't matter*.

Journalism was supposed to be the truth, not what people wanted to hear.

But the truth didn't matter if no one would print it. He could always take what he had to one of the bigger papers. The *Herald* made a good business bashing Grims. But he didn't have the proof. Even if he went with what he did have to one of the other papers, they'd likely take it and assign it to a senior journalist who already worked for them. They might slip him a check to go away, but it wouldn't be the story that made him.

"Well done. You're already smartening up." His editor recorked the bottle. "Now get out of my office and go write something our readers actually want to hear."

Chapter 41

THEO

The last place Theo had called home was the apartment on White Hart Lane.

Three small rooms that had always seemed flooded with daylight through the huge window that faced the woods. On a clear day, you could just see the tops of the trees. That apartment was where Alaric and Theo were born. Where they had both learned to walk and read and hold a sword.

It was where their mother had died.

She had been a kitchen maid at the Holtzfall mansion, wooed by a charming knight. And when they were wed, they had received permission from Mercy Holtzfall to move out of the barracks.

Their mother was gone long before Theo's memories started. An illness that swept her away in the space of a few days. Alaric had some memories of her, but Theo only had what was left of her afterward. The blue she had painted the walls in the small living room. A velvet chair with a large wine stain that she had dragged up six flights of stairs when Mercy Holtzfall had told her to discard it from the mansion. Against the blue wall, they had a single shelf of books from which his father taught them to read in the rare free time he had.

There were the classics. Battered copies of the various morality lessons. A few religious texts. But the rest of them were books about knights and their great exploits. Gyrard the Bold who slew the beast at Milstadt, Heward the Faithful who saved the maiden Clara from the witch's tower, Godfrey of the Many Deeds. And of course, the two they were named for: Alaric the Guard and Theodric the Trusted.

Theo and Alaric had pored over them as boys. Imagining themselves climbing towers and riding over cliffs. Even though their father warned both his sons that these days being a knight mostly meant keeping Holtzfall secrets and driving them around the city. The days of true knights were gone. They were confined to the covers of those old books. To the imaginations of boys in the apartment with blue walls. Before they had moved out to the barracks.

Driving a Holtzfall was what his father had been doing when he was killed. Nora's father, a Holtzfall by marriage. When their automobile was struck on a slick city road by a milk truck that had spiraled out of control. Both men were killed, as well as the truck driver.

His father had been buried among the other fallen knights. It was only when Theo had turned away from his father's grave that he had noticed Honora standing behind them. She was ten, wearing clothes that smelled of smoke. Her grandmother, Leyla, had insisted that her son receive a funeral pyre, as was traditional in *her* country, instead of a Gamanix burial. No matter who he was married to, he was desert born.

Even then, Theo had understood she had come to be with them in their grief. All three of them were grieving lost fathers. They grieved together.

Theodric the Trusted.

The Holtzfalls were supposed to put their trust in him, not the other way around.

Theo waited by the gleaming black door with the *13* on it. The day of the riots, Nora hadn't even hesitated in revealing this secret entrance. Why would she? Knights did not betray Holtzfalls.

Theo wasn't betraying her, he reminded himself. Nora might be deep in her grief, but she had never failed him when it mattered. When they were children and Modesty had tried to blame her injuries on Alaric, Nora had been the one to tell Mercy Holtzfall it was a lie. When whispers were going around, wondering how their father could have driven so carelessly, she had been the one to put a stop to them. Nora could be trusted.

Lotte would find her at Hugo Arndt's victory party this afternoon. She would tell her everything. And Nora and Leyla Al-Oman would end this. They could save Theo from breaking his oath.

The streets were quiet. Every worker in the city had been given the day off to vote in the governor's election. And the downpour wasn't helping. Headlights suddenly spilled out onto the wide avenue that led toward the LAO factory, briefly setting the rain alight as the truck trundled to a stop. Bright white letters on the side read WOOLFIN STEAM LAUNDRY CO. And not for the first time, Theo felt unsettled. Woolfin provided laundry services to half the high-end establishments of Walstad. There were Grims hiding in every hotel, every shop, every restaurant. That ancestral instinct rose in him again. Like he was surrounded by beasts in the woods.

The fox girl slid out of the passenger side of the truck. She wasn't dressed as a maid anymore. "We're a little far from the factory." Her voice carried a warning. There were two other men and a woman piling out of the truck. All were plain faced and wearing worker's coveralls. He doubted that he could pick them out of a crowd later. "Remember, we can slit your brother's throat like a pig."

Theo kept his voice steady. "You don't need a truck to transport plans for charms."

"You're right." Rain streaked down her wolfish grin. "We figured as long as we were here, we'd help ourselves to a few other things. The weapons the police are so intent on always using against us, for instance."

Their father had taught them to lay their lives down for the Holtzfalls. For their oath. Theo had always thought he would be able to do that. But laying down Alaric's life was different.

Theodric the Trusted.

His namesake belonged to stories from an era that was long gone now.

Everything had seemed simpler to a boy practicing at being a knight in an apartment with blue walls and a worn-out armchair.

Wordlessly, Theo turned toward the door, entering the code that he'd seen Nora put in just a handful of days before. Pushing the door open, he turned to the four Grims waiting behind him hunched against the rain.

Theo glanced down the road for some sign of Nora. For some sign she was there to stop him. But there was nothing.

"Waiting for something, knightling?"

Nora and Lotte would come.

He trusted that they would come before he became a traitor.

Chapter 42

NORA

Modesty had never worn her namesake well. But today, it fit her particularly scantily. In fact, Nora could see right through it.

Even from the opposite side of the party, Nora could feel the gloating oozing off her cousin as she told the story of her encounter with the troll for the fifth time, brandishing *two* rings. The temperance ring on her ring finger, a new one made of oak on her middle finger. Oak for courage.

She would have to have courage to wear *that* dress to the governor's victory party, Nora supposed.

The votes wouldn't even be fully cast, let alone counted, for hours. But Hugo Arndt had already won. After the disaster of the riots just two days before the election, it was quietly but unanimously decided among the upper circles that Governor Gerwald's days were numbered. It was time for one of their own to take charge.

For his victory celebration, the garden of the Arndt mansion had been made to look like the woods from a painted storybook. Trees made of glass and gold and silver were dotted through the manicured garden. From their branches hung fruits made of sugar glass, brightly colored drinks in each one.

Modesty was holding a glass apple she had plucked from a nearby tree, sipping at the red and gold-flecked drink inside as she dramatically told her story to the assembled crowd.

All in all, it was probably a good thing Nora hadn't won the Veritaz ring for temperance, because the rage coursing through her right now would have surely burned it straight off her hand.

Modesty winning one ring was a bad day. A fluke Nora could chalk up to any number of pieces of bad luck.

But a second ring . . .

It was possible Nora had underestimated her cousin. Or overestimated herself. No, that wasn't possible. It must be the first one.

Hugo Arndt, the new governor, was standing on the steps of the mansion, glad-handing. ". . . easy enough to round them up." She caught the edge of something he was saying to Albertine von Hoff. "All we have to do is wait and see who casts their vote for Isengrim."

Nora had heard that some countries had anonymous voting. Obviously that would never work in Gamanix, since wealth weighted votes. And the lack of anonymity would make it easy enough for Hugo Arndt to know who had voted against him. And then to *round them up*.

And suddenly Nora was desperately *bored*. She was so bored of all of this, of every single one of these people. They were all so predictably simple in their way of thinking. And not a single one of them really understood *anything*. People could accuse Nora of not caring about their problems, but they could never accuse her of not understanding them.

"I have a question for you, Governor," Nora interrupted. When a Holtzfall spoke, the governor listened. "Why do you think the lower circles might vote for Isengrim?"

"Well." Hugo chuckled, and Nora suddenly remembered the time this man had ridden a horse into a party because its coat matched his outfit. "Because they're poor, for starters." The crowd around him laughed, and Nora felt anger rise up in her.

"And so because they didn't *choose* you, they deserve to be rounded up and imprisoned? Perhaps that explains why so many more people would rather follow Isengrim than you." Nora could feel herself enjoying the attention, even as a mutter ran through the crowd.

What would she do with the heirship if she had it?

This.

Hugo Arndt's smile had become fixed. "Perhaps the Holtzfall Heiress and I could have a meeting in private about what best—"

"She's not the Holtzfall Heiress anymore." Modesty had meandered over from her rapt audience. "So if you'd like to meet with *me*, I'm certainly open to ideas of how to crush the Grims for good."

Nora didn't realize that she was turning to stride toward Modesty until suddenly there was a figure in her way. It took her a second to realize it was Lotte. Nora was briefly distracted by how incredible Lotte looked wearing the impeccably tailored white silk dress they had bought her. She should have paired it with pearls as well as the gloves perhaps.

And then her mind returned to Modesty.

"I've already proven I'm intemperate," Nora said in a low voice. "There's nothing to stop me slapping her now."

"Not even cameras?" Lotte was right, Nora realized. This was the governor's election party. There were journalists here. All of them armed with lenses and flashbulbs.

Reluctantly, she let Lotte draw her away, ignoring Modesty's smirk, until they were out of the crowd.

"I would say I owe you one." Nora shook dark hair off her face, trying to shrug off the unfamiliar feeling of being grateful to one of her cousins. "But I did save your life the other day, so we'll call it even."

"Well, imagine you did owe me one," Lotte said. "For standing me up last night, for instance."

Amidst infiltrating the Grims and being attacked by a troll, Nora hadn't had time to come up with a lie about why she'd failed to meet Lotte last night. And before she could, Lotte pulled something from inside her long white silk glove. "I found this at Johannes & Grete."

Nora recognized the charm instantly. "A bloodvenn."

Of course. Nora felt like a fool for not realizing that would be what to look for at Johannes & Grete. And then her mind pulled her back a few moments. "Wait, did you go back to Johannes & Grete last night *without me*?" She hadn't anticipated that.

"You thought I'd wait for you?" Lotte raised her pale blonde eyebrows, all pretense of innocence gone from her face.

"Yes," Nora added. "Or, honestly, I didn't think you'd be able to get in without me."

"In that case, it was extra rude to stand me up, wasn't it?"

Not as rude as trying to steal the information to sell out her cousin's secrets to Oskar Wallen, but Nora didn't say that. "Color me impressed, then." And she meant it.

"So what's a bloodvenn?" Lotte asked, holding the small glass charm up to the light.

"It's a charm to make sure that all Holtzfalls are in fact really Holtzfalls," Nora said drily. "If an impostor ever laid claim to the ax . . ." A cascade of consequences too terrible to even contemplate went through Nora's mind. She pushed them aside with a small shiver running through her. "About two hundred years ago, it turned out that Providence Holtzfall's wife had been unfaithful. None of her three children were his, and no one was the wiser until the day of the ceremony, when the Huldrekall had to break it to him that he had no heirs. *That* was the last time, before this generation, that a Veritaz was held between Holtzfall cousins instead of siblings, incidentally. In order to avoid such situations, a charmier created bloodvenns. You put two people's drops of blood on the glass. If they repel, then there is no shared blood. But if they share blood, then the drops will find each other in the charmed glass.

The closer they draw together, the more blood they share."

Nora held the pressed glass up to the sun. "Like they have here. The children of all Holtzfall fathers are tested at birth to make sure they really *are* Holtzfalls and not the result of straying wives. Before you ask, regrettably, yes, Constance and Clemency did both pass the test. But in your case, there would be *no* need to test for Holtzfall blood since you are obviously your mother's child. Which means this other drop of blood isn't meant to identify our side of the family. It's meant to identify the other one."

Nora had sworn off the hunt for her mother's murderer just hours ago. It was a distraction. It was the reason she had lost. The irony that she might now be holding the answer that Oskar Wallen wanted was not lost on her.

"So in other words," Lotte was saying, "this is entirely useless unless we know who the other drop of blood belongs to."

"Well, our grandmother isn't exactly in the habit of labeling her secrets." Nora squinted at the glass again, holding it up to the light, moving it back and forth, their reflection dancing over the glass.

She wondered . . .

Nora pressed her finger to the glass, summoning her Holtzfall gift. There was a flash of movement in the glass as the reflection began to wind back. They were silent as Nora searched in the small piece of glass. "It's a lot easier with mirrors," she muttered, keeping her attention on the glass.

Suddenly, Nora's reflection shifted, becoming Mercy Holtzfall's. A few years younger, but still the unmistakably steely Holtzfall matriarch. She was leaning over the glass, an eyedropper in her hand. A dot of blood fell onto the glass, obscuring her face. They waited for one beat. Two.

For the second drop of blood.

And then another figure came into the reflection.

Liselotte Rydder. Mercy Holtzfall's sworn knight.

Nora expected her to draw out another eyedropper. Some blood taken from some man who wasn't present. But instead she drove a small pin into her finger, the blood blooming on her finger before dropping onto the glass.

The charm sparked to life instantly, drawing the two blood drops together, obscuring the faces staring down at it. Nora pulled her finger away sharply, her breath catching as she released the old reflection, leaving only Lotte's and Nora's faces staring into the glass.

Nora had wondered, more than once, what scandal could be so great that it was easier to spirit Lotte away to a convent than for Grace to just *marry* the man.

She had even begun to wonder if Lotte really was half immortal spirit.

But her father wasn't a forest being. He wasn't a 1st-circle dalliance. He was a Rydder knight.

Which, out of all the possible options, was the most terrifying one.

There were a lot of secrets in the Holtzfall family. But there was one that hung over any other: why it was so fundamentally important for Holtzfalls never to fraternize with the knights. It was a lesson taught over and over again. But the real reason why it was so dangerous, that was only known by Heiresses.

Nora had been an Heiress, once.

She glanced at Lotte out of the corner of her eye, her whole being suddenly aware of her cousin. In a matter of seconds, Lotte had gone from some youthful indiscretion of Aunt Grace's to a weapon that could bring the Holtzfalls to their knees.

Lotte's mere existence threatened this family.

This wasn't a secret Nora could trade to Oskar Wallen, even if that *was* what had started all of this.

"Lotte—" Nora's hand brushed her cousin's arm as she reached for the bloodvenn. But before Nora could say anything, the emotions cascading across Lotte's face suddenly shifted, her brows furrowing. Like she was listening to something far away.

"You were going to *trade* my father's identity?" It took Nora a beat to realize those words had come from Lotte and not her own mind. "You manipulated me into finding out this information because *you* wanted to trade it?"

Nora's whole being felt like ice had just dropped over her. How could Lotte *possibly* know that? Had Modesty told her? No, impossible. Modesty was a tool in her manipulation, but she had no idea of Nora's endgame.

"Who were you going to trade it to?" Lotte's voice cracked and, to Nora's horror, she saw tears in her cousin's eyes. "To the gossip columns?"

"No—" For the first time in Nora's life, she felt like her mind wouldn't work properly, tripping over itself to find some lie even as she reeled away from Lotte's uncanny knowledge. There was only one way that Lotte could know that. "You're a mind reader," Nora realized aloud. It hadn't even crossed her mind that her cousin would have a Holtzfall gift. Constance and Clemency were born without them, after all. Let alone one of the most coveted Holtzfall gifts there was—

Before Lotte could deny it, movement caught the corner of Nora's eye, her head whipping around. But all she saw was the carefully manicured hedges that were dotted through the garden.

"Did you see—"

Nora didn't have time to finish before everything in the garden seemed to burst into motion. Thick green branches sprouted out of the manicured hedges that hemmed the garden, spreading in all directions. Nora and Lotte were on their feet even as the screaming started.

Grass rose up, twisting at an impossible speed around people as trees spread into walls, cutting Nora and Lotte off from the party.

Branches and brambles wove themselves into shapes, climbing out and upward.

Nora thought about running, but that was what had cost her the last trial.

Her heart picked up speed in anticipation as the hedges twisted and writhed up and up and up, shaping themselves into a maze around them. This was another trial, another chance for her to prove herself. Another chance to win a ring. Another—

Nora blinked.

And the garden was gone. Instead she was staring at a memorandum charm as it clicked shut.

Chapter 43

LOTTE

otte's vision tilted violently as the world shifted around her in a blink.

A second ago, it had been bright afternoon in the garden, a trial coming to life around them. Now it was pitch-dark outside the window of her grandmother's office. Lotte had the vertiginous feeling of having been wrenched from one time and place to another in the blink of an eye. She felt suddenly nauseous.

"I'm going to be sick." Clemency echoed Lotte's thoughts as the room continued to spin around her. Next to her, Nora was bracing herself against the desk, shaking violently.

"No, you're going to pull yourself together," Mercy Holtzfall's cool voice sounded. The older woman gradually came into focus. She was sitting at her desk, hands folded. Lined in front of her were four golden compact mirrors. Memory charms, Lotte remembered. Like the one her mother had used on the maid. Lotte looked down, finding a bleeding cut on her arm, with no idea how she got it. Her breaths started to come fast and shallow with panic.

Mercy Holtzfall had taken memories from her. From all of them. Hours and hours of memories, if the dark sky outside was anything to go by. She could have taken days or weeks for all Lotte knew.

Clemency and Modesty looked as disheveled as Lotte felt. Dresses ripped, dirt caked into their fingernails, hair snarled. But

Nora. Nora looked like she had clawed her way out of the hall of the Undermountain King. Her entire body was covered in welts and scratches, blood was smeared across her face, and she was coated with a thin layer of ash. Like she had walked through a fire.

"Why?" Nora's voice sounded scraped raw too, like she couldn't get any more words out. But the ones she didn't say echoed through Lotte too. *Why would you take our memories? What could be so bad that you would take this from us?*

"To protect you." Mercy pulled off a ring that stood out against the rest of the gleaming jewelry that adorned her. A plain wooden ring. This, Lotte realized, must be her own Veritaz ring. The one she had won in her own generation's trials. Distantly, it occurred to Lotte that she had no idea what virtues her grandmother had proven in her trials.

She pressed the ring to the wall next to her desk. The wallpaper gave way under the pressure of the wooden ring, a hidden keyhole seeming to appear around it.

And in the wallpaper, a door opened.

Cold, damp air rushed out of the door, washing Lotte with a sudden sense of familiarity that she couldn't place. Behind the door, a long stone corridor extended as far as the eye could see. The walls were lined with charm after charm. Hundreds of stolen memories held inside memorandums. Mercy turned as if to gather the four on the table. But Clemency interrupted suddenly. "Where's Constance?"

Constance. She was so interchangeable with Clemency that Lotte hadn't even noticed her absence in the confusion. But she saw it now. There were only four of them lined up across the desk. Only four mirrors. Only four sets of memories.

Mercy Holtzfall paused in the doorway, looking severe. "Constance did not survive."

Her words hit Clemency first, her breaths coming short and fast as she sank to the ground. Modesty moved down, crouching next to her, trying to hold her up as Clemency fell apart.

Constance was dead.

"The story has already gone out to the papers," Mercy Holtzfall carried on calmly. "The Grims, in protest of losing the election, tried to subvert the democratic process and staged an attack at the governor's victory party. A bomb. Thousands across the city will report seeing a great pillar of fire around nightfall. Constance died bravely defending the governor's life."

"That's ridiculous. Where would the Grims get a bomb?" Nora was still doubled over, but she sounded angry.

Lotte knew before their grandmother spoke.

"From LAO Industries, of course." Mercy rounded on Nora, even as Lotte felt a sudden surge of guilt. "There was a break-in today."

Theo. She had told him she would get Nora's help. And instead . . . she had asked about the bloodvenn first. She had thought there would be time enough for both. If she had anticipated that a trial would sweep them up before she could warn her about the break-in, would she still have gone after her own answers first?

"A break-in?" Nora looked up from the desk.

"Yes." Mercy's anger seemed real and sharp, directed at Nora now. "Who could say what inventions of Leyla's they stole. Charms. Bombs. Weapons we don't even know of yet."

"This wasn't a Grim attack," Lotte spoke up, clutching at something that would ease the guilt. "It was a trial."

"And how do you know that?" Mercy Holtzfall turned on her. "None of you have any new rings to prove that there was ever a third trial." Lotte's gaze dashed swiftly across her cousins' hands and her own. She was right, the only rings were the two on Modesty's hand.

"Holtzfalls have failed trials before." Nora's voice was unsteady with pain. "Contestants have died in trials before."

"And just days ago, Grims tried to kill your cousin. What seems more likely? That you all failed or that a Grim assassination succeeded?"

"If that's what Grandmother says happened—" Modesty started.

"Oh, shut up," Nora's voice rasped out, lunging toward Modesty.

Lotte saw her chance. She moved backward, as if jostled by the lunge. Letting her hand fall over the small charm where her memories were locked.

It was like reading a mind. Except it was her own.

IT WAS A TRIAL. LOTTE REMEMBERED.

The garden had moved with a mind of its own, until Lotte and Nora were standing in a maze.

Finally it stopped, leaving silence where there had been chaos. They both remained still, distantly aware of the sounds beyond the maze. Both waiting to see if some new threat would spring out of the brambles around them.

When nothing did, the next step of this trial had seemed obvious. To solve the maze.

Lotte and Nora hadn't spoken, the uncertainty of what had passed between them in the moments before the trial hanging there. It was that uncertainty that made Lotte turn and walk away from Nora.

She didn't want Nora to see the humiliation and the hurt written all over her face.

She had made the mistake of trusting Nora. Of thinking of her as a friend, when she'd only been using her. Exactly like Modesty had. Nora had just been cleverer about it.

If the trial was to solve the maze, Lotte was going to need a head start.

It was a matter of minutes before her path crossed with Nora's again. She walked past her. Only for a few turns later to find herself face-to-face with her cousin again. And again. Until finally the sixth time Nora had broken the silence.

She'd said she thought the maze was moving. She said she didn't think this was a test to solve the maze. Somehow, wordlessly, they fell into step together. Lotte remembered thinking that she saw shapes in the hedges. Like bodies had been caught there when the maze had taken form.

The sky above them drifted into late afternoon when Lotte finally had to stop. She sank to the ground, pulling off the shoes that were making her feet ache. Nora took a few steps before realizing she wasn't following.

She waited.

Then backtracked and waited.

And finally sank down to the ground opposite her.

And when Nora spoke again she told her the truth. She told her that her mother's murder had been staged, faked. Nora had only come close to speaking about her mother once. When she had told Lotte that life was not fair. Nora didn't wear vulnerability naturally. But she donned it, alone with Lotte in the maze as she told her everything. That she had toyed with the idea of trading Lotte's father's name for her answers.

It had almost sounded like an apology.

And in turn Lotte had told Nora about Alaric.

She told her about the Grims ransoming him for a ring. About the hold they had over Theo. About the factory and the choice he had to make, just like Nora had, between treason and loyalty.

When Nora had stood again she extended a hand to help Lotte up. And in her grip Lotte had read everything. That she intended to get Alaric back. That she would not betray Lotte.

That she could trust her.

The silence was different after that. Or perhaps they talked. Lotte's memory was faint on that. Because of what came afterward. They walked and walked until finally, as the sun was setting, the maze opened up for them.

For a wild, hopeful moment, Lotte thought it was a way out. But instead it was an open clearing with paths that led back into the maze at each corner. They hadn't found the way out; they'd found the very middle.

The clear area of grass was littered with leftover chaos from the party. Dropped glasses and canapés, discarded shoes as people had fled. And in the middle was one of the gold-and-silver trees. Glass apples filled with drinks still hung off it.

Moments later, three other figures stumbled out from entrances on the other side. Modesty, Constance, and Clemency. Looking as fed up and disheveled as Lotte felt. Nora somehow still looked un-fazed by the trial.

Until she didn't.

The moment all five of them were in the clearing, the pathways into the maze sealed behind them.

Now what? one of them asked. Reading the memory in the mir-ror, Lotte wasn't entirely sure who had spoken. But the second the question was asked, the maze answered. The hedges, which had been still since imprisoning them, began to grow again, closing in around them.

And all at once, everything descended into bickering. The five of them arguing over how to survive this. Whether to hack the maze back, or burn it, or try to break through it.

Until it became clear the only way out was up.

The panic and the fear in the memory made it choppy. But Lotte remembered them climbing. They'd pulled themselves up the immense silver-and-gold oak in the middle. Trying not to cut themselves on the jagged edges of the metal leaves even as the hedges closed around them. They reached down for each other, pulling up, giving leverage to climb. For a time, it seemed like the bickering had faded into actual cooperation. Except, as each hand Lotte clasped broke past the barriers of her hindern, she was overwhelmed with how much bitterness she tasted in their minds. Constance and Clemency lived with so much jealousy. They could not accept less than the heirship because it would mean they *were* less, which was already what their grandmother thought of them.

And Nora.

Lotte had never read a mind like Nora's before. It was like a burst of thoughts all exploding at once and meshing into one perfectly formed conclusion faster than Lotte could possibly track it. Nora had thought when they entered this trial that it was a trial of intelligence. That she would be sipping champagne at the exit with a ring on her hand waiting for the rest of them within an hour. But she had been mapping the maze's movement as she went. There was no logic to it. What was she missing? If this wasn't a trial of intelligence, what was it testing? Temperance and bravery were already gone. What did that leave? All the history of the Holtzfalls stormed in her mind at once as she considered past trials.

Justice. Selflessness. Charity. Wisdom. Honesty. Fairness. Prudence. Loyalty.

Unity.

It crashed to the front of her mind all at once. There had been a test of unity three generations ago. All four Holtzfall siblings had been trapped together. They had all come out of it with rings. In the history of the trials, that was the only generation where every competitor won a way into the woods.

Now this was their chance.

They could all get out of here with rings on their hands.

They were almost at the top.

The brambles were close enough that Lotte could feel them clawing at her arms as she dragged herself the last few feet up toward the top of the hedges.

Clemency reached the top first. She reached out, pulling Lotte after her. The brambles that made up the hedge were so densely woven together that it was like landing on solid ground.

Lotte turned, dragging Modesty after her.

And Modesty's thoughts cascaded through Lotte.

These weren't petty jealousies like Constance and Clemency. Loathing stretched like a vast burned field through Modesty. Years of resentment that had dug deep claws into Modesty's mind, making it bleed spite and rage that she hid with a smile. All of it was aimed at Nora, her cousin who had everything handed to her, while all Modesty did was work so much more for so much less.

Nora took everything. She never let anyone else have anything. And she'd had the *gall* to speak about the Grims and their poverty like she knew about wanting. It only stoked Modesty's determination to take everything from Nora.

She pulled her hand away as soon as Modesty was safely up, but she felt the darkness of those thoughts clinging to her. Lotte reached down for Nora, even as the walls of the maze closed around her.

Modesty moved faster than Lotte had thought she could. She lunged at Lotte, twisting her wrist hard, making Lotte cry out in pain as her fingers jerked open.

And Nora fell.

Knocking Constance down after her.

Lotte had screamed their names, but it was too late. The hedge had closed around them, swallowing them in the brambles.

And when Lotte had turned, Modesty was watching her with coldness in her eyes. *No one will believe you.*

After that, it was a blur. Somehow they reached the edge of the maze, clambering across the now-solid stretch of brambles. They made it back to the grass where, just hours ago, the wealthy of Walstad had gathered. It was empty except for Holtzfalls and knights rushing toward them, Lotte falling to her knees. Benedict knelt beside her.

Modesty burst into dramatic fake tears. Cries of how their cousins fell. How they tried to save them.

Liar! Lotte remembered the word ripping from her throat. She didn't care if no one believed her. *You killed them!* Somehow she was scuffling with Modesty.

Distantly, through the pain and the rage, she was aware of Theo pulling her off Modesty. She could feel his thoughts thrumming through his chest pressed against her back as she fought him.

And she felt his loss. She felt the agony of his disloyalty as he had stood by while the Grims took their fill of LAO. Because Lotte failed to tell Nora in time. Before this impossible trial took her. Killed her.

Lotte wasn't aware of what she was screaming incoherently when suddenly Clemency cried out.

It took Lotte a moment to see what Clemency had. There was smoke rising from the middle of the deep brambles. Just a wisp at first, but as they watched, it grew. And grew. And then Lotte saw the fire, the blaze growing inside the maze like a burning heart.

In no time, the whole maze was alight. Distantly, Lotte was aware of charms going up in the hands of the older generation of Holtzfalls, shielding them from the smoke as they all silently watched. Unsure if this was part of the trial or something else. Lotte was too afraid to hope.

Until finally, the fire died out, leaving only ash and petrified brambles behind where the maze had been. And in the middle were two forms.

Nora.

She was on her hands and knees, bloody and burned and covered in ash. She was clutching two of the metal leaves from that stupid golden tree in her hand. As Lotte got closer, she could see that she had carved symbols onto them. Crude makeshift charms to burn the maze and shield herself.

The other shape was what was left of the metal tree. It had warped and twisted in the heat into an ugly, gnarled ancient-looking thing. Branches melted so they drooped and dug into the ground. And gripped in its melted, gnarled fingers was a body.

It wasn't moving.

After that, all Lotte remembered was screaming. Clemency screaming her grief. Nora screaming accusations at Modesty. Modesty screaming her innocence. Screaming that it was Nora and her fire that had killed Constance.

Someone had loaded them all into automobiles. Got them past the cameras waiting outside and to the mansion.

AND THEN, JUST AS ABRUPTLY AS THEY WERE TAKEN, THE memories ended.

All of it, Lotte knew in the space of a blink. She withdrew her hand from the mirror as fast as she'd touched it. Unnoticed even as her grandmother flicked a finger, driving Nora and Modesty apart by magic.

"You will pull yourselves together *now*." Mercy Holtzfall's voice was raised. "You will tell the story I have told you. And you will trust that anything that I have done is for the good of this family. Like *everything* I do."

"Yes, Grandmama." But it was only Modesty who replied.

Clemency was still on the floor.

Lotte was choked with knowledge and anger.

Nora was the only other person in the room echoing Lotte's feelings.

Lotte reached for her cousin, but Nora's rage turned to action swiftly. And in a second she was gone.

Chapter 44
AUGUST

He sensed her before he saw her.

Like a snap of energy in the air before a lightning storm as she took the seat at the bar next to him.

"Are you going to offer to buy me a drink?" The rasp in Nora's voice drew his gaze up from the glass in his hand.

She was wearing her own face. No glamour, no disguise. She looked like Nora. Except not like he had ever seen her.

Her clothes were torn and singed. Her skin was riddled with bloody scratches. Her hair was caked in ash and grime.

And then there were her eyes.

All it took was one look at her for all of August's anger at her to evaporate.

He fought the impulse to reach for the bloody scratches across her face. "Nora . . ." One of the gouges was dangerously close to her eye. He clenched his fist on the bar. "What the hell happened to you?"

"I wish I knew." One of the cuts in Nora's hands had reopened, and August watched her wipe away the blood absently. "But I can tell you for sure it wasn't the Grims, no matter what the papers say tomorrow. And that it must be something terrible if my grandmother would rather give our enemies an invented victory than have us know the truth."

Just yesterday, she'd sworn up and down he'd never see her again. August had imagined her coming back. He'd practiced smug satisfaction and a smart comment for her when she did. But the only thing that he felt now was a deep pit of fear of whatever had done this to Nora.

"Fine, if you're not going to be a gentleman, I can get my own drink." Nora leaned over the bar, grabbing a bottle and a grimy-looking glass. The barman turned, a reproach on his lips that died the moment he caught sight of her. August waited as Nora uncorked the bottle and poured. Her hand shook, just for a second. He thought about reaching out, closing his hand around hers. But she steadied the lip of the bottle on the rim of the glass to hide her trembling.

"You didn't come a dozen circles out of your way for a cheap glass of whiskey," he said when she'd snapped the drink back.

"I had a thought." Nora poured herself a second glass.

August couldn't help himself. "You were bound to have one eventually."

Her mouth quirked up, a bit painfully. "There would be no Veritaz if my mother hadn't died."

"Insightful." August turned his glass thoughtfully against the bar. "You know, it reminds me of something I said days ago at the Veritaz Ceremony."

Standing in the garden on the first day they'd met, he'd told her that people besides the Grims had reasons to want her mother dead. People closer to her.

Finally, Nora looked up and said the last thing he expected to hear. "You were right. About my family."

Somehow he knew she didn't just mean about how the Heiress's death might benefit them. She meant about the fight they'd had on the river embankment. She meant about the accusations he had thrown at her about choosing to do nothing when she could do everything. She meant that she had been wrong. "I thought there were lines my family wouldn't cross. But my family did something terrible today that they don't want me to know about. I want the truth, no matter what it is. If it's Isengrim, then I will hunt him down. But if someone in my family killed my mother in order to trigger a new Veritaz and take the heirship . . . then I need to know."

Just hours ago, Mr. Vargene had made clear a story pointing fingers at the Grims for Verity's death would never see the light of day at the *Bullhorn*.

The murder of Verity Holtzfall was a story that might make August's name. He couldn't afford to be chasing unprintable stories. But the Heiress dying by the hand of another Holtzfall . . . August pushed his drink away. "Who are you accusing, exactly?"

"Aunt Patience," Nora said, not hesitating. "Uncle Prosper needs the money more, but he isn't smart enough. He's still at gambling tables every night, sure the next hand is going to pull him out of the hole. Aunt Patience, though . . . she gets things done. She pulled strings to get Modesty into the movies. And she's hated my mother since I can remember."

"What about Grace Holtzfall?"

"She hates Aunt Grace too," Nora said.

"No, I mean . . ." August tapped his fingers against the glass. Someone might go a long way to bring their exiled daughter back into the picture. To set her up to snatch back the victory that had eluded them seventeen years ago.

Nora was smart. She would be thinking the same thing. But she pressed her lips together. "Aunt Patience is more likely."

"And you're sure you're not just saying that because her daughter is currently winning the Veritaz?"

"Modesty will not be Heiress." Nora's eyes shot up, locking onto him so fast that for a second, August stopped breathing. And in that moment, for the first time, August saw all of her.

He had seen Nora, the girl who was brighter and funnier and more beautiful than anyone who saw her photograph from afar could possibly understand. But now she was showing him the dangerous side of Honora Holtzfall, unguarded.

The Honora Holtzfall he had first met . . . she wore diamonds and an unintimidating façade so that she didn't scare anyone.

But this Honora Holtzfall was pure power.

She was the intangible force that came from a family that had stood for centuries while kings and queens toppled around them. The heiress of two bloodlines that traced back centuries on either side. Deep into the roots of the enchanted woods and the blistering dunes of the desert. The power of someone whose blood overflowed with sheer magic.

Honora Holtzfall wasn't just a girl, she was a descendant of inventors, desert sultans, and honorable woodcutters. Of rulers and warriors and of survivors in a deadly game played generation after generation.

She pulled a paper napkin from over the bar, quickly scribbling a few words on it.

"This is the answer Oskar Wallen wanted. Who Lotte's father is."

The pull of the story was like a fishhook drawing August forward, back into Nora's game, but even he stopped at this. "You're sure you want to give him this?"

"I'm done being loyal to a family that has never been loyal to me. Give Oskar my message, and tell him a deal is a deal. I want the name of the cop who framed Lukas Schuld. And then you and I will be having a word with him."

PART V

FELICITY

Chapter 45

NORA

The Holtzfall family cemetery stood at the edge of the woods. Deep enough into the immense gardens that the mansion was no longer visible. The manicured lawns and carefully pruned rosebushes gave way to towering oaks and gnarled brambles. It felt right. To stand here amidst the wilder part of the garden, filled with wilder emotions.

Constance's body was wrapped in a shroud the color of new leaves, and lowered into the earth as the family watched. All of them wearing mourning clothes in Holtzfall green. As if they were unified.

Uncle Prosper and his wife stood like pillars of grief over their daughter's grave. Prosper was drunk, as always, but on a day like today, Nora couldn't hold it against him. Clemency, next to them, looked strangely out of place without her matched set.

Modesty clutched a green embroidered handkerchief to her face, dabbing at her eyes prettily. On the other side of the grave, Nora was aware of Lotte and Grace, even as she fought to avoid her cousin's gaze.

Nora had draped a gauzy forest-green veil over her head, held in place by a crown of green chrysanthemums. It fell down to her waist over a green velvet dress. She knew what the papers would say. That she was drawing attention to herself at someone else's funeral.

That she was hiding her lack of tears while Modesty wailed for the cameras.

And she was hiding. But not her lack of grief.

The gap in her memory yawned like a chasm, but the other side of it was clear. The naked hurt and accusation in Lotte's face as she realized that Nora had manipulated her. The accusation.

And the fact that it was all true.

That Lotte had seen her for who she really was at her worst.

Well, the damage was done now. Since Lotte already despised her for it, she might as well actually do it.

Oskar Wallen could blackmail her grandmother all he wanted. He would threaten to smear Grace's name in the papers, no doubt. Because he wouldn't know how valuable Lotte's parentage actually was. Why there had never been a child of a Holtzfall and Rydder before.

Barely anyone knew. That Lotte's mere existence could end the centuries-old alliance between the Rydders and the Holtzfalls.

Two gravediggers placed a sapling over Constance. It had been planted the day she was born, as was done for all of them. It was the same age she was to the day. Over time, its roots would grow deep and wrap themselves around the body, as trees had for generation upon generation of Holtzfalls before her.

Another newly planted tree set a few feet back marked Nora's mother's body. Tiny sprigs of new green growth had already started to spring up in the few short weeks since they'd last stood here, burying Verity Holtzfall. Behind that, Nora's grandfather's tree stood a few feet taller. And behind that was the uncle she had never met, Valor Holtzfall, dead in his own trials. They went back and back, taller for every generation before, until the tallest among them blended into the edge of the ancient woods.

Distantly, Nora became aware that her grandmother had stopped speaking. The weighty silence that followed was gradually filled with the sound of shuffling feet as the Holtzfalls began to make their way to the house.

The headlines had run this morning.

Innocent Heiress Brutally Killed
by Savage Grims!

Constance Holtzfall Slain
in Final Act of Virtue!

Killing Our Children!
Isengrim Must Be Stopped!

It occurred to Nora that if the Grims *actually* wanted to attack them, this would be the time. With every Holtzfall in the same place. No doubt that was why everywhere Nora looked, there was a knight. They flanked them like a military formation as they moved back toward the house for the wake. Behind them, the two gravediggers worked in tandem silence, covering over Constance's body.

Nora had skipped her own mother's wake. She hadn't wanted to listen to them all whisper about the passing of the heirship. She had stayed by the graveside.

Theo beside her, long after everyone else was gone.

But this was probably exactly what it had been like. Tiny canapés and champagne and gawkers from the outskirts of the family swarming around one of the Holtzfalls' many receiving rooms.

"Is that really *you*?" Freddie Loetze was suddenly there, offering Nora a champagne he was holding. "Or did you send a double in your place under that veil?"

Nora ignored the champagne and the temptation to throw it in his face again. But before she could make her escape, she caught sight of the rolled-up newspaper sticking out of his pocket, with her face on it. She grabbed it, moving out of the way before Freddie could snatch it back.

Constance Holtzfall KILLED
by LAO Bomb!

The headline was pointed. And the article below stopped just short of accusing Leyla and Nora of conspiring in Constance's murder. How, it exclaimed, had the Grims got into LAO if not with help from someone in the know? Who would want to kill poor innocent Constance Holtzfall, other than a rival, jealous heiress? And everyone had seen Honora Holtzfall question the new governor about the Grims that afternoon before the attack.

"Modesty." Nora closed the gap between herself and her cousin. Modesty was perched on a settee. She had dropped the act now and was laughing into a fizzing coupe of champagne surrounded by other 1st-circle cohorts. She tossed the paper on her cousin's lap. "I saw the most flattering pair of silk gloves in Muirhaus the other day. I should buy them for you. It would prevent you from leaving your fingerprints all over things like this."

"That's so thoughtful," Modesty simpered, pressing her fingers to her chin to show off her rings. "But I am simply *loath* to hide my favorite pieces of jewelry. Perhaps you should get them yourself, since you have nothing to hide."

Even if Nora could prove that false insinuation had come from Modesty, proof didn't matter in the circles they ran in. Nor did it to the public of Walstad. Perception did. Nora couldn't retaliate either. That would only look like petty jealousy over her cousin having two rings to Nora's zero.

There would be another trial.

If Nora were a patient person, she would have waited. She would have waited for another chance to prove that she was worthy. She would have waited for August to come to her with an answer from Oskar Wallen as to whether this twisted branch of her family had plotted her mother's death.

There were a hundred things she would have done if she were a patient person.

"Fine then, a duel, for the truth." If the gloves were off, then they were off. And she had the needling satisfaction of watching Modesty's face drop at the challenge. "Tonight, at the Clandestine Court."

Chapter 46

LOTTE

Lotte wondered if, deep down, Modesty suspected what she had done.

Modesty's graveside weeping was gone, replaced with insouciance as she perched on a settee, a green tulle skirt spread out below her, as if this were just another party. Not the funeral of someone she had killed.

She must know what she was capable of. She had done it so easily.

Lotte had made a mistake thinking that she and Modesty were using each other equally. Modesty had been playing her own game, trying to push Lotte out of the family. Trying to destroy Nora. She saw it now, how she had slid inside Lotte's mind. Planting an insidious seed that had grown there.

Lotte had spent her whole life with other people's thoughts intruding on her mind. But she hadn't mistaken any of them for her own thoughts. It had felt so desperate and so urgent, her need to find her father. But now she had no idea whether she'd ever truly cared or if that was Modesty's influence. And it made it hard to untangle how she felt now, knowing the truth.

Knowing that her father was a Rydder knight. That there was nowhere to turn for another life if she lost the Veritaz Trials.

Lotte had felt out of place in the Holtzfalls' world. Today more than ever as her family mourned a cousin she had only known for a few days. They shared a past with Constance that didn't include Lotte. She didn't have any stories to share. Or any grief to offer.

But she couldn't imagine herself among the Rydders either. Holding a sword, defending the lives of the Holtzfalls. Would that be what happened to her if she lost the trials? Would she be sent to train with Theo, be expected to die for Modesty and Nora and Clemency?

From the corner of the wake, Lotte found herself watching Benedict stand at her mother's shoulder. Hunting again for some resemblance between them.

The moment Nora had shown her the reflection of Liselotte Rydder dropping blood on the charm, Lotte had known. If a knight was her father, then it was Benedict. Benedict with his missing memories. Benedict sent to guard Grace while she hid her pregnancy in a convent. Benedict, who everyone said had been meant to protect the next Heiress, but stayed firmly by Grace's side years after she lost.

Did he suspect? Lotte wondered. That desperate surge of protectiveness she had felt when she first met him. She had thought then it was duty and oath. But maybe distantly, he remembered.

"You want to *duel?*" Modesty's loud scoff drew Lotte's attention from the other side of the room. "Over a *headline.*"

"Well, you know me." Nora was all haughty anger. "I'm a great proponent of truth in the press."

Nora had been avoiding Lotte all morning. The last thing she would remember was her betrayal coming to light. She wouldn't remember that Lotte had forgiven her. Or that the factory break-in splashed all over the headlines had been Theo's doing in a desperate bid to keep his oath. There would be time to tell her, after the funeral, Lotte thought. But now this was all about to go too far. Whether Nora wanted to listen or not, if she was planning on picking a fight with Modesty, she needed to know how dangerous their cousin really was.

Lotte moved toward Nora, but a servant cut across her path. "Miss Ottoline."

Lotte recognized her. It was Abigail, the maid who had taken Lotte under her wing when she had snuck into the mansion disguised as a servant. But the brief moment of gladness to see her faded fast as Abigail kept her eyes on her feet, her head bowed. Lotte was a Holtzfall now, not a fellow servant.

"Miss Ottoline, your grandmother has summoned you."

"Why?" Lotte's stomach dropped in fear, Nora and Modesty's squabble forgotten. Her grandmother must know that Lotte had read the memorandum charm. There was no other reason she would call on Lotte alone.

Abigail kept her head bowed. "Follow me, please."

Lotte dreaded walking down that portrait-lined hallway again. Generation upon generation of Holtzfalls sneering at the rogue branch in need of trimming from their family tree.

But instead, Abigail led her out of the house. Back through the gardens toward the distant corner where they had held the funeral. Past Constance's fresh grave, deeper into the trees that each marked the body of a Holtzfall being returned to the earth. Until the trees towered over them. The portraits weren't enough, apparently. Her grandmother wanted her to walk through the ancient grave markers of her family.

But when they reached the edge of the woods, it wasn't Mercy Holtzfall waiting for Lotte.

Two men stood in plain clothing.

One was about Lotte's age, the other had a graying beard and weary face. He was leaning on a shovel. It was only then that Lotte managed to place them.

The gravediggers from Constance's funeral.

A grin spread across the young gravedigger's face. And Lotte's heart kicked up in fear. These men hadn't come to dig Constance's grave.

But before Lotte could turn and run, the younger gravedigger was on her, pinning her against the nearest tree, twisting her arm hard enough to make Lotte cry out. "Quiet," he snapped. "Or we'll cut your tongue out too."

Behind him, the other gravedigger peeled himself off the shovel with the weariness of a man who'd had a long day at the job and just wanted to get this done. "What did we agree, a thousand?"

Abigail wouldn't meet Lotte's eyes as the older gravedigger counted out a thick wad of bills.

"Abigail." Lotte gasped out the other girl's name, ignoring the order to stay silent. She could tell by the thoughts leaking through the press of his hands against her that cutting out her tongue was an empty threat. Not because he didn't have the stomach, but because he didn't have the time. "Why are you doing this?" The young gravedigger jerked her back against the tree hard, but it was enough. Enough to draw Abigail's guilty gaze off the ground, even as she took the wad of bills.

"Edmund." The name came out small and choked. Edmund Rydder, the young knight who had been sent to guard her more than once. The one who tended to look bored while his sister, Hildegarde, jabbed him in the ribs to stand at attention. "I can't let him die in service to your family." Abigail desperately clutched the money to her chest. "I'm sorry, but we have to run before it's too late."

With that, Abigail was gone, vanishing back through the graveyard to the house, leaving Lotte alone with two men at the edge of the woods.

"All right, Miss Holtzfall." The old gravedigger rubbed his hand along his beard, then paused. "Or should I call you Miss Rydder?"

They knew.

They knew that her father was a knight.

Nora had sold her out after all.

He shrugged as if it didn't matter what her name was. "We should get started." And with the same weary efficiency, he drew a knife.

Chapter 47

AUGUST

There were many reasons that Oskar Wallen hadn't been arrested yet.

One of them was that there was no finding him unless he wanted to be found. But there were always ways to get a message to him. It hadn't quite been dawn when August had finally loaded Nora into the back of a taxi and watched her drive away. Back to her world.

While he went to work in his.

Luckily bakers started their work early. And Madleen Mendler was no exception. She had turned tricks when she was younger. Then Oskar Wallen had come along and she'd started killing men for him. It paid better, enough that she'd retired a few years ago. Became a baker. She was the only person in the city Oskar trusted to make him food he was sure wouldn't be poisoned.

She took the folded-up bar napkin and promised she'd hand it over with his morning's batch of rolls.

August didn't even remember getting home, but it was afternoon when he woke. Apparently he was keeping Holtzfall hours now.

Oskar, ever the gentleman, had replied to August's bar napkin via a cloth serviette. A nice one too, made of thick white cotton and a monogrammed *OW*.

On it was written simply:

Officer Eugene Knapp. 2146 Garden Street, Apartment 1309.
He has the ring.

Finally, they had it. The name of the cop they had seen in the photograph taking jewelry from Verity Holtzfall's body.

August attached the name and address to the emissary bird Nora had repaired the day they met. They were so close now. So close to answers. So close to the story. He made his way to the address to wait for her.

Garden Street turned out to be full of dull gray bricked buildings in an ugly newly built-up part of the city. Too far downtown to have any wealth, not far enough to be actually interesting. August lingered under the awning of the neighboring cobbler's, keeping an eye on the door since there was nothing else interesting to look at.

There was a newspaper stand across the street.

Constance Holtzfall was dead. Nearly every headline was pinning it on the Grims, just like Nora had said they would. She'd be buried today. August knew his message might not reach Nora before the funeral.

But it would reach her. They didn't need to speak to the officer today. They'd waited this long. He could wait until Nora was done mourning with her family.

Suddenly the door to the gray apartment building swung open, a man wrapped up in a trench coat against the rain emerging in a hurry. In a split second, August made his decision. He wasn't going to wait. Mr. Vargene had given them until tomorrow to come up with something that kept them employed. He needed to know now. Today. He lunged, catching the door before it could slam shut behind the man and quickly slipping inside.

Shaking off the rain, he scanned the mailboxes quickly in the entranceway.

E. Knapp, Apartment 1309.

Of course, in a building with no elevator.

Thirteen flights of stairs later, August arrived, out of breath, in the narrow hallway. He paused, unsure whether the rate his heart was racing was from the climb or the anticipation. He'd changed his mind about how he'd approach the man with every floor. If he ought to confront him outright or try to trip him into a confession.

Instead of magimek lightbulbs, the hallway bore the remnants of disabled gaslights lining the walls. Those had been made illegal about two decades ago. They said they were a fire risk, but everyone knew the governor at the time had been under duress from Leyla Al-Oman and her new magic-fueled lights. Passing a law that made the whole city use magimek lights meant more money in LAO and Holtzfall pockets.

The only source of light was coming from an open door, halfway down the hall.

August moved toward it carefully.

He was close enough now to hear music from a vox through the door that was ajar. Some singer August's mother loved crooning about her broken heart because her love had taken a ship across the sea. Her lilting tones eerily filled the quiet hallway, even as August reached out a hand, pushing the door fully open.

The first thing he saw was an overturned table. A cup smashed on the ground next to it. He knew then what he was about to find. But he couldn't stop. He had to see to be sure.

The door squealed treacherously as he pushed it fully open, unveiling the rest of the small apartment. It was cramped and miserable, even by August's standards. A ragged couch was crammed into a corner. A rug had been used to try to give the room a little bit of warmth but without much success. The kitchen cupboards were a garish peeling teal color. A kettle steamed on the counter, and the vox hummed gently, the crooning singer now giving way to a news bulletin. And in the middle of the room, Officer Eugene Knapp's body was sprawled across the floor.

Blood was still pooling beneath him.

He had been dead minutes, not hours.

Not dead. August processed. Murdered.

The sound of a door slamming somewhere else in the gargantuan building crashed through the ringing in August's ears, which was doing its best to drown out any coherent thought. A neighbor, probably, heading out on errands, who was about to discover the same thing August just had.

August forced himself to turn away from the body, fighting a wave of nausea. He couldn't be caught at a crime scene. He forced himself to walk at a normal pace back down the hallway. Back down thirteen flights of stairs. To not hide his face and break into a sprint as he passed a woman lugging groceries up the stairs.

Somewhere around the sixth floor, his thoughts began to catch up to him.

The ring. He should've looked for the ring. Looked for evidence. Or at least if it was a theft. If Oskar knew that this cop had a ring worth a few million, other people must know too. It would be easy to chalk it up to a theft. But August had seen too much to believe in coincidences. The timing. Who else could have intercepted Oskar Wallen's note to August? Was it someone on Oskar's side? Or was this August's doing? The note he'd sent Nora . . . What if she wasn't here because it had never made it to her? On a day like today, when her whole family was gathering for a funeral, any one of them could have intercepted his emissary. And if one of them was behind the murder and the setup—

It seemed like an eternity before he made it to the ground floor. Until at last, he was pushing the door open sharply and walking out onto the street.

And he stepped straight into a uniformed body. The police officer staggered back, the normal *Excuse me, didn't see you there* forming on his lips even as August prepared to say the same platitudes back. And then the officer's face changed as he glanced down, his brow creasing.

August followed his gaze.

Suddenly noticing there was blood on his shoes.

Chapter 48

LOTTE

The gravedigger's grip on her wrist was gentle for a killer. And he *was* a killer.

She knew that the moment his fingers touched her skin. The first girl he'd killed looked a bit like Lotte. Although that had been so long ago, he sometimes thought all the girls he killed looked like that one. She'd been one of his old boss's girlfriends who'd been making too much noise about what he was doing. She'd screamed so much when they came for her, he remembered thinking it was no wonder they had to kill her to keep her quiet.

But he wasn't here to kill her. He was here for another purpose that slipped in and out of focus in his mind too fast for Lotte to catch.

He had a new boss now, one who knew better than to mess around with noisy girls. Lotte caught a flash of expensive clothes and well-groomed hair, and the edge of a name that he tried not to look too hard at.

There was neither joy nor regret when he thought about the girls he'd killed. Just the deep pragmatism of a man who knew what his job was.

The knife in his hand sliced deep into Lotte's palm, making her cry out in pain.

"I said not to scream." The other gravedigger wrenched her tighter in his grip, his voice low and angry in her ear. The thoughts that poured off him were a world away from that of the older gravedigger.

Where the older man was slow and ponderous, the one holding her was a violent shock of jittery thoughts popping through his mind frantically like a photographer's flashbulbs.

Lotte grabbed on to one. *This has to work.* Lotte tried to draw the thread out further, to understand what they were doing here. But his mind had already skipped on. He liked his job. He was good at it. At killing people for money. But he had big dreams. He wanted to change the world, like Isengrim was always banging on about. And if he got this right—Lotte's grip closed over the thought more tightly this time—if this rich girl's blood could really break the bond between the Rydders and the Holtzfalls, then that would be a victory. There would be no knights to protect Modesty Holtzfall tonight when the Grims came for her.

"You can't blame her for a bit of noise. I heard you killing that girl on Market Street." The older gravedigger was as casual as if they were chatting over a drink at the bar. "You were cursing up a storm."

"That wasn't my fault," the younger gravedigger muttered. "She wouldn't stay still, slippery little eel, cut her ear off by accident."

Lotte could feel her hand tensing as blood welled in her palm. The older gravedigger drew her arm straight out ahead of her. They were at the very edge of the woods. And as he stuck her hand out straight, Lotte's fingers extended into the darkened line of the trees. The gravedigger turned her hand over, the blood from the slash dripping down, hitting the moss at the edge of the woods.

The Holtzfall gardens were all perfectly manicured grass lawns. Even around the graves. But at the border of the trees, the ground turned wild. Moss and stones and wildflowers spread backward into the shadow of the woods. Staining red now as Lotte's blood fell.

The men waited, watching. They seemed to be waiting for something she couldn't quite grasp in their minds. Possibly because they didn't seem to wholly know either.

Her blood. They were to spill her blood in the woods. If they did that, it would free the knights from their oath.

"Is that it?" the younger one asked. "Shouldn't there be a flash of light or a declaration from some woodland geezer or something?"

This was because of her parentage. She could read that much in the jumbled minds of the two men holding her. She didn't pretend to understand exactly what that meant or how that was supposed to free the knights, but that was why they were here. Because she was a Holtzfall and a Rydder at once. And something about her blood was important.

The older one didn't answer, but his mind was working. Grinding slowly with thought. The boss had said they had to spill her blood in the woods to break the bond. He'd figured that just meant a little cut. But maybe they were supposed to slit her throat.

The younger one was thinking the same. This was the first job he'd ever been good at, and he didn't want to lose it. He wondered if his mother would be proud of him.

"She wouldn't be proud." Lotte's voice came out strained against the knife as she saw her chance. "Your mother would hate what you're doing."

The young gravedigger jerked against Lotte violently, but he didn't loosen his grip. Not yet. But now Lotte had the edge of the thought, and she pulled on the string, trying to keep her own mind steady even as fear consumed her.

"Your mother would *never* have hurt a fly, you know that." She had to keep them talking, buy some time. Someone was bound to notice she was gone eventually. "She was always worried about you making your way in the world because you were never as gifted as your sister at school. But just because you couldn't read well or do sums, that doesn't mean she wanted you to become a killer."

"You're speaking to the dead." This time he staggered away from her, his face blanched, breaking the connection.

Lotte saw her chance, wrenching free from the older gravedigger, the blood that now coated her hand making her arm slick as it slid out of his grip. She was free. She moved to run even as the older gravedigger lunged after her.

Lotte turned, her hand meeting his chest, shoving him back, just as her blood activated one of the charms on her hand. The charm that was supposed to open doors. The gravedigger was blown back with the same force that she had blown the door off its hinges at the law office. A curse slipped out of his mouth as he slammed into a tree at the edge of the woods.

Lotte turned again, but the younger one was standing in her path. He still looked scared, but he was standing his ground. Her thoughts were racing, wondering if she had any other charms that might do her any good.

"You won't make it very far, little heiress." As she looked back toward the woods, the gravedigger was pulling himself up wearily. And then she saw it, behind him, from the darkness in between the trees. Something was moving.

At first it seemed formless, like a trick of the light moving through the branches. But then it resolved into a hand. Though not a hand like any Lotte had ever seen. The fingers were impossibly long, jointed in six places and pale like the bark of a birch tree.

The fingers closed around the older gravedigger's collar, wrenching him back so swiftly into the trees that he didn't even have time to scream.

At first.

The screaming came a second later. Deep, guttural cries from the dark of the wood. They reminded Lotte of the girl's screams in his memory. The girl who looked like her.

When Lotte turned back, the young gravedigger's face was slack with horror, the knife in his hand dangling loose.

And then he ran for his life.

Lotte stood, shaking, dripping blood on the pristine grass.

She found herself waiting, like they'd said. For a flash of light. For an immortal being to step out and make some grand declaration. That her blood had split the Rydder knights from their oath somehow. But nothing happened.

Lotte's mind spun, trying to make sense of everything. But amidst it all, she had one clear thought, plucked from the mind of the younger gravedigger: The Grims were going after Modesty. Tonight.

Thee Rydder knights had been on high alert all day.

The Grims were armed now.

Because of Theo. Because Theo had granted them a way into LAO. The guilt of that had etched itself into every muscle and bone in his body. But the papers were lying, he was sure of that. Whatever had happened to Constance Holtzfall, the Grims weren't behind it. The Grims had still been loading weapons out of LAO when she had died.

And yet, still knowing that, the guilt wouldn't leave him.

Finally, with dusk drawing in, the Holtzfalls were starting to dissipate, returning to their own corners of the city. That was when Benedict found Theo.

"Lotte," he said without preamble. "Where is she?"

The question caught Theo off guard. "I wasn't assigned to guard Ottoline—"

"I've seen you." Benedict cut him off impatiently. "Both of you around each other. I'm not blind, Theodric, and you're not the first knight to look at a Holtzfall like that, no matter what you might think. Now, do you know where she is?"

Theo had no reply for that. But he wouldn't do Benedict the disservice of lying to him. "I'll search the gardens" was all he said, folding himself back into duty, the way he had been taught to his whole life. "Someone should search the house."

"It will destroy you, you know." Benedict paused, heading back toward the house. "Being that close to her and knowing that any closer will be the end of you. It will tear you apart in ways you don't yet understand."

THEO HADN'T MADE IT FAR WHEN HE CAUGHT SIGHT OF TWO figures moving swiftly in the dusk. For just a second, his hand dropped to his sword. Something in the urgency of the way they moved set him on edge. And then they dashed by the windows of the house, the light catching them.

"Edmund."

Edmund Rydder had never had a knight's instincts, but at the sound of his name, he moved instantly, shielding the girl with him. A maid with curly hair tucked away under her cap, carrying what looked like a swiftly packed bag, a terrified look in her eyes.

Edmund took a breath, but the obvious lie seemed to deflate before he could speak it. "I'm making a break for it, and you should too, before it all goes down tonight."

Theo had always known that Edmund wasn't a natural knight. No matter that he was a Rydder by blood. But he hadn't thought he was a fool either.

"Edmund," Theo warned, his hand opening and closing on his sword. "If you run, you're sealing your death. Both of your deaths." The girl in maid's uniform, who Theo thought might be named Abigail, stood defiantly behind him, clutching her belongings. "Just like every knight before you who has run."

"Yes, but the difference is all of them were oathbound." Edmund moved forward into the light, his eyes bright with zeal. "And we're not anymore." He clasped Theo's arm frantically. "It's over. Can't you feel it?"

Theo felt the same as he always had. But Edmund was too far gone. Theo grabbed Edmund's shoulder. Steadying him, trying to make him make sense. "What do you mean we're not oathbound?"

"Ottoline," Edmund said fervently. "She's one of us *and* one of them. Her blood is the key—once it's spilled, our oath is broken."

Theo thought of the glass charm Lotte had clutched in her hand. But there would be time to make sense of that later. Now Theo's fingers tightened around Edmund's arm. "Edmund, where is she?"

"It doesn't matter! The Holtzfalls have no more hold on us. You don't need to save them. Our oath is broken! You don't have to fight for them, you don't have to die for them!"

"We have to go." Abigail's fingers laced with Edmund's. "Before it's too late. Please." Her eyes were pleading. "Let us go."

By my oath. The ancient promise that bound them all echoed through Theo. But his oath wasn't to keep the other knights to their duty. He only had one oath to keep. "Tell me where Lotte is and I won't stand in your way."

Abigail pressed her lips together for a moment. "The edge of the woods. By Honor Holtzfall's burial tree."

Theo was already running back across the garden, back to where the funeral had been held, and past it. He called out her name, but there was no answer. At the edge of the woods, he found blood staining the grass, still drying, along with a discarded knife and two shovels.

Theo felt his stomach twist, but if she was dead, they would have left her here. No killer would make it out of here carrying a body.

Theo raced back toward the house, ready to sound the alarm. But the moment the barracks came into view, Theo knew something had shifted. Knights were amassing in a circle, tension obvious in them. And as Theo got closer, he saw that Edmund hadn't made it far. Benedict had Edmund pinned to the side of the barracks as Commander Lis looked on. Two knights were holding Abigail back.

"He tried to come get his sister," Theo heard another knight saying as he drew closer. "He was a fool to think Hilde would ever leave with him."

Edmund's voice was raised. "Run! All of you! Run now before they find another way to enslave us. Before you die fighting the Grims tonight."

"Edmund," Commander Lis addressed him, "if you have knowledge of the Grims' plans, I command you to tell me now."

Edmund seemed deaf to her. "Run while the oath has no more hold on you!"

"You believe you're free of Hartwin Rydder's oath?" Mercy Holtzfall cut across Edmund's ravings like a knife. The Holtzfall matriarch stood behind them.

The knights parted dutifully for Mercy Holtzfall as she moved forward. She flicked her hand, an order for Benedict to release him. Benedict stepped back.

Instantly, Edmund drew his sword.

Several knights' grips flew to their own blades, but Mercy Holtzfall held up her hand. There was an eerie stillness to her before she spoke. "As ax bearer of the line of Honor Holtzfall"—Mercy Holtzfall's words bore the weight of an order—"I order you, Edmund Rydder, descendant of Hartwin Rydder"—Theo waited for her to order him to drop his weapon—"to drive your sword through the chest of your young lover." Theo saw it on Edmund's face, the moment the order closed its hand over his heart.

"I won't!" he called out defiantly. "The oath is broken! I won't!" But he was moving already, grip on his sword shifting as he turned toward Abigail.

The young maid didn't flinch. "He won't hurt me." She didn't run, she didn't try to shield herself. She was defiant in her certainty. Even as Edmund moved toward her, a twisted, pained look on his face.

Theo moved before he could think better of it. He was between Edmund and Abigail in a heartbeat. The sword driving toward her crashing against Theo's blade as he parried. He drove Edmund back easily. The boy had never been much of a swordsman, but he was still bound by their oath.

"Theodric," Commander Lis barked. "Stand down."

Theo moved his sword from one hand to the other, keeping his eyes on Edmund as the oath forced him back up from the ground, sword still in hand.

Mercy Holtzfall was silent, even as Edmund drove forward again, and Theo fought him back again. Unless he was ordered to, Theo couldn't stand by and watch this. He couldn't see Edmund punished like this. He couldn't watch the young maid die.

Treason should cost a knight his life, not anyone else's.

He caught sight of Abigail staring, face drawn and pale, incomprehension written all over it. He saw there that she'd truly believed they would escape. That whatever she had done to Lotte would break Edmund free of his oath.

And now his oath was forcing him to kill her.

Edmund got to his feet again, and his eyes met Theo's. "You have to stop me." His voice was loud enough for all the knights to hear. To understand.

He wanted Theo to kill him. Before he could follow Mercy's order. Before he broke past him and the blade went through Abigail's body.

No. There was another way. Theo parried again as Edmund lunged toward him, knocking him back again. He could keep Edmund back, protect Abigail without killing him.

But Theo would tire. And the oath would still be driving Edmund forward.

Edmund had never been willing to die for the Holtzfalls. But he was willing to die for Abigail.

The blade sprouted through Edmund's chest so suddenly that Theo drew back. A stifled cry that sounded like Hilde came from the crowd even as Abigail's screech split the air. Edmund's eyes widened in shock, but there was relief there for just a moment.

Before his face went slack.

When he fell to the ground, Commander Liselotte Rydder stood behind him with a blade in her hand, streaked in Rydder blood.

"There is no time for this." Her voice carried command through the silent shock of the assembled knights. She wiped her blade clean, as if killing one of their own was nothing to her. "If the Grims are coming, we need to be fighting them, not wasting time on traitors. Now, all of you, arm yourselves and get ready for battle."

Chapter 50
NORA

Dueling had been outlawed three centuries ago in Walstad. But in the days when humans lived among magic in the woods, they were the usual way to resolve a dispute. Back when people believed that the powerful immortal beings were never far and were always watching. And that they would guide the hand of the person in the right, to defeat the liar.

First it meant dueling with swords. Then magic.

Now they had courts of law to resolve disputes instead.

But for the 1st circle, "illegal" was really only a suggestion.

When Nora entered the Clandestine Court, it was already overflowing with the rich, young, and bored. Champagne bottles floated through the air, serving drinks to anyone with an empty glass. Sig Gossberg tipped his head back and let the bottle pour directly into his mouth as his table clapped and cheered. Freddie Loetze was in the middle of a glass of whiskey and a game of cards with two of the Bamberg brothers. He was reclined, lazily flicking chips forward with the charmed ring on his fingers so he didn't have to sit up. Onstage, a tall man puppeteered a woman with strings made of glowing magic. Modesty had changed out of her mourning clothes into an extravagant but uninspired silver evening gown. To anyone else, she might look at ease.

The Clandestine Court screamed jarringly with laughter as a

band of floating instruments played themselves off to one side, creating a raucous cacophony.

There were several blind bars dotted around the city, but this was the city's most well-hidden one. Anything that happened here remained invisible from the masses. The building was concealed from interlopers by money and influence and just a bit of magic. From the street, the entrance to the Clandestine Court looked like a dilapidated theater, with burned-out lights above the marquee and boarded-up doors. No one but the select few of the 1st circle knew it existed, let alone where it was.

Nora cut through the tables and the revelers, aware of the rustle that followed her even as she moved like a knife toward her purpose. She ascended the steps toward the stage, the performers quickly scrambling out of her way as she took the stage and turned to the crowd.

"Cousin," Nora announced loudly, as the music dimmed. "You promised me a duel."

The ripple that went through the crowd was immediate. Duels at the Clandestine Court were usually over something trivial. A spilled drink. An accusation of cheating at cards. Just another way for them to pass the time and spend their near-bottomless supply of magic.

But Nora was challenging Modesty for her reputation. She might not believe the immortals were watching, but she did believe that she had the ability to grind her cousin into the ground until she was revealed as a liar.

Modesty hesitated at her table, surrounded by her gaggle of hangers-on. That had been Nora once, surrounded by people clawing for a bite of the power.

She had been the Holtzfall Heiress then. And she would be again.

"Oh, come on, Modesty, don't be coy. Let's not waste our time pretending you don't crave the attention."

An unstifled laugh and a few jeers rolled through the crowd. It didn't leave Modesty much choice.

She put down her drink, and the jeers turned to whoops of anticipation as she moved to join Nora on the stage. She waved at the audience like she was at the opening of one of her pathetic pictures. But up close, Nora could see Modesty's perpetual ingenue grin was strained.

"Cousin." Modesty laughed loudly for the benefit of the crowd. "Really, all of this over some *silly* headlines . . ." She trailed off, leaving room for Nora to jab back. She wanted her to play along. She wanted to feed the people watching them some friendly cousinly rivalry.

She wanted grace. Nora had none to give.

By the time she was done with her, Modesty would confess to planting that story.

Ann Stoff, of the Stoff textile fortune, began an excited countdown from the front row. "Ready!"

Slowly, Nora began to pull off her perfectly fitted doeskin glove one finger at a time.

"Set!"

She had reached the last finger now.

"Go!"

The glove was off, and Nora flung it high into the air, drawing Modesty's eye, magic sparking off the charm on her wrist as it went. It transformed into a dove flapping violently toward Modesty's face, disrupting whatever charm she'd been preparing, before turning back into a glove that simply flopped onto her head. The crowd burst into uproarious laughter.

Nora didn't waste time reveling in it.

She already had her next charm lined up. A quick twist of her hand sparked the ring there and turned the floor below Modesty soft, sending her staggering to her knees. And suddenly the glove that

Nora had sent was slipping from Modesty's head and wrapping itself around her neck.

It squeezed, cutting off her air as effectively as if there were a hand inside.

Modesty's eyes went wide, her fingers dashing up to the glove. No doubt there were charms across her hands that would detach it. But in her panic, all her cousin seemed able to do was scratch at it like a charmless peasant.

Nora stepped forward calmly. "Are you ready to confess?"

Nora snapped her fingers and released the charm, the glove falling to the stage. Modesty doubled over, gasping.

"Are you really going to kill me?" Modesty spoke in a low voice, for Nora's ears only. "In front of all these people?"

The accusation reeled Nora's last charm back in, knocking back some of her anger. "You actually think I *would* kill you?" Even in her darkest thoughts, she had never considered actually hurting her cousin. But Modesty had. She saw it in Modesty's face. Modesty really would kill *her*. Not just that, she *wanted* to kill her.

That was what had happened in the maze.

Nora saw it suddenly, so clearly that she couldn't believe it was only occurring to her now.

Modesty had tried to kill her. The scratches and burns all over Nora's body, so much worse than anyone else's. Constance's body as collateral damage.

That was the only real answer to why Mercy Holtzfall would take their memories. Because it protected Modesty. The current front-runner for the heirship.

"Stop!" The voice from the crowd drew Nora's gaze. Lotte was moving through the tables, and Nora just had time to take in the blood drying down her cousin's arm. "You need to get out!" Lotte was shouting. "The Grims are coming. Everyone needs to—"

The burst of air hit Nora in the chest, knocking her back as

Modesty took advantage of Nora's temporary distraction. Nora hit the side wall of the stage, her spine connecting painfully. But she had already turned her attention back to the charms on her hands, pulling up a shielding charm as Modesty approached.

That was what saved her when the wall behind them exploded.

The room was filled with dust, and the explosion rang in Lotte's ears, drowning out anything else.

The back wall of the Clandestine Court was gone, and people with wolf masks were flooding in, the sleek charmed weapons they had pillaged from LAO drawn as they climbed through the debris and the rubble.

Silent shots went off, the metallic spark of magic filling the air as the Grims fired into the crowd. Mere feet away, a shot hit a girl square in the chest. Lotte watched the effects of the charm spread from her sternum to the ends of her fingers, stopping her in her tracks, a scream caught in her throat.

An immobility charm. Like the ones she'd seen the cops use to break up the Grims' protests. But instead of just immobilizing the girl, her fingers turned gray, the color spreading through her whole body as she turned to stone. A statue of a screaming girl.

Lotte's ears cleared, and now she could hear the screaming. Shot after shot, struck around the room, cries of pain rising to meet them.

The Clandestine Court had devolved into chaos, bottles and tables and glasses smashing to the floor. Ballgown- and tuxedo-clad figures pushed for escape into the street while their enemy poured in around them.

Lotte ducked down, taking cover under the lip of the stage where

Nora and Modesty crouched, hidden even as the Grims swarmed over them.

"We have to get out of here." Modesty's voice was spiked with panic.

"We have to get everyone out," Nora replied. She was already wrenching the brooch off her chest. The shielding charm she wore. Lotte had learned to recognize the bitter crackle of pouring too much magic into a charm. It tasted like burning metal in the air as Nora forced the charm past the limits of its intended use. It was meant to protect one person, and Nora was stretching it to protect everyone. Everyone who was left, everyone who was still scrambling. All of a sudden, a wall of invisible force sprang up in the Grims' path, blocking the wolves off from their 1st-circle prey.

"Go," Nora said, her voice strained.

Modesty didn't need to be told twice. She was on her feet, joining the rest of the 1st circle in a mad scramble for the door, through overturned tables and the statues of people caught by the charms.

Lotte didn't move.

"Go," Nora said again, and she could hear the strain in her voice. "Someone has to stay behind to hold the charm, but—"

"No," Lotte said simply. There was still blood on her hand from where the gravedigger had sliced her palm open. She closed it over the charm in Nora's palm, flooding it with the magic from her blood.

In a split second of contact, Lotte's mind was engulfed with Nora's thoughts, so fast and urgent that she could barely capture one, until the surprised realization rose to the top. Lotte really was staying. The rush of loyalty, of surprise and gratitude, almost overwhelmed Lotte. And Lotte felt the same rise in her chest in answer.

They stayed like that in the chaos of the room as the Grims hammered and raged against the shield. Lotte was aware of some of the Grims turning back, going the way they came, pursuing their quarry through some other path. But she couldn't worry about that now.

She could feel the charm in between their palms growing hot. Overheating as they pushed the magical circuitry far past its limits. They were not going to be able to hold this forever. Maybe not even long enough for help to come.

Looking down, Lotte saw a crack forming across the pattern etched in the gold between her bloody fingers.

"You should run now," Nora said quietly. The Clandestine Court was almost empty, and from the corner of her eye, Lotte was aware of the Grims coalescing on the other side of the shield. "I can hold it long enough for that."

Lotte looked up, her eyes meeting Nora's. But it wasn't sacrifice she saw there; it was intelligence. "You have a plan," Lotte said.

"I have an idea." The Grims were waiting for them to falter. "It's a few pieces short of a plan at the moment."

"Then let me hold them off," Lotte said. Nora hesitated. Lotte took a breath, ready to tell Nora that she could manage it. She might not be as well trained with charms as Nora was, but *this* she could do. Then she heard the rogue thought. It wasn't that Nora didn't trust her. She was unused to having an ally. She was supposed to do it alone.

"You don't have to do this alone," Lotte said. "I'm with you."

Finally, with a nod, Nora released the charm.

Honora Holtzfall was not in the habit of running from her enemies.

But she wasn't stupid enough to just wait for rescue either. In one quick movement, she vaulted over the bar, the buttons of her shirt scraping off and scattering among the ice on the other side.

A blast from one of the charms flew over the barrier and hit the mirror behind her, knocking a particularly good bottle of liquor from the top shelf, sending it shattering next to Nora as she worked a diamond ring off her finger and grabbed a fallen metal cocktail shaker.

She moved quickly. Her mind drew out the circuitry as her hand followed, as steadily as could be expected under the circumstances. She was aware that the shielding charm that Lotte was holding would overheat any second while she carved the circuitry into the metal.

"Nora," Lotte called out. "It's cracking."

"Just a little bit longer," Nora shouted back. She hadn't handled a luster in she didn't even know how long. If she had done it right, it would knock the magic out of anything within a mile radius.

And suddenly there was a cry. She saw Lotte drop the charm as it shattered into glowing metal pieces.

The shield dropped with it.

From the other side, a man in a wolf mask leveled a weapon at her head.

Nora looked him in the eye, then she twisted the cocktail shaker a fraction of an inch. Lining up the magical circuit she had carved into it.

The luster went off with a shock wave.

She heard the trigger of the weapon click.

The Grims' weapons went dead.

At exactly the same second, the lights did too.

Plunging the Clandestine Court into darkness.

Jails weren't new to August.

He had a few scattered memories of coming here when he was young, before his father had shrugged off the last of his criminal leanings. August had landed in here a few times himself. Usually for climbing over a police barrier or being somewhere else he shouldn't, in pursuit of a story. A bit of bail money, or a bribe, and August was usually on his way in a few hours. Although once he'd let himself be booked overnight in the 3rd circle. It'd been winter, and they hadn't been able to afford the heating in his mother's apartment that year. The police station in the 3rd circle had been a warm place to sleep, being in the upper echelons of the city.

Prison, on the other hand . . .

Being arrested for murder got you upgraded.

He'd told the same story over and over again to the cops. The truth. That he'd found the body. In fairness, if he hadn't been there, August wouldn't have believed the story either. The fifth time he told it, they had asked if there was anyone else who could corroborate that he was there looking for a story and not stabbing someone to death.

"How about Honora Holtzfall?"

He was pretty sure *that* was what got him sent to Wirr Prison. Who said the justice system wasn't efficient?

As the police van rolled through the city, August became aware of an unsettled feeling with every farther block they went. It was nearly nightfall, and the streets were still busy, even as voxes blasted reminders of the curfew. It felt like the precipice of something dangerous.

The police van rattled to a stop. An officer wrenched the back open, but his eyes were darting around. He looked distracted as he ushered August toward the flat gray face of the prison, which stared down with hundreds of barred window eyes. In no time, he was being pushed into a waiting area as the police officer disappeared again.

And now August sat, waiting to be processed as the sky outside darkened.

They were supposed to let him send a missive. Let someone know he was in here. He ought to let his mother know. Or maybe his editor. He was tempted to send one to Nora. He might need a recommendation for a good lawyer, after all.

August leaned his head against the wall of the waiting cell, turning his mind back to the story. The pull of it drawing him in even here and now.

They'd run into dead ends before, but this one felt especially defunct. And not just because it came in the form of a murdered man. August had a sinking feeling it wasn't a coincidence that Officer Eugene Knapp had been killed only hours after Oskar Wallen had given up his name.

August was just considering getting some shut-eye when, all at once, the lights went out.

For a second, he thought the bulb above him had just burned out. But it was too dark for that. August could hear faraway shouting. The panic that came with a blackout. He pulled himself to his feet, peering out the solitary barred window in the processing cell.

The whole prison had gone dark.

No, not just the whole prison.

The whole city.

Skyscrapers in the distance stood like pillars of black against a starry sky. On the road outside, cars had stalled. Something had knocked out the power in the whole city.

And that, August realized, moving quickly, would include the magimek locks on the prison doors.

Sure enough, the door pushed open easily under August's hand. He could go now, be out without there ever being a record of him being arrested for murder.

Or . . .

August hated the thing in him that made him pause. The thing that couldn't let a story go. That couldn't just *leave*.

He'd told Nora more than once it was impossible to get into Wirr Prison.

But he was here now. In the same prison as Lukas Schuld. The man who had falsely confessed to killing Verity Holtzfall.

The murdered cop had been a dead end. But here was a tiny opening in the brick wall he'd been staring at for hours. One last tiny hope for answers, however unlikely.

Cursing himself, Honora Holtzfall, and everything else in this stupid damned story, August turned on his heel, heading deeper into the prison.

Chapter 54

THEO

Three knights fell before the fighting began in earnest.

LAO weapons cracked out over the fleeing crowd even as the knights braced themselves at the mouth of the Clandestine Court. They moved around the panicked 1st-circle wealth easily, letting them pass to safety as the Grims came after them.

"Hold!" Benedict's voice carried over the chaos as two more knights were struck in the chest by the blast of magic from the Grims. "Hold!"

They stood united now, but Edmund's raving's still rang in Theo's ears. His wild false promises that their oath was broken. He had been proven wrong. But if Edmund had been right, if the oath had been broken, how many among them wouldn't be standing shoulder to shoulder with the rest of them now?

Another blast came, this time from behind, striking a knight in the back, who fell with a cry.

"At will!" Benedict's voice carried over the fray, and as one, every knight moved.

Theo had trained all his life with the knights who stood with him now. But he knew that training was not the same as a fight. Another knight fell in front of him. Even as his own sword swung up, breaking a weapon away from the Grim who had fired the shot.

They were heavily armed.

Because of him. Because he had been torn between treason and loyalty. Because he had tried to find a way out when there was none. Guilt weighed heavily on Theo as bodies fell around him on both sides.

Through the fray, Theo caught sight of Modesty.

He moved, fighting his way toward her as a Grim rounded on her. In a second, Theo was between them.

The Grim snarled at him from behind the mask. "So this is your choice, lapdog?" Theo recognized the man's voice. It was one of the Grims who had Alaric prisoner. He raised a weapon, aiming straight for Theo's chest.

Theo braced himself. This was how he would die. As a knight. Standing by his oath.

But as the man's finger went to the trigger, the streetlights were extinguished.

The whole city plunged into darkness.

There was a moment of chaos, of confusion, that lasted for only a beat as their eyes adjusted to the darkness.

As the knights realized that they had the upper hand.

Chapter 55

AUGUST

Prisons were meant to be hard to break *out* of.

Which made walking in fairly easy.

Whatever barriers had once been here were gone with the blackout. The only light in the prison came from the moon shining through into the open-air courtyard, illuminating the chaos of the prison break in progress.

With the magimek locks gone, some brave but stupid guards were trying to lock the cells the old-fashioned way, but they were too late. Prisoners were already overwhelming them, uniforms being dragged to the ground. Cries of pain echoed around the yard as men grabbed their chance at freedom.

August was the only one pushing the other way, his heart racing as he fought against the flow. He wasn't sure if it was fear or anticipation. He tried to make out faces in the crowd, looking for Lukas Schuld. The mug shot that had been plastered over every front page.

He found a different face he knew instead.

"Edvard!" The shock startled his name out of August. The hulking man's head shot up from the crowd, as he stood a foot taller than most of them. August had known Eddie Dahl since he was a boy. He and his father had come up on the streets together. He'd most recently been an enforcer for Oskar Wallen before he went down for . . . well, enforcing.

Eddie cracked a wide grin. "Little Wolffe," he called. "What are you doing here? I thought you were staying out of the business."

"I'm looking for someone." August pressed toward Eddie through the crowd. The large man squeezed his shoulder in greeting, as if they were just running into each other on the streets, not in the middle of a prison break. "Lukas Schuld."

"The Heiress killer?" Eddie's grin widened. "Oh yeah, I know where he sleeps. Come with me."

Eddie's considerable size made fighting the current of escaping prisoners almost easy. August followed him to a cell far down the block as Eddie elbowed men out of the way. It was unlocked, but a figure still lingered inside.

Lukas Schuld looked gaunter than he had in his mug shot from just a few weeks ago, but it was still unmistakably him. There was a hollow, haunted expression in his eyes as he pressed against the wall, watching the other prisoners race past his cell.

"Bit of a strange one, if you ask me," Eddie said in a carrying whisper before giving August one more sturdy clap on the back. "Good luck to you, boy. I'll see you on the other side."

Lukas Schuld's haggard eyes came up as August stepped into the cell. "Who are you?"

It was a fair question. In a prison of men either wearing guards' uniforms or prisoners' stripes, August was conspicuous in his rumpled white shirt and charcoal trousers.

August thought fast. "You know who sent me." He hedged. "It was the same person who paid you to be here."

Lukas's attention snapped to August, suddenly sharp. "He sent you to kill me."

He.

August knew the makeup of the Holtzfall family as well as anyone else in the city. The weak-chinned uncle always skulking in the back was the only living man in the Holtzfall line. Whatever his name was.

Profit? Progress? Prosper, that was it. But he didn't strike August as the sort of figure who would inspire this kind of terror from Lukas Schuld.

Had Nora been right from the beginning?

Isengrim.

She would be *insufferable* if she'd been right all this time.

"He didn't send me to kill you." August needed more from Lukas, he needed to push just a little harder. "He sent me to get you out of here."

August saw his mistake written all over Lukas Schuld's face the moment he said it. "No, he didn't. He wants me to die in here."

Damn. August had overplayed his hand.

Lukas Schuld made to move past August. They might be about the same height, but Lukas had a desperation that August couldn't match if it came to it. Besides, he hadn't been in a fight since he was six years old, and that ended with two black eyes.

But he couldn't just let Lukas go. Not after he'd come so desperately close to an answer. To the end of this story.

As Lukas Schuld pushed past him, August pulled the small diamond earring from his pocket. Nora's. The one she had planted on him the night of the Veritaz Ceremony. He'd kept it on him ever since. Just in case she needed to find him.

He dropped it into Lukas Schuld's pocket as the man fled, merging into the crowd.

Underground in the Clandestine Court, the darkness was complete. The only light was the moon, faintly peeking through the gap where the Grims had come through.

As she held perfectly still, Lotte could hear the sounds of the Grims shifting around them.

Their stolen weapons clicked uselessly, the magic knocked out of them. But they still outnumbered Lotte and Nora. And even in the dark, they would find them eventually. Lotte tried to get her bearings as the wolves shifted around them in the dark. Nora had been behind the bar. But there were dozens of knocked-over tables that would make noise if Lotte tried to move toward her.

And Lotte had no idea which way was out.

And then . . . a flash of light illuminated the room.

For a panicked second, Lotte thought it was the power coming back on.

Until it was followed by a booming crack of thunder echoing around the bar, shaking the bottles on the wall.

The first of the raindrops hit the Grims' metallic masks with a quiet, plinking sound, soft at first. And then faster.

Another strike of lightning flashed, and in the brief violent illumination, Lotte saw the unnatural clouds gathered in the ceiling, accumulated around the chandeliers of the Clandestine Court. The lightning hit a table, sending it cracking. More than one Grim let out a cry that was drowned out by the boom of thunder. The rain rapidly turned into a deluge coming so fast and thick that Lotte felt like she might be drowning. The torrent forced some of the Grims to their knees as the unnatural storm raged indoors.

Then a hand closed around hers.

Nora, her thoughts flooding into Lotte.

Her half a plan had turned into a fully fledged one. This was the same charm the Holtzfalls had used for good weather at the Veritaz Ceremony. But good weather was no good to them now.

The storm roared around them.

They had cover.

Now they had to get out.

They fought their way down the slick debris. A Grim moved toward them, but another fork of lightning crashed between them, driving him back.

Lotte pulled Nora after her, guiding her through the blinding rain. Lotte could still feel the echoes of Nora's desperate gratitude rattling around in her chest.

She wanted to tell Nora that of course she'd stayed.

That she would stay again because she knew Nora would do the same. And one clear thought from Nora seemed to overwhelm Lotte.

This was what family was.

They stumbled out of the Clandestine Court, bursting out of the storm and into the streets of Walstad, into the fray of knights and Grims.

As they broke free, Lotte hunted in the crowd for Theo, fighting among the knights in uniforms. Not daring to look for him in the bodies on the ground.

Finally, she found him in the fray, their eyes locking across the street.

They had made it, all of them had made it. The relief crashing through almost brought her to her knees as Theo broke away from the fray toward them. As the three of them stumbled to each other, slick with rain and blood amidst the death and the destruction.

And in Lotte, it echoed: *This is what belonging to someone is supposed to feel like.*

PART VI

UNITY

Chapter 57

NORA

Edmund's body was tied to the flaying tree.

The one where Sigismund Rydder had been tied after trying to flee. And had been commanded to lash himself to death. Nora knew her family's history. Her grandmother meant Edmund's body as a clear warning to any knights who might dare to defy her.

But Nora wasn't a knight. She could do whatever she wanted. And historically, she always had.

"Alaric is alive." Nora had known that once, apparently. But Lotte had been forced to remind her since their grandmother had stripped her memories, along with everything else she'd forgotten from the day of the election party. It was strange, having to trust someone else's mind more than her own. But she'd been right, Modesty *had* tried to kill her. *Had* killed Constance.

She turned away from the window from where she could see Edmund. There was no count yet on how many others were dead. On both sides.

Nora knew there had been finely clad bodies lying on the floor of the Clandestine Court alongside the Grims. There would be wealthy empires whose heirs had died last night. Or been turned to stone. And thanks to Nora's cocktail shaker turned luster, there were criminals roaming the streets.

The riots, the city had recovered from swiftly. This was a blow it would take longer to come back from. But through it all, the Holtzfall mansion stood untouched.

"So you're both telling me that I've been running around the city trying to find a way to reach Isengrim," Nora said to Theo and Lotte, "and we had a bargaining line open all this time." They were *we* now. The way that she and August had become too. Nearly dying together tended to do that.

"That's really your takeaway in all this?" Theo leaned back against the window frame in the turret room of the mansion. The wear of battle hung heavy on him. The battle against the Grims at the Clandestine Court last night. As well as the secret battle that had been waging between his two loyalties. Nora felt a fierce protectiveness rise in her toward him. Theo and Alaric had spent their lives saving her. It was time for her to keep up the Holtzfall's side of the oath made a thousand year ago.

"What were you expecting?" Nora asked. "Did you want me to throw a fit?" She understood why Theo had been afraid to tell her. She was a Holtzfall first. Maybe there had been a time, when things were simpler, she might have felt betrayed by this. She might have blamed him for the Grims in the factory. But loyalty and family were complicated. The maze trial had proven that.

Besides, it wasn't as if she was proud of everything she had ever done.

"As long as we're all sharing our secrets, I should tell you." Nora turned to Lotte, who was half-collapsed on the window seat next to Theo. "I sold the information about your father to Oskar Wallen. So do you want me to apologize *out loud* or do you already know that I feel guilty about that with your Holtzfall gift and we can move on?"

Lotte blinked in the beginnings of the daylight leaking through the window. "We can move on." Nora tried to hide her relief at

Lotte's words. "Although, you should probably know Oskar Wallen sent someone to kill me."

"Why would he do that?" Nora leaned forward sharply.

Lotte managed to shrug, lying down, but there was a challenge in her eyes. "I was hoping you could tell me. He seemed to think my blood would free the knights from their oath."

Nora hesitated. She knew they were sharing secrets, but this one was bigger than just hers. "The story of Hartwin Rydder," Nora said carefully, "is that when he pledged his sword to Honor Holtzfall, he swore that Rydders would serve Holtzfalls until one of our bloodlines ended. That's not exactly true." The words of the oath were written in ancient Gamanix on Hartwin Rydder's sword, hanging up in her grandmother's office. Nora's ancient languages were rusty, but it roughly translated to, "*The Rydder oath will protect the Holtzfall bloodline until the day our bloodlines are bound. Should mingled blood be spilled, the oath will be broken.*" Nora quoted from memory.

"That's what Edmund was raving about." Theo pushed himself away from the window, suddenly alert. "Saying that the oath was broken."

"Because my mother is a Holtzfall and my father is a knight."

"Then why didn't it work?" Theo's eyes went out the window again, to where Edmund's body was tied to the tree.

Dozens of possible answers came to Nora at once. Ancient magics were strange, perhaps the blood had to be shed with Hartwin's sword. Or on the same place where the oath was made. Or perhaps Oskar knew more than she did and the child of mixed blood had to be killed. But she gave the only true answer she could. "I'm not sure." And then she added, "And I also don't know why Oskar Wallen might care to liberate our knights for the Grims." She drew herself up straight. "But I do know I'm not letting Alaric die. If they want a ring so badly, we'll give them a ring."

"I don't think even you can make Modesty give up one of her rings." Theo's smile was rueful but resigned. "She'd admit to murdering Constance first."

"I know," Nora said. "But the rings on Modesty's hands aren't the only ones we have."

Chapter 58

NORA

There were only two people who were meant to have access to the office in the Holtzfall mansion: the head and their heir.

Nora was neither. But she had been the Heiress apparent for a long time.

"I did this with your mother," her grandmother had told her when she was eleven. "Usually she would be the one to do this with you, but your mother is not so much one for tradition as you and I." Using Hartwin's sword, her grandmother sliced Nora's hand open. Bright red blood welled there. Before it could spill on the pristine floor, Mercy Holtzfall pressed Nora's eleven-year-old palm against the gnarled door. Nora had watched with pride as the ancient wood soaked up her blood. As it must have for generations of Heiresses before her.

Her grandmother had done that because she had been certain Nora would be the Heiress. Because she trusted in that, and in her.

And now Nora was here to steal from her.

She stabbed a small pin into her finger and with just one drop, the branches bowed out of her way. It was strange, not seeing Mercy Holtzfall sitting there. She had been called away in the chaos to meet with the new governor and instruct him on how to respond to his first crisis.

The rest of the mansion hung heavy with portraits and tapestries.

Even a few modern paintings by artists the Holtzfalls had graced with patronage.

But only three things adorned the walls here.

Hartwin's sword.

The hooks where the woodcutter's ax sat when it wasn't deep in the woods.

And Honor Holtzfall's ring.

The trial rings were fickle magic. They appeared with a win—and at the end of the trials, they vanished from all but the hand of the victor. But Honor Holtzfall's ring was straight from the tree of the Huldrekall. It was everlasting.

The three steps to take it from the wall felt heavy. Nora was keenly aware of the weight in her hand. But it was that simple. She was holding the ancient Holtzfall artifact.

For a moment, Nora considered sliding it on her finger.

It would be so easy to lie. To claim she had won a trial. She could take this ring and walk into the woods, retrieve the ax, and become the Heiress again.

And then not only would her mother be dead, Alaric would be too.

And she would sit in this chair for the rest of her life, knowing that she had chosen the heirship over a life.

Nora closed her hand around the ring, pulling out the duplicate she had charmed and putting it in place. It was identical to the real ring in every single way. Except that it had absolutely no magic. But so long as her grandmother didn't suddenly fancy a walk in the woods, she wouldn't notice.

Nora left before she could change her mind, the branches of the office lacing themselves shut behind her tightly as she fled under the judgmental eyes of her Holtzfall ancestors.

She found Lotte and Theo waiting for her at the end of the hallway. As Nora approached, she was aware of them drawing a step farther apart then they had been, their conversation cutting off when they saw her. "No, by all means"—Nora rolled her eyes—"continue your nice chat while I risk my grandmother's wrath for all of us."

"Nora." Theo ran a hand over his face. "You can't really mean to hand over Honor's ring to the Grims. You can't give them a way in after everything they've done."

"We'll see." Nora turned the ring over in her hand. "After all, there's a reason our family made its fortune cutting back the woods. The things that are in there have a tendency to kill people. I'll be amazed if the Grims make it out alive. But if they do . . ." The Grims might be able to do what her grandmother Leyla had done: Draw magic out of the woods. Give it to the people, fulfill their promises of wealth.

Nora found she was not afraid of what that looked like. She was curious.

Over and over, when she asked herself why the world had to be the way it was, the only answer she came up with was because that was how it had always been. The rich were rich because they had been for so long. The poor were poor because the rich fought against any change, even as the Grims fought for it.

And last night was the first battle they had lost in the war against change. Nora would rather any more change came without bloodshed.

"Something has to give in this city, one way or another. And if Isengrim can deliver on his campaign promise, then I'm intrigued. Now we just have to let them know we have what they want."

PART VII

LOYALTY

**COMPETITION! TONIGHT!
DANCE UNTIL YOU DROP!
100 ZAUB TO ENTER!
LAST COUPLE STANDING WINS
1,000 ZAUB!**

The words were written in lights on the marquee of the dilapidated dance hall, reflecting off the automobile they pulled up in.

"Are you sure your journalist is here?" Lotte's skepticism echoed Nora's own. For one, she was reasonably sure just by looking at him that August wasn't a good dancer.

"No, I'm not." Nora peered down at the wristwatch in her hand. There was no denying that the locanz charm was pointing here. Nora, Lotte, and Theo had circled this dance hall enough times. The diamond earring Nora had planted in August's shoe the first day they'd met was inside this dance hall. Whether or not August still had it was another question.

The death count had been climbing all day. Upper-circle heirs had died. Grims had died. Innocent bystanders had died. The new governor had been on the vox, making vague promises of *measures* to be announced tomorrow.

But tonight, there was a frenetic energy in the air through the city.

A wild, untethered sense of freedom. Nora heard it even now in the frantic music pouring out of the dance hall. With the police dealing with the aftermath of the attacks, no one was enforcing stupid little things like curfews.

It was hard won and easily lost tomorrow.

If they had a chance of saving Alaric, they needed to get the ring to the Grims before whatever these *measures* were. But the Grims weren't exactly easily found.

Especially after last night.

Those who weren't locked away or dead had gone to ground.

The boarded-up betting shop where Theo had met them once was empty, and the girl who worked in the Paragon hadn't shown up for work this morning.

Which left August.

If the Grims could communicate with each other through the *Bullhorn*, Nora could do the same. She'd used the same code they had used in Isengrim's letters. Encoding with spelling mistakes and typos one short phrase.

I have the ring.

Crude but effective. Hopefully. Effective enough to lure the Grims out of hiding to find Theo. Except when she'd gone to deliver her article to the *Bullhorn*, August wasn't there. None of the other journalists had seen him since before the Grim attacks that had shaken the city.

"I gave all of them two days to get me something that made it worth keeping them employed here," the editor informed her, a sneer pulling at the scar on his cheek. "I guess I'll take his absence as his resignation."

"That seems like a poor employment strategy," Nora had commented.

The editor's eyes dashed up. "Who did you say you were again?" The suspicion that passed across his face was enough to make Nora retreat.

Which left Nora going back to the same way she had found him that first day.

The locanz charm.

She'd figured it might lead her to August's apartment. She was already formulating some lie to tell his mother as they moved through the city. But as the charmed watch led them here, Nora could slowly feel uncertainty taking hold. For all she knew, August might have sold the earring off days ago. And people had died in the attacks. It wasn't impossible a journalist too close to the action might have gotten hurt. Or worse—

"If you wanted me to take you dancing, all you had to do was say."

August looked like he'd just washed off a very long night. And there was a shadow across his rueful smile as he moved down the sidewalk toward them. But still, Nora felt relief crash over her.

"For a thousand zaub prize?" Nora tried to hide her relief. It wouldn't do to let on that she was glad to see him alive. "I'd need a higher price to make it worth my while."

She caught Lotte's raised eyebrows and found herself grateful her cousin wasn't reading her mind right now. "Lotte, Theo, August." She waved a vague introduction, feeling strangely like two very different worlds were crashing together. "And vice versa."

"I would shake your hand"—August nodded to Lotte—"but your knight looks like he might kill me if I get any closer."

"How did you find us?" Theo asked, eyeing up August suspiciously.

"You're two heiresses and a knight in an odd part of town. Word gets out." August shrugged. He'd been looking for her too. And he'd found her, no less. How very annoyingly competent of him.

"I could have saved you the trouble, if you'd just kept my earring." The watch in her hand was still firmly pointed toward the dance hall, not August. "I gave you that for safekeeping."

"Well, I figured it'd be put to better use tracking down Lukas Schuld."

Nora's attention snapped to August so sharply he almost took a step back. "You mean to say Lukas Schuld is inside this building?"

"Who is Lukas Schuld?" Lotte asked.

"He's the man who killed Verity Holtzfall," Theo said.

"He's the man who confessed to killing her," Nora corrected, an idea already sparking in her mind. "Big difference."

"He escaped Wirr Prison in the blackout last night. I figured we'd need a way to find where he's hiding out. Ask him some questions."

"What were you doing in prison?" Theo asked, still seeming suspicious.

"I got arrested because someone, who shall remain Honora Holtzfall, wasn't where she was supposed to be."

"That sounds right," Theo admitted.

"All right." Nora liked it better when Theo was suspicious of August. She couldn't have them ganging up like this. "How was I supposed to know where you were?"

"I sent you a note."

"I didn't get a note."

"Did the servants not pass it on because it wasn't on fancy enough gold-leaf paper?"

"Are we after a murderer or not?" Lotte interrupted, turning everyone's attention back to the dance hall.

"This doesn't seem like the most inconspicuous place to hide out," Theo remarked, nodding toward the building, where lights blazed on signs, inviting any and all to come in and spend their money.

"Maybe he's celebrating his freedom." August shrugged. "Maybe he's trying to win that prize money to make a run for it."

Competition! Tonight!

Last couple standing wins 1,000 zaub!

Nora had traveled a long and frustrating road of questions and half answers and suspicions alongside August, but they'd arrived here at last.

Lukas Schuld had confessed to a crime he hadn't committed.

Nora wanted to know why.

"I tried to get answers from him last night, but maybe a Holtzfall heiress might be more effective."

"Maybe." Nora knew what August had in mind. Bribery, probably. The old-fashioned way. But she had an even more old-fashioned way—a Holtzfall gift that hadn't been seen in two centuries. Her eyes went to Lotte at the same time that Theo's did. "But I'm not the right Holtzfall for the job."

Chapter 60

THEO

The noise and heat hit them before they were fully through the doors. Bodies were packed in so tightly that it was a struggle to press into the fray. People in work clothes or their evening best pushed to and from a bar that was slinging drinks sloppily. On the other side of the hall, a messy press of bodies crowded at a betting window, brandishing numbered paper slips and cash.

Somewhere in this chaos was the man who had taken money to confess to Verity's murder. And if that money had been from the Grims, he might have a way to reach them. For days, it had seemed to Theo the Grims were everywhere. Watching his every move. Waiting for him to deliver them a ring.

And now that he had it, had a way to get his brother back, they were nowhere to be found.

Even now, he caught himself hunting for the sharp angled face of the fox girl here, the way she'd seemed to be everywhere before the attacks.

She might not have made it out alive.

Or if she had, she might have written him off as a traitor and slit Alaric's throat.

Theo pushed that thought aside.

The raised voices mingled with the music that clanged through the dance hall, a red-faced band in the corner playing loudly. The dance floor was dug out a few feet below them, ringed on all sides with a viewing platform where people crowded against the railing to watch. Dozens of couples danced feverishly. At the edges of the dance floor, a few couples were sitting down, breathing hard. One woman's ankle was propped up with ice on it.

DANCE UNTIL YOU DROP!
100 ZAUB TO ENTER!
LAST COUPLE STANDING WINS
1,000 ZAUB!

These were the couples who had already dropped. They looked miserable, their precious 100-zaub entry fee gone, and their shot at winning 1,000 vanished. Every single one of these couples was willing to push themselves to the brink of exhaustion for a shot at that amount of money.

But the viewing gallery was having the time of their lives. The viewers were doubled over laughing, pointing out different couples and placing bets. A man hanging over the railings with a glass in his hands slopped his drink carelessly, sending a splash of beer across the dance floor as a dancer twirled his partner straight into it. Naturally she slipped, crashing to the floor.

"Whoopsie daisy!" a voice boomed over the magical vox through the room. A man was hanging louchely over an announcer's booth. The master of ceremonies in all this. "Better luck next time, couple twenty-five." Around the platform, a few people booed the young couple, throwing balled-up betting slips as the young man helped his teary girlfriend off the floor.

Fighting against the crowd, the four of them moved through the dance hall, following the hands of the watch in Nora's hands, their gazes darting around. As if Lukas Schuld might be leaning up against the bar, drink in hand.

The charmed watch led them through the other side of the dance hall. A small inconspicuous door was marked NO ENTRY.

Obviously Nora took that as an invitation.

The door opened easily under the lasa charm on her hand.

The laughter and music dulled behind them as they made their way into what appeared to be a stockroom. Wooden crates filled with bottles lined the walls, with one corner dedicated to piles of betting slips.

The watch on Nora's wrist pointed directly toward a wall lined with crates of champagne.

"Anyone want a drink?" August joked.

Theo stepped forward, already pushing up his sleeves, ready to lug the wall of crates out of the way one by one.

"I don't drink warm champagne," Nora said shortly.

Theo realized what she was going to do a second before she did it. He just had time to step back, shielding Lotte, when Nora slammed her hands down. Six crates exploded, flooding the stockroom with alcohol and glass and shards of wood.

Revealing a door behind where it had been.

Nora climbed over the debris with the casualness of arriving at a party that had long awaited her.

That door opened as easily as the one to the stockroom had.

And behind it, illuminated by one stray oil lamp, was Lukas Schuld.

Chapter 61

LOTTE

As the light from the stockroom flooded into the small dark room behind Lukas Schuld, Lotte's eyes fell on a woman and three sleeping children.

"Don't hurt him!" The woman had thrown her body over the three children when the crates crashed down. "He didn't do anything. I swear he didn't!"

"I know he didn't." Nora's voice was calm, but she never took her eyes off Lukas Schuld. "That's why I'm here. I want to know why he confessed to a murder he didn't commit."

Lotte didn't have to be a mind reader to see the naked fear that flashed across his face at Nora's words. "No, no, I did it." There was a tremor in his voice. Whoever Lukas Schuld was covering for, that person scared him more than even Honora Holtzfall. "I killed Verity Holtzfall. I didn't mean to, I—"

"No, you didn't," Nora cut him off. "When I find out who your employer is, I'll let them know to hire a better actor next time they need someone to take the fall for a murder."

Even without taking her hindern off, Lotte knew there were too many jumbled minds in here for her to get the truth. She could practically feel the fear and defiance radiating off the woman, and the sleeping children were beginning to stir.

She caught Nora's eye, jerking her head toward the champagne-drenched hallway.

"Let's speak outside, Mr. Schuld."

When he stood to follow, Lukas Schuld was shaking like a leaf. His eyes darted between Lotte and Nora and then toward Theo and August standing in the back.

"You!" Lukas Schuld's eyes widened as he saw August.

"Me." August shrugged ruefully. And not for the first time, it occurred to Lotte that August was not at all what she'd expected from Nora's journalist. But she liked him.

"Let's save reunions for later," Nora said. "I want the truth, Mr. Schuld."

Lotte felt everyone's attention on her as she passed the hindern charm off her hand. A dozen minds piped up at once. The half-formed dreams of the children in the next room, and the gnawing monstrous fear from their mother, scraps of thoughts coming from the dance hall. But she focused on Lukas Schuld standing in front of them, champagne pooling at his feet.

He was worrying these were his only shoes.

And suddenly Lotte saw Nora as Lukas Schuld did. Not a girl desperate for answers about her mother but a gleaming figure of vengeance. Lotte had always thought Nora's resemblance to Leyla was strong. But for the first time, through Lukas Schuld's eyes, Lotte saw a flash of Mercy Holtzfall in her cousin.

She was going to kill him.

He thought he had run from death when he escaped from the prison, but he would die now at the vengeful hands of the Holtzfall Heiress. A storm of panic rolled over his mind, obscuring any other thoughts Lotte might have been able to find there.

"Mr. Schuld." Lotte stepped in between Nora and the man. "Tell me the truth."

"I killed her."

She has to believe me. I need her to believe me.

"What happened that night?" Lotte said, keeping his eyes on her. Drawing his mind away from Nora. From the fear of what she would do to him.

"It was late." Lotte seized onto the truth of that thought, trying to pull it out of his mind like a thread. "I was leaving a bar." That was a lie. He'd been home with Maggie and his girls. He hadn't touched a drop of drink since the twins were born, although the damage of years of drinking and gambling was already done. But the words he was saying aloud clapped their hands over the truth, silencing it even as it threatened to rise up in protest. He was repeating the story the way he'd been instructed to tell it. He had to lull the truth to sleep.

"And Verity?" Lotte prompted.

He'd heard about Verity Holtzfall's death the same way everyone else in the city had: newspaper headlines. But he'd barely heeded them. There were other things on his mind. It had been days and the baby's fever was getting worse. And there was no money for medicine. He was striking with the rest of the crew, and Maggie had lost her job as a maid in a house in the 5th circle when she'd married him. The mistress of the house said she wanted a maid who would be working, not rushing home to coddle babies. Lotte could feel him sinking back down inside his mind even as he told the story he was supposed to. She followed him down. He'd been desperate. Terrified of what would happen if he didn't get the baby her medicine.

So he'd done something stupid. He'd gone out one last time, with their last hundred zaub, for a game of cards.

And he lost. And he lost. He lost again and again. He lost bad. Always hoping he could win the next one. But he just sank deeper and deeper into the hole.

"I was walking home, and I saw her in her fancy clothing," Lukas was saying, drawing out the lies just like he had practiced them. Just like he had told the police. In the depths of his mind, the truth huddled conspicuously, even as he tried hard not to look at it. Even as Lotte dove deeper for it. "I didn't know who she was, except that she was dressed way too nice for the thirteenth circle. I'd already drunk my whole paycheck for the day, and I couldn't go home to my wife empty-handed. I was desperate." *I was so, so desperate*, the truth inside him echoed.

A man in a fine suit approached him as he left the card table in defeat and despair. The man had offered to wipe his debts out. And more than that. He offered him money. An impossible amount. It would clear his debt at the table and leave *plenty* to take the baby to a healer. And there'd be more money too, every month for Maggie and the girls. For the rest of their lives.

All he had to do was tell a lie.

"She was all dressed up in her emeralds."

When the cops came for him, the man in the fine suit told him, they'd have her jewels to make the story convincing. They'd pretend he'd had them all along. All he'd have to do was confess to murder.

"I needed the money, bad." Lotte could feel it all, his grief, his desperation, echoing in her mind. He'd taken the deal. It was an easy choice. Between his freedom and the baby's life. When Maggie had asked where he'd gotten the money, he'd told her the truth. She'd sobbed and begged him not to do it. They would find another way. But it was too late.

He'd already struck a deal.

And the person holding the purse strings wasn't someone to be trifled with.

Lotte snatched at that edge of the thought. *Who? Where was the money coming from?* But his mind was already racing ahead. The next day, the police came with the jewels, and Lukas told the lies he'd been instructed to tell. He let himself be locked up, his face plastered over every paper in the city. It was worth it. 2,000 zaub a month would be coming Maggie's way for the rest of her life. It was the best thing he'd ever done for his family in his whole worthless life.

Lukas had told himself he could live with it.

Until he was sentenced to death.

Maybe he'd been stupid for not seeing that was the way it would go. Killing an Heiress was a crime too big for life in prison. No one would believe him if he changed his story now. And if he did, what would happen to Maggie and the girls? It would be more than just the money. They'd hurt them. Bad.

Who? Who would hurt them?

But if he was executed, would the man in the fine suit keep his word?

So when the blackout came, he'd run, along with the rest of the prison. He'd gone straight to Maggie and the girls, packed what they could, and taken them away from that tiny apartment, through the blackout.

By dawn, they were here. The dance hall was run by an old friend, one who'd clawed his way up in the world. He would hide them, albeit for a price, until they could make a run for it. They would go to the countryside—to the sea, maybe, take a boat on the Great Crossing. Even a man like *him* couldn't follow them there.

"A man like who?" Lotte resurfaced from his thoughts. Lukas's gaze snapped to her, even as he shied away from the question, the name he wouldn't speak.

"Isengrim?" Nora pressed. "Is that who set you up?"

No.

"Was it another Holtzfall?" Nora pressed again. "Was it Modesty or Patience who bribed you? My uncle Prosper?" She hesitated before she said the next name. "Aunt Grace?"

No. The name slipped out of Lukas's mind, unbidden. It spilled over Lotte's lips.

"Oskar Wallen."

Chapter 62

NORA

Nora had always thought she was too clever to fool.

But now she saw how easily Oskar Wallen had done it.

He was a criminal. Anyone would have told her not to trust him. But his world had seemed so far away from hers, she'd never imagined they could even touch.

And only now, too late, all the pieces of his game dropped into place. He'd made them come to him under the pretense of knowing nothing of the cover-up. He'd praised her cleverness for figuring out his charms. He had never offered too much. Never enough to spark her suspicion.

Nora had imagined wild conspiracies that led to Lukas Schuld's confessions. Aunt Patience killing her mother to give Modesty her shot at the heirship. The Grims coming for her mother in their quest for a ring to get into the woods.

The truth was simpler.

A criminal who knew how to cover his tracks.

Who knew that a false confession would keep the heat off him.

Any gangster worth their salt would have cops on the payroll. And even if all Oskar took was the one missing ring, leaving the rest to be false evidence, it was still worth millions.

And when August and Nora had come knocking, he'd sent them

in the direction of Officer Knapp, then made sure the man was dead by the time they got there.

Nora had made a bad trade. Her loyalty to her family for a dead man and a dead end, which was all part of a setup to throw her off his scent. And she'd almost gotten Lotte killed in the process.

"Why?" Nora asked, pressing past Lotte as she forced her scattered thoughts to pull together. There had to be more to this. She believed Oskar had been honest about one thing: killing an Heiress was an expensive risk. And this was an expensive cover-up. "Why did Oskar Wallen kill my mother?"

"He doesn't know." Lotte gave the answer easily. Of course he didn't. Oskar Wallen wouldn't be the sort of man to confess his plans. He wasn't the mustache-twirling villain in a children's comic strip. He was a dangerous criminal who'd tricked Nora. Who had taken information from her and then used it to try to break the Rydder knight bond to her family.

"Nora," Lotte said in a low voice, "he doesn't know anything else."

Nora believed her cousin.

She watched Lukas Schuld, pressed back against the wall in panic. She had hated him from the moment she'd seen his face in the paper, even after she knew that he'd been lying. He had been a part of this. But she couldn't find any of that hatred now. He wasn't really a player in this game, just a piece on the board.

"You should get out of this city," Nora said. She saw tentative hope break over Lukas Schuld's face. "If we found you this swiftly, Oskar Wallen won't be far behind."

She had about 10,000 zaub on her. She'd started carrying money since it came in handy when she was with August. "You are going to run *now*, and you're going to run fast and far." Lukas stared at her, his mouth opening and closing, and he took the money. "Go!" Nora said. He didn't have to be told again. He scrambled away, back to his family.

"Oskar Wallen isn't an easy man to find, you know," August said as Nora turned back toward the other three.

She knew what he was saying.

Oskar *would* come for Lukas Schuld. If he didn't flee the city, he would be bait. An easy way to find Oskar Wallen.

And then a scream rent the air.

Chapter 63
LOTTE

The smell of smoke reached Lotte first.

They pushed their way through the crowd on the viewing deck as piercing screams from the dance floor eclipsed the music and the hubbub of the hall.

Lotte got to the front a second before Nora did.

A girl with pinned-up curls in a sea-glass-colored dress was twirling frantically in the middle of the dance floor. Her partner had collapsed on the floor, tired legs giving out below him. But she was still dancing, and there was frenzy to her pace, cries ripping from her throat.

"Well, ladies and gentlemen"—the announcer's too-bright voice bounced around the room—"it looks like our friend in couple forty-three has stopped dancing, which means that he and his lovely partner are out, out, out. But maybe she hasn't got the message . . ." A laugh rippled through the gallery, briefly covering the girl's screams.

Something was wrong. The girl was sobbing, and her arms were flailing. And the burning smell was getting stronger. Smoke was rising from her heels, Lotte realized.

And then the dancer's feet burst into flames.

The crowd that had been pressing forward turned to panic.

But Lotte stayed rooted, her breath suddenly coming short and fast.

She had almost forgotten that there was one final trial left.

And here it was, only two days after they had all failed in the maze.

Lotte could feel the Huldrekall's eyes on the back of her neck, watching what she would do. The eyes of the Holtzfalls, sure that she wasn't worthy of them. The eyes of the Sisters of the Blessed Briar, sure that she wasn't worthy of anything.

And they were right.

She had not been good enough to keep her temper.

She had not been good enough to stand her ground.

To be loyal to a family she didn't fit into.

And now she stood immobilized as, without hesitation, Nora moved.

Chapter 64
NORA

Nora had done a lot of things to liven up a boring party in her time. She had used Sabina Lehnert's yacht to board a shipping vessel that was coming in from Alba when they had run out of refreshments. She'd released all the Skvaders at once at a hunt. But she hadn't tried lighting herself on fire yet. She would have to keep that one in mind. She had never seen every eye in a place turn to someone so quickly.

She grabbed an ice bucket off the railing where it was balanced, pulling out the champagne bottle as she went. Half the crowd was pressing closer for a better look, the other half was pushing away. There was no time to wonder what kind of trial this was. This was the last trial. The last chance to prove herself.

To prove she was worthy of the heirship.

She landed without slopping any melting ice onto her dress. Champagne ice bucket handling was a talent she had perfected.

The dance floor was in chaos now, every couple around the dancer screaming and staggering to get away. Nora pushed herself swiftly up, largely ignored in the commotion as she pushed toward the girl. But the girl's partner got there first, stripping off his jacket, throwing it at the girl's feet to smother the flames.

It did nothing except burn his hands.

"Move!" Nora pushed by him, kicking the burning jacket aside and dumping the bucket of melting ice over the dancer, extinguishing the nascent flames.

But it did nothing for the dancer.

The girl continued to sob, her feet flailing violently as two men grabbed ahold of her, trying to still her. And then, all at once, her legs collapsed under her, and she staggered to the floor.

There was a beat of relief.

And then the two men who had seized her began to dance with the same frantic unwillingness the girl had.

It was spreading. And Nora was running low on champagne buckets.

And then she saw that the closest dancer's shoes were red.

Nora was sure they had been a black patent leather before. She would have noticed if his shoes didn't match. And now they were the color of a burning ember in a fireplace. The boy surged forward, grabbing the arms of two of the couples who had been dancing a moment before. Nora read the word *Help!* on his lips. And suddenly, they were dancing too, even as he collapsed.

The chaos was spreading like wildfire. The unafflicted dancers were trying to run, but the gates to the upper level had been closed, trying to keep this dancing curse at bay. As the affected dancers barreled into the crowd, they infected more people as they rid themselves of the curse.

She watched another man's feet catch fire. More people's feet were smoking, sparks flying from their heels. It was spreading too fast. She needed it in one place.

She grabbed the arm of the nearest man with red shoes. And she watched as the color leeched out of his shoes. Her own shoes turned red.

Good grief, red was a vulgar color for shoes.

And then Nora felt her feet begin to move against her will, like they were being tugged by puppet strings that ran all the way through her. Almost in time with the music. And then Nora reached out an arm to a nearby girl, who was twirling and sobbing. "Take my arm!" Nora called out. She didn't know if the girl heard her or if she just latched onto her out of desperation. The girl stilled, the red leaving her shoes too. Nora released her, and she grabbed another girl, then a young man, catching him by the sleeve and pulling him to her so that she could take on his curse.

One after the other, she gathered the curse, consolidating it into herself, fighting to control her body even as it moved against her. The red had spread everywhere now, her stockings, her dress, they were all the same shade of scarlet, and she was whirling, whirling.

She was getting dizzy, and she didn't have any idea how to stop this thing.

Her stockings were beginning to smoke, and she could feel the heat rising.

She kept spinning, her mind whirring for an idea. Why couldn't she think of one? As she whirled, she caught sight of Lotte again, who was shouting something she couldn't hear over the music.

Her skin was getting hot. Not just her feet, her whole being.

Her body was weary, her vision starting to blur.

And it suddenly occurred to Nora that she was going to die.

For the first time in her life she wasn't smart enough to outwit a problem. She couldn't think of a charm, or a clever plan. She was going to burn alive.

But at least everyone else would live.

And then her legs collapsed under her. Like a marionette whose strings had been cut.

Nora was on the floor.

Staring up at hundreds of gaping faces on the balcony above.

An arm with typewriter ink on the cuff reached down for her.

August pulled her to her feet.

He turned her hand over in his. "Nice ring."

Chapter 65

The knight's oath took over everything else.

Theo's only focus was getting Nora and Lotte out of the building in one piece. It was too late for them not to have been recognized. They were Holtzfalls. But he could get them clear before someone recovered enough to do something about that.

They could sell the story of what they saw to the paper later.

They broke free from the dance hall and the heat of bodies and the smell of burning into the cool night air of the city.

Nora stopped, spinning around.

"Here." It took Theo a second to realize she was holding out the ring to him. The one she had stolen from Mercy Holtzfall. "It's better if you have it, in case they come for me now."

Nora's eyes darted to the new ring on her hand and then away again. As if she was afraid it might vanish at any moment. Theo had never stopped thinking of Nora as the Holtzfall Heiress, even with two rings on Modesty's hand. Nora had been the Holtzfall Heiress his whole life. He had always known that he would serve her as a knight one day.

Hartwin Rydder had tied his life to Honor Holtzfall because he was a good man. Because the man who shielded so many people needed a sword by his side. The Rydder knights had stood by the Holtzfalls for centuries because the Holtzfalls had proven themselves time and time again.

And as she held out the ring to him, Theo knew he would be proud to be bound to the Holtzfalls if it meant Nora was at their head.

"Are you *sure*? You are giving the Grims a way into the woods."

"If they make it out alive, then I guess they'll be worthy of their spoils." Her tone was light, but her eyes were serious as she dropped the ring in his hand. The key to getting Alaric back.

Theo watched the certainty flicker off Nora's face as she turned to Lotte next. Nora visibly steeled herself against the bitterness she had come to expect from her cousins. But Lotte offered Nora a small, sad smile. "You'll make a better Heiress than I would. Our grandmother was right about that." Her eyes went to the ring. "I only ever wanted a family. I don't need to lead it."

"You're the only member of this family I actually like, so I'm not letting you escape us now." Nora deliberately rested her hand on Lotte's arm, and Theo could only guess what thoughts she was pressing into Lotte's mind. "As long as I'm wearing a ring, you'll have a place in this family."

"Don't get too confident now," Lotte said. "You still have to beat Modesty to the ax before you start making promises."

Nora scoffed. "I would never dare. Pride is a terrible vice, isn't it?"

The girls embraced.

NORA CHOSE TO WALK HOME, HER JOURNALIST BY HER SIDE.

Theo put up a nominal fight, seeing as August didn't look like he'd be much use if the Grims came after Nora and her ring. But as usual, Nora got her way, and Theo drove Lotte back to the Paragon in silence.

Lotte was deep in thought, gazing out the window, until finally they stopped.

Theo hesitated, on the edge of saying something. But he was unsure what to say to a Holtzfall who knew she had lost her chance at the heirship.

In the end, Lotte spoke first. "Since I'm unfit to be an heiress, maybe when this is all over, you can train me to be a knight."

"A sword-wielding Holtzfall, that would be something." Theo searched her face. He had done this a dozen times today since finding out that Lotte's father was a knight. But no matter what, he couldn't find any Rydder in her features. She was Grace through and through. She looked like a Holtzfall.

He tried to imagine her next to them in the barracks. Training to fight under Lis. Training with one side of her family to give her life up for the other side.

He found himself wanting to reach for her now, to bridge the gap between them.

It will destroy you, you know. Being that close to her and knowing that any closer will be the end of you. It will tear you apart in ways you don't yet understand.

The rain started, tapping gently against the roof of the car. "Here." Theo didn't reach for her. He shrugged his jacket off, passing it to Lotte. And then she was gone, slipping out of the car, wrapped against the rain in his knight's coat.

He watched until she had vanished safely back into the Paragon.

He was about to drive away when he saw her. The figure lingering in the dark. Watching him. Theo stepped out of the car as the fox girl emerged into the streetlight. She had the signs of a fight on her, bruises marking her face. But she was still standing.

"Is my brother still alive?" Theo asked evenly.

"It would serve you right if he wasn't," she hissed. "I *saw* you fighting for them. But Isengrim is a man of his word. We gave you until the final trial before we slit his throat—"

Theo cut her off, holding up the ring.

And suddenly her face split into a wolfish grin.

Chapter 66

NORA

The night was young still, and once upon a time Nora would have been heading out, not heading home. She'd have been pretending to have fun at Rik's Café or perched at a table at the Clandestine Court waiting for something interesting to happen.

Definitely not walking down the street with a *journalist*, of all people, unable to clear the smell of burning from her nose.

August walked next to her, quiet for once, as they headed uptown. They hadn't spoken about it; they both just fell into step, heading in the same direction. She was grateful to have him there, though she would never tell him that. And grateful he understood her silence. Tomorrow they would talk about Oskar Wallen. Tomorrow she wanted to know everything he knew about the man who had killed her mother. And tomorrow they would formulate a plan. But for now . . . Nora found herself compulsively checking her hand for the ring. It was still there. No matter how many times her hand dropped out of her sight and she jerked it back up, it was still there.

She'd thought she would feel relieved.

Or maybe victorious.

Smug was a definite possibility.

But all she felt encircling her hand was an immense weight of responsibility. Not just to her family anymore, to the whole city.

They walked all the way into the 1st circle until they reached the corner of the block that the Holtzfall mansion dominated. August's hands were deep in his pockets as they lingered in the light spilling out through the windows. Nora didn't move to go inside, and August didn't move to go home either.

Still neither of them spoke.

Finally, August made an annoyed noise at the back of his throat. "No, really, it was no trouble at all, this was on my way home. You're welcome."

Nora felt a smile tug at her mouth. "I didn't say thank you."

"I assumed you were thinking it and too proud to say anything."

Nora was feeling reckless. Reckless enough to wonder if she kept pushing, would he fall with her or move out of the way. "If you must know, I was wondering if you were ever going to get around to kissing me."

August could usually keep up with her, and Nora took pride in the moments when she was able to trip him up, like when she won their little game of verbal jousting. And she felt the thrill run through her now as he stumbled for just a second.

But he found his footing fast. "Are you really that vain that you just assume everyone always wants to kiss you?"

"It would only be vanity if I was wrong."

"I don't think that's what vanity means," August replied. "I ought to know, I spend enough time with you."

"Are you sure? I know it's an awfully big word. And mostly you're good with pictures—"

He cut her off with a kiss.

His hands finally came out of his pockets, cupping her face on either side as he pressed his mouth to hers, as he smothered the smells of the dance hall with his own scent of newspaper ink and coffee. He kissed her just like he argued with her, like he knew just how to match her, their rhythms falling into sync as easily as they had when they talked. She felt the same thrill that she did when they were hunting down a story together. He kissed her like he knew her.

He broke away. "Fine, you're not that vain."

"Really? You're sure you don't want to define that word for me?" Nora was smiling. Aunt Grace had always told her not to smile in pictures, that it would make her face look too wide. But now it drew August's eyes to her mouth, and then he was kissing her again.

It was only when the rain started that they broke apart. Droplets smacked onto the sidewalk around them. August pulled Nora into the shelter of his coat, wrapping his arms around her as they tried to take whatever cover they could, pressing near the wall of the mansion. Nora tipped her head forward, pressing her forehead into his chest, feeling her breathing ease. Huddled this close, Nora could feel the warmth of him through the thin silk fabric of her dress, the straps of his suspenders against her skin. They were temptingly close. She knew she ought to ask him inside.

That was what bold, reckless rich girls like her were expected to do. And Nora was *excellent* at exceeding expectations. But then, inevitably, they accepted, and she lost interest at the *obviousness* of that answer.

She dreaded losing interest in August.

"I'd better go." August's voice was as casual as if it'd just been another day. As if the thought of coming inside had never even crossed his mind. "Seeing as when I told you that this was on my way, I technically meant that we are actually twelve circles *out* of my way and it's past curfew."

Nora tipped her head back to look at him, this boy who wasn't what she'd expected him to be any more than she was what he'd expected. "So you're not so good with what words mean? That's what you're telling me."

"I guess I'm not." August tilted his head down to hers. "You'd better come by and check the paper tomorrow."

"Didn't I hear that you'd quit?"

"I'm hoping they might be lenient when they hear I was in jail."

"Then I guess you'd better take this with you." She handed him her scrawled-out article, the code meant for the Grims buried in her words.

"You owe me for this." August took the paper from her.

"Oh, how will I possibly afford your exorbitant journalistic rates?" Nora rolled her eyes.

He placed one last kiss on her mouth before dropping his arms to his sides and releasing her from the embrace of his coat.

They lingered, neither of them making a move to go. And then, at last, August headed back down the street. Nora watched him for as long as she could before he rounded a corner, and the rain drove her into the mansion.

Nora's smile lasted all the way up the steps.

It lasted until a few seconds after she'd opened the door.

She found her grandmother waiting in the darkened foyer.

All of Nora's reckless joy drained in a moment.

Mercy Holtzfall didn't wait for anyone.

Chapter 67

LOTTE

The rain that had been threatening through the day had resolved into a real storm that was battering against the glass of the suite at the Paragon by the time Lotte got inside.

She expected the suite to be empty, like every night. But her mother was there, in a gown made of draping checkerboard black and white silk that pooled around her feet. She was pouring herself a drink. She looked like she'd been out already and returned, her hair a little disheveled.

And for the first time since she'd found her in the garden on the night of the ceremony, Benedict wasn't with her.

Instead, in the middle of the room, Liselotte Rydder was waiting. A suitcase at her feet.

Grace stood, recorking her bottle. "Oh, good, I was beginning to think we would have to send out a search party."

Lotte was still getting used to being someone's daughter. But while other mothers might worry about their daughters being missing for a whole day, Grace Holtzfall wasn't that kind of mother.

Lotte held herself still. "What's happening?"

"The final trial has taken place. There was some sort of dancing fit at the governor's speech tonight, with Clemency and Modesty in attendance. A few people caught fire, but that will heal. And then they all just . . . stopped. So everyone knew the ring had been won elsewhere. And since it looks like it's not on your hand, good news," Grace said flippantly. "You're going home."

It took Lotte a second to realize what her mother meant by *home*. Gelde.

"You're sending me back." Lotte almost choked on the absurdity of those words.

Letting go of the heirship had been like shrugging off a costume that had never fit. She had watched Nora accept death to save others, knowing that she didn't have that in her. That she wasn't selfless enough.

The truth was, she wasn't worthy enough to be the Heiress. And she *resented* having to be in order for them to want her. When none of them but Nora had ever made her feel like a Holtzfall. But the idea that they could send her *back* had never crossed her mind. Like she was a dress her mother had tried on before deciding to return it to the shop.

"Not my decision." Grace waved a hand vaguely toward Lis. As if with one flighty gesture, she could cast the blame away.

Hatred burst through Lotte's chest. Hatred like she'd never felt for anyone. Not even the Sisters. At least the Sisters had never pretended to care for her. "Just like it wasn't *your* choice to send me there in the first place." The words felt thick and bitter in her throat, seeing the discarded memories play out in her mind. "Just like you wanted me all along?"

Grace didn't meet her eyes. "Maybe if you'd won a trial, my mother would let me keep you, but—"

The scoff Lotte let out echoed loudly around the apartment. "I don't need you to care for me, Mother, but at least you could stop pretending that you ever did." And it was true, she saw it clearly now. In her time in Walstad, Grace had done nothing for her. Nora, even *Modesty*, in her own self-serving way, had done more to help Lotte through the city than her mother had. Her mother had just brought her here and expected her to be some imaginary perfect daughter. A daughter who didn't need her to be a mother. Who could serve *her* interests instead.

Grace raised her eyebrows, fine lines appearing in her brow where Lotte had never noticed them before. And for the first time, Lotte wondered if she was seeing the real Grace Holtzfall. Not Grace pretending to be more frivolous and silly than she was. Not the woman brightly pretending to be her mother, but the woman who had birthed her and left her.

"I gave up everything for you." Grace spoke in a low voice that was almost lost to the storm pounding the window. "Believe it or not, I was once the next Holtzfall Heiress. My mother was grooming me for the role, just like she did Nora. I won four trials before going into the woods. Verity only won a single ring. And I made it to Honor's ax before she did. It was right there in front of me, my entire future ready to grab, and I hesitated. Because of you." She said it like an accusation. "I had grown up for *years* with the unbearable weight of being a Holtzfall. Of seeing my brothers and sisters as competitors more than family. Of resenting them more often than I could love them. I imagined saving you from all that. And as I stood in the woods, I saw Verity. She was running, looking so desperate to prove her worth to our mother. She was so *hungry*. She wanted everything it meant to be a Holtzfall. I was worthier. I was better. *I*"—Grace's voice rose—"was my mother's heir! But I let my sister take everything, because I thought I had another life waiting out there for me. One with you and your father."

Lotte felt a shock go through her. It was the first time they had spoken of her father since Grace had denied knowing the truth.

She took a sip of her drink. "It turned out I was wrong."

"So you're not just a coward and a liar," Lotte said, her voice shaking, "you're selfish too. You were going to make Benedict break his oath and run away with you?"

Edmund Rydder's body, tied to the tree, blazed angrily in Lotte's mind. The consequences of trying to leave the Holtzfalls on full display.

"Benedict?" The shock that went over Grace's expression was real and raw for a moment.

"Enough," Liselotte Rydder said at last. "You asked for your chance to say goodbye and you were granted it." She drew a knife, moving toward Lotte. Lotte stepped back, only to slam into another figure behind her. Before she could turn, a hand went over her mouth. The knife went to Lotte's chest.

And then Lotte's world went dark.

Chapter 68

Mercy Holtzfall's eyes drifted to Nora's new ring for just a moment, a small flicker that Nora had learned from years of lessons to recognize as pride passing over her face. Once, she might have reveled in that, but now all she felt was apprehension. Once, she might have believed that her grandmother would never hurt her. But she had taken her memories. She had protected Modesty, knowing she had murdered Constance. And she had tried to kill Lotte on the road here. Nora had no doubt about that now.

"We'll speak in my office."

Nora hesitated. Mercy raised one hand, clicking her fingers. As casual as if she were calling for more ice in her drink. And as if from thin air, bronze and iron charms clamped themselves to Nora's wrists and ankles, shackles without chains. The charms forced Nora forward like she was a toy soldier being marched by an immense child's hand.

Mercy took a seat delicately in the office chair that had been in the family since the days of Capability Holtzfall. The charms forced Nora into the chair across from the desk.

"Well." Nora didn't bother trying to move her arms, even though the charms had positioned her to perch like an awkward doll across from her grandmother. "These won't go with any of my outfits."

Her grandmother didn't raise her voice, pulling out a slip of paper from her desk. "Who is Isla Brahm, and what exactly has she done to deserve fifty thousand zaub of our hard-earned money?"

Whatever Nora had thought this was going to be about, this wasn't it. She had arranged it the morning after she and Lotte had broken into Johannes & Grete. Lotte had told her about the lawyer who had died on the road trying to get Lotte to Walstad. It had been easy enough to find his widow. Nora wasn't sure what a fair payout for a death by mechanical wolf on company time, so she had arranged was for two years of his salary to be sent to the widowed Mrs. Brahm. She hadn't thought anyone would miss it. Nora could spend fifty thousand zaub on a bad day in Muirhaus Department Store, but she figured it would last Mrs. Brahm long enough for her to find a job of her own, or maybe a new husband. Whichever she preferred.

"Why?" Nora asked. "Can we not afford it? Because if that's the case, I have some dresses I'll need to return."

"I thought you were intelligent, Honora." Mercy Holtzfall's eyes flicked to the ring on Nora's hand. Applewood for selflessness. Not a virtue Mercy had ever held in high regard. "So tell me, do you truly think we should be handing out charity to every person in the city who has a sad story about her dead husband?" She already knew who Isla Brahm was. Of course she did. It had been a test. And Nora had failed.

The mansion was silent as Mercy Holtzfall watched her granddaughter, the rain drumming its fingers at the window. "Let's try again." Mercy twisted her hand, and Nora took in a strangled breath. "Care to explain, for one, what you were doing at Johannes & Grete when you were being tested by that rampaging troll?"

So. Her grandmother didn't know everything. She assumed it had been Nora there, not Lotte. And Nora wasn't about to correct her. To tell her she had been at a Grim rally.

"I figured I'd make sure my affairs were in order in case I died in the trials. I left all my best dresses to Modesty because they'll clash with her hair horribly. I didn't know she would try to kill me for them, though."

Nora had the brief satisfaction of having the upper hand on her grandmother. *I know*, she wanted to scream. *I know what you took from my mind*.

"Funny," her grandmother said, sounding as if she had never encountered someone less amusing.

"Do you think the papers would think so?" Nora challenged. Of all the grandchildren, Nora knew best that Mercy Holtzfall ought to be feared. But she was also by far the hardest to intimidate. "Do you think the people of Walstad would find it *funny* that one of the Holtzfalls is a murderer and that you're covering up her crime?"

"What would you have had me do, Honora?" Mercy sighed. "At the time, your mediocre performance meant that Modesty was my only option for Heiress. I couldn't have the people of Walstad questioning whether or not we were truly virtuous enough to rule over them."

"She killed Constance!" Nora's voice rose this time.

"You never even liked Constance." Mercy Holtzfall sounded exasperated. As if Nora were being deliberately obtuse.

"The world has changed since the days of Honor Holtzfall," Nora said quietly, the unsettled anger that had been with her finding firm footing now. "Maybe it was enough once that our existence shielded them from the dark things in the woods, but now we *sit* like dragons on our hoard of wealth. You've dragged me in here to berate me for giving a pinch of what we have away, while Modesty is walking around having *killed* someone in our family."

"Is it your journalist who filled your head with those ideas?" The mention of August drew Nora up short. Her grandmother seemed to sense she had Nora's attention. Silently, she slid open her desk drawer. Out of it came a small metallic bird. Nora recognized it as the emissary that she had repaired the first day she had met

August while sitting on his desk fiddling absentmindedly. It held a small note scrawled with August's handwriting. It was an address and a request to meet him. The message he had sent that she had never received.

That had led to him getting accused of murder. "This came looking for you during Constance's funeral. A cousin whose death you express to be so outraged over. But you would have abandoned your family to go on a tryst with your little journalist." She shoved the drawer shut. "I'm surprised you didn't find it while you were in here earlier rifling through my belongings."

It took everything in Nora's being for her eyes not to flick traitorously to the duplicate ring on the wall. Her grandmother knew she had been in here. But she couldn't know why, or else this conversation would be going very differently. If she found out Nora had given a ring to Theo to save Alaric, heads would roll. Theo's, specifically. Her grandmother would see his actions as treason.

The lie came easily. "I wanted my memories from the maze trial."

There was a long moment of silence before Mercy pulled her own Veritaz ring from her finger. The one that had been there since she won her own trial at just sixteen. Silver fir, for cleverness. "There is another memory you would have been better off stealing from me, perhaps. You might have learned more."

She pressed the ring to the wall like she had the day she had stolen their memories, opening the vault where the memorandum charms were kept. The air that came from the vault smelled damp and colder than anywhere in the Holtzfall mansion.

Mercy returned, brushing dust off a mirror.

She placed the charm on her desk, and with one more small gesture, Nora's left hand was released.

"Go on." Mercy folded herself back into her throne behind the desk. "You shouldn't waste your gift."

Once upon a time, Nora would have done whatever her grandmother wanted. Now she wanted to turn away from it out of sheer pique. But curiosity got the better of her.

Nora pressed her finger to the mirror. She couldn't read it like a mind as Lotte would, couldn't absorb it all in the blink of an eye. But the charm sparked with long-held memories that seemed to whisper to Nora. Mirrors always worked best for her gift. Better than photographs or glass. And all at once, the memory came to life inside the small circle of the mirror, like figures on a film reel, even as she heard it whisper in her mind.

She saw Grace Holtzfall. Younger.

Seventeen years younger.

Stepping into this same office wearing a voluminous dress and a bright smile.

Chapter 69

THEO

The Passenger Hotel stood as a crumbling monument in the 17th circle of Walstad. Far away from any of the other hotels in the city. Georg Bauer, a shoe salesman from the middle circles, had put everything he had into it.

But the Otto-Raubmessers owned just about every other hotel in the city, and Mercy Holtzfall's sister Temperance had married into their family. She had complained to her sister about the competition. And the Holtzfalls, who owned the land, like they owned all the land in the city, had raised the rent.

The Passenger was closed within the year. It had stood empty ever since.

The fox girl led Theo silently through the arched stone entryway. He was barely over the threshold when two mechanical forms lurched out of the dark, sharp jaws gnashing. Theo's hand flew to his weapon, but the fox girl twisted something on her wrist and the wolves stilled, then retreated, sitting back on their haunches on either side of the door.

Theo felt the now-familiar sickening twist of guilt. That was another spoil of the Grim break-in at the factory. The lights in the hotel were dim and flickering unsteadily, making the wolves look like they were still shifting.

The fox girl made it a few more steps before noticing Theo

wasn't following. "I thought you wanted to see your brother."

"He can be brought here." Theo stood his ground, the entryway at his back.

The fox girl considered him. "Alaric is not being surrendered before Isengrim sees that ring. And Isengrim is not coming to you. So either you come to him or we send Alaric's body to the Holtzfall mansion."

Theo was all too aware of how foolish it was to follow her farther into their lair.

But he had come this far.

He was holding a thousand-year-old ring in his hand for his brother's life.

They passed what had once been the ballroom, and Theo saw figures milling around a large map of the city. Weapons stolen from LAO were stacked against the wall. Hundreds of Grims had been rounded up after the attacks, but there were still a lot of them here, free. And they didn't seem to be licking their wounds.

Nora seemed content to hand the ring over. To leave the Grims to their fate in the woods. Let them eke out what power they could. But there was a feeling here of preparing for war.

A girl with pinned-back blonde hair glanced up as they walked past, her eyes tracking them until they turned right, down a hallway lined with doors. Theo could feel the walls closing in around him. A smart man wouldn't let an enemy leave after seeing this. And Isengrim didn't strike Theo as stupid. His hand tightened on his weapon.

One way or another, he would go down fighting.

The fox girl came to a stop in front of a door.

She rapped a quick, careful pattern. A moment later, the door swung open.

Theo had been prepared to find his brother bound, beaten bloody. Worse than he'd seen him a week ago. Instead, Alaric was looking in a mirror, straightening the cuffs on a knight's uniform. He looked up when they entered, smiling at Theo a second before a jolt of power went through Theo's body, sending him to his knees.

Through the sudden ringing in his ears, Theo heard his brother say, "Easy there! He's not the enemy."

Theo had been trained as a knight since he was a child. His instinct to fight back overpowered everything else for a moment, drowning out the shock and betrayal as he tried to pull himself up. But his legs didn't work. "A gift from LAO Industries," the fox girl said above him. "You'll be able to stand again in a few hours."

"Alaric—" Some part of him was still reaching out to his brother for help even though he understood it wouldn't come.

Alaric crouched down across from him. "I'm sorry for the deception, little brother." He clasped Theo's shoulder reassuringly, the way he had a million times before. "It was the only way."

"You were never a prisoner." He should have seen it the moment they had first dragged his brother out. Alaric Rydder, the greatest knight in their generation, would never be subdued by a rabble of Grims. He would have fought them.

Fought them to the death.

It had been a trick.

This was how the Grims had known about the Clandestine Court. How they had known where and how to come after the Holtzfalls. The answer, over and over again, was Alaric.

"It's for your own good, Theo. I don't want you getting killed running to their rescue. Not until it's all over." He sounded so much like the brother who had corrected him time and time again on the handling of his sword. "You moved mountains and Holtzfalls for me. To get us into the woods. We'll take it from here, but you need to stay safe."

"You're breaking your oath." Theo wanted to stand in front of his brother. Wanted to be able to look into his eyes and see the treason there. He wanted to see if everything their father had instilled in them, everything Lis had trained them for, had all meant nothing. He wanted to know when his brother had chosen this cause over his oath. He wanted to know if it had been an easy choice, when Theo's battle the last few days had nearly ripped him apart.

His brother's expression darkened. "I never swore any oath, Theo. Neither did our father. Neither has any Rydder since Hartwin a thousand years ago. But we unthinkingly serve them anyway. When Verity died, I saw my chance to be free. To join a fight I chose. Not one a long-dead ancestor chose for us."

"This isn't you," Theo pressed. "Isengrim has brainwashed you."

Alaric straightened. "I'm doing this for you, little brother. For all of us." And even as Theo watched, a glamour slipped over his brother, changing his appearance. Theo's own face smiled back at him, a mask over Alaric's real face. "We were made to be wolves, not lapdogs."

Chapter 70

NORA

*T*he bright green-and-gold tulle of Grace's gown swished across the polished wooden floors. Benedict followed Grace into the office, her eternal shadow. A shadow who was being given the slip more and more these days. But he couldn't exactly do much about it except protect her when she would allow it. There were nights, though, when he would lie awake, tortured by the Rydder oath, which urged him to go and pull her back from the shadows between the blazing lights of a Walstad night.

But some part of him knew that it was better. That the truest, most immediate danger was the way every part of him was pulled toward her. Ached to protect her beyond the oath.

Grace flounced into her mother's office, dropping into a chair across from her. Mercy was already sitting. Lis was at her shoulder, as always. She caught Benedict's gaze as he entered, a silent signal passing between them as fellow knights. Something bad was happening.

"All right, Mother, let's have it." Grace puffed hair out of her face, apparently oblivious to the tension in the room. "What have I done that can't wait until after the celebrations?"

Tonight's ball was to close the Veritaz Trials. For the past three days, Benedict had stood, tense, at the edge of the woods, aware that Grace was enduring things he couldn't protect her from. The trials of the woods had been known to go on for weeks in some generations, mere hours for others. Finally, just as the sunset was burnishing the tops of the ancient trees on the third day, Grace and Verity had stumbled out of the woods, side by side.

Verity's hair, which had been in a long sweeping braid before she went into the woods, now fell to her shoulders, the ends of it slightly singed. Grace was soaked through and shivering, claw marks across her arms. But they were alive, and Benedict felt his heart leap with relief—and with another emotion he knew was too dangerous to admit to himself. That would drive him mad if he did.

There was a quiet moment as the assembled crowd watched the two Holtzfalls with bated breath. And then, a smile splashing across her face, Verity held the ax aloft.

She was the victor of the trials. The crowd cheered and clapped. And Grace embraced her. The winner of a very long race. One that had many casualties, including their own brother.

Benedict had taken off the jacket of his uniform, moving to drape it over Grace's shoulders. He'd expected her to be devastated by her loss, but she was smiling as wide as her sister. Her real smile—the one from ear to ear that she never showed the cameras because she said it made her face look too wide.

By the time the Holtzfalls gathered that evening to celebrate their new Heiress, newspapers were lining the stands, showing two beaming heiresses. Several accused Grace of faking her joy to mask jealousy. Patience Holtzfall, their younger sister, was doing a delightfully bad job at hiding her own spite.

But Benedict knew Grace. He knew her joy was genuine, even if he didn't understand it yet. There were moments where she had talked about leaving the family, fleeing her life to live wild on a mountain or anonymously in some foreign city. But those were empty words. There was no other life when you were born a Holtzfall. Like there was no other life when you were born a Rydder knight.

"You seem to be having a fine time at tonight's celebration, considering you just lost everything I ever sought to give you." Mercy echoed

Benedict's own thoughts, her fingers drumming on the table. She was in Holtzfall green. A few wisps of pale hair escaped her pompadour.

"I read that sulking gives you wrinkles. If you'd like to speak to someone contrite, I suggest you summon Patience. She's so pinched with bitterness she's going to look like a prune by next week."

Mercy Holtzfall didn't laugh. And she didn't waste any more time with small talk before getting to the point. She pulled open a drawer of her desk to reveal a stack of photographs. She tossed the first one down on the desk in front of Grace.

Benedict only had to glimpse a corner of the image to know it wasn't meant for his eyes. A glimpse of bare skin and blonde hair fanned out across a pillow. He averted his gaze, aware of the blush climbing up his neck as one image after the other was slapped down in the otherwise crushing silence.

He wouldn't do Grace the disrespect of looking at her like this. Out of the corner of his eye, he could see Mercy watching the mirth leech out of her daughter's face.

"How did you get these?" she asked so quietly Benedict barely heard her. And then she seemed to remember herself. "Because whatever spy of yours stole them, Mother, it was just a bit of a laugh with a friend. I'm not planning on escalating it to the gentlemen's clubs or—"

Mercy slid the pictures back together into a neat pile. "Well, the so-called friend you were 'laughing' with came to me while you were in the woods. He gave me the choice to pay him three million zaub, or The Walstad Herald would print these on the front page."

"He wouldn't do that." Grace wanted to sound flippant, careless. She wanted to sound sure. She didn't.

"It's amazing how often people you love will surprise you," said Mercy Holtzfall, a calm anger settling over her. "For instance, until your friend came to me yesterday, I would have thought any daughter of mine clever enough to win the Veritaz ring for intelligence wouldn't be stupid enough to let a journalist, of all people, slip past their guard!" Holtzfalls were trained from a young age to only ever show journalists what they wanted seen by the entire world. Grace's face turned red, and the beginnings of tears were in her eyes. "But no matter how foolish you've been, I've taken care of it. I understand his ambition was to report to our fine city's paper from abroad. We agreed to three million ʒaub and a one-way passage out of Walstad. His ship left this morning, in case you have any illusions about going to find him."

Grace's head shot up, revealing she'd meant to do just that.

"Now." Mercy's anger slipped off as quickly as she had donned it, leaving her impassive again. "We'd best get back to the party. Let this be a warning to keep your future scandals from having a paper trail. Especially once I'm gone. Verity doesn't share our guile, she won't be able to cover things up for you this seamlessly. That's why I wanted you as Heiress. But I suppose the Huldrekall sees all. He could tell you weren't worthy."

She moved to brush by her daughter. But Grace reached out suddenly, grabbing Mercy Holtzfall's arm. "Mother," she said in a low voice. "I—" The tears cut off her next words. The desperation of a girl who had gone from growing up far too quickly to desperately needing her mother. Benedict had never seen Grace look so needy before. Her hand dropped to her midsection. "I need your help."

THE MEMORY ENDED THERE.

And Nora was slingshotted seventeen years forward again, sitting exactly where Grace had the moment her path had fallen out from under her feet.

Her thoughts pulled in every direction.

Lotte wasn't Benedict's daughter. Or the child of a Rydder knight at all. That was why their oath hadn't been broken by Lotte's blood. Her father was just some man—a *journalist*—who had manipulated and used her family for money. She could almost hear herself saying the words *August wouldn't do that*. Echoing Aunt Grace in the memory.

But then—the bloodvenn.

Child O. If it wasn't Ottoline, then was there another Holtzfall child out there with Rydder blood? The key to breaking the knights free of their oath?

"Lotte deserves to know who her father is," Nora said. "Even if he's . . . that." Nora's father had been dead for seven years. Some of the details were starting to fade, like whether his hair fell over his right eye when he laughed and what his laugh sounded like. But he was still a part of who Nora was. She saw him every time she looked at herself in the mirror. Lotte deserved to know that part of herself too.

"Ottoline is the least of our worries for once," Mercy Holtzfall said dismissively. "I've already sent her back where she belongs."

Nora jerked against the restraints. "You can't do that! She's one of us."

"The trials say differently." Mercy sighed. "I'm disappointed in you, Honora."

"I'm devastated." Nora's eyes were just about the only thing left she could move. She rolled them back as far as possible, knowing it would irk her grandmother.

"I can see the road you are heading down more clearly than you possibly can, Honora, and it only leads away from your family," Mercy said. "I already caught one of my would-be Heiresses too far down it to stop her"—she tapped at the mirror—"this time, you will not get any further. I intended for Grace to be my heir, and she let me down. And I don't care for Modesty." Mercy gazed out the window toward the woods. Through the darkness and rain, the towering trees were still visible. "She only performs well when she is on display. I thought she might serve a useful purpose as a competitor to make you rise to the occasion. Other than that, she is about as valuable as a show pony. What I have always admired about you, Honora, is that you are at your best when you're not being watched."

Nora *hated* that even now, shackled to a chair, the family's lies unfolding, she still wanted her grandmother's praise.

"And there will be things that you will need to do as head of this family that must be done . . . quietly. I have invested a great deal of time into you, Honora, and I don't enjoy having my investments squandered. That's not how you become rich."

"We're already rich."

"And I intend for us to stay that way. It's going to begin with some rules for you. These"—Mercy snapped her fingers, and the charms pulled Nora's arms up like a puppet—"will stay on. And they will keep you from going anywhere without my permission. You will be confined to this house until the final trial in the woods in four days."

"You can't keep me here." Her grandmother might be powerful, but no matter what their rings said, Nora knew she was smarter. And now her mind was ignited by bright, blooming rage. It would maybe take her a day to figure out the charm circuitry on her manacles and undo them.

"And once you're Heiress," Mercy said, seemingly ignoring her, "you'll have the influence needed to save Leyla's good name."

Nora felt her body jerk forward almost involuntarily at the mention of her other grandmother. "She doesn't care about her reputation."

"But she might care about going to prison." Nora understood the threat that was unfolding all at once. But just like with Oskar, she understood too late. "The Grims who attacked the Clandestine Court were using LAO weapons. Everyone saw them. It lends credence to that *dreadful* article saying that the break-in was set up by Leyla to allow them to plunder her factory in peace." She had accused Modesty of planting that story in the paper about the break-in.

She had never imagined it might have been Mercy. "Especially since they used those weapons to come after Modesty."

"I almost died in the Clandestine Court," Nora shot back.

"And what if they were to find out it was LAO magimek wolves that tried to kill Ottoline on the road here . . ." Mercy trailed off significantly. "All Leyla's granddaughter's competitors . . . targeted by LAO technology."

The anger that rose through Nora was hard and cold. "You've been building a case against her in secret. Because if I'm not Heiress, then you needed an excuse to wrest LAO out of her grip."

"We have to keep it in the family."

"It belongs to *my family*." Nora jerked against her constraints, her voice rising.

"And it will continue to—if you win."

Nora didn't like being threatened. "I *am* going to win." The words tasted bitter. She wanted to win because she was better than Modesty. She knew she could be a better Heiress too, even if it wasn't the sort of Heiress her grandmother wanted. She could be one who actually did something for this city. But the only thing that she could do to gain any power back from Mercy Holtzfall was exactly what she wanted her to do. The only way for her to win this war was to capitulate in this battle.

"Good." Mercy Holtzfall's smiles were rare, but a faint one played around her mouth now. One of real amusement, tinged with weariness. "You don't know nearly as much as you think you do, Honora." It was just enough that the lines in Mercy's face were visible, making her look her age in spite of all the money she spent on looking younger. "Lucky for you, I still have decades left to teach you."

The Tale of the Woodcutter

The Woodcutter's Heiress

The woodcutter was close to despair, but he had one more child, his daughter. The kindest of his three children. Though surely she, soft-hearted as she was, could not succeed where his sons had failed.

Nonetheless, on the third day, his daughter took the ring and her father's second-best ax and headed into the woods. Soon she crossed paths with the weeping woodsman. He told her his sad fate. The daughter looked at the ax in her hands, and without hesitation, she gave it to the desperate woodsman. After all, her family had not wanted for anything her whole life. His need was far greater than hers. And then she continued on her way.

Before long, she, too, came across the Lindwurm wrapped around the clearing. Like her brothers, she was afraid. But she had made a promise to her father, and she could not stop here. The daughter climbed a tree as close to the sleeping Lindwurm as she dared, and from there, she leaped over the beast without disturbing it.

In the clearing, she found her father's ax. It was as her father had said, tangled in the branches of the tree. The daughter had no ax of her own to cut her father's prized ax free, for she had given it to the weeping woodsman. But as she looked at the branches, she realized they looked like one of the puzzle boxes her father carved on idle days by the hearth. Slowly, she got a grip on the ax and carefully began to thread it through the branches, choosing her path carefully, dodging dead ends and snares until, after many hours and several wrong turns, the ax was free in her hands.

And finally, the honorable woodcutter's daughter returned home, holding her father's ax. She presented it to him, apologizing for not having the ax she had left with, telling him she had given it to someone in greater need than them. And when the woodcutter held the ax in his hands, he knew that this one was truly his.

His daughter had triumphed because where her elder brother had proven he was clever, he had not shown himself to be anything more than that. Her younger brother, too, had only proven he was honest. The woodcutter's daughter had been clever like her brother, in solving the puzzle of the tree. And honest too, in admitting that she had given away the first ax. She had also been patient, spending hours getting it free. And brave, daring to pass the Lindwurm when neither of her brothers would. And she had been selfless, helping the woodsman in need.

And because of all these virtues, she was worthiest to inherit. And so the woodcutter's daughter became his heiress, while her unworthy brothers got nothing.

So ended the first of what would come to be known as the Veritaz Trials.

PART VIII
HONESTY

Chapter 71

NORA

"They've caught Isengrim."

Her grandmother delivered the news on Nora's third morning of imprisonment with the casualness of reporting the weather. Nora paused for only a moment in the doorway to the Blue Salon, a thousand thoughts racing through her mind at once.

"Did they?" Nora forced the same casual tone in return.

They were the first words Nora had spoken since the night she had won her ring. She knew the silent treatment was petty and childish. And that it was costing her more than it was Mercy. But everyone she would actually *care* to talk to was gone anyway.

Nora was alone.

She had been alone before the trials too.

But then there had been August.

And Lotte.

And Theo.

And now . . . being alone again was far worse than the first time. Like being pushed back out into the cold after enjoying a warm hearth. Lotte had been tidied away. The family's disgrace swept into obscurity. The *Herald* published a fake story that she had retreated to the countryside to dedicate herself to the convent in which she was raised. Nora wanted to believe that Lotte was still alive. But she couldn't be certain with her grandmother.

Nora's code had been printed in the *Bullhorn* the day after the dance hall, so at the very least she knew that August had made it to the paper alive to deliver the missive. But she had no way to know if the Grims had received the message. If Theo had been able to trade the ring for Alaric's life.

And August—

Last night, Nora had stood on one of the house's balconies and screamed. Screamed at the top of her lungs. Hoping that someone might tell a newspaper. That somehow that would be enough for him to deduce that she hadn't kissed him then abandoned him.

But all the papers were printing was that Honora Holtzfall was finally taking the heirship seriously. Now that she had a ring, she was forgoing her frivolous ways. Secluding herself in her duty. Determined to win.

That, at least, was true. And one way or another, it would be decided tomorrow. When she and Modesty entered the woods for the final trial.

"Isengrim was turned in by a tip from a neighbor," Mercy informed her, sliding the newspaper across as she sank into her seat. The same one she had sat in the morning of the Veritaz Ceremony, when she had bound her magic to Honor Holtzfall's ax. "For all they pretend to stand unified," Mercy Holtzfall said, "it didn't take them long to turn on their own."

"Well, starving people out does tend to work in a siege." Nora pushed the paper away.

New governor Hugo Arndt had promised *measures* after the night of the Grims' attacks, and he had delivered on them.

Checkpoints and blockades had gone up throughout the city. Lower circles were refused entry to the upper circles, even those who had jobs in the 1st-circle houses and hotels. Those who were depending on their paychecks to feed themselves and their children. Supplies from outside the city were redirected to the 1st circle only.

Rewards were offered for anyone who would turn a Grim in. The largest one, of course, was promised to anyone who could unmask Isengrim.

The new governor was truly 1st circle, through and through.

"Don't be dramatic, Honora." Mercy Holtzfall sighed. "Be ready to leave by six."

"Leave?" That drew Nora up straight. The charmed manacles hadn't even allowed her to set foot outside the house since she had entered it. Now her grandmother was talking about her being allowed to leave like it was nothing. Like she wasn't a prisoner in her own ancestral home

"The governor will be giving a speech. We are expected to attend."

IT DIDN'T SEEM TO MATTER TO HUGO ARNDT THAT HIS HOUSE had been turned into wreckage by the maze trial, he simply moved into the governor's mansion. Where the previous governor had gone, Nora had no idea.

He had set up the steps of the grand house to look like a stage.

Hugo Arndt stepped up with a grin to applause and cheers from the crowd. His voice boomed through the zungvox as he made his speech. Nora barely heard any of it. *Blah blah blah, return our city to safety. Blah blah blah, end of the plague of the Grims.*

Instead, her eyes were scanning the crowd. She had spent the day waiting for her chance. Pacing, preparing. Changing clothes three times. The *Bullhorn* must have sent *someone*. Not August, maybe, but *someone*. Someone to whom she could slip the note that she had scrawled on a ripped-out page of a book from the Holtzfall library, in the hopes it *might* make it to August.

The rest of the crowd had eyes firmly trained on the stage. They were all waiting for the same thing, a glimpse of the man himself.

Of the legendary Isengrim. And finally, Governor Arndt got to it. "Here, to stand trial for his crimes," he said, announcing him like the newest attraction at the circus—and Nora couldn't help it, even her eyes were drawn forward—"is the man who calls himself Isengrim."

A shackled man was pulled onto the stage. The assembled crowd burst into a cacophony of hisses and boos.

He was just a middle-aged man. Sun-hardened skin around a scar over his face that had taken an eye with it. Muddy-brown hair going gray at the temples. He shuffled along the stage, shoulders slumped.

And with a cold wash of certainty, Nora knew.

This wasn't the man who had spoken at the rally on the day of the second trial.

She wanted to be rational. It was impossible to compare the man in the mask speaking to his disciples to a shackled prisoner. A wolf in the wild wasn't the same as a wolf in a trap. But this man, she was sure, wasn't Isengrim.

And then a shot went off.

A knight grabbed Nora and pulled her down as the man onstage crumpled like a rag doll, blood spreading over the front of his shirt. All Nora could think was, *Who had a gun?* Those had been illegal in this country since they were invented.

"Murderer!" The cry carried over the crowd. "Murderer!"

Franklin Otto. Nora recognized him. His son had been among those killed by the Grims at the Clandestine Court.

Franklin handed the gun over without a fight, cameras capturing the scene as Governor Arndt stepped back up to speak. "Well, we *were* going to go through a trial," Governor Arndt spoke over the cacophony that followed as Franklin Otto was pulled away. "But this was where things were inevitably headed." A chuckle ran through the crowd, and Nora felt that old burning anger rise. "I suppose I should thank Mr. Otto for his expediency."

And just like that, it was over.

Isengrim was dead.

No.

An impostor was dead.

It was possible that it was a misunderstanding. That someone had turned this false Isengrim over just to collect the reward. But something scratching at Nora's brain told her that wasn't it. There was something else happening here, another reason the Grims wanted the city to believe they had lost their leader.

"Grandmother." Modesty closed in on them in a whirlwind of an ugly yellow dress. "I think this calls for a celebration. We are all going to gather on Angelika's barge for a little river cruise. Nora *must* come!"

Nora knew exactly what was happening.

She was a prisoner in the Holtzfall mansion, but to Modesty, Nora's invitation to live with her grandmother looked like favoritism. Modesty wanted Nora out of the mansion for the night. Away from their grandmother. Usually, Nora would rather have been anywhere but with Modesty. But since her alternative was to be locked in a mansion, for once, she and Modesty wanted the same thing. She just couldn't let her grandmother know that.

"Must I?" Nora didn't quite dare roll her eyes. Mercy Holtzfall would never grant her permission to do this if she looked like she wanted to. But she couldn't oversell her disdain either. Her grandmother would see right through that.

"Yes, you must." Nora felt a sting of satisfaction that turned to disgust as she realized how much her grandmother had trained her to think like she did. "But you will be home by midnight." Mercy gestured absently to the charms on Nora's wrists. "Or you will be brought home."

Midnight. That would have to be enough freedom. Because tomorrow she entered the woods. And she would either come out the Heiress, or she wouldn't come out at all.

Chapter 72

LOTTE

She dreamed of the Ice Heart Girl.

Once, in the days when stories were real, there was a girl with a stepmother.

The girl was beautiful, as all girls in stories were.

And the stepmother was jealous, as all the stepmothers in stories were.

One day, the stepmother sent the girl out into the snow to search for holly to hang above the hearth. The stepmother sent a knight under the pretense that he would protect her. But really, he had orders to kill her and return with her heart.

The knight was loyal. He followed orders.

The girl's heart dripped blood all the way home.

If she wasn't a girl in a story, that would be where it ended. But in this story, she was found lying in the snow by a Vettir, an immortal spirit who was both born of winter and the maker of it.

He was so taken by her beauty that he crafted her a new heart out of ice. The girl rose from her deathbed of snow and followed the drops of blood that had fallen from her own stolen heart all the way home.

When she got there, she couldn't find her heart. She searched every chest and every cabinet and every drawer. And when she was done with those, she started searching the inhabitants of the home.

One by one, she ripped out the hearts of every person living in her father's great hall, to see if any of them were hers.

It didn't matter how they pleaded for mercy. The girl had been kind once, but her heart was ice now.

Her stepmother was the last person she searched for the heart. She didn't think she would have it. The girl had offered her heart to her stepmother many times before, and the woman had refused it. The stepmother begged like everyone else had, but with her dying breath, she finally told the Ice Heart Girl what they had done with her heart.

They had thrown it in the fire.

And so, the Ice Heart Girl plunged her frozen fingers into the last embers of the fire, and there she pulled out the smoldering lump that was left of her first heart. She put it next to her new ice heart. And then . . . none of the stories agreed on what happened next. Whether the ember melted the ice, or the ice doused the ember, or whether they both burned the other one out and the Ice Heart Girl simply died.

Lotte's hands flew to her chest, fingers clawing at her breastbone until she found her heart, beating frantically in her chest.

She was awake.

She was alive.

Drugged. Not dead.

She remembered what her grandmother had said the first time they'd met. That she would never kill her own blood. Lotte hadn't believed her then. And she hadn't believed her when Lis had closed in on her with a drawn knife.

Maybe Mercy Holtzfall didn't have the guts of the Ice Heart Girl's stepmother. Or, more likely, there was some other reason she was being kept alive.

She didn't have to open her eyes to know where she was. She had slept in this bed for sixteen years. At least, on the nights when she hadn't been confined to the briar pit. Now, as she fought her way out of the last of the drugged sleep, she was aware of dusk's light leaking through the small window of the cell.

She used to rise at dawn here in the convent. Now she was rising at sunset. It seemed she had picked up some things from the Holtzfalls after all.

Lotte struggled to sit up, her body weak.

She had no idea how long it had been since her fight with her mother in Walstad. Hours, days . . . months. It might be all over. The last trials of the Veritaz gone.

Nora might be Heiress.

Or she might be dead.

She managed to pull herself out of bed, stumbling toward the door. Nora's last words to her echoed in her mind.

As long as I'm wearing a ring, you'll have a place in this family.

The door rattled, firmly locked under her hand.

The old familiar anger and fear that Lotte always felt in the convent began to rise. The feeling of helplessness. Of being trapped here. Of being alone and unwanted.

Except she wasn't.

She was Ottoline Holtzfall.

The thought occurred to her so suddenly and so simply that it caught Lotte off guard.

She was Ottoline Holtzfall. She wasn't powerless.

A handful of charms, courtesy of Nora, had adorned her hands when she'd stood across from her mother. But they'd taken those. Lotte moved toward the suitcase she saw in the corner. But as she rifled through it, she realized that it had nothing but the plain dress she had worn when she arrived in Walstad. There was nothing else in there. Nothing left of her life in the city.

And then something sharp pressed against her breastbone. Right above her heart.

For the first time, Lotte took stock of what she was wearing.

It was the same dress she had worn to the dance hall, still smelling faintly of smoke. And over it was Theo's jacket. The jacket she had worn that day on the balcony, when Nora had first tried to teach her how to activate charms.

Lotte felt around the collar of the jacket until her fingers closed over it. The tiny silver pin that was meant to light a candle. Lotte turned the silver pin in her hands, the charmed symbols catching the last of the light through the window, desperation cracking into hope. She would rather have been accidentally left with the lasa charm she had used to open the door at Johannes & Grete.

But this would do.

And her dress already smelled of smoke anyway.

Lotte plunged the pin into her index finger, her blood blooming scarlet and beading down the surface of the pin, the symbols on the surface drinking it up hungrily.

She turned the charm toward the door a second before the fire poured out.

Far more than was needed to light a candle.

The ancient brittle wood of the convent door caught fire like a tinderbox.

Lotte wrapped cloth from the bed around her face as the smoke started to billow in.

The Sisters might retire before sunset, but that didn't mean they were too deep in meditation to notice the convent was on fire. As the room filled with the smoke and the wood cracked violently, Lotte heard voices outside, panicked, calling for water. By the time they'd started dousing the fire, it had already charred the wood black.

She didn't need a lasa charm. All she had to do was shove.

The scorched remains of the door collapsed at the feet of three startled Sisters of the Blessed Briar holding empty buckets.

Lotte regarded them calmly from where she stood in the doorway. She waited to feel afraid of them. She waited for her body to tense in anticipation of a punishment. But the only fear was what she saw on their faces.

They had been fools to think that she could be held in this cell.

That cell had held Lotte, the motherless orphan. Unwanted. Cursed.

It wouldn't hold Ottoline Holtzfall.

"I knew they would send you back once you were no good to them."

This voice was one Lotte knew well. Sister Brigitta's face was soured with satisfied venom as she appeared in the light of the embers outside the door.

"The knight said you would sleep for a week, but I suppose she made a mistake and only dosed you for three days. You'll start by getting out of that whorish dress, of course." The pendant around Sister Brigitta's neck swung in and out of the light. Her hindern. "The dishes from dinner need scrubbing. And if you finish quickly, you can give penance until the sun rises. And tomorrow—"

Lotte's hand snapped out, latching onto Sister Brigitta's wrist, bypassing the charm.

The vitriol of her mind hit Lotte like a wave. The Sisters had always heaped punishment and penance on Lotte, but none of them had reveled in it as much as Sister Brigitta. Because Sister Brigitta hated the Holtzfalls with an ancient and festering resentment that she had nursed in the dark corners of her mind for seventeen years.

Lotte saw it now. The whole truth. Of a girl growing up, watching the Holtzfalls through the papers. Prosper Holtzfall, the daring gambler always out on the town. Patience Holtzfall, always in the same circle of rich children who went to all the places they were supposed to. Then Verity and Grace, who never went where they were supposed to. A perfectly painted matched set, always out at bars and clubs. And once, when they were kicked out of the Swan Salon, they were photographed throwing an impromptu party in the middle of the street, closing down three blocks as they invited every passing car to join the fun and served champagne to the whole city. And finally Valor Holtzfall, the gentle youngest child, too young to be in on the fun, but not too young to compete when the trials came. And when young Brigitta Kleiner saw them sipping champagne in their bright dresses, the hunger of poverty would twist in her stomach a little more painfully.

They had everything, everything in the world. And still they had taken Nik from her.

In the years since he had died, his face had faded a little, blurred by memory. And his voice too. But never the sound of his laugh. Never the warmth that spread to the tip of every finger and toe when he smiled. Like when he had taken her hand that morning on the ice. She had been wobbling on her skates when he elbowed her, pointing excitedly at the edge of the lake. Where the famous Holtzfalls were stepping out on the ice. And in the middle of the fabled Veritaz Trials too. One of them was showing off, doing spins, her blonde curls splaying out around her like sea-foam. And Brigitta Kleiner had envied her.

Grace Holtzfall was landing a perfect spin when the ice cracked.

Brigitta barely had time to panic before she was plunged into icy water, taking Nik with her. She had held onto his hand as long as she could, but with fingers numbed from the cold, she wasn't sure if she was still holding him when she fought her way back to the surface, only to find the ice had sealed above their heads. Freezing water flooded her lungs as she screamed, as she panicked, banging on the ice.

Later she would learn that above the ice, crowds had gathered at the edge of the lake, panicking, screaming, but unable to break through. This was no normal ice; this was a trial, and it wasn't one meant for anyone but a Holtzfall—even if it had been inflicted on so many who weren't playing their games. Journalists had been poised, waiting, waiting, until at last Grace Holtzfall broke back through the ice.

She had barely dragged herself up before she turned back to the frozen surface in a desperate bid to get to her brothers and sisters. She'd been fast. Fast enough to save almost all the other Holtzfalls.

But not fast enough to save everyone.

The newspapers only ever remembered that trial as the day that Valor Holtzfall drowned. His name, his young face, on every paper, as the city seemed to be expected to mourn him. They never mentioned the names of the two dozen others who had been killed.

Certainly not Nik's. There were no photographs of him printed day after day, saying how tragic it was to die so young. There were no pictures of the mourners at his funeral under headlines about how brave the Holtzfalls were to go on with the trials without him.

As usual, the Holtzfalls didn't know what they had cost others, and they didn't care. They didn't care that they'd taken Brigitta Kleiner's whole future. Forced her out of the city to swear herself to a convent to avoid starving to death.

And even here, she hadn't been free of the Holtzfalls.

Grace Holtzfall had arrived in a sleek black car, wrapped in furs and pearls, with a knight at her shoulder. As if she had come to taunt Brigitta. That *her* little problem could be solved by coming here for a few months. And then she could just leave, wrapped in those same pearls, shedding her shameful child like an accessory that wasn't in fashion.

Brigitta could feel her resentment swelling to fill her entirely, burning her to rot inside. They might not care about the child that she left behind any more than they would care about Brigitta or the boy she lost to the ice. But this girl was still a Holtzfall. The closest Brigitta Kleiner would ever get to having her revenge for what they had taken from her.

"Let go of me, you wretched girl." Sister Brigitta yanked her hand out of Lotte's grip, splashing candle wax across Lotte's palm as she pulled back. But it was too late.

Lotte knew everything.

All this time, she had thought of herself as nameless.

All the time in the city, she had struggled to believe she was a Holtzfall.

But she had always been one.

She had pulled away from the heirship because she had believed she was unworthy. Because no matter how far away she was, there had always been some small voice whispering that she was unworthy of it. Unworthy of her family.

But now she was looking that voice in the face. And she saw her for who she really was.

She saw herself for who she really was.

"You know who I am," Ottoline said calmly. "And you didn't have a choice in what my family cost you on the ice." Sister Brigitta's face blanched at the mention of what she had seen in her mind. "So I'll give you a choice now: Move out of my way or I will burn the whole convent to the ground."

Sister Brigitta hesitated for just a second. And Lotte found herself wondering whether her hatred of the Holtzfall family really would get the better of her. Whether she would stand her ground. Whether she might think Lotte was bluffing.

And then finally, Sister Brigitta moved.

It was the right choice. Because the Sisters had been right about Lotte her whole life. She wasn't very virtuous. Certainly not virtuous enough that she would have felt guilty setting this place alight.

N ora couldn't decide whether being stuck on a boat was worse than being stuck at the Holtzfall mansion. She had tried to break away from the knight her grandmother had sent to guard her at the pier, but that had come to nothing. And now she was stuck here, floating in the middle of the Wald. Wearing a dress of stained glass. It was patterned for the silk to look like the panels of a window in a chapel and charmed so the setting sun glowed through it. It had been enough to draw Modesty's jealous gaze, and hopefully make her regret inviting her. But now the sun had set, her dress had gone dark, and Nora had taken up a position on the stern, watching the city go past, glaring at anyone who was stupid enough to make conversation with her.

"Champagne?" The familiar voice jolted Nora out of her boredom.

August was wearing a waiter's uniform, doing a bad imitation of a bow while holding a tray carrying a single glass of champagne. Out of sheer habit, a comment was on Nora's lips—*I see it didn't work out in journalism after all*—before she remembered that he couldn't be here.

"August." She grabbed the champagne off the tray before he could tip it over and draw more attention. She felt her heart drop, quickly glancing around for anyone else who might have seen him. She sidled up to the barrier, pulling him after her, away from curious ears. "You can't be here," Nora whispered urgently, eyes darting around. She had wanted to get him a message. But even she knew seeing him was too dangerous. If her grandmother found out she had been anywhere near him . . .

"You're going to want to hear this."

There was nothing she wanted to hear more than she didn't want to risk being caught with him. "August—"

"I know where Oskar Wallen is."

Except that.

Nora had been given a lot of gifts by a lot of suitors in her time, but this was easily the best. "I could kiss you right now."

August's smile widened. "I wouldn't stop you."

The thrill of danger went through her. What was she doing? She knew how far her grandmother would go. She needed him to leave. But not without answers.

"Where's Oskar?"

August pulled a scrap of paper from his pocket, his face turning serious. "Nora, if I give you this, you've got to promise you're not going to do anything rash. You have enough proof. If you give it to your grandmother, she can have him arrested." There was no way Nora was telling her grandmother a thing about Oskar Wallen, she thought, turning the constraints on her wrists. "Nora, you have to be careful. He's dangerous."

"I'm dangerous," Nora countered.

"Nora," August said, pressing the piece of paper into her palm. "Promise me."

Nora felt a rush of warmth where his hand touched hers. She leaned forward, pressing her mouth to his quickly.

"I promise," she lied.

As she pulled away, a sad smile seemed to cross August's face. A smile so unlike him that it made Nora draw back.

And even as she watched, August vanished like an illusion.

Chapter 74

LOTTE

There were no automobiles in Gelde. But Lotte would walk back to Walstad if she had to. It would take days. But she would make it eventually.

By my oath.

Benedict's voice flashed in her mind suddenly.

Lotte whipped around, her eyes darting through the familiar hallways of the convent. It was as empty as it always was at night. No sign of Benedict. No sign of anyone.

But she was sure that she knew his voice.

Lotte closed her eyes. It was a strange thing, to be standing in the convent, not trying to push the voices away for once. Instead trying to draw them in.

"What are you doing here?"

It took Lotte a second to realize that the voice wasn't in her mind.

Her eyes snapped open to see the girl standing in front of her. She looked both familiar and like a fading memory.

"Estelle."

It had only been—well, Lotte had no idea how long it had been since she had been driven away, leaving Estelle in the square of Gelde. Standing here, Lotte felt like she had lived several lifetimes. But Estelle looked just the same. Except the stricken look on her face when Lotte had refused her a ride to Walstad had turned to fury now.

"You left without me," Estelle accused. "You *knew* how much I wanted to go to Walstad. And you left me behind." There was once a time when Lotte would have reached into Estelle's mind, desperate to find the answer that Estelle wanted to hear.

"You were going to leave *me* behind," Lotte replied instead. "You and Konrad and your plot to run away to the city together."

Lotte realized her mistake the moment Estelle's eyes narrowed. "How do you know that?"

Lotte had forgotten. In the city she had forgotten how afraid she had been in Gelde. Afraid every single day that Estelle would find out about her curse—her gift—it didn't matter what she called it. Find out that everything in her friendship with Estelle was a lie. That she would find out that Lotte had craved her friendship, craved belonging so badly that she had stolen thoughts from Estelle's mind over and over again.

Once, when they were children, a younger girl, Ada Reiss, had stayed up all night making cherry tarts because she had heard they were Estelle's favorite. She had pretended they were for everyone in their small schoolhouse classroom. But Estelle had found out that Ada had stayed up all night just in hopes of impressing Estelle. No. She hadn't found that out. Lotte had *told her* that. To keep her friendship from drifting over to Ada.

Estelle had scorned Ada in front of the whole class for trying to win popularity with her. For *wanting* anything so much that she would go to those lengths. Ada had cried as Estelle threw the cherry tarts on the ground. And Lotte remembered the sickening, terrified twist in her stomach imagining if Estelle ever found out how much Lotte wanted too.

Even now, all these years later, she felt shame curl her shoulders, aching to shield that desperate child she had been then. Lotte hated that part of herself. She hated that she was here in Gelde with it again.

In the city she had survived trolls and climbing brambles and yet she was most afraid of this. This had lived in her since she was a little girl. The lie that she had managed to belong somewhere, when all she had done every day was try and want and lie. And Lotte was sick with lying.

"I read your mind. I read your mind for years. Because I wanted to be your friend." The truth came out all at once, like a long-dammed-up stream of words finally breaking free. "And then you were able to leave me behind so easily, I realized how little you cared about me. And it hurt me more than anyone has ever hurt me." The words felt like exposing a raw nerve of vulnerability. She felt like little Ada holding out cherry tarts knowing Estelle would smash them on the ground. But she felt herself peeling off the last of Lotte, the girl who did things because she wanted to be liked. Because she wanted someone, *anyone*, to want her.

And underneath, Ottoline Holtzfall came fully into the light.

"And I left you here because I wanted to hurt you back."

Lotte could already hear the scorn that was poised on Estelle's tongue. She felt it twisting in her stomach. But the smile that crossed her face wasn't Estelle's. It was gentler than any expression she had ever seen on her face.

And in a blink, Estelle was gone, like an illusion vanished into thin air.

Lotte suddenly stood alone in the hallway of the convent, her heart racing in her ears.

She had seen magic over and over in Walstad, but here in Gelde, it seemed wilder and out of place. Lotte reached into the air, as if she might somehow find Estelle there, solid but invisible.

And in the faint light, she saw there was a wooden band on her ring finger.

It had been a trial.

A final *damned* trial when she hadn't been expecting one.

It was meant to be one trial per contender.

There were four of them left.

There had been *four* trials already. Temperance. Bravery. Unity. And selflessness.

But there had been five of them once. Before Constance died. And now a fifth trial on the eve of their entry into the woods. A trial of honesty, which Nora had just badly failed by lying to August . . . or some illusion of August conjured by the Huldrekall.

Nora forced her mind to slow down, to tamp down her self-recrimination, touching the ring she still wore. She had a way into the trials tomorrow no matter what. And—she was still holding the scrap of paper. It hadn't vanished when August had. It was still solid in her hand. And when she opened it, there was an address scrawled on the inside.

She wondered if a trial meant to test her honesty would lie to her.

She had to be home by midnight.

The charms on her wrists and ankles were a keen reminder of that.

Which meant Nora had an hour.

Nora climbed up on the railing of the boat. Before she could think better of it, she dove into the Wald. She just had time to hear screams from the boat, a knight calling her name, before she hit the water.

SHE CUT THROUGH THE CIRCLES QUICKLY, MAKING HER WAY downtown. Ignoring the looks that passersby gave her, a soaking-wet heiress. No matter where the Rydder knights thought to look for her it wouldn't be here.

The address was for a modest house in the 7th circle. A boring middling part of the city. Looking at the brick-and-white-fronted house, amidst all the others just like it, you'd never know it belonged to the most notorious criminal in the city.

But from where she stood in the street, Nora could see some of the charms embedded in the walls. To keep the house from burning down. To avoid break-ins. There was a single light in the window on the second floor. It was quiet this late at night. No cars roamed the roads. No one out for a stroll.

She pinched her own charm between her thumb and forefinger, flooding it with magic.

And then she ripped the façade of the house off.

None of his charms guarded against that.

The bricks shattered with a terrible noise, mortar, concrete, and pipes all crumbling into dust. Until all that was left of the street side of the building was a cloud of slowly settling dust.

Nora waited. There was shouting from the nearby houses, doors being yanked open, people screaming. No doubt someone would contact the police soon. But she still had time before they arrived.

Time to deal with him.

If Nora had learned anything from the past three days locked up in the Holtzfall mansion, it was how to wait.

Finally, emerging from the cloud of dust over the debris, coughing, stumbled Oskar Wallen. He was wearing paisley-printed pajamas in yellow and blue.

"Mr. Wallen." Nora greeted him, feeling her blood run cold with rage. "Thank you for meeting me at this late hour."

Oskar Wallen's eyes were almost as big as his ears. She had caught him defenseless. Whatever charms he wore wouldn't be enough. Nora had magic to burn. Tomorrow she would either be the heiress to more magic than anyone knew what to do with or she would be stripped of any she had left. She might as well spend it now.

Nora reached for another of her charms. "See, here's the thing. I didn't realize when you said you were sorry for my mother's death that you were actually apologizing to me." A burst of flames emerged just in front of his feet, sending Oskar staggering backward.

"Miss Holtzfall," Oskar Wallen started, sounding more composed than a man in pajamas standing in the rubble of his house had any right to be. "I'd love to be able to tell you I know what you're talking about. Really, I pride myself on having the best inform—" He was cut off as the next jet of flames blasted up, singeing the toes of his slippers.

"Explain to me, then"—the flames sprang up again, this time encircling him—"why you were paying off Lukas Schuld?"

Oskar Wallen paused, the façade slipping. "Miss Holtzfall." His voice was darker now, not the man who she had exchanged pleasantries with in the Silverlight Market. "I believe platitudes are for the weak-minded, and neither of us is that. So I implore you, listen closely when I tell you again: I *wish* I were able to tell you that I know what you're talking about." His teeth were gritted, and his voice carried a weight and significance that made Nora pause, even in her rage. "You are here because there are some things you already know," Oskar Wallen said, his eyes boring into hers. Like he was trying to tell her something wordlessly. "But you must also realize you don't know everything yet. You should have come to me when you had all the answers."

Nora felt restless. "Since I'm here so early, why don't you just give the rest of them to me?"

Oskar Wallen was at her mercy, his house in ruins behind him. She could kill him at any moment. And he had the nerve to laugh, a sound that traveled down the street, merging with the sirens approaching. "I would if I could, Miss Holtzfall." And then he looked her squarely in the eyes. "By my oath, I would tell you if I could."

By my oath.

They were words that had followed Nora her whole life. From every knight on the heels of a Holtzfall. Every time her grandmother gave an order, those words were echoed back. As they protected them. As they pledged to them. As they obeyed.

"It's true what they say, you know," Oskar said. "It doesn't matter how powerful one is in this city. So long as there are Holtzfalls." He bared his teeth in an angry smile that looked like an ugly caricature of his gentlemanly affectation. "You'll make an excellent heir to your grandmother one day."

Somewhere in the city, a clocktower struck midnight. Nora felt the charms on her arms and legs spark to life, wrenching her away from Oskar Wallen.

Dragging her back through the streets of Walstad. His words echoing in her ears like a taunt over and over again.

By my oath. By my oath. By my oath.

Chapter 76

LOTTE

y my oath.

Benedict. His voice came again, like a distant whisper, snapping Lotte's attention away from the ring on her shaking hand. She had sworn to herself she would walk back to Walstad if she had to, but a ring—that changed everything.

Everything.

By my oath.

Lotte followed Benedict's voice now, closing her eyes and pulling on it like a thread through a labyrinth. A thousand other whispers began to draw closer as she moved. Until suddenly her hand met solid wood.

Lotte's hand was resting against the door to the briar pit.

She had woken in the briar pit the morning her life had changed. The day she had learned she was a Holtzfall. But she had woken here many other days before that. Spent countless nights curled on the icy stone floor, surrounded by thorns on all sides, listening to the whispers of the dead who had dared to come to rip the princess from the Bergsra.

Or so she'd believed.

Nothing the Sisters had ever said was true. She had learned that from Benedict. But she had never thought back on the whispers from the briar pit.

I swear on my oath. I will not—You wouldn't—Did my mother
She will not—I'd rather die.
I never—If you don't, I'll always—How could you—
I saw nothing.
You will never understand—

She knew those voices. They didn't belong to the dead. They were stolen memories.

Thousands of stolen memories. Whispering. Like the mirrors that had sat on her grandmother's desk after the maze trial. She remembered her grandmother opening the secret door in her office. The way the air had tasted familiar in a way she couldn't place.

Air that tasted of turned soil and old stone that wasn't found in the sparkling new city of Walstad.

It came from here. From the place where Holtzfalls put the things they wanted kept secret. Inconvenient memories. Unwanted daughters.

A thick wall of briars greeted her at the bottom of the stairs.

In all her sleepless nights, she had been careful to steer clear of the walls. But Lotte knew now how the Holtzfalls guarded the things they wanted to keep secret. She reached out, her hand passing through the briar, thorns scraping at her arm. Drawing blood.

It was always about blood with the Holtzfalls.

Her palm met solid wood, even as the briars withdrew, like they were bowing out of her way, revealing a perfectly circular keyhole. It was a twin to the one on the secret door inside Mercy Holtzfall's office.

And now she had the key.

The wooden band fit perfectly. It turned as if this door and all its secrets had been waiting for her.

Behind it, the corridor stretched what must be all the way below the convent; lined row upon row were memorandum charms. A cacophony of whispers rose to meet her.

Another door waited at the end of the hallway.

That one would lead into Mercy Holtzfall's office. A byway.

This was Lotte's way back. Back to Walstad. Back into the game.

She moved swiftly down the hallway, even as the voices she passed tried to snag at her. Memories begging to be remembered by someone.

Some mirrors were covered with dust. Lotte's fingers brushed against them. Maids witnessing indiscretions of long-dead Holtzfalls. Secrets that wouldn't hurt anyone anymore. Small humiliations that seemed petty now.

But the closer Lotte came to the byway, the more she began to recognize faces. Memories of her mother, of Mercy Holtzfall's other children. And then their children. Memories of secrets belonging to Nora, Modesty, Constance, and Clemency.

A memory of a rainy night in Walstad.

Of a dark alley.

Of a woman stepping out of an automobile.

Of a knife.

Lotte knew who had killed Verity Holtzfall.

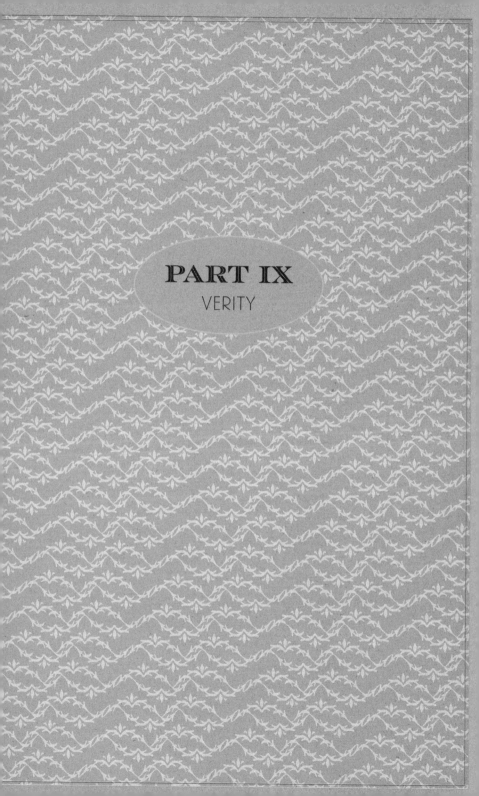

PART IX

VERITY

Chapter 77

NORA

*S*tay out of the woods, little one.

There you will find dangers you do not yet know how to face.

Nora's breath misted in the predawn spring air at the edge of the forest. It had only taken her three hours to disarm the cuffs after they had forced her home. She left them on the carpet in the front hall for her grandmother to find. It didn't matter anymore; she wasn't going anywhere.

She hadn't slept. She'd waited as the salve worked to heal the scrapes across her body from being dragged through the city.

Away from Oskar Wallen.

Away from her answers.

By my oath. By my oath.

Knights' words. From the man who had killed a Holtzfall. Taunting her with some piece that she was missing still.

She was the first one to the edge of the woods that morning. Before her grandmother. Before even the cameras. Nora couldn't see much past the first line of trees in the dark. That invisible barrier she had never been able to pass, which had haunted the periphery of her vision her whole life. Nora didn't know what awaited her in the woods.

She was wearing a black leather-paneled skirt that was gathered at her waist on one side, showing off the close-fitting black leggings below. Voluminous silk cloth sleeves poked out from underneath a black jacket and black leather shoulder squares drew attention to her face.

Stay out of the woods, little one.

No. At long last, Nora was ready to face the woods.

The journalists arrived as the sky lightened. She didn't glance their way as they filed into the pen set up for them a few feet from the starting line, even as their cameras began to click. They'd think she was here early for their benefit. She wasn't. It turned out she didn't really care what they thought.

"Waiting for dawn here at the border of the Old Woods, ladies and gentlemen," a vox host started to say into his machine, filling the dead airwaves until the sun came up and they would be able to enter the woods. All over the city, people would be turning on their voxes to listen to the start of the trials. Waiting for news of who would be the next Holtzfall Heiress.

The light crawled across the ground. Once it touched the base of the trees, they would be able to enter the woods.

The rest of the family, along with most of the 1st circle, was gathering on the opposite side of the gardens from the journalists. They were perched on delicate garden furniture in crisp morning suits and bright dresses, being served glasses of champagne and platters of food.

Nora found herself looking for Theo. Looking for a nod that would let her know Alaric was safe. That the Grims had kept their bargain. But she couldn't see any knights among the crowd.

Instead she spotted Aunt Grace lounging in a silk nightgown with a sleep mask pointedly on her head. Lotte had been sent away, and Aunt Grace wallowed in indifference.

Nora kept her feet rooted at the edge of the woods. There would be time for anger later.

Anger for how much she had imagined Aunt Grace cared for her, and been proven wrong. For how much of herself she still saw in

Aunt Grace. And in Mercy Holtzfall. In the ugliness of both winning and losing.

Modesty arrived. She was bright-faced, as if she might actually have slept. That movie-star smile was splashed over her face as she waved magnanimously at the cameras snapping her way.

"Our second and final competitor, Modesty Holtzfall, ready to join her cousin at the starting line," the vox host yammered on as Modesty came to take her place next to Nora.

Nora's mother had stood here seventeen years ago. Next to her sister.

It should be Lotte here next to Nora. The way it had been Grace next to Verity.

"May the best heiress win!" Modesty dashed Nora a winning smile as she sidled up next to her, flashing the dual rings on her hand. Maybe it would be harder if it were Lotte here. Even allies became competitors in the trials.

Two rings, Nora suddenly realized. Modesty was only wearing two rings.

Temperance and bravery.

Two trials won by Modesty. The trial of loyalty lost by everyone. And Nora's victory in the trial of selflessness.

But as of last night, there had been five trials.

The trial of honesty.

That left one ring unaccounted for.

Clemency stood in the crowd with the rest of the Holtzfalls. If she had won, she would be strutting right up here. It was possible that yet again they had all failed. That they had proven themselves to be the most dishonest family that ever lived.

Mercy Holtzfall emerged from the house, and a hush fell over the garden until she came to stand face-to-face with Nora and Modesty. She touched her fingers to the charm on her throat, sparking it with magic.

"A thousand years ago," Mercy said, her voice reverberating around the garden and through the voxes across the city, "our great ancestor Honor Holtzfall sent his three heirs into the woods, granting each of them the chance to prove they were worthy of inheriting the great burden of being the bearer of the blessed ax. In the woods, each heir's truest virtues were shown. Today, it is two of my granddaughters' chance to show—"

A crisp whistle pierced suddenly through the dawn, slicing across Mercy Holtzfall's words. A murmur ran through the crowd at the audacity of someone interrupting her, heads craning, hunting for the source.

They all saw her at once, blonde hair tangled and blazing in the beginnings of daylight as she moved across the garden.

"Ladies and gentlemen," the vox host said in a hurried hush, "Ottoline Holtzfall has suddenly appeared." Lotte was wearing the same dress she'd had on four days ago when they'd parted ways in front of the dance hall. "As we all know, the newest Holtzfall retreated to the bliss of the countryside a few days ago, choosing to live a simpler, more virtuous life. And it seems she is wearing . . . as she approaches the starting line . . . could it be . . . ? Yes, it is, ladies and gentlemen—"

"She has a ring." Nora felt her heart leap in a confusing mix of joy and apprehension. But already she was beginning to move toward Lotte. Competitor or not, she was glad to see her. She walked on even as her grandmother barked at her to stop, her voice echoing around the whole garden.

Lotte and Nora embraced as they met, Nora pressing to the edges of her mind how glad she was to see Lotte, hoping her cousin could read it. *I would have come for you*, she promised in her mind. *If I'd won, I would have saved you.*

She pulled away, eyes roaming over her cousin.

There was something different about her. Not just the ring.

"Ottoline." Mercy Holtzfall's voice was the same bright artifice that it had been when she had first appeared on the day of the ceremony. "I see you won a trial in spite of your best efforts."

"Turns out I'm the most honest Holtzfall," Lotte replied. When Nora had first set eyes on Ottoline in this same garden, she'd resented her for looking like every Heiress who had ever preceded her. For looking more like Nora's own mother than Nora ever could. But this, she realized, was the first moment that Lotte was carrying herself like a Holtzfall.

Lotte's gaze met their grandmother's unforgivingly. "I was going to give you the chance to try your hand at it, but I don't think honesty runs in the family." Lotte turned to Nora, and there was pain written on her face. "There's something you need to know." Lotte pressed a memorandum charm into Nora's palm.

Nora looked down at the small mirror, a sudden sinking feeling of dread in her stomach.

The sky was rapidly lightening. They didn't have much time. But whatever this was, it was important—Nora could feel the urgency radiating off Lotte. Whatever this was, it couldn't wait.

Nora flicked the memorandum charm open, pressing her fingers to the mirror.

Her Holtzfall gift sparked to life as she played the memory.

Chapter 78

NORA

The first thing she saw was her mother.

At ease in a chair in Mercy Holtzfall's office. Nora was seized with the urge to reach for her, to crawl through the glass and into her mother's arms. She heard herself choke out a sob, but the image just played under her fingers like a film reel.

Verity Holtzfall couldn't hear her daughter's grief. It hadn't even happened yet.

The memory, Nora realized, was playing from over Mercy Holtzfall's shoulder. This was one of Liselotte Rydder's memories.

Mercy was saying, "That's not amusing, Verity."

"It's not meant to be, Mother," Verity replied. Nora felt her mother's voice crawling its way into the broken pieces that her death had left behind, forcing them farther apart. "We have enough magic stored to last a hundred heiresses' lifetimes. Why shouldn't we share some of it among the poorer circles?"

"You want to insult them with handouts?"

"Generosity is a virtue, Mother. I gained my ring because of it. We could pay for every child in Walstad to go to school, and we'd still have money to burn. We could give every tenant in the city a chance to buy their land from us so that they aren't indentured in rent to the Holtzfalls for their whole lives. We could give medicine out for free. We could—"

"And then what, Verity?" Lis could only see the back of her mistress's head, but she could sense the anger in the set of her shoulders. "I've spent my tenure at the helm of this family regaining what my father squandered with his kindness. All for the sake of this family's legacy. If you give handouts today, they'll just want more tomorrow. Do you plan to bankrupt us?"

"Grandfather hardly made a dent in the fortune. And even if he had, there's more money coming in every day."

"Have you considered what you are leaving behind for Honora?"

"I'm leaving her plenty." Verity sighed, exasperated.

There was a long moment before Mercy Holtzfall spoke again. "I made a mistake not preparing you equally. You have never understood what it means to be head of this family. Not like Grace would have. Not like Honora will."

Verity Holtzfall's smiling mouth pressed into a thin line. "None of us could ever be good enough for you, Mother. Grace let you down by losing, I've let you down by not being Grace, and one day Nora will let you down by not being *you*." The truth of that echoed through Nora even now as, in the memory, her mother stood up with a sigh. "Fine, Mother, it's your money, for now. But one day your portrait will be up on that wall too . . ."

"Wishing death on your mother so you can inherit, how nice."

"I'm not wishing you dead." Verity sounded exasperated as she turned to leave the office. "But things are going to change when I inherit, with or without you, Mother."

Painful silence stretched out as the branches of the office door wove themselves back together behind Verity Holtzfall. Liselotte waited. Finally, without turning to face her knight, Mercy spoke.

"Summon him."

Nora knew what was coming the second before she saw him.

As every single piece fell into place at once, forming a clear picture.

Oskar Wallen stepped into her grandmother's office.

I wish I were able to tell you that I know what you're talking about.

His words rang around her mind.

By my oath, I would tell you if I could.

He wore a garish tie and a plethora of jewelry. In his own world, he might have looked wealthy, but here, across from Mercy Holtzfall, he seemed to Nora to be playing pretend.

"Am I here to be *ordered* to kill your daughter?"

His fingers tapped across the head of the cane.

The stolen bloodvenn. Shared blood with Liselotte Rydder. A knight.

Child O.

Not *O* for Ottoline. *O* for Oskar.

Oskar Wallen, the son of a laundress and an unknown father.

But very little was unknown to Mercy Holtzfall.

Here, he wasn't a gangster running his own empire, he was just another knight summoned to serve his mistress.

"No." Mercy waved behind her at Lis. "Liselotte will take care of that." And then she intoned the words. "As ax bearer of the line of Honor Holtzfall, I order you, Oskar Rydder, to find someone else to take the blame. You will cover up this murder and not speak a word of what you have done."

Oskar Wallen's face soured as the order closed its jaws around him. As the order gripped him.

It didn't matter that he was raised on the streets, not in the barracks. It didn't matter that he'd been trained as a gangster, not to wield a sword. It didn't matter that he had no loyalty to the Holtzfalls. He had the blood of Hartwin Rydder, and that was enough. He was as bound to Mercy Holtzfall as their most loyal knight.

"By my oath, I will obey," he sneered back. "Have her at the intersection of Brosmar Road and the border of the thirteenth at midnight."

When he departed, Mercy spoke to Liselotte without turning. "You know what needs to be done." It wasn't a question. And in the memory, Nora sensed that Lis knew this was not the first time she had been asked to do something like this. Although of course, she had forgotten those times as well. As she would this one.

There were always *signs* after a member of the family died.

After Mercy's husband had died, Lis had tasted poison on her fingers. When Verity's husband died, Lis had found instruments for tampering with an automobile. As if she had left them behind for herself as clues, knowing that her memories would be taken.

Clues to what she had done in the name of obedience.

She had fought to be the best knight of her generation because she had believed in a life of honor and duty and service. But there was no honor in these deaths.

For the first time in the memory, Liselotte spoke. "And Alaric?"

Nora understood. Lis Rydder had practically raised Alaric and Theo after their father died. She wanted him to be spared, unlike his father. She wanted him to be sent elsewhere and kept ignorant of what they were doing here.

But either Mercy didn't understand or she didn't care. "I'm sure you can manage to dispatch him as well as my daughter."

Nora's fingers were shaking now as she spun the memory forward and forward, quickly passing by Lis's memories of the rest of the day. She saw flashes of other faces, of her own, of Theo's and Alaric's.

Until, finally, she was there. Driving through a rainy night in Walstad. Alaric in the passenger's seat, restless and bored. Lis's fingers shifted uneasily on the steering wheel. He was too good for this. Too talented to be wasted like this. Lis drove slowly downtown through the storm. She glanced in the rearview mirror, checking on Verity in the back, who was looking anxiously out of the window.

"Are we nearly there?" Verity asked.

"Nearly," Lis said as the car's headlights splashed along the rain-slicked walls of a narrow alley. "Nora sent the emissary from a bar a few streets over," Liselotte lied, pointing down one small alley. "But it's too narrow in these old streets to get the car through. We'll have to go on foot."

Lis stopped the car, stepping out into the rain. She pulled open the car door, opening an umbrella as she went, to let Verity out.

"Which way is it?" Verity asked anxiously as she let Liselotte help her out of the car, pulling her coat tightly against the drizzle.

The knife went through her stomach like it was nothing.

A cry ripped out of Nora now, as her mother tumbled to the ground in the memory. Alaric was at her side in a second, on his knees next to Verity, her blood all over him even as she gasped, dying. His face turned up to Lis in the rain. She expected to see confusion there, but she saw understanding. He had never been a fool, this boy, her dear sister's grandson. He had seen the world for how it was far sooner than most did. Especially knights.

"Are you going to stab me too?" He straightened, facing his great-aunt. "Or do you need to make it look like I put up a fight?" He looked so much like his grandmother. Like Lis's sister. More than their father or Theo ever had.

Lis moved like a whip. No matter how much she trained them, she was always the best of the knights. The knife slashed across his forearm, drawing blood before he could even draw his sword.

"Bleed a trail to the river," she instructed. "Make it look like your body was tossed in and swept out to sea. They'll think you're dead. Mercy will never send anyone out looking for you. But you will have to go far, far away."

"What will you tell Theo?" Alaric let the blood run down his arm.

"Nothing."

Alaric nodded. He was gone, into the storm, leaving a bloody handprint on the wall behind.

Lis waited by Verity Holtzfall's slowly dying form.

"You may come to regret that." Oskar Wallen's voice came from behind her. "My mother thought she could get me out too. And yet here we are."

"I have many regrets." Lis didn't look up, watching Verity die. She remembered the day Verity had been born. "Alaric should have a life without the same regrets."

"Tell her it'll be taken care of." Oskar's voice was bitter. "By my oath. Now you should leave. The cops will be here soon."

And Lis watched as the woman who would have been head of the Holtzfalls finally died.

Chapter 79

NORA

Last night, face-to-face with Oskar Wallen, she had been pure power, burning and destroying. But what overcame her now was colder as she raised her head from the memory and came face-to-face with her grandmother.

"You killed my mother." She said the words out loud, to see how they tasted. How they landed.

Mercy Holtzfall had the gall to look exasperated.

She had taken away Nora's entire life. Her father. Her mother. Her place in the family. Her identity. She had made her grandchildren fight for the heirship. To the death.

She had destroyed this family. Because she couldn't stand to see it change. Even as the city, the world, changed around it.

And she just looked annoyed.

Almost against her will, Nora felt magic flow out of her with a scream.

If she usually lit her magic with a spark, this was a firestorm. It hemorrhaged out of her with raw anger, flowing straight for Mercy.

Mercy Holtzfall moved wildly, taking a staggering step back as she fought to shield herself from the storm that crackled out of every inch of Nora's being, even as the crowd screamed. She wasn't sure what she was aiming it at. Not sure what she intended to do. Not sure how far she was willing to go.

But she was burning white hot.

Mercy had more magic than she did. Nora sensed her fingers twitching, ready to pin Nora back. Or maybe force her into the woods. Force her to compete as the sun slowly crept above the horizon.

A shadow fell across Nora from behind. "Is that true?" It was Aunt Grace's voice. She was still in her silk pajamas, but now she looked wide awake. "You killed Verity?"

And then another voice, Aunt Patience. "Answer her, Mother!"

"You killed one of *us*." Uncle Prosper's voice shook.

What was left of the previous generation lined up in front of their mother, each of them seeming to gather a piece of anger from Nora. A piece of understanding at what their mother had done. What she was capable of. Aunt Grace moved Nora and Lotte behind her as Aunt Patience did the same with Modesty, who looked torn now, her eyes darting to the edge of the woods. As if this might be her chance to get a head start.

Because what was building now, on the edge of the final trial, was all-out war. Anger and magic on both sides.

And then, somewhere deep in the woods, there was a noise. Like a starting shot at a race.

Nora's eyes moved up in spite of herself, catching sight of a flare rising from the trees, deep in the woods.

Like a signal.

And as it exploded above the treetops, Nora felt something pull at her.

At the magic in her bloodline, even as it sparked in rage.

And then she felt her magic begin to unravel.

Chapter 80
LOTTE

The flare dissipated in the sky as Nora and Modesty fell to their knees, both crying out in pain. Across the garden, Clemency folded in on herself with a shout of agony.

Lotte's gaze shot to her grandmother. But Mercy was on her knees too.

Something terrible was happening.

Patience Holtzfall was calling for a healer. For a knight. For someone to help her daughter.

The knights.

Lotte had always known the knights to stand between the Holtzfalls and even the smallest hint of danger. Lotte searched in the crowd, looking for Theo. And there, she saw a flash of uniform. And for one moment, she thought it was him. But even as she watched, his face shifted ever so slightly into one she didn't know.

"On my signal!" the figure in the knight's uniform called out.

And suddenly dozens of servants and attendants were snapping to attention. Dropping their trays of champagne, weapons appearing in their hands.

Grace's hands found Lotte's, a desperate pulse of urgency running through her mother's mind. Now was their chance. She had failed to escape with her daughter all those years ago. But she could escape now. She was running and pulling Lotte after her.

The knight pulled his fist down to his side, a silent signal.

And then the attack started.

Chapter 81

THEO

He saw the flare go up over the top of the trees, through the small window of his makeshift prison cell. He saw it burn through the sky with a blazing triumph, announcing the end of the Holtzfalls. The end of their power.

There was a time when knights hunted monsters.

Then there was a time when knights protected heiresses.

And the world was changing now.

Chapter 82

AUGUST

The sound of a champagne cork popping jolted August awake at his desk.

For one half-asleep moment, the sound made him look for Nora. But it was Mr. Vargene, the editor of the *Bullhorn*, wielding an open bottle with an uncharacteristic grin stretching the scar on his face.

"Cheers!" Mr. Vargene called out, raising the bottle. "To the end of the Holtzfalls."

It was then that August saw the flare in the sky.

Chapter 83

NORA

Nora had wondered, in her worse moments, what her life would look like without the heirship. But she had never taken much time to think about the moment of loss. The second where her magic would be drained out of her if another hand closed over the handle of the ax before hers . . .

But the moment her legs dropped out from under her, she knew that was what was happening. Her magic spinning out like a spool of thread on a line, reeled out by a force too strong for her.

It shouldn't be happening. The final trial hadn't begun yet. No one was in the woods.

Except for the Grims.

They had claimed to want a way into the woods to tap into the magic in the earth the way Leyla did. To draw from the bottomless well of magic. Nora had told herself this wouldn't matter. They could have all the wealth they wanted; it wouldn't take any away from the Holtzfalls.

She had never even thought that they might head for the ax. For their vast fortune tied to Honor Holtzfall's relic. Waiting in the woods.

Enough magic to rule over an entire city.

Shots went off, striking person after person, Holtzfall after Holtzfall turning from flesh and blood into solid marble. Eons' worth of Holtzfall magic ripped away, turned against them.

All the better to kill them with.

Nora pulled herself to her feet as Modesty staggered next to her. There were already Grims closing in. A man in the white shirt and black tails of a waiter fired a charm, the spell hitting Aunt Patience, turning her to stone in an instant. Her face froze in shock, arms raised to shield herself even as a scream ripped out of Modesty's throat.

Nora found herself casting around for Lotte. For Aunt Grace. Instead, she found her grandmother. The rising sun glinted off the wolf mask of the figure closing in on her. For the first time, Nora thought her grandmother looked her age. The Grim pointed at Mercy Holtzfall like an accusation. And in the light of the rising sun, Nora could only watch as her grandmother, the most powerful woman in the city, turned to stone.

There was nowhere to run. The Grims encircled Modesty and Nora, the morning light bouncing off their metallic masks.

Nora stood up straight. If she was about to be turned to stone, she'd at least like to make an elegant statue. She wasn't going to be frozen forever running like a coward.

And then she saw him, moving through the press of Grims like a general among his troops.

"Alaric." Nora's voice sounded preternaturally calm, even to her own ears. He looked the same as he had appeared in Lis's memory.

He had never been a prisoner of the Grims.

That was clear now.

"Where's Isengrim?" She cast her gaze around the garden. "Is your wolf too much of a lamb to come lead his troops himself?"

"Nora." Alaric's smile was patronizing. "You're a bit too old to believe in the big bad wolf."

The big bad wolf. A made-up figure to keep little children in line. To scare them away from the woods, where there roamed far worse things than wolves.

Isengrim wasn't real either.

Of course he wasn't. He was a figurehead so perfect there would be no choice but to follow him. A big bad wolf to scare the wood-cutter's descendants. It could be any man with a mask. He could be anyone. Impossible to arrest. Or kill. Or defeat. Because he was an idea.

Unlike the Holtzfalls, whose faces were splashed everywhere. Who could be rounded up and destroyed.

Alaric smiled again. The kind of smile he used to grant Nora when her mother was being demanding or when she was dragging her feet on the way to some Heiress lesson with her grandmother.

She wanted to rip it off his face.

"Following an idea instead of a person," Nora scoffed. "That's always ended well."

"You won't be around to find out." He raised a weapon.

In a moment, she would be stone.

And in spite of herself, she winced.

But it didn't strike her.

It struck an invisible shield, bouncing off and hitting one of the Grims, turning him to stone.

For a moment, it felt like an immortal being had reached out of the woods and slapped away the killing blow. That she had been saved like the worthy girls in stories from centuries ago.

And then Lotte stepped in front of her.

Her dress, which had been white silk once, was smeared with ash. And blood.

The same blood coated a shielding charm in the shape of a golden hairpin, topped with a tiny pearl swan. Nora recognized it as belong-ing to Aunt Grace.

She shouldn't be eligible, Clemency had whined at the unfairness of it all. *We all had to wager our magic. She should too!*

Nora had never been more grateful for anything in her life than she was that Lotte hadn't been at breakfast the morning of the Veritaz.

Who even is she? Clemency had demanded.

She was a Holtzfall.

The only Holtzfall in all of Walstad with any magic.

Chapter 84

LOTTE

Lotte had tried to flee this family before.

On the night of the second trial when she had broken in and found the bloodvenn.

She thought then that she was holding a way out of this family.

But her mother had been right the first time.

There was no way out of being a Holtzfall.

They stood now. Three Holtzfall heiresses. On the edge of the woods.

Modesty, Nora, and Lotte, together, their rings on their hands.

The boy in the knight's uniform who looked like a strange echo of Theo clenched his jaw. "We haven't met," he said to Lotte now. "You must be Lotte."

"It's Ottoline Holtzfall to you."

She could feel her blood coating the charm.

She could hold it for now, but not forever.

Lotte met Nora's gaze, looking for a plan there. Or *part* of a plan.

Nora held her eyes a long moment, as if considering, before glancing behind them for just a fraction of a second. Glancing toward the woods, where the sun had just touched the edge of the trees. Toward the only place that they could run and no one could follow them.

Stay out of the woods, little one. There you will find dangers you don't yet know how to face.

They turned, even as Lotte dropped the shielding charm.

The Grims staggered forward, but they were too slow.

As one, the three surviving heiresses entered the woods.

Epilogue

efore the collapse of the House of Holtzfall, Trudie Junge had never tasted champagne. Now there was a whole crate of it below her desk at the *Bullhorn*. The wine cellars of the Holtzfall mansion had been raided within hours of the Grim victory, as celebrations rolled out across the city. And tonight they were celebrating another victory. The *Bullhorn* was the last newspaper left in Walstad.

First, the *Herald* had gone. They'd accused the Grims of being dictators, running a headline that read: *NO ONE VOTED FOR YOU! WHY SHOULD WE OBEY?* That was the end of them.

The *Gazette* had followed.

The Charmed City Times had been shut down for printing a picture of the three surviving Holtzfalls on the front page, suggesting that they were in hiding somewhere, planning their return. But it had been months, and they hadn't returned. They were dead, everyone knew that, claimed by the woods like so many others.

What was left of their rule was being dismantled. Their knights, who had been drugged to sleep by one of their own the day of the Grims' attack, were being held for trial. To see who among them were truly loyal and who had only been trapped by their oath.

One by one, in the three months since the coup at the Holtzfall mansion, one paper after another had tumbled. Now all the news in the city came from the *Bullhorn*.

A cork popped loudly, flying into the ceiling as the assembled staff cheered. The fancy glasses they were filling had been taken from another house in the 1st circle. Karl, who used to write obituaries, downed his drink before smashing the coupe on the floor to cheers from the bullpen.

Trudie sipped her champagne slowly, enjoying the heady feeling of the bubbles. When she'd moved to Walstad from her little farming town, she'd imagined a life in the city of sipping drinks in glitzy dresses and dancing the night away. Now, with no more Holtzfalls hogging the city's luxuries, she had the life she'd always wanted. Trudie wasn't even sure she liked the taste of champagne all that much, but she liked the feeling of holding a drink that would've once cost her a whole day's salary.

Out of the corner of her eye, Trudie caught sight of August Wolffe.

He was just coming into the office, head down, ducking around the celebrations, seeming deep in his own thoughts.

"Did you hear the news?"

August looked up as Trudie came to the edge of his desk. "The news?" he echoed. For a moment, she had the strangest feeling that he was looking at her but seeing someone else. And then the confusion on his face was gone. He cracked that sideways smile that always made Trudie flush. "We make the news."

"Oh, no." A little bit of Trudie's champagne slopped out of the glass as she transferred it from one hand to the other. "It's a turn of phrase. You know, like an expression or—"

"What news?" August asked, cutting her off before she could start to ramble.

"We win!" Trudie beamed. "We're the last newspaper standing!" She raised her glass to cheers August before she realized he wasn't holding a glass. "Oh, let me get you some champagne!"

She followed his eyes as they drifted to the case under her desk.

The Holtzfall crest stamped on it had split in two when they'd pried it open. There'd been rumors floating around about August and one of the Holtzfall girls. One of the older journalists swore up and down that he'd seen August in a bar with Honora Holtzfall the night of the election.

Which was totally absurd, of course.

Holtzfalls didn't consort with journalists.

"I don't drink warm champagne," he replied. His mouth tilted up again, as if enjoying some private joke.

Another cork popped loudly. After that, Trudie lost track of him.

By the time their glasses were empty, it was far past Trudie's normal leaving time. The sun had set, even now at the height of summer. Some of the streetlights flickered as she made her way home, hoping the air might clear her head. The lights had been doing that lately. But Trudie was sure the Grims would fix it soon enough. If LAO had always managed to keep the lights on, so could the Grims.

Brehmer Street was lined with people waiting for their dose of magic. The Grims had promised magic and money for all, and they were upholding that promise—you just had to wait your turn, was all. Trudie cut down a small side alley to avoid the crowds. A lot of people were looking to move now that there was no more rent to pay.

After all, Mercy Holtzfall was gone, so no one owned the land they lived on.

But Trudie liked her little apartment. It was a short walk from the office. And now it was all hers. And that made all the difference in the world.

"Help . . ." The small voice startled Trudie out of her tipsy thoughts.

It had come from the mouth of the doorway up ahead. "Hello?" she called back warily.

"Help me." The voice came as a reedy whisper this time. A child's voice. Night had fallen fully now, and she couldn't see into the shadows of the doorway ahead.

Suddenly Trudie was a little girl again, her mother tucking her into a warm bed next to the hearth, telling her stories. *Stay out of the woods, little one*, they all began. *There you will find dangers you do not yet know how to face.*

There weren't many woods near Harlund, where she'd grown up. It was miles and miles of grazing land for the cattle, no trees in sight. But Trudie had still been frightened by the tales of the things in the dark trees that used to hunt little girls. Before the Holtzfalls and their ax came to keep them at bay.

All of those tales were hundreds of years old.

But . . . there had been rumors recently.

Things that looked like the Nokk swimming in the waters of the Wald.

Scratches like claw marks gouged into buildings.

Screams in the night. Some of Trudie's neighbors had started to whisper that Walstad had forgotten the things they feared before the Holtzfalls. But when she'd heard August mention it to Mr. Vargene, he'd brushed it off. And since they were the only newspaper in town, that meant it wasn't news for anyone.

"Help me," the little voice whined again.

Trudie took a wary step back, her breath catching in her throat.

And then a small figure stepped into the light.

It was a child. Small and pale, with large haunted eyes. It was clutching something that looked like a ragged doll to its chest. All at once, Trudie's fear gave way to a sudden rush of embarrassment.

Was she really such a little girl, still afraid of the dark, that she would run away from a child in distress? She took a step forward, crouching down unsteadily on her heeled office shoes. "Are you lost?" she asked.

It was only as the child opened its mouth to reply that she saw its teeth. Rows and rows of sharp teeth bared at her in a nasty grin, caked with blood. Trudie stumbled backward, her anxious heartbeat picking up to a panicked pace as she scrambled away.

"Help me." The child cackled.

Then it leaped.

ACKNOWLEDGMENTS

The Notorious Virtues is a long book that has traveled an even longer road. And many, many people have guided it along the way to find its home in your hands now. So here's hoping I have enough pages left to thank everyone who helped it get here.

Firstly, this is a book about family, so I'd like to start with mine. My very first book is dedicated to my parents, and really, every book I ever write will be for them in some way. This one is no exception. Mum and Dad, without you, I wouldn't have made it to the end of this road. Or if I had, I wouldn't still be standing. I am here, in every way, because of you.

I have a brother who would unquestionably win a trial of intelligence over me (and has in the form of winning University Challenge in 2018, small sister brag there). If you were at all impressed by the code in chapter 33, he is the one who cracked that. Max, thank you for being the science one so I can be the arty one.

While this book has had many guides, it's only had one agent: Molly Ker Hawn, who has been there from the beginning and is still standing here with me at the end, even though the road was longer than expected. I wouldn't want to make the journey with anyone else. And of course to the excellent team at the Bent Agency who supported this book to this point: Martha Perotto-Wills, Emma Lagarde, and Aminah Amjad.

To my editors past and present: Alice Swan and Kendra Levin, who acquired this book. Stella Paskins, who saw its infancy. And

Kelsey Murphy, Jenny Glencross, and Natasha Brown, who so patiently and caringly guided this book to maturity. Good editors are those who are able to see what you're trying to achieve and help you get there. But the best editors are those who can see what you are able to achieve even when you don't think you can. When I couldn't see the woods for the trees, my editors were better guides through than a magical ring ever could be. Thank you all.

But it also takes an editorial village, and this excellent village is made up of Claire Tattersfield, Want Chyi, Ama Badu, Krista Ahlberg, Andrew Hodges, Abigail Powers, Jack Bartram, and Crystal Watanabe. The devil is in the details, and with this many words, and writing a book in a world I started building over a decade ago, there are a lot of devils, and I am grateful to have had such an expert team to help me tackle them.

I also want to extend a huge thanks to Jen Loja, Jocelyn Schmidt, Tamar Brazis, Ken Wright, Leah Thaxton, Shanta Newlin, and Emily Romero.

If this book caught your eye, it's because of the incredibly talented cover artist Katt Phatt. And the cover designers Samira Iravani and Theresa Evangelista, as well as art director Emma Eldridge. And if you thought the inside looked nice, that's because of the hard work of text designers Kate Renner and Lori Thorn.

If you heard about this book, it is probably because it has had incredible publicists work on it. Olivia Russo, Bethany Carter, Aubrey Clemans, Simi Toor, Elyse Marshall, and Hannah Love: thank you all!

Or it's because it has had an incredible marketing team. Thank you to Alex Garber, Felicity Vallence, Shannon Spann, James Akinaka, Christina Colangelo, Bri Lockhart, Amber Reichert, Jordan Francoeur, Jessie Clark, Lisa Kelly, Courtney McAuslan, Maggie Searcy, Kelsey Fehlberg, Michael Hetrick, Megan Parker, Dana Mendelson, Carmela Iaria, Vanessa Carson, Trevor Ingerson,

Summer Ogata, Danielle Presley, Judith Huerta, Gaby Paez, Carmella Lowkis, Sarah Connell, and Sarah Lough.

And if you were able to buy this book, it's because of sales teams both at Penguin and at Faber. Thank you especially to Becky Green, Emily Bruce, Kimberly Langus, Mark Santella, Mary Mcgrath, Kate Baron, Kim Lund, and Sam Brown.

To the production teams that made sure this book got where it was going: Vanessa Robles, Amy White, Miranda Shulman, Gaby Corzo, Mia Alberro, Alex Aleman, Katie McLean, Sarah Stoll, and Hassan Ali.

And to the rest of the team at Faber and Penguin, Alex Bradshaw, Robyn Bender, and Pete Facente, as well as accounts: thank you!

To my Waterstones family: James Barber, Sarah Bland, Chloe Bunch, Malachy Conlan, Alina Darmo, Emma Golay, Steven Hughes, Lara Kantardjian, and Emer Walsh. Your support as I tried to juggle it all means I can actually almost juggle it all, and your collective passion for books makes me fall in love with books every day all over again.

I also want to thank booksellers in general. Those of you who I have met, those of you I haven't. You have been incredible champions for my books, and I know how much passion you have for your work and am eternally grateful for it.

Thank you to Elle Serpis, Andrew Subramaniam, Katy Humphreys, Michala Chostikova, and anyone else whose understanding of taxes has kept me from accidentally going to jail.

This book is about family, but I want to thank my friends who have been there throughout. For the little things and the big things.

Three friends in particular spent hours with me at various points in this book, letting me work out how the plot all clicked together, sometimes multiple times as the book changed. Amelia Hodgson, who let me brainstorm various options for virtues and their matching trials at a very early stage of this book. Nina Douglas, who let me take her through an entire desk full of Post-it notes of plot points and decide which ones I actually needed at the dark-night-of-the-soul stage of this book. And Jonathan Andrews, with whom I had many late-night phone calls while he walked to and from the shops in Bristol, on which he let me explain how I'd broken my book again this time and helped me talk through fixes.

Meredith Longridge-Sykes and Jakes Longridge, Renée Ahdieh and Victor Ahdieh, and Janet Hamilton-Davies and Paul Davies for giving me refuge in the storm. As in literally letting me stay with them when I needed to escape the UK and get some mental space.

Samantha Shannon for somehow being an even more incredible friend than she is a writer, as well as the most generous reader. The annotated bound manuscript I will treasure forever, and your encouraging words about this book helped me believe in it when I started to spiral.

Jennifer Bell, who is a glowing sun of a human being, and is some-how always writing three books at once, and still finding time to be encouraging of her friends' books and bringing joy into the lives of others. Look at us, we got through them!

Bea Fitzgerald and Alexandra Christo for incredibly kind early reviews. And Catherine Doyle and Katherine Webber for excited texts about this book when I needed to hear encouragement most.

To Holly Bourne, Laure Eve, and Krystal Sutherland for being wonderful lockdown COVID support.

To my West London lads Alice Sutherland-Hawes, Catherine Cho, and Rhiannon Trip, who are always around to make sure I'm getting fed while talking books or watching shows about murder, or boats, or both.

My *Housewives* girls, Laura Dodd, Kate Keehan, Laura Sebastian, and Martha Waters. There are few people who I can talk with both about copyedits and about receipts, proof, timeline, and screenshots, and who will get it.

For general emotional support, authorial or otherwise, thank you to Lucy Ivison, Anna James, Elle McNicoll, Zanib Mian, Lucy Strange, Ross Montgomery, Lisa Williamson, Kate Dylan, Katherine Dunn, Saraa El-Arifi, Rosie Talbot, Kiran Millwood Hargrave, David Fenne, John Moore, Rachel Chivers Koo, Kat McKenna, Rosie Talbot, Annabel Steadman, P. M. Freestone, Natalie Bunch, Len Chapman, Lauren Williamson, Darryl Andrade, Anne Murphy, Sophie Cass, Tammi Gill, Katherine Berry, Noirin Collins, Meave Hamill, Elisa Peccerillo-Palliser, Roberta Lima, and Isabella Elliot.

And especially to Rachel Rose Smith and Justine Caillaud for being there for such a long time. Always.

The pit in my stomach is telling me that no matter how wordy this is, there are definitely people I have forgotten along this long, long road. Good news, if it's you, you can use this omission to guilt me into buying you a glass of champagne next time I see you. But know that if you supported me in any way through this book process, I am grateful.

And finally, to you, the readers. Those of you who waited so long for this book. Those of you who came back. Those of you who are new. All of you, I am so grateful to you for being here at the end with me.